THE PAST CATCHES UP

Samantha showed him the victim's photo. "Do you recognize this woman?"

Lucan studied the image. "Yes, but I don't know her name."

"How do you know her?"

"I had sex with her several weeks ago." He sat back on the edge of his desk.

"You were lovers?"

He smiled. "We were strangers."

"Do you often have one-night stands with strange, nameless women, Mr. Lucan?"

"Three nights." He drained his wineglass and straightened, moving a step forward.

"What was that?" Samantha asked.

"It was a three-night stand. I kept her in my bed for three nights." He bent closer, and his voice dropped to a bedroom murmur. "How many nights would you last, Detective?"

Was he hitting on her? "None." Sam felt strange, rooted to the floor. "I don't have sex with strangers."

"Then let's get better acquainted, shall we?"

DARK NEED

A NOVEL OF THE DARKYN

Lynn Viehl

A SIGNET ECLIPSE BOOK

SIGNET ECLIPSE
Published by New American Library, a division of
Penguin Group (USA) Inc., 375 Hudson Street, New York, New York 10014, USA
Penguin Group (Canada), 90 Eglinton Avenue East, Suite 700, Toronto,
Ontario M4P 2Y3, Canada (a division of Pearson Penguin Canada Inc.)
Penguin Books Ltd., 80 Strand, London WC2R 0RL, England
Penguin Ireland, 25 St. Stephen's Green, Dublin 2,
Ireland (a division of Penguin Books Ltd.)
Penguin Group (Australia), 250 Camberwell Road, Camberwell, Victoria 3124,
Australia (a division of Pearson Australia Group Pty. Ltd.)
Penguin Books India Pvt. Ltd., 11 Community Centre, Panchsheel Park,
New Delhi - 110 017, India
Penguin Group (NZ), cnr Airborne and Rosedale Roads, Albany,
Auckland 1310, New Zealand (a division of Pearson New Zealand Ltd.)
Penguin Books (South Africa) (Pty.) Ltd., 24 Sturdee Avenue,
Rosebank, Johannesburg 2196, South Africa

Penguin Books Ltd., Registered Offices: 80 Strand, London WC2R 0RL, England

First published by Signet Eclipse, an imprint of New American Library,
a division of Penguin Group (USA) Inc.

First Printing, June 2006
10   9   8   7   6   5   4   3   2   1

For Edward,
my light in the darkness

What need to clutch with iron grasp
What gentlest touch may take?
What need with aspect dark to scare,
So awfully, so terribly,
The weary soul would hardly care,
Call'd quietly, call'd tenderly
From thy dread power to break?

—Caroline Southey, "To Death"

Chapter 1

Men did not dump Lena Caprell. She dumped them. That was how it went. That was how it *always* went.

Yet here she was, walking out of her lover's ridiculous club and into the night, no limo waiting, no private room and dinner at Baleen in the Grove, no elevator ride to the penthouse suite that she had already started redecorating in her head. No long hours of flickering candles or dark wine or orgasms she didn't have to fake.

What had he said? *You're good, darling, but I'm not. It's time we saw other people.*

No, no, no. This was not how it was supposed to work. Not after only three dates. She was *too* good for this.

She'd let him cool off for two weeks after he'd told her it was over, but enough was enough. Today she'd gotten serious. Three hundred at Galleria for the new dress, then two hundred at the stylist's for hair and nails and a Brazilian wax. Esme had squeezed her in, too, so an extra fifty for the tip. Almost six hundred dollars. She'd never spent so much for a man, not even that commercial director who'd gotten her a reading for the Pollo Tropical people.

She thought it had been worth it. By the time she'd given herself a finishing spritz of Glow before leaving the condo, every inch of her *had* glowed, delicious and wicked and ready for love.

She'd gone early, but they'd made her wait. When she finally got in she didn't make a scene. No. She'd impressed the bartender with a cherry stem, and then as soon as he showed up she'd hurried over to give him a big, wet kiss. In front of everyone, yes, so they wouldn't make her hang around next time, but also because *she* couldn't wait. He was like a fat line of coke in a guest bathroom; she had to have him.

Only no kiss, no hug, no nothing. He'd pulled her off him as if she were some kind of groupie and told her to leave. *I'll order a cab to take you home.* Just like that.

Hadn't she cried—real tears? Hadn't she confessed how much she loved being with him? So much that she would have even settled for one more date. It hadn't been a lie.

You're beautiful when you're determined, darling, he had murmured, *but one more night with me might be the death of you.*

The death of *her.* The bastard had no idea. Lena wished she carried a gun, so she could go back in and shoot his balls off. How *dared* he do this to her.

"No." She stared at the cab pulling up to the curb, unwilling to accept that he had called it for her. "He can't do this. Not to me."

"*Oye,* lady, need a ride?" the young Cuban driver yelled out over Ricky Martin's latest hit.

To get in the cab would be the same as accepting the fact that she had been permanently, solidly, irreversibly dumped. Which was not happening to her, oh, no. Lena shook her head and strode off, the spike heels of her favorite Manolos hammering the pavement.

Why had he sent her away? Not that she had done anything wrong, but what had she done? What had she had *time* to do?

I shouldn't have gone to bed with him that first night, she told herself. *I should have made him wait.*

That was such an old rule with her that the morning after she'd been astounded that she had broken it. Too much champagne, probably—or too many nights alone. It has been so long since she had met anyone tempting that she'd had to change the batteries on her vibrator twice.

Maybe it *was* the sex. The chemistry between them had been like spontaneous combustion—one minute they were flirting; the next he had her on her back. She shivered, thinking about the things she'd let him do to her. He hadn't gotten rough, exactly, but he'd pushed her past hot and hungry right into wild and kinky.

Lena pressed a hand to the flawless skin on the side of her neck. He'd regret dumping her. She knew how much she was worth. Did he think high-quality, well-maintained, gorgeous women walked into that dreary freak club of his every day? Lena had gone in only by mistake, thinking it might be a new salsa place. The cute bartender she'd stayed to flirt with had told her about the new owner—handsome, British, filthy rich—and that he hardly ever left the place.

Lena shivered as she remembered when she first saw him. He'd taken one look and smiled across the room, and she'd forgotten all about the freaks and the bartender and salsa dancing.

Come with me, he'd bent down and whispered against her hair. *It's so much better than coming alone.*

No, this wouldn't do. At all. She'd go down and have a cup of coffee at Casablanca's, and maybe a tiny slice of their fabulous house cheesecake, and calm down. What she needed was to think of an excuse to go back, and talk to him, and make him see how wrong this was. Something to make him feel sorry for being such an ass to her.

"Excuse me, young lady," someone said from behind her. "Did you drop this?"

Lena glanced back and stopped at the sight of the cross. God, it was a nasty thing, a crucifix covered in muck, big enough to hang over a door. "No."

"Are you certain?"

The glitter of yellow metal under the dirt caught Lena's eye. Probably gold plate, she thought as she took a step toward it, but maybe not. The dirt she could scour off. "Where did you find it?"

"Just behind you, here," the man holding it said, gesturing to the sidewalk. "Do you recognize it?"

The gold was flashing in her eyes, distracting her from what he was saying. Under the grime was something round and glittering—rhinestones? Jewels? Lena reached out her hand, and he placed it on her palm. It felt heavy and cold, and if the big dark cabochons were fake she'd eat her purse, tortoiseshell handles and all.

She turned it over, saw what was on the back, and smiled. "No, it's not mine, but I know who it belongs to." She closed her fingers over it. "I'll take it to him."

"I thought it was an unusual name." He smiled at her. "Is this man a friend?"

"He's my boyfriend." She preened, feeling the pretty cross growing warm against her skin. All it needed was a little cleaning, which she could do in the ladies' room at the club. "Thank you."

He stepped closer. "You are most welcome."

Lena would have turned and kept walking on to Casablanca's, because it was getting cold, but that would mean moving out of the streetlight, and the cross would stop shining. A beautiful piece like this was meant to be seen—just like her.

"Allow me to give you a ride, young lady." He took her arm and guided her over to a long, dark car sitting at the curb.

Lena wanted to explain that she didn't need a ride, but the gorgeous, glittering cross absorbed her. She rubbed off some of the dust with her thumb and counted seven dark jewels on it, like red and black sapphires, if there were such things.

What if they're real? Does he have that kind of money?

"You like it, don't you?" the man said as he walked her to the curb.

"Yes." Lena climbed into the back of the dark car, feeling very grateful that the nice man had found the cross. He had given it to her without any fuss, too, and that was how it should be. Beautiful women deserved to be showered with pretty things.

The man chatted with her about nothing in particular as they rode slowly through downtown. Lena had to smother a yawn a few times—she was so sleepy—but nodded and listened absently as she fingered the filigree gold settings around the red and black gems in the cross. Almost all the dirt had come off, and she felt sure it was museum quality, or at least the only one of its kind.

She pressed it against her heart, gratified to know no other woman in the world would have one like it. Fitting, too, because only she had the style to carry off wearing it.

Why her new friend brought her to a church instead of Casablanca's, she didn't know. She hadn't been to Mass in ages. But he insisted she go in with him, and once inside showed her how lovely the stained-glass windows were. Lena thought they looked chintzy compared to the radiant colors of her cross, but was too polite to say so.

The inside of the church was peaceful, though, from the holy water in the large white marble baptismal font at the side of the altar to the racks of votive candles, all lit tonight and throwing out a rosy glow from their fluted crimson glass holders.

Lena caught her breath, surprised how quickly sadness had extinguished her happy mood. Standing there before the altar made her feel worse than opening her credit card statements. She should have come to church more often than simply for Christmas, Easter, and her mother's weddings. How many years had it been since her last confession? She couldn't remember. Too many. Far, far too many.

"You seem so unhappy," her new friend said, patting her shoulder. "Go and light a candle and pray, my dear. It will make you feel better."

Lena nodded and went to kneel on the little padded step in front of the votive candles. She didn't want to set aside her cross, so she carefully eased the thong over her hair and let it rest against her heart. There. It hung too long for the neckline of her dress, but she could change when she went home.

She picked up a taper and touched it to a candle's flame, but the weight of her sorrow doubled. Terrible, really, how many of the candles were lit. So many broken hearts in the world. They came here to pray for those who didn't love them. The ones who didn't deserve to be loved.

Like her.

Now Lena could see how it was her own fault that she'd been dumped. If she had been prettier or younger or better in bed, he wouldn't have pushed her away. He'd seen through her. He'd kicked her out because she'd acted like a whore. A cheap, common whore out to get his money.

Tears streamed down her face as she gripped the cross in her hand. "Forgive me. Forgive me."

Her new friend came to stand over her. He seemed to understand why she was crying. "You paint your face and dress like a harlot, and that is how men will treat you."

Lena looked up at him and took in a sobbing breath. "What can I do?"

He smiled and gestured toward the font. "Wash yourself in the holy water, my dear. Cleansing yourself of sin is the only way to know true absolution."

Lena was so grateful that she sobbed all the way to the font. She paused only long enough to remove her shoes, so they wouldn't get wet. She planned to return them to Galleria tomorrow and buy something humbler, more befitting a modest woman.

Awkward but eager, Lena climbed up on the bottom rim of the font and leaned over the pool of cold, clear water. First she'd scrub the cosmetics from her face and wash the gel out of her hair. Then she'd splash herself all over to rinse away the perfume and the scent of his hands from her skin.

"Yes, my dear." Her new friend rested a gloved hand on the top of her head. "All of it must be washed away."

Lena sensed that her friend was impatient, but he was obviously a busy man and had much more important things to do than stand here and watch her. She really shouldn't keep him. If he'd just help her take the cross off her neck; it had gotten so heavy—

Cold water.

Lena's eyes opened wide and bubbles escaped her mouth on a scream. She didn't know where she was. Her head was in something white filled with water, and she couldn't jerk it out. Bathtub? Pool? Too small. The weight around her neck felt like a concrete block, and the hands holding her to the rim of the font wouldn't let her push herself out. She was paralyzed, helpless. She screamed, choking as she inhaled water into her nose and mouth. She forced it out with the last of her breath and realized she wasn't going to breathe again, ever.

Not like this. Not like this.

Her hair floated in front of her eyes as her struggles slowed. Her lungs wanted to burst out of her chest, and then they did, and water filled her, cleansing her, cooling her, taking her away from the pain and the fear, from him, from everything.

"Enough, my dear."

The hands let go of Lena, and she wrenched her head out of the water, and air blasted into her lungs. She was rolled over and something pummeled her back, making her vomit the water she had swallowed and cough up what she had breathed in. She groped, trying to hold on to her savior.

He picked her up, wiping the wet hair from her face. He smiled down at her, as if pleased she was breathing. "Are you clean now?"

Lena stopped coughing and stared down at herself. Her dress was ruined. Her hair hung in long, wet clumps in front of her face. And her hands—she'd held on to the edge of the font so hard her palms were bruised. Her stomach rolled as she realized the hands that had held her down had been her own. She'd almost drowned herself in that damn font.

I've been drugged.

"What's wrong with me?" She turned on the man with her. "What did you give to me?"

His smile faded as he stepped back. "Only the cross. Sins cannot by cleansed away by anyone but the sinner. You know this in your heart."

"No." To her horror, Lena turned slowly, like a toy on remote control, and walked toward the font.

"'And whosoever shall offend one of these little ones that believe in me, it is better for him that a millstone were hanged about his neck, and he were cast into the sea,'" the man said softly.

"Stop it." She stepped up and placed her hands on the rim, gripping it tightly. "Don't make me do this." Her back arched and her fingernails snapped as she dug them into the cold stone with all her strength. "Please, God, I don't want to die!"

Just before Lena shoved her head back under the water, she heard him say, "Then you shouldn't have let him touch you."

"Okay, look." Fort Lauderdale Homicide Detective Harry Quinn took out his bronchial inhaler, but didn't stop talking between wheezes to use it. "A swimmer who drowns in the ocean doesn't wash up on the beach, then roll four hundred yards to climb up on a bus bench." He coughed. "No way in hell. She was *put* there."

His partner, Detective Samantha Brown, silently agreed. The body was clearly visible, sitting as it had been found, propped on a bench, ankles crossed, hands primly folded in her lap. If not for the wet hair and the cocktail dress plastered to her body, she might have been just another woman waiting for a bus. Victims of drowning never looked so tidy.

Sam's nerves had been on edge since taking the call from Dispatch. Seeing the body as it had been left didn't soothe them.

"First impression?" Harry asked.

"She wasn't swimming," Sam murmured. "Not in that outfit."

"Maybe she fell asleep with her head back and it rained real hard." Her partner laughed at his own tasteless joke, then coughed uncontrollably until he put the end of his inhaler between his lips and pumped a shot of medication into his lungs.

Harry was two weeks from retirement, and hanging on to his job by sheer willpower. His asthma had grown so severe that most of the physical aspects of the job were out of the question. Sam's boss, Captain Ernesto Garcia, had offered to let Harry ride a desk to his pension and assign her someone else, but Sam couldn't do that to her partner. Harry was proud of having worked Homicide for thirty-three years of his FLPD career; the least she could do was stick with him through the last fourteen days of it.

After Harry retired . . . She didn't want to think about it. Harry knew about her deal. A new partner wouldn't.

"We're not sure what happened," the patrolman at the scene said. He paused for a moment to watch Sam walk toward the body, his eyes warming as he checked out her long, ripe form. "Someone might have brought her up here to get her away from the seagulls."

Harry looked up at the empty sky, just now turning pink and purple. "No gulls around here. That's a little weird."

Sam spotted a local news channel's van pulling around the corner. "Officer, set up some screens and barricades, and keep those cameras on the bar side."

"Yes, ma'am."

She went back to her car to retrieve two Styrofoam cups filled with coffee, and almost felt the patrolman checking her out from behind. Being a fairly tall woman with straight, dark brown hair and warm hazel eyes got her some looks, but it was the rest of her that snagged men's interest. Sam was, as the polite men on the squad put it, built. The plain suits she wore didn't completely disguise her curves, which daily exercise only kept toned. Keeping her hair in a braid or ponytail gave her a no-nonsense look, but she still drew too much attention for her own comfort.

"You're going to give yourself an ulcer drinking that stuff the way you do." Harry nodded at the coffee in her hands as they walked over to the bench. "I thought you were going to cut back."

"No one will sell me any speed." She stopped and looked at the victim's body. "What's your take?"

"Deliberate. Kind. Could have been a tourist." Harry used the inhaler again as he contemplated the dead woman. "Say he's out jogging or walking down to get another layer of skin cancer, he trips over body, panics, picks her up, carries her over to the bench to do, I don't know, mouth-to-mouth?"

"Civilian trips over the body, he panics, he runs away, he yells for help, he throws up. But he doesn't touch her or move her. They all watch *CSI* these days." Sam ducked under the yellow crime scene tape and walked around the carpet of Visqueen encircling the bench.

Harry kept speculating as he followed her in. "Yeah, but if it was a smart-ass kid, or a drunk . . ."

"Look around." She gestured with one of the cups. "No footprints, and no seaweed or sand on her. She's not bloated, either." She looked at the concrete pad under the bench. "Big puddle of water down there. I'd say she's only been here an hour at the most."

"Only one way to know." His gaze moved from the dripping dress to the woman's hands.

Sam saw the broken, bloodied fingernails, and checked the perimeter to assure the uniforms were cordoning off the area. She was just about to touch the body when a white van pulled up to the curb, blocking the view of the bench from the street.

"Hold it, the walking smokestack's here." Harry coughed. "I'll go make nice to the media."

Sam watched as Dr. Evan Tenderson jumped out of the van and stomped over, a scowl puckered around the unfiltered cigarette in his mouth. The assistant medical examiner was a militant smoker. "Morning, Doc."

"Morning, my dick, it's five-fucking-thirty A.M.," he said, removing the cigarette and baring nicotine-stained teeth his parents never bothered to have straightened. He squinted at the dead woman as he dropped the butt and pulled on a pair of thin latex gloves. "Now I've seen everything. How the fuck did she get up here?"

"We're trying to determine that. Here." Sam gave him one of the coffees she carried. "Black, one sugar."

"If you wanted me to move faster, Brown, you should've brought doughnuts. Or a hooker with a tight mouth." A sour smile covered his yellowed buckteeth. "No sexual harassment intended by that remark." He shoved a pair of gloves from his case at her.

Sam let it go. "I need an ID if she's got one."

"Everyone's got one." Tenderson set down his bag and gingerly braced himself on the edge of the bench as he leaned over the body. "Caucasian female, approximately twenty-five to thirty-five years of age, deceased." He looked down. "Hair, clothing, and skin are saturated with water." He used a pair of long-handled tongs to unzip the purse hanging from her shoulder and extracted a wallet, which he handed to her along with an evidence bag.

Sam placed it in the bag before she released the snap and unfolded the wallet. The sun sparkled on the seal holograms imprinted on the lamination over a smiling headshot of the dead woman. "Lena Caprell, twenty-seven years old, Fort Lauderdale resident, safe driver."

"Told you." Tenderson turned his attention back to the body. Sam was about to walk over to update her partner when the medical examiner yelped and pulled back his hand, holding it by the wrist as he swore loudly and at length. When he saw Sam watching, he yelled, "Bitch shocked me."

"I thought you'd seen everything." She stepped up as far as she could without moving off the protective plastic, and saw the dull glint of old metal and shriveled leather.

"I mean it. Felt like getting zapped with household current," Tenderson insisted, shaking his hand.

"She's wearing some kind of necklace." She took the pen out of her jacket pocket and slipped it under the crinkled thong, fishing out the pendant attached to it. Even with the gloves on, she took care not to touch the dead woman's hands. She couldn't risk it now, not with Tenderson hovering beside her.

The crucifix that Sam tugged out of the dress was eight inches long and and very dirty. It looked to be an antique or a knockoff of one. On an archaeological dig it would have been a marvel; on a dead young woman in a boutique evening dress it was almost obscene. Then again, so was seeing the body of Lena Caprell sitting here, clean and pale and unmoving as a statue. Yesterday she had been a person. A handful of hours before now, she would have looked up at Sam and spoken, or smiled, or breathed. Now she was as animated as the concrete bench beneath her.

O death, where is thy sting? O grave, where is thy victory? Sam looked at the victim's hands, folded so neatly in her lap, the only discordant note. What had torn up those lovely, manicured nails so badly?

She glanced at Tenderson and sighed. There was no way he was leaving. "Check out her hands."

"Oh, sweetheart, you get me some skin off this bastard that did you?" Tenderson crooned as he examined Lena's fingers. His eyes shifted to the cross. "You think she was a big Catholic?"

"Could be." The weight of the cross bothered Sam. "Or she needed weighing down."

"Jesus is a heavy dude." He went back to nursing his hand. "Frigging thing still hurts. Latex doesn't insulate worth a shit."

Sam needed a few moments alone with the body, but it didn't look as though she was going to get them. As she lowered the crucifix, the weight of it caused it to flip over. On the back of the crossbar were five letters rendered in an old-fashioned script. "There's something engraved on the back."

Tenderson looked up from sulking over his hand. "What?"

"Just one word." Sam used the pen to turn it toward the sunlight, but that only made the engraving look deeper and darker. " 'Lucan.' "

Chapter 2

Lucan, former chief assassin of the Darkyn high lord Richard Tremayne, suzerain of a newly formed and still nameless *jardin*, and greatly loathed pariah among his kind, looked out at the gathering darkness. Despite seven centuries and more of walking the earth, first as a man and then as a creature who preyed on mankind, Lucan had spent scant time in the tropics. Here night came as would a stealthy lover to a balcony, climbing the cloud lattice to enfold the pastel innocence of day in his midnight cloak.

How easy it would be to walk into that singular darkness, follow it around the world, and dwell in it forever.

Before using his talent to eliminate the high lord's enemies, Lucan had flirted with such an existence. For many decades after he rose he drifted aimless and unfettered, shunning his immortal kindred and using humans only for food. He hadn't been happy, but he had been left alone. Now he had risen higher than he had ever thought possible, and still he was the shunned, the despised, the mistrusted—and as plagued by both humans and Darkyn as was a pharaoh enslaving Jews and defying their god. He knew he would be no more welcome here than any other place he had tried to make his home.

It was ludicrous. It was fitting. It made him want to kill something.

"My lord, there is a delivery."

Lucan smelled mentholated cough drops and turned from the oceanside window of his suite to see someone he did not especially wish dead yet: his recently acquired *tresora*. "As I have told you some two thousand times before this, you need not call me 'my lord,' Burke. That is for the Kyn to do, not you."

"I apologize." Herbert Burke was a thin, small man with an anxious face. Plagued with allergies, he emanated the scent of the sickroom, and carried a wealth of tissues, nose sprays, and other medicinal paraphernalia on his person to treat his perpetual congestion. "The delivery is somewhat unusual."

Lucan's silvery brows rose. "Is it a woman?"

"No, my . . . no."

It never was, more the pity. No one seemed to know how to pay proper tribute anymore to a newly appointed suzerain. "Then put it in the office, and I will attend to it later."

"Thank you, my lord." Burke paled at his mistake and fled.

"Good God. I cannot imagine what I have done to intimidate that human so much." Lucan's gaze shifted to the dark-haired man sitting and skimming through a stack of correspondence. "Do you know what it was?"

His seneschal did not stop reading. "It may be your reputation among the *tresori,* my lord."

"I have not taken a human servant for two hundred years." Nor would he have, given a choice. He felt a twinge of idle curiosity. "What do they say about me?"

Rafael glanced up. "That you would kill and eat a man simply for annoying you."

"That is what Hannibal Lecter does," Lucan said. "I would only rip out his throat and drink his blood."

His seneschal set aside the letter he was reading. "Three nights past, when you became angry over Burke spilling a little wine while serving you—"

"That was very good wine," Lucan pointed out.

"—you did speculate aloud on how difficult it would be to drown a human in a bathtub filled with his own urine." Rafael's bland expression shifted one degree toward disapproving. "Burke was frightened."

"Burke is an idiot. Obviously it would take far too long for him to fill a tub with enough urine to drown in." He yawned. "Better to use the excess mucus he is always blowing out or coughing up."

"I would beg you be more tolerant, my lord." Rafael opened an envelope and removed a long contract form. "He has never actively served a Darkyn suzerain. He does not know you are

merely jesting with him. You are, in fact, making him more nervous by the day."

"Indeed?" He allowed a little of the irritation he felt to color
his voice. "How fortunate I am to have you as my seneschal,
Rafael. I might never understand my servants, or any damned
thing that comes out of my mouth."

Bored, Lucan turned back to the window to watch the night.
Rafael silently finished reviewing the interminable amount of
mail.

"Here is a list of the local bands that are available for Friday
and Saturday nights, and papers you must sign for the new con-
tractor, my lord, on the lines where I have placed an X." The
seneschal handed him a folder containing the information. "The
construction manager has written to request a meeting with you."

Lucan stroked his jaw. "Should we risk it? After all, some
careless word of mine may make him believe that I have abom-
inable intentions toward his liver."

The broad shoulders moved. "Perhaps he will work faster."

"Don't develop a sense of humor now, Rafael. It would be
the undoing of me." He removed a gold-and-platinum fountain
pen given to him by the grateful suzerain of Monte Carlo and
uncapped it. It took a moment for him to remember how he had
been signing this name—he had used so many over the centuries that he routinely forgot—and then scrawled his signature
across each paper. "There." He thrust the contract back at his
seneschal. "What other absurdity must I attend to?"

Rafael nodded toward the window. "A woman was found
dead near the beach this morning. Drowned, one of the waitresses said."

"I didn't kill her." Lucan looked at his second with renewed
interest. "Did you?"

"No, my lord. But the woman"—Rafael's gaze shifted toward the titanic bed in the adjoining bedchamber—"was one of
the humans that you used several weeks ago."

He occasionally indulged himself by taking a female patron
from the club, but they rarely lasted more than a day or two. He
made sure of that. "The blonde or the redhead?"

"Neither." His seneschal checked his watch. "She was
brunette. Very pretty, and quite elegant."

"The actress. I remember. God, what a waste." She had been a well-tended beauty, and as avaricious as a Venetian noblewoman bent on bettering her family fortune. Her scheming had amused him so much he had taken her for three consecutive nights. "She didn't strike me as suicidal." She had wanted to kill him, though, after he had ended their tête-à-tête. "Find out what happened to her."

"Yes, my lord." Rafael turned and headed for the door of the suite.

"One more thing." He enjoyed seeing his seneschal stop and stiffen his shoulders. "Call Alisa and send her to my office when she arrives. As *soon* as she arrives."

"As you wish, my lord." Rafael left the suite, closing the door silently behind him.

His seneschal didn't approve of his appetites, Lucan decided. Doubtless Rafael's idea of the proper suzerain for this collection of misfits was one who played the role of vicar and made the rounds of the *jardin* every night, holding hands, listening to troubles, and doling out sage advice. Strong but benign leadership that would keep them sane and united through the difficult centuries ahead.

For this they had Lucan, who was as benign as blood rot and ten times as lethal.

The nightclub had worried the members of Lucan's *jardin,* but they had spent two hundred years ingratiating themselves into the landscape of South Florida, trying to appear as just another group of immigrants. Anything that called attention to what they really were was to be avoided at all costs, so they had become business owners, community leaders, and other pillars of respectability.

Lucan saw Infusion as more appropriate camouflage. What better way for the new Darkyn suzerain in town to blend in than to open a gothic-themed tavern and dance hall that catered to the young and self-absorbed? He didn't even have to invest in a new wardrobe.

The drama of his new setting suited him. If one was to be a fiend, Lucan thought, one might as well flaunt it. His private suite might resemble a guest room at the White House, but downstairs the atmosphere was crimson blood and black midnight from ceiling to floor.

Many of his young patrons came dressed as characters from the horror novels they loved to read, and he encouraged this by having his employees hand out free drink coupons and gift certificates to local costume shops. Specialty Bloody Mother Marys were a nightly special, served in black glasses decorated with pairs of plastic fangs and sipped through IV tubing instead of straws. Every other drink on the menu was named for a famous creator of dark fantasy, from the Stephen King Kahlua and Cream to the Straub Berry Margaritas.

Lucan was also planning a summer concert for his patrons, featuring local bands and a special performance artist who turned her body into art through subtle self-torture. Burke had advised against it, as he advised against everything that gave Lucan any amount of personal pleasure or amusement.

"There hasn't been a goth club on Fort Lauderdale Beach since the early eighties, my lord," he had told Lucan. "Better to open a coffee shop or a salsa club."

"I can't drink coffee or eat salsa," Lucan had replied easily. "Goths, on the other hand, I find quite digestible."

Burke had employed one of his nasal sprays and wandered off muttering to himself.

Lucan decided, despite all the advice against opening Infusion, that the results of his labors were most pleasing. As he left his lordly suite and took the elevator to the club level, he thought about opening another theme club in Miami and commuting between the two, as more than half the *jardin* dwelled in Dade County. Perhaps a salsa club might do for his southern base.

If he could stay this time. If only he could stay.

The club would not open for another two hours, and the entire first floor stood silent and empty. Lucan followed the scent of cherry-eucalyptus cough drops to his office, and entered the pass code that released the vault-quality electronic locks on the steel door. Inside Burke had left the lights on, and atop the desk that had once belonged to a shipbuilder in Ireland was a long white-and-lavender box from a national flower-delivery service. On the front were printed the words, SOMEONE IS THINKING ABOUT YOU.

"Then someone should have sent me a woman," Lucan murmured as he used his palm blade to cut through the box's taped sides. He flipped open the top and examined the contents.

Two dozen dead flowers lay inside, brown and withered.

"Lilies." Lucan reached in the box to take out one of the flowers. A knock sounded on the door, and he set the box to one side of his desk before drawing a throwing knife from his vest. "Come in."

The young woman in the purple-and-green-plaid cloth coat who entered the office was not as poised as the dead brunette, or as noisy as the plump blonde before her. Her features bore a faint resemblance to those of a rodent, which she did her best to disguise with thick cosmetics and a short, layered bob of eggplant-purple hair.

"You sent for me?" Alisa, also known as Alice Nora Kruk, asked in her prim, polite voice. She kept her coat on and stood by the door, and, if he told her to, she would leave without protest. It was one of the reasons he used her more often than the other human females he encountered.

Throughout the centuries, the Darkyn had enjoyed professional courtesans the same way children did candy. Since Lucan had come to South Florida, this human had quickly become his favorite infrequent confection.

"Yes, darling Allie." Lucan replaced his knife and sat down in the wide-backed leather chair behind his desk. "Are you wearing anything under that unfortunate clan's tartan?"

Alisa neatly unbuttoned the coat and opened it to display a merry widow, garter belt, and fishnet stockings, all in shades of reddish purple. She left the narrow strip of black curly hair over her pubic mound natural, but the small gold ring piercing the top of her labia sported a dangling heart-shaped amethyst.

"How enchanting." He sat back and enjoyed the precise way she approached him, every movement subdued yet provocative. Another reason she had lasted as long as she had: Allie possessed the gift of utter, ruthless self-control. "Tell me, who did you beat senseless today?"

"No one. I had a businessman in Boca scheduled for a paddling, but he came all over my lap after four whacks." She removed a wad of pink chewing gum from her mouth and flicked it into the waste can by his desk. "Got me all icky. I had to shower before I came to you."

He removed a folded linen handkerchief and a tube of

medicinal salve from his desk drawer and placed them within reach. "I would hope so."

"I might get out of the 'trix trade soon." She knelt down in front of the chair and unlaced the top of the merry widow, pushing her hands inside the cups to slowly fondle her implant-enhanced breasts. "Go into specialty anal instead. Guys are much more interested in ass-fucking these days."

"Yours," he said, tipping up her chin, "or theirs?"

"Doesn't matter. I make money either way." She breathed in and her pupils dilated as she released more of the lacing between her breasts. "Unless you want to change your mind about us."

Lucan was tempted to make their arrangement more regular and permanent; he could certainly afford her lease rates. Allie's skills were also professional quality, and even under the influence of *l'attrait*, she retained a remarkable amount of self-possession. Yet even he could not break the ancient traditions involved with the oath of loyalty. No human outside the ranks of Darkyn was ever invited in. Burke might fumble the occasional wine bottle, but he came from a long-established *tresoran* family who had trained him from boyhood to serve.

"I would not deny you the delights of sodomy," he murmured as he bent to put his mouth to her right shoulder.

"Oh, God." The young woman closed her eyes and moaned as his fangs lightly pierced her flesh. "This hurts so much better."

As Lucan swallowed the warm blood that welled up from the punctures in her soft, thin skin, his eyes shifted to the box of withered lilies. Why would someone go to the trouble of sending him dead flowers? Was Richard trying to make another of his cryptic points?

A trembling hand touching the back of his neck made him lift his mouth. He applied pressure to the punctures his fangs had left with the folded handkerchief, and after a few moments, a dab of the antibiotic ointment.

"Please," she moaned, spreading her thighs wide and pulling at his hand. "I need it."

The blood of a woman in his belly always gave him an erection, and Lucan saw no reason to dismiss it. After all, he did pay

Allie double her standard rate. But as he unfastened the front of his trousers, he wondered how much longer he could go on using her. Delightfully jaded though they were, even her shop-soiled charms might push him into blood thrall.

No, it wouldn't be Alisa. It would be the emptiness eating away inside him. The space nothing could fill, not blood or sex or death.

"I need it right now." She scrambled up onto her knees, and in her haste she knocked the box of lilies off his desk. Lucan heard water gurgling and lifted Alisa out of the way while he used the toe of his shoe to nudge open the box lid. Two broken pieces of a thin terra-cotta vial fell out, splashing water onto his carpet.

"I'm sorry," Allie said, emerging from the haze of *l'attrait* to look down with dismay at the mess. "Was that something important?"

Rust-tinged water slowly soaked into the carpet at his feet. He smelled copper—one of the few things in the world that could kill him—and saw that every lily in the box had its stem inserted in a thin, easily broken clay vial of the same contaminated fluid. "Not to me."

"I do not tell my life history to humans," Marcella Evareaux said as she watched the tiny puncture wound in the bend of her elbow vanish.

"I'm not human. I'm your doctor." Alexandra Keller capped off the tube of blood she had just taken from the other woman, marked the label ME-1, and placed it in an upright rack filled with other blood samples. The tower room in Marcella Evareaux's Victorian mansion was so large and sparsely furnished that every word she said echoed faintly, making Alex feel as if she were standing in an auditorium rather than a home. "Why do you live here by yourself?"

"Why do you wish to know," the tall, black-haired French-woman countered, "when it has nothing to do with your tests?"

Alex shrugged. "I'm trying to be friendly. You're only the fourth female vampire I've met so far."

"The Darkyn are not vampires. We are *vrykolakas*." Marcella draped her shoulders with a gray burnout velvet wrap, which was a shade darker than the plain silver rings she wore around each finger. Every movement she made created a faint, exquisite scent of wisteria.

"So I've been lectured." Vampires were so touchy about what you called them. "What's your talent?" All of the Darkyn had some strange psychic ability that affected human beings. Alex and Jema Shaw, the only humans to survive the change to Darkyn since the Middle Ages, had gifts that worked on humans *and* vampires.

Dark eyes glittered. "I don't kill humans who ask too many annoying questions."

"I hope that goes for former humans, too." Alex grinned. "And would you be my best friend? Please?"

Instead of showing amusement, Marcella's expression tightened. "I do not take women . . . friends."

"Aw, it's really fun. We get to go shopping together, swap old-boyfriend stories, watch chick flicks, and borrow each other's clothes for hot dates." She waited, but the other woman didn't reply. "Or not. You know what this means. I can make you pee in a little plastic cup. Or listen to more annoying questions, like did you grow those fangs on your own, or did someone infect you?"

"It was another time, another life." Marcella moved her hand through her long black curls in an idle, sexy gesture Alex couldn't have imitated even if she'd practiced in front of a mirror for ten years. "What does it matter?"

"If you're worried about me gossiping, I can keep my mouth shut," Alex assured her. "Ask your brother; he'll vouch for me."

The other woman rearranged her long limbs in a negligent pose. "Arnaud's opinion of you was less than favorable, Doctor."

"Called me a mouthy little bitch, did he?" She grinned. "He just hates everybody. Except that girl out in the swamps he keeps going to see." At Marcella's blank look, she added, "The one whose father keeps shooting him in the ass."

"I cannot speak of that." Long fingers toyed with the wrap's crystal beaded fringe. "I still know nothing about you, or how you came to be one of us."

Alex's change from human to Darkyn had been the stuff of

bad soap operas, in her own opinion, but she didn't mind sharing. "You mean you didn't get the *jardin* monthly newsletter? I was minding my own business, working as a reconstructive surgeon in Chicago when your boss, the Evil One—"

"The seigneur."

"That's him—had me kidnapped and flown to New Orleans, where he sweet-talked me into giving him back a face. I did; he went nuts, bit me, gave me his blood, and passed out; his minions hauled me back to Chicago and left me to die." She took a breath. "Only I didn't."

Marcella sighed. "I have trouble believing this. If it is true, you and this other woman in Chicago are the only humans to survive the change—"

"In half a millennium, yeah, it was kind of like winning the fang lotto," Alex agreed. "Anyway, four million dollars later, I fell for the Prince of Night's bullshit again, came back here, operated on some of his tortured friends, and fell in love with him, dumb bitch that I am, then made him change me the rest of the way to keep from becoming the King of Pain's lab rat."

"That would be Richard," Marcella guessed. "Why did you go back to Chicago with the seigneur?"

"That trip was to chase down Thierry Durand. I had been able to reconstruct his legs, but his mind was another matter completely. He was insane after surviving the Brethren's torture, and we were trying to keep him safe while he recovered. But he escaped. That's when we found Jema Shaw, the other was-human like me and got into her shit." Alex still wished she could have done a thousand things in Chicago differently. "From what I can tell, she was infected with Darkyn blood when she was a baby. For some reason it didn't kill her, and then another crazy man used drugs and lies to keep her from changing for thirty years."

The other woman rested her hand on her chin as she stared at Alex. "Incredible."

"Disgusting. Anyway, Jema fell in love with Thierry—who recovered his sanity better when he was free than when he was locked up at Michael's—there was a party, a shoot-out, a sword fight, arms and heads being hacked off, people dying—the usual Darkyn idea of a good time. Thierry got sane, killed the

crazy man who had been drugging Jema, Jema finished changing, I made repairs on the survivors, and then we all came
home." Alex sighed. "Somewhere in there I got shot in the
chest with a copper bolt, but that's basically it." She spread out
her hands. "Ta-da."

"So." Marcella stared at her for a moment. "This would be
why I live alone."

Alex laughed, and as she did, the scent of lavender mixed
with wisteria. Before she could take advantage of the female
vampire's improved mood, a large, heavily muscled man with
light brown hair and a scarred face slipped into the room.

"Hey, Phillipe." Alex hailed Michael Cyprien's seneschal
with a slight frown. "I thought you and Mike were going into
the city to look for the new torture chamber the Brethren are
setting up."

Marcella's eyebrows lifted. "Mike?"

"She means the seigneur, madam," Phillipe said to Marcella
in French, which Alex was still learning from Michael. To her,
he said in careful English, "We have just returned, and met
Beauregard Paviere downstairs. He would speak to you."

"He would? A vampire—excuse me—a *vrykolakas* who
wants to talk to me? That's a first." Alex eyed Marcella as she
packed up her case and sample rack. "You owe me one life
story when I come back to tap your veins again."

Marcella's lips twitched. "Assuming I will be a willing
donor."

Arnaud's sister accompanied them downstairs, where a tall
man with a long, pensive face framed by tousled brown hair
paced the entry hall. He stopped as soon as he saw them descending the curved staircase and hurried up to the bottom step.

"You are *le docteur, oui?* You are needed at my home right
away." He was in so much distress that he seemed to vibrate
with tension. "Faryl, my younger brother, he is in serious
trouble."

Michael Cyprien, Alex's lover, stepped into the hall. The
most powerful *vrykolakas* in America, he had recently been el-
evated to the status of seigneur, to rule over all the Darkyn
jardins within the United States, which was why all the vampires looked at him the moment he spoke. Alex looked because

he was usually the hottest man in the room, and because he was hers. "Faryl is alive? Where has he been, Gard?"

Paviere looked ashamed. "I cannot say, seigneur."

Alex saw Michael's tall frame tense, and glanced at Phillipe, who looked startled. "What sort of trouble is your brother having, Mr. Paviere?"

"His flesh is rotting and falling off his body."

"Rotting *and* falling off." Not another insane vampire. Alex had just finished dealing with all the insanity she could handle for one immortal lifetime. "That would make your brother a corpse, and contrary to popular fiction, no one can raise the dead."

Beauregard looked up at Marcella and rattled off something in a dialect of French so ancient and obscure that Alex felt certain it had never been spoken by the human citizens of the continental United States.

The female vampire shook her head. "Faryl is not dead. Gard means that he has the fleshrot. Ah . . ." She groped for the next word, and then snapped her fingers. "The leprosy."

"Unlikely," Alex said, "seeing as the Darkyn spontaneously heal." She noted the sudden shuttered look on the three other vampires' faces. "Oh, come on, don't tell me there's *another* thing I don't know." Michael had already neglected to tell her that the inviolate Darkyn in a weakened state could be cut and hurt by metals other than copper.

"I will explain later," Michael promised.

"She must come to my estate," Beauregard pleaded with the seigneur. "Before today I had not seen my brother in two hundred years, but I think he is dying."

"Rotting flesh will do that to you." Alex looked into her lover's gold-rimmed turquoise eyes. "Looks like I've got to make another house call."

Michael nodded and turned to the agitated man. "How did this come about, Gard? Why has Faryl been hiding from us all this time?"

Paviere's head drooped. "I had thought he would end it when he left us, but it seems he has kept the faith. He has been feeding in the swamps."

Michael swore under his breath. "Alexandra, we must attend to Faryl immediately."

Phillipe drove them from Marcella Evareaux's lakeside manor into the bayou country, passing through the small towns and fisheries until the asphalt disappeared and the dirt roads turned narrow and muddy. Gard and Michael exchanged a few polite words, the way men who hadn't seen each other in years would, but it was the tension radiating from her lover that convinced Alex to keep her mouth shut.

Later, though, Cyprien owed her some answers.

The Pavieres lived on an old Southern plantation, in an antebellum mansion that looked a little worse for the wear. Weather-stained marble columns crawling with kudzu marched along a decrepit wraparound porch, surrounded by lawns of knee-high grass punctuated with bunches of flowering weeds.

Inside, Alex knew from experience, it would be spotless. A little outward decay discouraged tourists and neighbors from becoming too friendly, or figuring out that the Darkyn had moved in long before Sherman had burned Atlanta.

A tiny black woman dressed in a gorgeous flowered dress rushed out to meet the car. "Welcome to La Moisson, Seigneur Cyprien. Madam, I am Ruby, *tresora* to the Paviere family." She bobbed her head at Alex and turned instantly to Paviere. "Master Gard, Master Faryl is gone."

Gard's gaze shifted to one of the upper windows. "How did he get out?"

"He smashed the locks on the door." The black woman wrapped her arms around her waist. "I could not stop him."

Gard's expression turned hopeless. "It is done, then. He goes to south, to *le tueur*." He put an arm around Ruby and walked slowly into the mansion with her.

"*Le* what?" Alex glanced at the two men beside her. Phillipe only shook his head.

"*Le tueur* means 'the assassin.'" Michael's face emptied of all emotion. "It means that Faryl has gone to Lucan."

"The guy who attacked my nurse?" Alex didn't have to fake the shudder. "Why would he go to him?" Her eyes went wide as Michael stalked into the house after Gard and Ruby. "Phillipe, what did I say this time?"

"Faryl goes to Lucan for help rather than to the seigneur." The seneschal grimaced. "It is a grave insult."

"The guy's rotting; maybe we should see it as a favor." Alex still couldn't make sense of the situation. "And why go to Lucan anyway? He's not a doctor, is he?"

"No. Faryl goes to him because of his faith," Phillipe said softly. "To Catholics suicide is a sin."

"Yeah, like they need more hang-ups." She rubbed the back of her neck. "So Faryl went to Lucan for what? Sympathy? Confession? To hide from his family?"

"No. Faryl wishes Lucan to kill him."

Chapter 3

Living in a third-floor apartment at Palm Royal Place allowed Samantha Brown three things: privacy, peace, and a room with a view of a canal instead of another apartment building. Walking up and down three flights of stairs wasn't much fun, especially on the days she went grocery shopping, but she liked the exercise.

The peace and privacy had come with more of a price tag.

Sam had moved into her latest apartment a few weeks after she and Wesley Dwyer became partners. She'd been forced to give up her old apartment and obtain an unlisted phone number as soon as Dwyer had started harassing her, mainly because he scared her, and she didn't want him knowing where she lived.

There were three other apartments on her floor. Two were expensive three-bedroom rentals that were leased by elderly couples who used them only for vacations and holiday visits. The other apartment, a twin of her own, was occupied by Keri-anne Lewis, an attractive single blonde who had a computer sales business and, like Sam, was hardly ever home.

Sam hadn't been too friendly with her neighbor at first. The job killed most potential friendships, and she was convinced she had about as much in common with the pretty, polished Keri Lewis as she did with Laura Bush. Then one weekend she found Keri struggling to get an old, heavy armchair down the stairs, and gave her a hand with it. Keri had invited her back to her apartment for a drink. Sam admired her place, which she had decorated with a modern, funky style in red, black, and white.

"How do you like being a cop?" her neighbor asked as they

sipped iced tea out on her postage stamp-sized balcony over-looking the other half of the canal below.

Sam shrugged. "It's okay. I'm trying to get a transfer over to Homicide." Anything to get away from Dwyer, who by that time had become a real nuisance.

"I never see you with any guys," Keri mentioned.

"No time." And, after putting up with Dwyer's continual harassment, even less inclination.

"You could change your hair." She nodded toward Sam's ponytail. "Put on some makeup, dress up a little. You've got a great body. Very earthy. What are you, a size eight?"

"Ten. Twelve if the top isn't roomy." She looked down at herself and grimaced. "I'd trade it all for a size two and the chance to go around braless."

Keri chuckled. "While I'd love to be stacked like you. Why do we always hate ourselves?"

Sam had left a little later not knowing much more about Keri than she had before, but from that day on her neighbor treated her like an old friend. She'd invited Sam over for dinner a few times, and then they went to catch a movie together. Sam was just starting to like having a woman friend when Dwyer had finally pushed her too far by cornering her and nearly raping her, and she filed a formal complaint against him with IA.

The grilling Sam had taken on that particular day had left her angry and sick. One of the IA cops had insinuated that by not reporting the earlier abuse, Sam had been giving Dwyer "silent permission" to harass her. She'd been forced to take four vacation days off while the complaint was filed and investigated. She'd stopped at a liquor store for orange juice and vodka, intending to get thoroughly drunk as soon as she got home. When she met Keri in the stairwell, she invited her inside to celebrate the disaster.

Keri hadn't drunk much, but she'd listened while Sam bitched her way through four screwdrivers and two straight shots of Stoli. Finally she'd taken the vodka away and put it in the freezer.

"You need to do something else besides sit here and be miserable about a man," Keri said.

Sam, who had never been much of a drinker, had been enjoying her first real binge. "Like what?"

What happened after that had told her all she ever needed to know about Keri Lewis, and a week later had ended their friendship in a spectacular scene in front of most of Sam's coworkers. These days Keri took special pains to avoid her, but Sam still could never walk past her neighbor's door without feeling guilty. She'd tried to apologize, too many times, but that had only made the situation worse.

The phone ringing woke up Sam two hours after she'd gone to sleep, and Garcia's secretary told her to report in for a shift change. Tired but resigned to one of the downsides of being a cop, Sam dressed, nuked a cup of leftover coffee, and headed out the door.

She'd almost made it to the stairwell when she heard Keri behind her. "Samantha. I thought you were working nights."

Sam closed her eyes for a moment, forcing a smile onto her face and turning. "I was. Now evidently I'm not. How are you, Keri?"

"Same old me."

A doll maker might have fashioned Keri Lewis from porcelain and golden silk. A small, hard smile displayed her pearly teeth, only slightly less dazzling than her big green eyes. The sienna suede jacket, pencil-legged faded denims, and white tank top were too severe for her cameo looks, but as Keri put it, she preferred leather over lace.

"I tried to call you," Keri told her, "but someone changed their number."

"I forgot to give you the new one." No, she hadn't. "What's up?"

"I'm subletting my place for the summer while I close on a house. Girl named Christian. A little wild-looking, but she paid the deposit in cash. She's moving in this morning." A car horn sounded downstairs, and Keri glanced that way. "That's my ride. I won't be back here again." She gave her a thorough, insulting once-over. "It's been interesting."

"Yeah." Sam almost held out her hand, but decided a smile was less offensive. "Good luck with your new place." She didn't flinch as Keri's palm connected with her cheek, and she didn't try to hit back. "I'm sorry."

A petite girl carrying a purple beanbag up the stairs stopped to watch.

"No, you're not, you bitch. You love this." Keri stepped forward as if to hit her again; then she swore and stalked past the girl standing with the beanbag on the landing. Before she started down the stairs, she looked back. "I hope one day someone gives you what you really need, Samantha, and takes it away from you the minute you start enjoying it. Just like you did to me."

Sam watched her hurry down the stairs and out to the parking lot, where she climbed into a black sports car.

"Well." The girl came to stand beside her. "I'd say she's pissed at you."

Sam gave her a sideways glance. What she had thought was a blue wool skullcap was actually the girl's hair. Silver rings pierced her right nostril, left eyebrow, and middle of her lip, and a black tattoo of a Chinese character graced a spot on her neck. Her fingernails were bitten down to the quick, and there were dark bruises on the knuckles of her right hand.

Sixteen or seventeen at the most. Sam knew their landlord didn't run background checks on sublets. "You're Keri's tenant."

"Chris." She rubbed her head, revealing one small ear that had been pierced from top to lobe with studs and more rings. "You'd be the numb-cunt bitch of a cop who lives across the hall?"

Sam coughed to hide the laugh that was startled out of her. "Is that what Keri called me?"

"Lady, that's the *nicest* thing she called you." Chris sat down on the beanbag and hugged her knees. "I like it up here. If someone's going to break in, they'll hit the first or second floor, right? No way they're going to climb three flights."

The kid thought like a cop. Or a thief.

"Wait till you have to carry down trash, or haul up furniture," Sam warned her. "Then you'll be wishing you were closer to the ground." Maybe she'd run a background check on the kid, see what her story was.

"I'm using Keri's stuff until she gets back from her trip," Chris said. "Looks like a diner in there, doesn't it? All you need is pie under glass and a fat waitress carrying around a pot of coffee." She sniffed the air. "Do I smell French roast? Maybe there's a little extra a supernice neighbor would be willing to share?"

With a sigh Sam handed her the Styrofoam cup she held. "Enjoy. But I wouldn't get used to having Keri's stuff. It's expensive; she'll be back for it."

"I've got some things." Chris curled her hands around the cup and shifted, making the beanbag scrunch under her weight. "Lots of people around here throw out perfectly good stuff, too. I already scored a bag of clothes and shoes from the Dumpster." She sipped the coffee and grimaced. "Sugar, ugh. I take it black. I know—beggars can't be choosers. Anyway, the clothes are guy stuff, but most of it's wash-and-wear, and I can cut it down to my size."

"Better wash before you wear."

Chris squinted up at her. "I'm a poor beggar, Officer, not stupid."

"It's Sam," she corrected. "How old are you, anyway?"

"Why?" Chris stood and picked up her beanbag. "Do you have to be of age to drink coffee?"

"No."

"Then I'm twenty-one, Officer." The ring in her lower lip glimmered. Her smile was pure lightning, there one moment, gone in a blink. "See you around."

Eighty-seven men and eleven women were assigned to Fort Lauderdale Criminal Investigations Division, but only six of those worked homicide cases, with Sam as the only female officer in the unit. She and Harry had volunteered for a permanent assignment to the graveyard shift, as it allowed the other homicide detectives—all of whom were married with children—to work mornings or afternoons.

With half the murders in the city being committed at night, Sam and Harry ended up with the lion's share of Homicide's caseload.

Homicide was one of seven units under CID, with only six detectives allocated to investigate an average of twenty murders each year and to assist the Violent Crimes Unit, as they worked ten times as many cases. As a result, the squad room was one of the smallest within the department. Detectives routinely used their desk time to reduce the endless piles of paperwork or interview witnesses and gather information via phone. Now and then a detective from Juvenile Crimes or Auto Thefts would wander in to steal some of the dark brew from the five-gallon coffeemaker that was never allowed to run empty, but the atmosphere within CID could hardly be called social.

Some blamed murder, others the chilly management style of the captain of CID, Ernesto Garcia.

Sam viewed working in the squad room as a necessary evil. She didn't like the tight maze of desks that had been crammed into a space designed for half as many, or the fact that Garcia had renovated the one interview room in Homicide to serve as his personal office. Still, it was fairly quiet, and only rarely did she and Harry run into Garcia or the other four detectives working day shift.

Today was an exception, as Lena Caprell's body had been discovered by the Beach Patrol thirty minutes before Sam and Harry went off duty.

"Overtime, must be nice," Jeff Peterson called out as Sam went to her desk. He was a short, slim weapons fanatic who had moved to Homicide to wait for a range instructor slot to open up at the police academy. "What are you pulling down now, Harry?"

"More than I get," Ortenza, Peterson's partner, grumbled. The father of four, he'd been in a bad mood all month, since the day his wife informed him their fifth child was on the way.

"Quit your bitching," Harry said in a genial way as he ambled over to the coffeemaker. He didn't drink the dark brew, the caffeine of which interfered with his breathing medication, but kept a hot pot on the table to heat water for the decaf tea his wife supplied him. "Sam, you coffeed out?"

"No such thing." Sam picked up her phone and dialed Evidence Processing. Tenderson had grudgingly allowed her to take the cross and wallet they had found on Lena Caprell's body, and on her way to the squad room she had left them with one of the techs in EP for analysis. "This is Detective Brown. I forgot to add a dating request to my processing request."

"We'll have to send out that cross you left here," the tech told her. "It's solid handworked copper, you know, and these might be real beryls and onyx."

"No, I didn't know." Sam had wondered why it had been so heavy, but what she knew about old jewelry could fit comfortably inside a thimble. "Where do you think she got it?"

"They don't carry stuff like that at Ron Jon Surf Shop," the tech said. "I kind of wonder if she didn't steal it. I mean, I'm no expert, Detective, but I grubbed around some archaeology digs when I was in college. This cross belongs in a museum. It's definitely the oldest religious object I've ever seen."

"How old?"

"I can't say." The man sucked some air through his bridgework. "Wild guess? It might date back to the Middle Ages. Maybe before that."

What was Lena doing with something so old? "Let me know what you find out."

"There's one more thing," the tech said. "We found the stem of a cherry in her wallet. It was fresh and, uh, tied in a knot."

"Got it. Thanks." Sam jotted down some notes on the conversation and switched on her computer terminal. She knew the old bar dare of tying a cherry stem in a knot using only tongue and teeth; men thought it was sexy when women did it. Which meant Lena might have stopped somewhere for a drink last night. "Harry, what was the name of that nightclub across the street from the crime scene?"

"One word. Something short." He dropped a tea bag over the side of his favorite mug, a gift from his wife that sported a miniature bass serving as a handle and the words I'D RATHER BE CASTING.

Sam did a search of Fort Lauderdale nightclubs with single-word titles and began reading them out loud. "Hotshots, Infusion, J.T.'s—"

"Infusion," Harry said as he came to the desk and picked up his phone. "That was it."

"Thanks." Sam's gaze moved from her screen to watch their boss walk in through the door that led into Violent Crimes. "Morning, Captain."

"I need to see you two," Garcia said as he passed by Sam's

and Harry's desks and continued without stopping to his corner office.

Harry stopped dialing a number and replaced the receiver. "You get mouthy with Tendernuts?"

"Do I ever?" Sam printed out the info sheet on Infusion before following Harry into their boss's office. Out of deference to her partner's seniority, Sam let Harry take the only chair in front of Garcia's desk and assumed her usual spot next to the door frame.

Ernesto Garcia's office was as tidy as the captain himself. Rows of framed citations he had earned over the years marched up and down one side wall. He had occupied the former interview room in Homicide for three of the seven years Sam had worked there, but to date he remained something of a mystery man. He had a reputation for running a tight, efficient division, and had zero tolerance for time wasting or bullshit.

Despite that, everyone agreed that there was something a little off about Garcia.

Unlike other ranking Cuban-American officers in the department, the captain didn't waste time establishing rapport with his subordinates or projecting himself as a friendly or kindly authority figure. He was also a bachelor, lived alone, and never spoke of family or friends.

"He's gay," was Jeff Peterson's theory. "And his boyfriend is a drag queen. A flaming drag queen."

"Nah, I bet he lives with his sweet little old silver-haired *mamacita*," Ortenza argued. "Mine would move in with us if we had a spare room. Only I think my wife would poison her."

Sam didn't care about her boss's love life or living arrangements; she figured he was entitled to some privacy. A body-conscious man, Garcia kept his big frame in shape by lifting free weights and running five miles on an indoor track every morning before work. She knew because she used the same gym herself. Harry had speculated that Garcia shaved his head to look older and tougher, but Sam suspected the captain didn't want to waste time in the A.M. fooling with his hair.

"Prelim on Caprell, Lena." He held up a file from the coroner's office. "Cause of death was drowning."

"We figured—" Harry began.

"She drowned in tap water," Garcia continued as if he hadn't spoken. "Both lungs were filled with it. The ME also found a minor ligature mark on the neck, ten broken fingernails, and extensive bruising on the upper sternum."

No one had to state the obvious: Lena Caprell had been murdered.

"We don't believe that she was killed on the beach," Sam said, and described the condition of the victim's remains. "The positioning is too deliberate; he must have posed her."

"Talk to the men in her life." Garcia pushed the file across the desk. "Pull her photo off DOT and run copies, show them around the area. Check with next of kin; see if she's dumped someone recently. Quinn, excuse us for a minute."

Harry gave Sam a quick look of concern before he retreated back to the squad room.

"Sit down, Brown."

Sam didn't like being invited to sit; it meant bad news. Still, she took Harry's seat. "If this is about a new partner, Captain, I'd like to fly solo for a while."

A flicker of surprise crossed Garcia's dark features before they smoothed back to impassivity. "That's against department policy. Peterson got his academy post approved, so I have two new transfers coming in next week."

Sam knew then that her boss had already chosen someone to take Harry's place. "Anyone I know?"

"Adam Suarez from Economic Crimes, and Wes Dwyer from Metro-Dade Traffic."

Her entire body went cold. Three shots rang out in her memory, while a phantom burn scorched across the back of her left hand. She didn't remember the bullets that had struck her in the abdomen and upper arm. Just the one that nearly took off her hand.

A handsome face leered at her from an ugly past that wouldn't go away. *I'll fix you, bitch.* Another, less attractive visage grinned from behind a street piece. *Wes say to tell you this from him.*

"I've been briefed on your history with Dwyer," Garcia was saying over the dull roar of Marqueta's laughter in Sam's ears. "I thought I'd tell you before he signs on, so you can prepare yourself."

"Prepare." She peered across the ten thousand miles of desk between them. "The last time I worked with Wesley Dwyer, I ended up in the hospital for six weeks. The first two I spent in intensive care. How would you suggest I prepare? By wrapping myself in Kevlar?"

Garcia leaned back in his chair. "Dwyer didn't shoot you, and he was never implicated in the shooting. You killed Marqueta."

Deep and abiding outrage melted the ice encasing her limbs. "If that's the way it is, I'll make it easy for you." She stood up and reached into her jacket for her badge.

"Sit down, Samantha."

She sat. Garcia got up and shut the blinds before coming back around to perch on the edge of the desk. Although he didn't look sympathetic, his voice went quiet. "I need to know how bad this thing is between you two."

"Bad." She forced herself to recite what constituted the worst moments of her life. "I filed a sexual harassment charge against Dwyer two months after we became partners. There were never any witnesses, so he wiggled out of all of it by saying it was all a big misunderstanding. Ever since, every guy in the department has considered me a tight-ass."

Garcia didn't deny this. "Did you misunderstand his intentions? Maybe he was being friendly."

She regarded him steadily. "If your partner made obscene phone calls during the middle of the night to your residence, or dropped in so often that you had to move, or referred to you only as 'my suck bitch' while speaking to other officers, or left sex toys covered with scented lube in your desk, or cornered you in a restroom in order to shove his tongue in your ear and his hand down the front of your pants, and threatened to set you up for a drug bust if you didn't give him a weekly trip around the world, would you consider those intentions friendly?"

The captain's full mouth tightened. "No."

"The chief down in Burglary did, but he was a hard-ass who didn't like women on the force." Sam rubbed her temple. "He kept us paired until the Marqueta case."

"The IA reports state that Marqueta shot you while Dwyer was requesting backup." Garcia crossed his arms. "Your ex-partner said you went in alone."

"Dwyer *left* me alone in that warehouse and took off. Marqueta was waiting for me." She toed the carpet with her shoe. "It was my word against Dwyer's, but this time IA treated it a little more seriously. I was the one who took three bullets and nearly bled to death after shooting Marqueta."

Garcia glanced out at the rising sun and went to shut his outside window blinds. "What about the complaint you filed with IA on him once you were released from the hospital?"

"One of the guys over in VC found a hooker who said she saw Dwyer and Marqueta together the afternoon before the shooting," Sam told him. "She disappeared an hour before she was scheduled to come in and make a formal statement. They found her three weeks later with her throat cut in a landfill out in Davie."

"You wore a wire and tried to get him to admit to killing her."

"I pushed hard, but he wouldn't," Sam admitted. "He must have been expecting it, too, because right after IA ran the tape, his union rep showed up yelling about entrapment. Division settled things with a transfer down to Metro-Dade's Traffic Unit."

"He's gotten a couple of citations for community service, talking to kids about bike safety and that kind of thing," Garcia told her. "He also did the mandatory psych eval and came through clean."

Sam felt like throwing her weapon and badge at him. "You think I'm lying to you about this?"

"I know Dwyer's been dogging a transfer back here for the last two years. He's kissed ass from here to Homestead to get an assignment to Homicide." He sat down behind his desk and folded his hands. "I'd say, yeah, he's coming back for you."

Some of the panic inside her loosened. "You partner us, I'll be dead in a week."

"I'm not assigning him to replace Quinn," the captain said. "You'll get Suarez, and Ortenza can have Dwyer while I work out how to bust him down to patrol. Until I do, you need to keep your mouth shut about this."

She had been harassed, stalked, assaulted, and shot three times because of one unbalanced cop with a grudge, but she couldn't tell anyone. "Right."

Garcia held up a hand. "I'm on your side, Brown, but that's not enough. You have to see it through their eyes." He nodded toward the squad room. "You're young, attractive, and you've made rank faster than any man here. Some of the squad already think you're a slut for promotion. You also levied a sexual harassment against your own partner, and when that didn't stick, you went for attempted murder, and wore a wire."

And the squad would believe whatever Dwyer said over her. That was the way it was. "Dwyer made me want to puke from day one. As for my rank, I earned it with my brain, not my ass."

"I know. Which is why you're going to keep your head down until I can boot this nutcase off my squad." He produced an ugly smile. "You're not the only one who's had to swallow shit to make rank."

"Dwyer isn't just shit, Captain." She looked at the bullet-wound scar creasing the back of her left hand and got to her feet. "He's psychotic. The real deal. Whatever you think about me, don't underestimate him. I did, and I almost lost a kidney."

"I'll handle it."

"You do that. But if I turn up dead, do me a favor. Don't believe him when he says he didn't kill me." She walked out of the office.

When Sam got to her desk, Harry handed her the sheet she had printed out on the nightclub. "Guess what?"

She couldn't think about Dwyer, or she'd spend the rest of the day emptying her stomach in the nearest toilet. "I don't know, what?"

"That building with the nightclub just changed hands." Her partner nodded toward the sheet in her hand. "Check out the name of the new property management company."

Sam focused on the sheet, and found the paragraph about the sale of the property. "I'll be damned. Lucan Enterprises."

"Yeah." Harry grinned. "So, are we going dancing tonight, honey, or what?"

Chapter 4

John Keller had felt the air change as soon as the bus passed Orlando. What had been cold and dry in Georgia suddenly softened and warmed, easing the tightness in his chest. By the time the Greyhound pulled into the Hollywood station, he was tired, hungry, and hopeful.

Tired and hungry were nothing new, but the hope was something he hadn't felt in a long time.

The driver, a lean black man with distrusting eyes, took John's one suitcase from the cargo bay and set it down in front of him. "You got a place to go, my man?"

John nodded and reached for the case.

"I just wanted to say how I appreciate you looking after the old lady," the driver said, nodding toward the frail, elderly woman being escorted from the station by the middle-aged daughter who had come to meet the bus.

Helping the lady in and out of her seat and escorting her to the tiny restroom on the bus had been simple courtesy, nothing more, but the other passengers had stared at John as though he had lost his mind.

"It wasn't a big thing. Have a safe trip back," John told the driver, and then paused as the man held out a business card. "What's this?"

"My brother's got a roofing business in north Broward. Steady work for a man who ain't afraid of heights." The driver gestured toward the northwest. "You need a job or something, call him, tell him Maurice said you're okay."

John took the card and shook the driver's hand. "Thank you."

"Like you said, no big thing." Maurice grinned, flashing gold caps. "You take care now, my man."

John walked into the station and stopped at one of the vending machines to get a can of soda. He studied the card and wondered if he might have to make the call to Maurice's brother. The bus ticket to Florida had left him with seventeen dollars in his wallet. If Mercer didn't show up, it was enough to buy a couple of meals, make some long-distance phone calls, or rent a cheap room for the night. After that he would hit bottom: broke, homeless, and unemployed.

It didn't frighten him. Hitting bottom had been a regular occurrence in John Keller's life since leaving Chicago.

Working his way to Florida had been harder than John had expected, but the economy was on a downslide, and no one wanted to hire a grim, quiet ex-priest with no practical job skills. He had been forced to spend a month in Kentucky working labor-pool jobs and living in a homeless shelter simply to save up for a bus ticket here.

John took a long drink from the ice-cold can of Pepsi and felt too many eyes watching him. He didn't blame the passengers waiting for their buses or relatives to arrive. It was getting dark, and night brought out the caution in people. He'd lost more weight, so much that now his worn, thriftstore-bought clothes hung on him, and he badly needed a haircut and a beard trim. He probably looked like a bum. If Mercer showed up, he might not even recognize him. He was a ghost of his former self.

At least I'm not a vampire.

His sister, Alexandra, had become one. It was ironic, in the sense that John had worked for years to keep his sister out of his life, using his vocation as the wall between them. John had once thought he and Alex might someday reconcile their difficult relationship, once he had overcome his shame over his past mistakes, and she stopped pretending she was an atheist in order to hurt him.

Before John could begin the healing process, he had been lured from his sister and his calling as a parish priest to become an initiate of *Les Frères de la Lumière*, the Brethren of the Light. He had gone to Rome for his training, where the former Catholic priests had brainwashed, brutalized, and virtually tortured him. Not, as John had been told, to transform him into a warrior of God. No, John had been taken simply to be made into bait for his sister, for by then Alexandra had already sacrificed her humanity to play physician for her immortal vampire lover and his kind.

Now that his little sister had become something beyond his understanding, something that made a mockery of everything he had believed in, John didn't know what to do. Most of his beliefs and all of his faith had died over the last year. Still, John could not have a relationship with a creature that fed off the blood of the living—even if she had been his sister.

We are on opposite sides of this thing. We can never be brother and sister again.

John had left the priesthood, because as repulsive as the parasitic needs of the Darkyn were, the horrendous practices the Brethren used to hunt, torture, and kill them were just as horrific. He did not know what Alex and the Darkyn intended to do, but the Brethren's mission was clear. They would do whatever was necessary to win the centuries-long struggle to wipe out the Darkyn. John knew they were not above using anyone—street thugs, runaway children, or even other Darkyn—to hunt down, torture, and kill the vampires.

These are demons sent up from hell itself to torment mankind, Archbishop Hightower, John's sponsor and mentor, had told him. *They use whatever they can to manipulate us, to turn us against one another.*

Alex hadn't done that. To date she had stayed away from John, and the one time they had been alone together since her transformation all she had asked for was a vial of his blood. She claimed she needed it to keep searching for a cure for herself and the Darkyn, whom she believed were victims of an ancient viral mutation.

Hightower had warned John that he was a target of the Darkyn. *If these creatures have Alexandra, then the Order is the only thing that can keep you safe now.* He had given him incriminating photographs the Darkyn had taken of John when he had been out of his mind on drugs, so much so that he had raped one of the female Darkyn working for the Brethren. *They won't rest until you are back in prison.*

John hated to admit it, but he missed Hightower as well. He didn't trust the archbishop, and sometimes he despised him, but Hightower had wielded tremendous positive influence over his life. The last time he had seen his mentor, Hightower had paid him the ultimate compliment: *You're the closest thing to a son that I'll ever have.*

His adopted parents had died while John was in the seminary. Alexandra was as good as dead, and his mentor had betrayed him time and again. That was why John had contacted Mercer. All he really had left in the world were a few friends, like Mercer Lane.

"Father John Keller, please come to the ticket booth," a woman said over the PA system, making him swivel toward the glassed-in booths at the far end of the station. A man in a plain dark suit stood next to the middle window and was scanning the faces of passengers walking in from the bus lot.

John had met Mercer Lane at a Benedictine conference two years ago. Mercer had transferred from his parish in Manchester to America, and had been looking for a post in Florida. His wry, self-deprecating humor had made an otherwise dull event lively, and John had corresponded with him for several months after the conference. Those happy memories made John seriously consider walking out of the station and sparing his friend any involvement in his complicated life.

Then Mercer saw him, and John was caged by the genuine smile that appeared on his face as he hurried over.

"Saints, John, you look like the devil himself with that beard." Mercer embraced him as a brother might and stepped back. He had long, floppy light brown hair and the patrician features of the youngest son of an old, moneyed family, which was exactly what he had been before becoming a priest. "How was the ride?"

"Fine, Merc. I'm glad to see you, too." He picked up his case. "Are you sure this won't be a problem?"

"Not for me; I run the place." Mercer grinned like a boy and took his suitcase. "I'll wager you're starving, and there's a smashing little deli down the street that's open late. You can have a bite and then we'll head back to home base."

The deli turned out to be kosher, and John renewed his acquaintance with a proper Reuben sandwich.

"You really went bugger-all? Handed over the collar and the cross for good?" Mercer asked before taking a sip of his mineral water.

"I did." John felt his stomach clench and willed himself not to turn lunch into a confessional booth. "I'd like to keep a low profile while I'm here, if that's possible. I'm using my middle name, Patrick, as my last name. Like I told you over the phone, I've had enough upheaval in my life."

John hadn't informed his friend about the details of what had made him leave the church. As open-minded as Mercer was, even he'd have a hard time swallowing the story of how John and his sister had been victimized and made enemies by the immortal demons known as the Darkyn.

His friend nodded. "We're not a nosy lot at the abbey." He smirked. "The brothers are more interested in seeing how much work they can get out of you while you're with us anyway. Tote that barge; lift that bale—that sort of thing."

The brothers. John's appetite vanished. "You never mentioned your affiliation with the church. What order governs the monastery?" He prayed it was not *Les Frères de la Lumière,* the Brethren of the Light, who had used him repeatedly in their battle against the vampires known as Darkyn.

"We're Franciscans," Mercer said. He tugged at the lapel of his jacket. "I wear street clothes when I drive into town, mostly in hopes that I'll be mistaken for Hugh Grant and kidnapped by a deranged supermodel, but on our grounds it's all about the robe and rope."

Franciscan monks were among the poorest and most dedicated of God's servants, and some of John's tension automatically eased. "No worldly goods at all? Somehow I expected a continental like you to end up running a Benedictine order."

Mercer laughed. "Brown is bloody hot enough. I'm not wearing black in the tropics."

After they finished their sandwiches, Mercer bought some bagels, lox, and cream cheese to take back to the monastery.

"I've often regretted not being born a Jew," he explained as they went to his ancient station wagon. "Their food is so much better. I'd trade ham and pork chops for kugel and matzo-ball soup any day."

"You'd have to marry," John pointed out. "Single rabbis are frowned on."

"After all these years of celibacy, I expect I'd need a spot of coaching." His friend shrugged. "Then the bird would want to meet my parents, and Mum would finally die of shock the way she's been threatening to all these years."

In his letters to John, Mercer had confessed to an extended battle with an addiction that had ruined his ability to stay in England. His parents, wealthy supporters of the Catholic church there, had not been sympathetic. In his last letter, which had caught up with John in Chicago, Mercer had told him he had a new vision of his faith and his role in the church. How that vision had led him to become the abbot of a Franciscan monastery, John wasn't sure. He'd never imagined a lively and intelligent soul like Mercer retreating to the cloister.

It's not as isolated as the North of England, thank the Almighty, and we're involved with the local community on a regular basis, Mercer had written of his new post in South Florida. *Feeding the homeless, helping out the elderly, guiding the kids, that sort of thing. I feel like I finally have a place in the world, John.*

John, who had never found his place, had tried not to envy his friend.

"You speak Spanish, don't you?" Mercer asked now.

John nodded.

"Good, because half of our people don't understand anything else."

John wondered if his friend had some agenda to repair the damage that had destroyed his calling. "I'll help however I can, but don't think it will change my mind. I'm done with the church."

"I got that loud and clear over the phone, Johnny," Mercer said. "I've all the friars I can handle anyway. What we could really use is a procurator. Over time we've inherited a dozen lifelong monastics, and you know how hopeless the old guys are at dealing with the outside world. I'm so busy I can't babysit all of them. You'd make a great go-between."

John wasn't going to commit himself yet. Not even for

Mercer. "I'm really not sure what I want to do. Let's take it one day at a time."

His friend nodded and chuckled. "That's my motto."

Lucan dried his face with an ivory hand towel and straightened to face the space on the wall where the mirror had been removed. Despite legend and Hollywood propaganda, Darkyn could see their reflections just as well as humans could, although many avoided mirrors. Guilt, perhaps, over the fact that time weathered every human face around them but left theirs untouched, or the old superstition that they would see the devil grinning at them over their shoulder.

We are all variations on Dorian Gray, my friend, Gabriel Seran had told him once. *We simply have not yet found our portraits.*

Lucan personally didn't particularly like or dislike mirrors; he had them removed only because, thanks to a minor side effect of his talent, they had the unfortunate tendency to shatter around him. If the old superstition about receiving seven years' bad luck for every mirror one broke were true, he would need to live an eternity to work off his.

A knock on the door made Lucan reach for his gloves. "What is it?"

"A call for you, master," Burke said from outside.

He dropped the gloves. "Tell whoever it is that I died during the last Crusade."

Lucan dragged his fingers through his damp hair. The other reason he didn't need mirrors was because his face had not changed in seven centuries. He had been considered handsome in nearly every age he had lived, thanks to whatever titled adulterer had impregnated his mother, Gwynyth, a minor lady-in-waiting at a forgotten court. That randy nobleman had gifted him with strong, defined features and an abundance of fine fair hair that had begun turning silver in his fourteenth year. His mother's eyes had been a limpid cornflower blue, so he assumed his sire had also endowed him with his strangely colorless eyes. Given his lack of color, Lucan occasionally wondered if Gwynyth had spread her legs for an albino.

Ask me about your father again, sweeting, his mother had

purred during one of the rare interviews she had granted him while screwing her way into the queen's service, *and I'll cut out your tongue.*

Gwynyth's people had been little more than gentrified farmers, the descendents of landholders and by-blows left behind by raiding Norsemen. From them Lucan had inherited a broad, heavy-boned frame and a peculiar quickness usually confined to smaller, lighter men. During his eighteenth year he had suddenly gained another four inches in height, growing so quickly that his joints stiffened and ached for months. That final surge of adolescence had given him an impressive length of limb and made him the tallest of his master's squires. His size, agility, and reach had caught the attention of a visiting Templar, who had convinced Lucan that God had endowed him thusly to save Jerusalem from the infidels.

Thou art made to be the strong arm of God, the warrior priest assured him. *Come to the temple and pledge thyself to be my brother in arms, and I will train thee myself.*

Lucan shrugged into a white linen shirt with full sleeves. How pitiful his life would have been if he had not abandoned his mother to her court intrigues. When he had told her he intended to take his vows, she had threatened to send him back to his grandfather's farm to work the fields. There he might have lived thirty or forty years, long enough to spawn the next generation of plowmen and die of some dismal disease or injury common to his birth era.

How much trouble Gwynyth might have saved him, if only she had carried out one of her threats.

A timid knock interrupted his thoughts. "Master Lucan?"

"What now?" he asked through clenched teeth.

"Lord Tremayne says that he is aware that you died after the last Crusade," Burke said, "but he would still like to speak with you. He is on hold for you."

Lucan jerked open the door and glared down at his *tresora.* "You put the high lord of the Darkyn on *hold?*"

"He said he didn't mind." Burke erupted into a spate of sneezes.

Lucan snatched the cordless receiver out of his hand, stepped back, and slammed the door in his *tresora*'s face. He switched the phone on and lifted it to his ear. "My apologies for keeping you waiting, seigneur. I vow I will strangle my human servant at the next opportunity."

"Do not deprive yourself of that congested jester on my account, Lucan." Richard Tremayne's silken voice curled inside his head like a contented, purring feline. "When he is not evacuating his orifices, the fellow doubtless has his merits. Do you know, has he tried Sudafed? My humans claim it a miracle drug."

"I shall inquire of him." Burke would have to die for this. "Your generosity is unexpected and deeply appreciated, seigneur."

"That I doubt," Richard said. "How are you finding your first taste of suzerainty?"

"The bureaucracy may drive me to frenzy." Why were they chatting as old friends long parted? Lucan had abandoned Richard without warning or permission. "I have gathered nearly a hundred, not enough for a proper *jardin,* but I suspect there are others waiting to see what I will make of it."

"Michael is among them."

"I owe Cyprien nothing." Agitated by the mention of the one Kyn he would kill for nothing, Lucan walked out to the wall of security camera monitors in his bedchamber that displayed different views of the entire nightclub. "I believe you are owed a proper explanation for my disobedience."

"It is a little late to be inventing pretty excuses for leaving my service." His voice took on an edge that scraped fine, sharp claws against Lucan's ear. "You served me faithfully for many years. I knew one day you would tire of it." The high lord's tone changed slightly, neutralizing the piercing effect. "My rule may soon come to an end, and I could not have deeded you like a castle or a fortune to my successor."

On the monitor Lucan saw a young woman and older man enter the club together and approach one of his bartenders. The odd couple both wore suits and showed his employee their identification. Bitterness rose in his throat. "You still intend to have Cyprien take the reins."

"My intentions are not your concern," Richard reminded him. "Cyprien, however, is. I have reason to believe that he and his people will be paying you a visit very soon."

Lucan would have replied, but the young woman had turned toward the camera. His fingers fumbled with the monitor controls for a moment until he could zoom in on her features.

Frances.

"If Michael does appear on your doorstep," Richard was saying, "you will not kill him."

He sat down on the carpet and stared up at the monitors, following the young woman's progress through the club. "I told him to stay out of Florida."

"Whether you recognize his authority or not, Michael is now your liege lord."

She was the image of Frances. Oh, Lucan could see that she was not an exact match, for she did not possess the same length of hair or languid grace of movement. Frances had dressed like a princess of the realm; this girl's boxy garments and ugly shoes desperately wanted burning.

But her face? The very image of Frances, who had been buried two hundred years ago.

"I wish you to do something for me."

"Anything." Lucan tore his gaze from the monitors and forced himself to attend Richard.

"Michael will bring his *sygkenis* with him."

Richard referred to Dr. Alexandra Keller, the first human to make the change in many centuries. How Cyprien had managed it, Lucan knew not, but he had seen the woman with his own eyes. He had also lusted after her pretty little body and greatly feared the passion with which she burned.

Not that it mattered now. Not when he had Frances's living twin downstairs, ripe and ready for the taking. "What would you have me do, seigneur?"

"Contact me if you find yourself with unexpected guests. Do not allow Cyprien or his *sygkenis* to leave Florida until I arrive."

Lucan was confused; Richard had made the dangerous trip from Ireland only a year ago. "You are coming to America again? Why?"

The line clicked, and a dial tone answered him.

Chapter 5

As soon as Sam met Harry at the department they drove down to the nightclub across from the bench where Lena Caprell's body had been left. According to the data Sam had pulled off the Internet, Infusion opened its doors at sunset and didn't close until dawn.

The sun had disappeared, but the usual breeze off the ocean had dwindled down to nothing, leaving the beachfront to bake a little longer in electric and neon lights and the exhaust fumes from bumper-to-bumper night traffic. Despite the ninety-degree heat and soup-thick humidity, a long line of patrons was waiting outside Infusion. Sam found an empty space halfway up the block, parked, and flipped down the visor to display the unit ID card. Harry was busy staring back at the club line.

"What is this place, like that *Rocky Horror* movie?" he asked, disbelief escalating his bushy eyebrows.

"You're stuck in the seventies, pal." Sam noted a couple passing by them; a young man who had tricked himself out to clone Marilyn Manson. His sulky companion, a Cuban girl, had affected more of a Daisy Fuentes–on-acid look. "This is beach goth." And not the kind of people or place she'd have expected a class act like Lena Caprell to frequent.

Harry grumbled all the way from the car to the front entrance of the nightclub, where a sign by the door indicated the cover was twenty bucks. The doorman, a muscular tank in a surprisingly nice tux, stood up as Sam and Harry cut the line.

"Turn it around." A meaty hand came up to make a stop sign. "You have to wait like the rest of them."

"But we have special invitations from the city." Sam flashed her shield, and the bouncer rolled his eyes before he jerked open the club's steel front door. "Thanks."

It took a moment for Sam's eyes to adjust to the near total darkness inside, and then she took in the basic layout. Infusion was cavernous for a beach club, lighting and sound equipment hanging from a flat black ceiling thirty feet above her head. There were plenty of tiny tables and stools crowded around a huge gray slate dance floor, and polished chrome-and-glass bars that stretched the length of three walls. Bunches of red, oval-shaped lights glittered from the shadows, giving the impression of hundreds of watchful, vicious eyes.

"Welcome to my nightmare," Harry muttered.

Like the bouncer, the bartenders also wore beautifully tailored tuxes, and had their hair slicked back from handsome, bored faces. The waitresses sported abbreviated black French-maid outfits, but without the usual mini white aprons and mob-caps. No, the decor was definitely red and black—heavy on the black.

Music started up unexpectedly, and Harry flinched as Nirvana's "Smells Like Teen Spirit" came screeching out of the oversize speakers above their heads.

"See the office?" he shouted to be heard over Kurt Cobain.

Sam spotted a plain door off to one side. "Over there, I think," she yelled back.

They found the door locked, and a shouted inquiry at one of the bartenders nearby revealed that the owner had not yet arrived.

"I don't know when Mr. Hell will be in," the young man bellowed at Sam.

She frowned. "Mr. Hell?"

"L," the bartender repeated, emphasizing it. "L for Lucan."

"Christ, he only has one name?" When the bartender nodded, Harry made a disgusted sound and jerked his head toward the entrance. "Sam, this shit is gonna blow out my eardrums. I'll go canvass the line."

She nodded and caught the arm of a passing waitress, showing her and the bartender Lena's photo. "Either of you recognize this woman?"

The bartender shook his head and went to deliver two

screwdrivers to a couple of middle-aged women at the end of the bar.

"Sorry, no," the waitress said before she hurried off with a tray heavily loaded with murky-looking mai tais.

That was the same answer Sam got from everyone, although she thought a couple of the employees recognized the photo and were lying to her. After an hour of coming up empty, she was ready to leave. The pounding music and clouds of cigarette smoke had given her a brutal headache, and if Lena Caprell had ever come to Infusion, the owner didn't want it known. They'd have to find out why.

"Sam." Harry appeared and watched the gyrating bodies on the dance floor for a moment. "No luck outside. You?"

"Manager still hasn't shown up. I think we'd better . . ." A huddle in one corner caught her eye. "We got a deal going down over there."

Harry squinted. "Yeah. Take two o'clock; I'll come up from nine."

The five men and women grouped together in the corner stood shoulder-to-shoulder, half-hidden between a square column and one wall of the club. Sam strolled up, peered over one shoulder, and saw a woman in the center. Ten hands were doing various intimate things to the woman's body.

"Hey." Sam prodded a back. "Time for a cigarette."

"I don't smoke." The thirty-something man glanced over his shoulder and bared some fake plastic fangs. "Would you care to join us?"

"You talking up my date?" Harry asked as he came up on the man's other side. He peered at the guy's mouth with mocking astonishment. "Halloween was over a long time ago, buddy."

One thing Sam hadn't been seeing was any sign of drunkenness or drug use, two favorite activities at the downtown beach clubs.

"Let me talk to her." She pushed two sets of shoulders apart and stepped into the huddle. "You okay here, lady?"

The woman's hair was a tangle, and her button-up dress was open to the waist, but nothing was hanging out. Her eyes focused on Sam after a couple of seconds.

"I'm fine." She leaned back against one of the men, who cupped her breasts. "So fine."

Everyone smiled at Sam and Harry. Everyone wore plastic fangs.

Swingers playing oversexed vampires. It took all kinds. "Look," Sam said, "why don't you folks find a nice hotel?"

"Is there a problem here, Officer?"

Sam swiveled and nearly slammed into a broad chest. She looked up into ghost-gray eyes. "Who are you?"

The man took her hand in his, the touch of the black velvet gloves he wore shocking her. "I'm Lucan, the owner of the club. You wanted to speak to me."

What kind of man wears velvet? In July? Sam tugged her hand from his. "Detective Brown, Fort Lauderdale Homicide. My partner, Detective Quinn. We need to ask you a couple of questions, Mr. Lucan."

"It's simply Lucan." His thin lips curled into something between a sneer and a smile. "Shall we go to my office?" His pale eyes briefly flashed up at the speakers. "It's the only place you'll hear my answers."

Sam heard Harry wheeze and saw more people lighting up cigarettes around them. She leaned close to him. "Let me handle this; you go outside before you have an attack."

Harry scowled but trudged off.

Lucan waited until she looked at him, turned, and walked through the crowd to the office. Sam followed, studying him from behind. He didn't match the description of the suspect; he was too big. She figured him to be at least six-four and two-twenty. He wore his silver-blond hair like a lion's mane, which should have come off stupid but didn't. Even the silly velvet gloves didn't seem prissy, but he had huge hands.

How would it feel . . . Sam shoved aside the mental image of black velvet on her breasts. *Quit thinking with your crotch.*

The interior of Lucan's office matched the club in style, decor, and darkness. He removed his jacket, turned on a small desk lamp, and offered Sam a drink, which she refused. She inspected him up close as he poured some wine for himself. The full-sleeved white poet's shirt and plain black trousers were retro nineteenth century, but it was a goth club; he probably considered it a uniform. He wasn't Cuban, not with the corn-silk hair and spooky eyes. His voice sounded British, but only vaguely.

"How did you know we were cops?" she asked him as he came to stand with her in front of his wide, spotless chrome-and-slate desk.

"You're not wearing black lipstick." He sipped his wine before returning her inspection. "Judging by your suits, you were either bill collectors or police officers. How may I be of service, Detective?"

"We're investigating an incident that happened nearby." She showed him Lena's photo. "Do you recognize this woman?"

Lucan studied the image. "Yes, but I don't know her name."

"How do you know her?"

"I had sex with her several weeks ago." He sat back on the edge of the desk.

"You were lovers?"

He smiled. "We were strangers."

Sam tried not to jump on that, but it was irresistible. "Do you often have one-night stands with strange, nameless women, Mr. Lucan?"

"Three nights." He drained his wineglass and straightened, moving a step closer.

Sam smelled night-blooming jasmine, but couldn't identify the source. "What was that?"

"It was a three-night stand. I kept her in my bed for three nights." He bent closer, and his voice dropped to a bedroom murmur. "How many nights would you last, Detective?"

Was he hitting on her? "None." Sam felt strange, rooted to the floor. "I don't have sex with strangers."

One velvet-covered finger touched her dry lips. "Then let's get better acquainted, shall we?"

Her entire body flushed. How could he heat her up so fast, just by stroking her mouth with a velvet fingertip? And why did she feel as if she were going to puke flowers?

I'm sick. Summer flu or something. She took a step back, and then another. "I'm only interested in your relationship with Ms. Caprell."

"Only?" Lucan watched her face with all the concentration

of a cat at a mouse hole. "I don't interest you? Not even a little, Detective?"

"I'll come back tomorrow." Her feet didn't want to leave the floor now, so she shuffled, sliding them like a skater going backward.

"I think you'd rather stay." He extended a hand. "It's what you want, isn't it, Detective? To come to me now. No one is here. No one will see."

He was hypnotizing her. Sam reached out blindly, and her hand connected with the wineglass he had left on the desk. The cold crystal against her hot skin helped her, but not enough to get her legs moving. "My partner is waiting for me."

"Let him wait," Lucan murmured, lowering his hand and moving toward her. "I'll tell you when you can leave."

The hell he would.

It took every ounce of strength Sam had to turn away from him. "Good-bye." She couldn't get more than that out of her mouth, not with the sunlight flowing through her, not with the jasmine growing inside her mind. She couldn't even put down the wineglass. Some part of her underneath of it was furious and shrieking, *No, I don't want this.*

Sam felt him coming up behind her and her legs stopped working.

"You don't want to go." Large, strong hands touched her shoulders before stroking down over the front of her jacket. Hands pressed her back, and she felt the bulge of his erection against the curve of her spine. "You want to stay, don't you? Stay and please me."

Sam wanted to punch him. "No."

Delicate crystal shattered.

She looked down at her bleeding hand, covered with gleaming shards. It didn't seem to belong to her, but there it was, attached to her wrist. "That should hurt."

"Bloody hell."

As he jerked her around, she looked up at him, bewildered. "Why doesn't it hurt?"

Lucan curled his fingers around her wrist and began plucking the slivers of crystal from her lacerated palm and fingers. "Because you've got a damned will of iron, you stupid bitch, that's why." Furious gray eyes bored into hers. "Who the devil are you?"

At that moment, she wasn't sure of anything but her name. "Samantha." Nothing seemed to matter but breathing in the waves of jasmine rolling over her, which silenced the angry voice deep within. "I didn't mean to break your pretty glass."

He sighed, as if relieved. "At long last." Black velvet touched her chin, lifting it so that she couldn't do anything but look into his eyes. "You didn't break it; I did. Now, tell me why you came here tonight, Samantha."

Sam knew she should be the one asking the questions—she was the cop; he was the suspect—but Lucan was such a kind man, and so gentle. He wouldn't ask unless it was really important, so of course she'd tell him whatever he wanted to know.

"Your name," she heard herself say. "The word *Lucan* was engraved on the back of an old cross we found on the victim's body." Something funny was happening. His pupils shrank down to splinters of black, while the ghostly irises had turned to chrome. "Something's wrong with your eyes."

"It's the smell of your blood. I haven't . . ." He looked away from her. "Give me a moment."

His voice sounded as tight as his hand on her wrist. He needed something, something she could give him. She'd give him anything he wanted—immediately—all he had to do was ask. She began to tell him that and then noticed that something else was wrong. "You have fangs."

They flashed when he spoke, and made him lisp a little. As perfect as he was, she liked that tiny flaw. It made him seem more human.

But he's not human, not with those vampire teeth. "Are you going to bite me?"

"You've saved me the trouble by piercing a vein." He lifted her injured hand to his open mouth.

Sam didn't feel fangs sinking into her palm. She felt his lips and his tongue, and a gentle suction that made her thighs ache. He wasn't simply cleaning the blood from her hand with his mouth; he was taking more—drinking it from one very deep cut.

He lifted his mouth from her hand, turned it over, and touched the bullet scar. "What did you do to yourself?"

"A contract killer shot me." She didn't want to think about Marqueta. Not with this drowsiness stealing over her, and the full heat pulsing between her thighs. "Is that all you want from me, Lucan?"

"No." His gloved hand moved into her hair and cradled the back of her head as he brought her face close to his.

He was kissing her, his open mouth on hers, his tongue gliding between her lips. He tasted of blood and tears and wine, and his hand tightened, pulling her hair. The sharp tug brought a moan from her throat.

What felt like an iron bar slammed into Sam's back, and her feet left the floor. Dimly she heard things falling to the floor, and then she was on her back, hard flat wood against her shoulders and buttocks, and he was looming over her, his shaking hands pushing her legs apart. She felt his erection through her trousers, and the answering rush of liquid heat that instantly soaked her crotch.

Lucan lifted his head and breathed in. "Christ Jesus, you smell like a jungle in the rain. What I could do to you, Samantha." Velvet stroked over her cheek. "What I will do."

Some of the delicious heat seeped out of her limbs, replaced by knots of tension. She needed more than his sexy promises and soft gloves, but she didn't want more. Part of her was still screaming for her to fight and get away from him. "Let me up."

His hand palmed her, and his thumb pressed in, making the dampness seep through. "You're wet for me. Let me have you."

"No." Sam got a hand on his chest and gave him a weak push. "I don't want this."

Lucan's mouth tightened, and he lifted her from the desk back to her feet. Before he released her, he ran his hand slowly down the length of her body.

"Why did you have to be a member of the police? Why could you not have been a waitress or a teacher or a stripper? No." He rested velvet fingertips against her mouth before she could answer. "Don't tempt me further; I am ready to drag you down and have you on the floor whether you wish it or not. Look into my eyes."

She looked.

"I have answered all of your questions," he commanded. "That is what you will remember of our encounter. Nothing more. Say it."

"Your answers. That is what I'll remember. Nothing more." A fierce ache twisted inside her. "Why?"

"Because you—" He broke off and cursed in a language that sounded old and blunt. "You will suppress that annoying will of yours and do precisely as I have told you. Rejoin your companion now, and continue your search for the one who killed this woman. When I ask you, you will tell me everything you have learned about the murder." His gloves pressed against her cheeks. "Obey me, Samantha."

She didn't want to, but . . . "I will."

She watched him do something to his wrist and hold a handkerchief to it, and then take the damp, warm cloth and wind it around her hand. When he had made a makeshift bandage, Lucan moved away from her to open a window behind the desk. The night air was thick and hot, but it blew some of the cobwebs out of her head.

The scent of jasmine faded. She had to . . . Harry was . . .

Sam glanced down at her left hand, which was throbbing, and frowned. It was covered with a bloodstained cloth, but she couldn't remember how she injured it.

"Did I answer all of your questions to your satisfaction, Detective?"

"Yeah." She'd blanked out for a minute, but everything he'd said about Lena Caprell came back with a vengeance. Her eyes went to the only inexplicable thing in the room, the remains of a shattered wineglass. "Sorry, did I break that?"

"Just now." His mouth curled. "It was an accident. Come. I believe my assistant has the largest first-aid and medical kit known to man."

Chapter 6

Gard Paviere's driver remained silent as he navigated through the empty streets to the Garden District, which gave Michael Cyprien a much-needed respite. Hours of trying to provide some solace to Gard and his devastated family had taxed him. He sympathized with the Pavieres, but Faryl had brought this upon himself. Now he wanted nothing more than to find his *sygkenis,* take her into a dark room, and lock out the many growing problems in their world. She would want to know about Faryl, however, and he would have to tell her something to explain away the fleshrot.

What he would tell her was his present dilemma. The truth was out of the question.

Alexandra was already obsessed with finding a "cure" that would transform Kyn back into humans, and learning of Faryl's self-inflicted disease would only fan the fires of her determination. Michael had yet to tell her that even if she did find some treatment with which to reverse the process, the Kyn would summarily refuse it. Alex might still think of herself and them as human, but the Kyn had shed their humanity a long time ago.

His lover refused to accept a very basic fact: None of them *wanted* to be human again.

Except Alexandra, Michael thought, *who would cure herself and condemn me to an eternity of loneliness.*

He could use his talent to make her forget Faryl Paviere and his hopeless condition, finding a cure, or anything else he wished. Although like nearly all Kyn talent, Michael's only affected humans, Alex had never developed an immunity to it.

What that meant troubled Michael even more than Alex's dogged ambition to turn their world upside down.

She is not human, or Kyn. She is becoming something else.

The electronic gates outside La Fontaine, Michael's home and the heart of the New Orleans *jardin,* parted silently for Paviere's driver. When the chauffeur came to open the door for Michael, he said in French, "Seigneur, forgive me, but may I speak?"

Michael rarely conversed with another Kyn's human servant—away from their masters, they were to be seen and not heard—but he knew Faryl's actions had Paviere's entire household on edge. "What is it?"

"Master Gard is so distraught," the driver said. He was an older Creole, and his dark eyes looked as if they missed little. "Gard is a faithful son, you see, and would do anything for his family. No one knew Faryl was still alive. I would beg you to remember this in the days to come. He is . . . a desperate man."

He was upset, even terrified for his master. Such devotion was common among the Kyn, who had lived under feudal rule for seven centuries, but very rare in their modern human servants.

"I know." Michael rested a hand on the chauffeur's shoulder. "Your concern is a testimonial to the sort of man your master is. I assure you that I will attend to this matter with Faryl as quickly and as mercifully as I can. Go home, and do what you can to care for the family."

The driver bowed and departed.

Michael followed the long, manicured hedge of white tea roses that Alexandra kept threatening to dig up and replace with hibiscus to the square marble footstones leading to the front of the house. His roses served as camouflage for the rosy brick of the privacy wall surrounding the old Victorian mansion. A *tresoran* architect had traveled from England to design his home, which resembled a Victorian fantasy on the surface but served as a fortress underneath stucco-concealed casing stone.

Perhaps he should have commissioned something more dignified to suit his diminutive castle than the carved white marble fountain in the center of the fore yard. But Michael liked the sound of bubbling water, and as a boy had been very fond of sketching the fish that swam in the river on his parents' country estate.

So often now he longed for those days, when nothing was more important than sunlight, silence, and peace.

He sat on the edge of the fountain's enormous basin and looked up at the fountain's top piece, a pair of angel fish with their long, flowing fins entwined. Cella Evareaux had sculpted them for him out of a block of old ivory-and-gold marble she had brought back from Greece, and silently presented them as her tribute when he was made suzerain of New Orleans.

How can I thank you for this? Michael remembered asking her.

Her reply had been identical to his own secret desire: *Leave me to my art, my lord. Leave me in peace.*

His growing awareness told him it would be midnight soon, and he looked up at his bedchamber window. Alexandra was up there waiting for him. The night and day did not have as much effect on her as it did Michael and the other Kyn. She would want answers he could not give her, reasons he dared not explain.

He had no choice but to make her forget Faryl Paviere.

Michael went into the house and up to his bedchamber. There he found Alexandra curled up asleep in their bed, swathed in one of the satin nightdresses he had given her, her fiery chestnut curls spread over his pillow. He stood watching her breathe, but when he reached out to rest his hand on her slim throat, her eyelids lifted.

A smile slowly curved her lips. "Hey, handsome."

He sat down beside her. "I didn't mean to disturb you."

"Then you should never have kidnapped me." She struggled up into a sitting position and pushed her hair away from her face. "You just get home?" When he nodded, she rubbed her eyes. "Gard all right?"

"As much as can be expected."

"Poor guy. What a shit thing to happen to his brother. I liked meeting Marcella, by the way." Alex rubbed her eyes. "I thought she might be as stuck-up as her brother, but she's all right, for a gorgeous, somewhat grouchy hermit artist."

"Cella prefers her solitude, and rarely speaks to anyone. You should feel flattered." He brought one of her small, clever hands to his lips. "When was the last time I told you how I love you?"

Her smooth brow furrowed. "You've never told me that."

"No?" His cock grew thick and heavy as he opened the front of her nightdress and exposed her small, pretty breasts. "I distinctly remember saying the words."

"Well, when I took a copper bolt in the chest for you that day in Chicago I think you mentioned it, but you were babbling a lot of nonsense." Her gaze shifted to the window. "What is it, about midnight? We'd better get busy if we want to get going before dawn."

"Indeed." He bent to kiss her, but she wriggled out from under him.

"You can have your wicked way with me on the jet," she assured him as she stood and walked to the armoire. "How many suits should I pack? And do you want all Armani, as usual, or should we be more daring this time and pack a few Calvin Kleins?"

"Pack." He thought she was jesting with him until he saw her remove two cases from the bottom and place them on the bed. "Where are we going?"

"To Florida," she said with exaggerated patience. "Faryl's on foot, as far as we know, right? We should be able to beat him to Lucan's place." She picked up her medical case and checked the contents. "I need time to make up some darts, in case he wants to pull a Thierry."

Michael went to the open suitcase and closed it. "We are not chasing after Faryl, Alexandra."

"Of course we are. The guy is in serious trouble. Parts of his body are falling off him." She looked up, exasperated. "You can play nice with Lucan long enough for me to tranquilize the guy and have Phillipe haul him back to the plane."

"Faryl is not like Thierry. What Faryl did to himself, he did deliberately." He reached for her throat, but she glided out of reach.

"Wait a minute." She breathed in, and outrage flared in her eyes. "You don't smell like that unless you're hunting or trying to use your talent. You want to lift my memories? After all we've— How fucking *dare* you?"

He shook his head. "It is better this way, *ma belle*. Let me help you."

"Help me what? Forget what I know about the Pavieres?" She glanced down at his erection. "I get it. You can't screw me into submission, so you'll mind-wipe me? Is that the deal here?"

"You can't save everyone," Michael shouted.

"Why the hell not?" she yelled back, and then her eyes narrowed. "What did Faryl do? What's going on? God damn it, Michael, you say you love me, then trust me enough to *tell* me."

All the anger drained out of him. He couldn't bring himself to lie to her, or to erase her memory. She was right: He loved her too much. All that was left was the truth.

"Faryl was a devout Templar, but unlike most of us the change did not destroy his faith. He has remained a Catholic ever since he rose from his grave." He went to the window to close the curtains against the first light of dawn. "He is like many were in the beginning. He despised being Darkyn, and loathed our dependency on humans as nourishment. Over the centuries Faryl tried to accept his needs, but the struggle between faith and survival became too much for him. Two hundred years ago he disappeared. We thought him dead, but he isolated himself in the swamps away from people. He has been feeding on the creatures that live there."

"He's been drinking animal blood for two centuries?" Alex demanded. "Nothing else?"

Michael nodded. "You know from your own experience that to do so makes us ill. However, we can feed on animals for very short periods of time. It is the last resort. If a Darkyn continues to feed exclusively on animal blood . . ." How could he tell her this?

"Let me guess." She closed her eyes briefly. "They get something like leprosy and their bodies begin to rot."

It was not far from the truth. "Something like that, yes."

"Okay, so Faryl is falling to pieces because he hates being a vampire, but he has to go to Lucan and ask Mr. Badass to kill him because Faryl is a Catholic and can't commit suicide. Which makes him as dumb as a brick." She eyed him. "Have I got this right?"

Michael went to her. "I know Gard and the Pavieres would wish it differently, but it would be best for everyone involved to allow Lucan to dispatch Faryl, as he wishes."

She gnawed at her bottom lip. "This leprosy condition, is it irreversible?"

"I cannot say." The only other living Darkyn with Faryl's condition would not thank him for revealing too many details about the beast drinkers. "All who have suffered it have never . . . recovered."

"The Darkyn have never had me on the payroll." Alex slipped her arms around his waist. "If I'm going to understand what is happening to me, and has happened to the rest of you, I have to analyze everything about our condition. Even something as repulsive to you as this thing with Faryl. As for him, if he really wants to die, he'll find a way no matter what we do."

He felt a cautious sense of relief. She was listening to him, and trying to understand. "What do you propose?"

"We go to Florida and find Faryl and talk to him," she said. "He may let me take some blood samples. If the deterioration of his body isn't too bad, and there aren't any toxins present to prevent healing, I might even be able to reverse it."

"There is also Lucan," Michael reminded her.

"What is it with you and him?"

Michael thought of the centuries he had spent locked in a silent battle with Lucan for Richard's favor. "We are old enemies. He will not thank me for invading his territory."

"You're the seigneur of America. I'd say he doesn't have a whole damn lot to say about it." She pressed herself against him. "Come to bed."

"I thought we were packing."

"I can't remember the last time we were in that bed together." She brought his hand to her breast. "So we'll pack later." There was a polite knock on the door, and she looked over his shoulder and saw Phillipe appear. "I'm sorry; where's my tranquilizer gun?"

"Je suis désolé." Michael's seneschal gave them an apologetic look. "There is a call from Chicago for you, master. It is Jaus."

Reluctantly he dropped his hand. He had asked Valentin

Jaus, the suzerain of Chicago, to keep Luisa Lopez, one of Alexandra's former patients, under guard. "Forgive me. Jaus has been trying to locate the men who attacked Ms. Lopez—"

"Don't worry about it." She touched a finger to his lips, silencing him. "I'll pack. Tell Val I said hi, and to give my love to Luisa."

Sam was winded by the time she reached the second landing, and felt like crawling the rest of the way to her apartment. Her hand was throbbing like a tooth in dire need of a root canal, like both sides of her forehead. There was a place on the back of her head that she was pretty sure was going to explode any minute. She had saved some pain pills from her hospital stay, and the promise of that chemical relief got her up the last set of stairs.

The door across from hers opened, and a blue-haired head looked out. "Evening, Officer Sam."

"Hey, underage brat." Sam fumbled for her keys.

"You look like crap warmed over. Did you bring me some coffee?" Chris stepped out into the hallway. "I guess not. What's up with your hand? You get shot? You shoot back?"

Sam looked down at the hand Lucan's assistant, a funny little man with a bad head cold, had bandaged for her. The bullet-wound scar throbbed more than any of the cuts. "Yes. No." She leaned forward until her brow touched the door. "I had an accident with a glass." She turned around and for a moment thought she was hallucinating. "What's all this?" She gestured toward Chris's clothes.

Chris looked down at the leather cutout vest and silk leggings under the dozen or so silver-studded belts wrapped around her waist. "It's my look."

"Kind of, uh, black."

"I'm only wearing black until they invent something darker." The navy-blue lipstick she wore made her teeth look snowy. "You don't get it. Okay. I'm a goth."

That explained the hair, the piercings, and the attitude. "Aren't you a little young for that? What happened to grunge and punk?"

"It's postgrunge now. I think punk is buried next to disco.

And, in my opinion, you're as old as you want to be. Steady." Chris reached out and grabbed Sam's arm, and only then did Sam realize she was swaying. "I am not making a pass at you, just so you know. Now let's get you inside, Officer."

With Chris's arm supporting her, Sam found her door key and unlocked the two dead bolts and knob lock. "I'm not gay," she told the kid. "And if I were, you'd be too young for me."

"I'm so relieved. Is that why Keri was so pissed at you?"

"She had the right." Sam couldn't get her key out of the bottom lock. "I didn't discourage her when I should have. Just so you get the gossip straight."

"I don't blab, and that shit can happen easy whether you're straight or gay." Chris pushed open the door for her. "You're kind of paranoid, though, huh?"

"Goes with the job. Thanks for the hand." She wandered back to her bathroom. When she had taken a pain pill and came back out, she found Chris standing in front of her bookcase.

"You're really into poetry," her neighbor said. "Old stuff, too. Keats, Byron, Shelley. Who's Rainer Maria Rilke? Is that a guy or a chick?"

"Rilke is the only one who makes sense anymore." Sam opened the sliding glass door to the balcony to let in some fresh air, dropped into her favorite armchair, and pushed it into recline. "He was a man."

"His mom fucked up his name, then. I bet Keri hated your place." She gazed around at Sam's shabby furniture. "What do you call this look? Early American yard sale?"

Sam considered smacking the kid, but she was too far away, and Sam wasn't getting up from the armchair again until Thanksgiving. Maybe Christmas. "Aren't you going somewhere, dressed up like that?"

"Down to the beach. They don't card as much, not that it's a problem for old chicks like you and me." She winked at Sam. "There's a new goth place my friends want me to check out."

"Infusion?"

Now the kid gaped. "How did you know?"

"I'm a cop, and this is my town. Don't go there." Sam cradled her sore hand against her chest. "A woman who was there a couple of nights ago was murdered."

"Oh, I can take care of myself." Chris put back the book she was reading and walked over. "Jesus, you're really pale. Like Snow White from the dwarf movie. Should I call nine-one-one or something?"

"No, I'm okay. I lost a little blood and it hurts, that's all." The pain pill was starting to work its magic, but Sam forced herself to focus on Chris. "I'm serious about that nightclub, though. There are some scary characters there. It's not a place for a young girl to hang out."

Another lightning smile flashed. "Good thing I'm not a young girl."

"I could run your ID just to verify that," Sam said. "Our lease agreements state that a sublet tenant has to be twenty-one years of age or older. We wouldn't want you to put Keri in danger of losing her security deposit."

Chris held up her hands. "Okay, Officer Do-Right, I won't go there. By the way, you left these in the door." She dropped Sam's keys on the side table. "I'll throw the bottom lock on my way out. Mind if I borrow that Rilke book?"

"As long as you bring it back." Sam's eyes began to close on their own. "You don't, I shoot you."

The last thing she heard before she fell asleep was her blue-haired neighbor chuckling.

Taking blood from two beautiful human females who came to dance at Infusion didn't satisfy Lucan. Neither did pacing the floor for several hours after the police had left. He considered sending for Alisa, but to use her twice in one day would be foolhardy, if not fatal for her.

That he was in such a state was not his fault. Detective Brown had done this to him.

He had been pleased by the suspicion and determination Samantha displayed as she confronted him about Lena Caprell. America was his country now; he was glad the humans put some effort into policing themselves. Shaking her composure had been mildly amusing as well. He so enjoyed disconcerting a woman of conservative sensibilities, and he suspected that the detective had inhibitions atop reservations wrapped in reticence.

If only he hadn't touched her.

Lucan could still taste her blood, still smell her skin; she was all over him. Taking another shower erased the physical traces, but wouldn't remove the lingering memories of her from his head, or ease the hunger surging through him.

What did the stubborn little bitch do to me?

All of this upheaval was because of the cross. Someone within his *jardin* thought to taunt their new suzerain by unearthing that relic from his past and using it to kill the human woman. What they did not realize was that the cross was now as meaningless to Lucan as Lena Caprell had been. He would have it retrieved from the police and then use it to ferret out whoever had thought to frame him for the woman's murder.

As for the detective, her resemblance to Frances was the only reason he'd temporarily lost his control. He had no interest in a paltry human female wasting her youth on avenging the dead. Her blood was sweet, and under her ugly clothes she had the body of a goddess, but other than that, the detective had offered little in the way of temptation.

Lucan was a connoisseur of some of the world's most beautiful women; Samantha Brown did everything but put a brown bag over her head to disguise her assets. She didn't smell of floral perfume or enticing spices, but of rich, dark-roasted coffee. Her pale mouth had certainly not offered any inducement, not until he had touched it and watched her lips tremble and her eyes go dark.

Frances had never done that. Frances had never permitted him to put one finger on her person, not until the night before she died.

Samantha had made things worse by resisting and then trying to run away from him. Nothing brought out the predator in him more than a female he couldn't have. He hadn't felt such a surge of lust since seeing Alexandra Keller for the first time in New Orleans.

Yet unlike Cyprien's *sygkenis,* Lucan could have Samantha Brown. As much and as often as he liked. He had only to bring her under his control. He remembered thinking that as he had taken her blood. Feeding from her hand had invigorated him. It was kissing her mouth afterward that had been his ruination.

Samantha Brown's mouth was as much a hidden banquet as her body: all heat and pleasure, lush and endless.

One moment he was tasting her; the next he was knocking things off his desk and stepping between her legs. His cock still ached with the memory of pressing her taut thighs apart and rubbing against her soft mound. Even as she had refused him, he had smelled and felt her body's response, even through the velvet of his glove. He had come very close to ripping off her ugly trousers and putting his mouth to her to taste it.

Permitting her refusal and allowing her to walk out had been a terrible waste.

If he'd had a shred of wit left in his skull, he'd go out, track down Samantha Brown, and drag her back here. Why had he let her go, when he could have her under him right now? She was nothing to him. No, he should have kept her, and laid her out on his desk, and fucked her until he had purged himself of this needling, infuriating desire.

"My lord."

Lucan strode out into the front room, where Rafael stood with yet another file. He had ordered his seneschal to discover everything he could about Detective Brown, and it had taken him a damnably long time. "What have you learned?"

He opened the file. "Lena Caprell was drowned in freshwater at an unknown location, and then transported and left on the bus stop bench across from the club. The cross was found around her neck, which bore ligature marks."

"He used it to kill her."

"It would seem so, my lord. I have also retrieved the information you requested on the detective. Samantha Brown is thirty-one years old, unmarried, childless, and dwells alone in an apartment two miles from here. She has worked for the Fort Lauderdale Police Department for twelve years." Rafael gave him a brief outline of Samantha's turbulent career.

Despite the lust maddening him, Lucan felt a twinge of pity for the human female. *Small wonder her eyes look as if someone has been taking bites out of her soul.* "What of her family?"

"At age three, Detective Brown was abandoned by her unmarried mother, now deceased, taken into state custody, and raised in a foster-care facility known as a group home until the age of eighteen." Rafael looked up. "There are no indications of contact with any other relatives. She lists her partner, Harold Quinn, as her beneficiary on her insurance policy."

He doubted the old man with the breathing problem was anything more than a colleague. "What of her current lovers?"

"Our man in the department says no," his seneschal said. "Popular opinion has it that Detective Brown is a lesbian."

Could that be the reason for her resistance to him? Lucan had never had a woman under the influence of *l'attrait* defy him as Samantha had. "I want to know who has bedded her. Everyone who has been between her legs."

Rafael inclined his head. "May I make a suggestion, my lord?"

"Why not?" Lucan rubbed the back of his neck.

"Retrieve the cross and terminate the detective."

He stared, thinking his seneschal was making a poor joke, but Rafael's expression appeared completely serious. "Now why would I wish to *kill* her?"

"Our man indicated that she is tenacious, defiant, and unrelenting. From what little you told me, I assume she demonstrated some resistance to *l'attrait*." The file closed, and Rafael set it on a side table. "If this woman has some immunity to the Darkyn, she may cause a great deal of trouble for us, my lord. For you especially if she manipulates your . . . attraction to her."

There were rare individual humans who did not respond to *l'attrait,* the Darkyn's primary means to lure and control humans. Resistant humans also tended to build up a tolerance to *l'attrait* with each successive exposure, so in time she would become immune to it. Often such tolerance was a genetic trait, passed from parent to child. The Kyn valued such humans, and recruited them and their families to serve as *tresori.*

Detective Brown could not be made his human servant, but that did not entirely exclude her from serving him. In centuries past, the Darkyn would take humans who proved resistant to *l'attrait* as *kyryas,* the household lovers.

There, that is how I will do it.

"She would be of more value as a *kyrya* than a corpse." Lucan didn't kill the innocent; nor would he waste such a woman on the fear of what she might discover about the Darkyn. "Forget about the cross; it is a counterfeit. Instruct Burke to conduct an extensive background investigation on the detective. Find something with which I can convince her to work for us."

"I will see to it at once." Rafael's black brows arched. "Do you really believe that you can bring a strong-willed woman like that under your control?"

"I foresee very little difficulty." Lucan remembered how, despite the fact that he had barely touched her, she had made his glove damp. "What is the address of her apartment?"

Chapter 7

Too impatient to endure Burke's careful driving or continual nasal evacuations, Lucan took one of his cars to Samantha Brown's apartment complex. Most Darkyn disliked operating vehicles of any sort, and a few still kept horses for their personal use where possible, but Lucan enjoyed the technology of this new era. No nag on the planet could cross two miles in less than a minute, but his black Ferrari devoured the road.

He parked the car in a shadowy section of the lot, and looked up at Samantha's building. Cheaply built, narrow, and joyless, it had neither aesthetic or practical appeal. There was no elevator; one had to traverse a narrow zigzag of stairs to access the upper-level apartments. He found it puzzling that so reticent a woman chose to live in a dormitory of humans rather than her own home.

"Where are you?" he murmured as he mounted the steps. Some helpful soul had posted numbers next to the doorways of each apartment; from the series it would seem his future *kyrya* lived on the third floor.

Lucan found apartment 303 at the very top of the stairs, but a number of strong locks prevented his entry. He looked out at the back of the building, and saw a ridiculously tiny balcony that promised easier access. He swung out over the short wall blocking the stairwell and jumped the eight feet to grab the wrought-iron balcony rails and hoist himself over.

Lucan turned to deal with the glass door to the apartment, but it had been left ajar. Just inside, not six feet away from him, lay Detective Brown, asleep in a reclining chair. Silently he stepped over the threshold and sniffed the air. Another female had been here recently, but at the moment Samantha was alone.

Alone, asleep, and all his.

It bothered him to see her like this. He turned and closed the glass door, perversely annoyed with her for leaving it open. Did she think herself invulnerable to intruders? Her weapon lay on the minuscule dining table; had a villain entered he would be on top of her before she could reach it.

"I *am* a villain," he murmured, amused by his own anger and protective feelings. He certainly wouldn't mind climbing on top of her, either.

With deliberate steps he walked past her to see the rest of this, her home. She seemed to favor strictly functional furnishings in drab colors and posters of mountains and waterfalls instead of inspired art. Her bedroom was hardly more than a nun's cell, with its too-small bed and walls of bookcases. Dust coated her television, and her kitchen appeared to be used for two things: making coffee and reheating it.

He turned around, taking in everything that was not there. "You live here as if you never live here."

It was perplexing. Samantha Brown was a female, and yet there was nothing feminine at all to be found in the surroundings. Not even a single flower—or the photo of a flower—anywhere. Frances, an avid gardener, would have loathed such a colorless place.

Lucan slipped into the bath, which was the most intimate and telling room in a woman's home. Samantha Brown's was almost empty. She possessed no cosmetics or perfumes, and her toiletries encompassed, like her furniture, only the necessities. A single scented candle sat on the edge of the tub, and when he lifted it to his nose he smelled cinnamon. Frances had despised strong and piquant scents, which she claimed were vulgar and assaulted the nose.

"Who are you?" Lucan murmured as he replaced the candle and looked around the stark room.

A search through her dresser revealed no silken lingerie or negligees; Samantha preferred simple, serviceable underthings. The thought of that magnificent body being clad in nothing more than plain white cotton and the scent of soap oddly stirred him, and he walked back out to where the human female slept.

She lived as if she might be forced to walk out and leave this all behind her with but a moment's notice—exactly as he did.

Lucan knelt down by the chair to have a better look at Samantha's face. Her straight, dark hair fanned one cheek, contrasting sharply with her fine skin. Nothing enhanced her curling lashes or delicate lips; her skin had a faint bloom of sun but smelled dusky, as if she bathed in the night. She was not beautiful or girlish or even pretty, and yet her features were more mysterious and enticing than Frances's open, guileless countenance had ever been.

He leaned over to breathe in her scent, which was as rich and unexpected as the cinnamon in her bath. Samantha might dress herself to avoid notice, and live like a nun, but she smelled of the green, earthy depths of the Amazon, where dangerous things roamed the dark hours.

The woman was a complete mystery.

Alone by choice, in this place that could barely be called a home. Was she more than she appeared to be? Did she long for a companion who understood that loneliness, as he did?

A pulse point ticked in the slim column of her throat, and he couldn't resist pressing his mouth there for a moment, touching his tongue to the strong throb. Her blood flow was strong, like her body. Despite having fed well not an hour past, he felt his fangs ache for her. He had not taken the pleasure of biting her when she had come to question him, and he wanted his teeth in her, to feel her flesh yield to him.

Lucan lifted his head and heard her soft sigh as she shifted in her chair, turning toward him, baring her throat like an invitation. It took most of his will not to climb atop her and have her right there.

"Are you like me?" he whispered. "Better to be lonely than unloved, reviled?"

"Lucan," she muttered.

He smiled. She slept, but on some level she was aware of his presence, and that gave him a certain amount of influence over her. He couldn't enter dreams, the way Thierry Durand did, but while she slumbered, she was more susceptible to *l'attrait*. He could begin the process of coaxing her away from this dismal life of hers.

He stroked his velvet-covered fingertips along the side of her neck. "You are young, and strong, and healthy. You belong in the arms of a lover who understands you. I think I may do, Samantha."

She frowned. "Lover?"

"Yes." He saw her eyelids opening a fraction, and rested his hand over her heart. "Do not wake. Listen to me." For a moment he thought she might rouse, and then her breathing slowed and deepened. "I want you to dream of being in my arms. Of being with me. I will do the same. In our silences and our solitudes, we can burn for each other, Samantha. Would you like that?"

She sighed, shifting closer to him. "Mmmmmm."

He was massaging the full, ripe mound of her breast, Lucan discovered, and the rest of him ached to do much more. If he didn't leave now, he wouldn't until he had her a dozen different ways.

He caught the end of her breath with his mouth, brushing it back over her lips. "Come to me again, Samantha. Whenever you want me. I will fill every emptiness you feel."

Father Mercer Lane wound up the tour of the grounds of Barbastro Abbey by climbing the three flights of stairs in the back of the cloister so his friend could look out over his tiny domain.

"This was all alligator- and snake-infested swampland forty years ago," he told John. "Nothing but sawgrass and palmetto bugs, as far as the eye could see."

John went to the railing. "How long has the abbey been here?"

"We celebrate our thirty-ninth groundbreaking anniversary in November." Mercer took out his cigar case. "I don't suppose you've taken up the filthy habit since leaving the church?"

"No, but go ahead."

"This is the only place I can have one without worrying about Brother Ignatius sniffing me." Mercer used a pocketknife to trim the end before lighting the cigar and puffing on it until the end glowed crimson. "This land was supposed to be a great investment for the archdiocese of Miami. They bought up a couple hundred acres here in North Broward dirt cheap shortly before the Gold Coast and Miami were built out. Resold them twenty years later for millions."

John nodded. "Why didn't they sell this property?"

"I've only been here a few months, so I'm not really sure." Mercer shrugged. "We're right on top of the Everglades, so everything to the west is protected by the National Parks and can't be developed. Brush fires set by the Indians on their land have always been a pain in the arse, too. Whatever the reason, the church hung on to this parcel too long, and the developers passed them by. That's when they sent Bromwell, the abbot before me, down here to build the abbey."

John looked out at the zero-lot-lined communities that encircled the abbey's property. "And none of this was here. It must have seemed like the end of the world."

"Bromwell must have thought so." He pulled in a mouthful of smoke and released it in a series of small rings. "He insisted on naming this place after Father Luis Cancer de Barbastro, a priest sent to establish a mission in Tampa who was slaughtered by Indians in 1549. You Americans have barbaric taste in monuments."

"I suppose we do." John looked over the railing at the ground. "Maybe Bromwell meant it as a tribute."

"You can't jump off, old chap; it's not high enough," Mercer said, watching John's face for a reaction. "You'll only break your legs, your spine, or your neck."

His friend didn't twitch a muscle. "I wasn't thinking of jumping."

"Well, if you're going to push me off something, at least tell what the bloody hell happened to you in Chicago." Mercer waited, but John remained silent. "You know, according to some of the older brothers here, Bromwell was a joyless stickler for the rules. He ran this place like a dictator, and made sure every brother who came here suffered right alongside him."

John crossed his arms and leaned back against one of the roof supports. "And?"

"Bromwell hated people, but not even he could stop the

march of progress. Housing developers invaded this place twenty years ago." Mercer nodded toward one of the crowded satellite communities. "Everyone with money stayed in the east, so this became a magnet for lower-income families, transients, and the like. Bromwell tried fencing off the abbey's land and built that bleeding monstrosity of a wall around the monastic buildings"—he nodded toward the seven-foot-high brick enclosure beyond the chapel—"but he couldn't keep the brothers cut off from the outside world any longer."

Mercer told John how property values had plummeted even further after the Mariel Boatlift of 1980, leaving the brothers in an ever-deepening melting pot of multiracial Cuban, Haitian, and Jamaican poor.

"I know from the paperwork Bromwell left behind that he had repeatedly contacted the head of his order to request reassignment. It never came." He looked out at the night sky. "Evidently he hated the immigrants and the fact that the other brothers wanted to become involved in the community, and started embezzling money from the abbey's funds. About a month before I was sent down, one of the younger brothers accidentally discovered it and confronted Bromwell." He nodded toward the chapel. "They found him hanging from a roof beam just before vespers."

"Is that why they offered it to you? Because of his suicide?"

"You know how superstitious the Benedictines are," Mercer said. "It tainted Barbastro for them, so they turned it over to the Franciscans. I was happy to take up the reins, as it were."

"So what are you going to do here, Mercer?" John was asking.

"The work," he said simply. "The brothers have become involved in dozens of community projects. They've raised the funds to help build and staff a low-cost day-care facility to help welfare mothers go back to work, as well as hiring a teacher for a halfway house for pregnant teenagers to enable them to finish out their schooling. They're also getting involved in programs at the local Catholic church to help keep young children from being lured into using drugs and joining gangs."

"What I meant was, what are *you* going to do out here, Mercer?" John asked. "Of all the places I imagined that you'd end up, this isn't even close. This is more like . . ."

"Mars?" Mercer laughed. "Maybe it is, my friend, but I'll tell you a secret: I don't mind playing the part of a Martian." He saw the doubt in John's eyes, but couldn't blame him for it. The last time they had spent any time together, he'd still been in one of his bleak moods. The Mercer Lane whom John had known had been a tired man. "To tell you the God's truth, I needed a place like this. With all that has happened to me since I joined the priesthood, I needed something good and simple, like this place." He didn't mind adding a small white lie. "That's why I came here. It doesn't get any simpler than this."

"If you wanted simple, you could have gone over to a third-world mission," his friend suggested.

"Like you did?" Mercer shook his head. "I'd have been bitten by a mosquito stepping off the plane and died of some horrid foreign disease. I couldn't have brought the Word to the ignorant savages anyway. My calling—my mission—requires me to dwell among the civilized unwise."

John's mouth flattened. "I wish I'd been that realistic before I went to South America."

"Well, now you're a ruddy private citizen, able to drop the beads and get on with your life. I don't envy you the prospect of dating. Women today are far more demanding than Mum ever was." He saw John flinch. "Is that what it was that drove you out? A woman?"

"I can't talk about it, and please don't ask me." John Keller, who never pleaded or showed weakness, sounded as if he were begging now. "Please."

"I'll remind you of something a very wise and exhausted young priest once told me: If you don't get it out, it will eat you up inside." Pleased to hit John with his own advice, Mercer turned and saw the gleam of a bald head. "Here." He thrust the cigar in John's hand. "Cover for me."

Brother Ignatius emerged from the stairwell and gave John and Mercer a stringent, sour look. "We do not permit smoking on the grounds of the abbey, Brother Patrick."

"Sorry." John ground out the cigar on the sole of his shoe. "I didn't know."

"Now you do." The older friar eyed Mercer. "Father Lane, it is after midnight. Shall I show Brother Patrick to his room?"

"Yes, thank you, Ignatius." Mercer slapped John's shoulder. "Get some rest. I'll see you at breakfast in the morning."

Mercer stood looking out at the abbey's grounds until John and Ignatius disappeared from sight, and then went from the cloister to the abbot's house, where there was always paperwork waiting for him to review and sign.

He was nearly finished with the day's correspondence when his guestmaster appeared in the open doorway.

"Brother Patrick refused a dinner tray and has gone to bed," Brother Ignatius said. "I have put him in the south hall of the hospitium."

"Call him John," Mercer said as he signed off on a purchase order for cleaning supplies. "He's not one of us."

"Yes, Father, I gathered that. May I have a word?" At Mercer's nod, he came into the office and closed the door behind him. "I know it is not my place to criticize your decisions, but is it entirely wise to bring one of the flock under our roof?"

Brother Ignatius prided himself on keeping close watch on the conduct of everyone at the abbey, and reporting any violations of the rules back to the abbot. He had never before questioned any of Mercer's decisions, but Barbastro had never before opened its gates to anyone outside the order.

"The sheep are safest when in the fold," Mercer responded dryly. He appreciated his guestmaster's vigilance, but sometimes Ignatius could be as annoying as a tattling five-year-old. "John is struggling with life and faith. God does not wish us to turn our backs on a brother in crisis, even after he has left the church."

"But still . . ." Ignatius clasped his hands together and twisted them as he sought the right words. "We were commanded to remain aloof. I am sorry to be the one to say this, Father, but you flirt with violating the oath."

"Rest assured that if I have, I will be removed from my position and another will take my place." Mercer saw a light blinking on his phone and punched the button that connected him with the abbey's switchboard operator. "Yes, Brother Jacob?"

"A call for you, Father." Jacob's voice sounded strained. "It is on the secured line."

"Lord have pity on us." Ignatius gasped.

Mercer hadn't suffered cold sweats since he'd left Europe, but there was no denying the chilly sensation that inched down his spine. "Thank you, Brother Jacob." He glanced up at the guestmaster. "If you will excuse me, Brother?"

The older friar pressed his hands together, bowed over them, and fled.

Mercer took a moment to regain some composure. He had not yet received a call on the secured line. At times he had even allowed himself to forget about it, as much as he was able. Still, there was no need for hysteria. The call was likely some matter to do with the order's new administration; many things had changed since the pope had died. Likely this was nothing more than some sort of official notification that could not be entrusted to a fax like all the others.

Mercer's hand still shook a little as he picked up the phone. "Abbot Lane."

"Wasn't that a song by the Beatles?" a man with a New York–accented voice asked. Before Mercer could reply, he added, "You take your time answering your calls, Brother."

He couldn't place the voice at all. "Who is this?"

"I keep the Light of the World shining," the man snapped. "Don't tell me your fax machine is broken."

"I . . . I live for the Light," Mercer said, giving the traditional response. "Cardinal D'Orio, what an honor it is to speak with you."

"You're not going to speak, Brother. You're going to listen." D'Orio uttered a belch. "Pardon me. I know better than to drink Coca-Cola—it always gives me gas—but I love the stuff. Now, we have a report that one of the *maledicti* has established one of their infernal nests in your territory, Brother."

"I don't see how," Mercer said uneasily. "My predecessor eradicated the last of the demons some twenty years ago, did he not?"

"Your predecessor was a thief and a liar, but that's beside the point." D'Orio drank something. "You have the problem now. Capture what you can and burn the rest."

Kidnapping and arson, Mercer thought, all in the name of the Almighty. "Your Holiness, there may be some difficulty in carrying out your orders. I am prepared, naturally, but this cell has never been activated."

"Consider this your wake-up call, Mercer. I expect a full progress report in two days. Don't lose sight of the light." D'Orio hung up the phone.

Mercer pulled open his desk drawer and looked at the bottle of wine inside. He never drank here at the abbey, preferring to indulge himself away from the poor brothers under his care.

They didn't deserve to be exposed to the ugliness of his work. They'd done good things here, the sort of ordinary things that Mercer had once wished he could do.

They aren't like you, the ghost of his novitiate master in Rome whispered inside his skull. *They're demons, and you were created to fight them.*

Mercer knew what his mission had cost him. He'd lost his way—and almost his soul—trying to do the work and then forget the unspeakable things involved with what he'd done. But the work had to be done, and he had been chosen by God to do it. While he was convinced there was no heaven waiting for him after death, surely the majority of what he had done here would outweigh the bad and earn him purgatory.

He ran his fingers over the bottle's hand-printed label, and closed his eyes. "God help me. God help us all."

"More pink," Alexandra said as she looked around the beach house. "Holy Toledo. Is there some state law that says every other thing in Florida has to be pink?"

The men ignored her, but they had been doing that since they'd left New Orleans.

She wandered around the first floor of the light, airy house that had been provided for their use by some unnamed local ally of the Darkyn. To be fair, the house was not entirely pink; the decor included sea colors of blue, turquoise, and green to go along with artful touches of seashells and driftwood that accented the casual furniture. Large glass windows looked out over a long stretch private beach, and beyond that, the gently rolling surf of the Atlantic.

It should have been soothing, but something had been nagging at her since they'd left Louisiana. Alex couldn't quite put her finger on what it was, but it made her feel as if her temper—or something—was ready to snap.

"To think I would have sacrificed a limb to have a time-share like this two years ago." She stopped in the kitchen and checked the contents of the refrigerator, which had been stocked with four full shelves of bagged blood, wine, and the perishable medical supplies she'd sent ahead. At least they wouldn't have to hunt for willing donors while they were here. "What, no keggers?"

"Ale makes you vomit," Phillipe said as he carried her instrument bags into the room. "Do you wish me to place these in the cabinets or the drawers, Alexandra?"

"I'm not planning on operating on the countertop." She frowned. "Maybe we should set up one of the spare bedrooms as a treatment room, the way we did at Val's place in Chicago. Assuming we have a spare bedroom. Have we heard back from Val about them moving Luisa, and is she doing okay?"

"Ms. Lopez is now safely installed in a rehabilitation hospital, where the Kyn may watch over her. Suzerain Jaus says she is well." He stowed the cases in the large walk-in pantry and reemerged. "As for the bedchambers, there are three in addition to the master."

"A little smaller than what we're used to, huh? After rattling around in *le* mansion, though, it's kind of cozy." She followed him out to the front room, where Michael was still rattling off things in fast French to Gard Paviere. She cleared her throat. "Some people should speak English when the non-French person is in the room."

Philippe smothered a chuckle as he went back out to unload more luggage from the limousine.

Alex waited impatiently as Michael finished whatever he was telling Gard. After Paviere clasped Michael's hand between his, he gave her a short bow and left them alone. "You want to repeat all that in the only language I'm fluent in now?" she asked sweetly.

"No." Michael dragged a hand through his hair and looked around him as if seeing the room for the first time. "You do not like something that is pink, you said?"

"That was thirty minutes ago. I'm used to it now. Val has

Luisa out of the hospital and into a Kyn rehab place, where she'll be safe." She flopped down on a wicker love seat upholstered with palm-leaf-patterned fabric. "When do we go meet with Dr. Doom? Do I have to dress up and be nice, the way I did with Val?"

"We will arrange a meeting for tomorrow night. You may wear whatever you wish." Michael sat beside her, his expression serious. "You go nowhere near Lucan unless I am with you."

"Not a problem," Alex assured him. She had no desire to be alone with the high lord's former chief butcher. "Does he know we're in town, or is this like a surprise inspection where we show up and shock the bejesus out of him?"

His beautiful mouth flattened. "He knows."

But not because you told him, she guessed. "Okay. Are you going to teach me to hunt other vampires, or whatever it is you do, this time? It took us forever to find Thierry in Chicago."

"You said you do not hunt."

"I don't hunt for necks to bite," she reminded him. "I'm okay with going after a prospective patient, as long as I don't have to treat him like a sippy cup." The mental image of having to feed on a leprous vampire made her wrinkle her nose. "Euuwww. I think I just grossed myself out."

"Alexandra, this will not be as it was in Chicago," he said, and put an arm around her. "Valentin has always been a friend, but more important, he accepts me as his seigneur. Lucan has been trying to kill me almost since we rose to walk the night."

"Boy, you two really don't like each other." The look in his eyes killed the chuckle rising in her throat. "You *are* kidding about him . . . really?"

"Lucan and I have fought in tourneys, on battlefields, and anywhere else it was necessary to prove ourselves. In every instance, I prevailed over him and won Richard's favor." He lifted her onto his lap. "He came to despise me for it."

"It's been a couple hundred years since you two hung together, right?" When Michael nodded, she rested her cheek on his shoulder and played with the ends of the silk handkerchief peeking out of the breast pocket of his jacket. "Maybe he's gotten over it. Even Darkyn grow up eventually, right?"

"When the first colonies in America were established, like

so many of us Lucan wished to come here to begin his own *jardin.* Richard refused to release him from his service and chose to send me instead to New Orleans." He removed the clip holding her curls in a loose knot at the back of her head. "For Lucan, it was the final insult."

"Bitch-slapped down by the boss." Alex winced. "I bet he just loved that."

"Indeed, he did not." Briefly Michael's arms tightened around her. "He slaughtered the human servants I had left behind in France, and burned my estates to the ground."

"No way." She lifted her head to stare at him. "Is that what he was trying to do to Nurse Heather? Is that why he broke into the house in New Orleans?"

"I cannot say. All I know is this: you are my *sygkenis,* and that makes you a prize target for him," he warned. "If he can lure you or take you away from me, he will. By seduction or any other means."

She couldn't believe it. "All this because he couldn't beat you at swords, and you got the cushy overseas assignment that he wanted?"

"Yes." He spanned her jaw with his hand, using his thumb to trace the curve of her upper lip. "Now do you understand why I wish you to go nowhere near Lucan?"

Suddenly a lot of things that had been going on since they had returned from Chicago made sense to her, and she sat up straight. "This is why you've been playing knights in shining armor with Phil four nights a week. You think he's going to come after you for real."

"In this case, *ma belle,* I have come to him." He stood, still holding her in his arms. "Richard may have convinced Lucan not to assassinate me, but he may yet use any opportunity he can take to torment me. When he broke into La Fontaine, somehow he must have seen you. Later he made it clear to me that he wanted you." He nudged open the door to the master bedroom and carried her inside.

Alex tried to process all this. "Why didn't you tell me about this before we came here?"

"We had real concerns to deal with, Alexandra. My oldest enemy in the world may wish to seduce you, but that does not mean he will." Michael placed her on the net-draped bed and shrugged out of his jacket. "If by chance he does manage to have a private moment alone with you, simply remember what he did to your nurse. To take his revenge on me, he would not hesitate to do the same—or worse—to you."

"Meanwhile, you're giving him a *jardin* and treating him like one of the old vampire family." Her head was starting to hurt, so she pushed herself off the bed and began walking the floor. "You're not going to take him out, either, are you?"

"If I kill Lucan, Richard will be seriously displeased." Michael began unbuttoning his shirt, and the scent of full-blown roses filled the room. "He might even decide to kill me. It is ironic; Lucan has always been jealous of the attention and favor Richard has shown me, but he is the one the high lord truly considers his surrogate son."

Alex watched him undress down to his black silk boxers and reach for the lighter, more casual clothes Phillipe had left on the edge of the bed. She breathed in his scent and felt the edginess inside her recede a few inches. "You going somewhere?"

"No, but I must make a few phone calls and do some computer work," he said as he shook the folds out of his khaki trousers. "If you are tired from the journey, you should sleep."

Alex wasn't the one in need of rest. Ever since they'd returned from Chicago, Michael had been completely wrapped up in reorganizing the American *jardins* and establishing diplomatic relations or whatever with Darkyn clans in Canada, Mexico, and Central and South America. They'd barely had time to exchange a couple of words, much less relax together.

Relaxation—that was what he needed. And she knew one way to give him a little.

"It's nighttime. I'm a vampire. I'm not tired." She crossed the room and locked the door, and then took the trousers from him. She threw them aside before resting her hands flat on his bare chest. The scent of lavender blended with the unseen roses enveloping them. "I'm thirsty."

"There is blood." He watched as she slid down the front of him to go down on her knees. "Unless you wish something else."

She moved her hands up his thighs, over the silk of his boxers, and tucked her thumbs under the waistband.

"I don't want to keep you from your phone calls." She eased the boxers down, freeing the rising, thickened shaft of his penis. "Very long."

He groaned as her breath touched him. "I do not think you will."

"It's okay, though, isn't it?" She tipped her head back. "I mean, I *am* really thirsty."

Michael threaded his long fingers through her curls. "Then open your mouth for me, Alexandra." The golden rim around his turquoise irises expanded even as the black pupils in their centers contracted to slits. He curled his free hand around his cock. "One time when we did this, you left me standing hard and naked in the rain."

"I remember." Alex took the smooth, plum-shaped head between her lips, closing them around the base and sucking lightly before releasing it. "You never called in that IOU."

"This is true." His fingers curled into a fist, urging her mouth to him. "Take me there again, *ma belle.*"

Alexandra had never minded performing oral sex on a lover, but she had never found it particularly physically arousing for herself. In the past she had enjoyed the feeling of power it gave her to set aside her own satisfaction while she devoted herself to her lover's pleasure. What she liked most was observing the effect what she did had on her partner. Yet as Michael filled her mouth, for the first time the slick friction created an altogether unfamiliar blend of heat and sensation. It moved from the sensitive surfaces of her lips and tongue down her throat and infused her breasts, making them swell and her nipples tighten.

This is new.

She looked up at Michael as she rubbed his shaft with her tongue and sucked. His gaze was fixed on her face, and the sight of his cock between her lips and the feel of her mouth must have excited him, because his fangs appeared, and she could feel him getting harder.

"Let me in," he murmured, thrusting a little farther inside. "Yes, *ma belle*, like that. Your tongue feels like velvet on me."

Now she groaned around his cock. The need was expanding over her, making her clit as erect and hard as her nipples, reducing her to a triangle of throbbing, aching points desperately in need of attention. She gripped his thighs, digging her finger-nails into the tight, hard muscles there. *No, this is for him. I can get off later.*

"Touch your pretty breasts for me, Alexandra," he urged as he thrust gently in and out of her tugging mouth. "I want to see your hands on them."

Was he reading her mind? Alex didn't know, didn't care. Gratefully she cupped her breasts, massaging the painfully hard nipples under her palms, and willed her own fangs not to emerge. Now was simply not the time to have two sharp points pop out into her mouth.

"Suck harder, *chérie*," Michael said, his voice as deep and slow as the movements of his cock. "Take me in. As much as you can. Like that, *oui.*" He started muttering in French, gliding in and out of her, and then he jerked himself out of her mouth.

Before Alex could do more than whimper, she was flat on her back on the bed, with Michael climbing on top of her. He inverted their positions so that the damp head of his penis was nudging her lips even as he grasped her knees to tug her legs open to his mouth.

His tongue pushed into the top of her labia and flattened against her exposed clit, which he rubbed with his tongue back and forth in a slow, continuous massage. The effect was like throwing jet fuel on a bonfire.

Alex couldn't scream; his cock was pushing deep inside her mouth again. The tips of her fangs extruded and she was terri-bly afraid the sharp points would lacerate him, but she couldn't let go. She needed to suck on him as much as she needed to feel him kissing her between the legs. That wasn't all he was doing, either. She could feel two of his fingers rimming the slickness of her vagina, and then working slowly into it, penetrating her. She prayed she could hold on to her self-control as she fought the snowballing need to come under his mouth.

Michael decided matters for them both by pushing the entire length of his cock into her mouth at the same time he thrust three fingers into her and sank his fangs into her labia.

Alex shook as she came in waves, writhing on his fingers, vibrating under his mouth, and then semen and blood jetted into her mouth, cool and dark and thrilling. She had bitten him, too, and swallowed everything he pumped into her, enjoying the way his body jerked atop hers while his mouth and fingers never stopped working her until she careened into a second wet, pulsing climax.

It might have gone on forever, Alex thought, and neither of them would have cared.

At last Michael lifted his head and gently drew himself from her clinging lips. She caught him and held him long enough to see the twin punctures on the head of his penis closing before she released him.

They'd bitten each other a few times during sex, but not like that. Not where it could do real damage. She reached down and gently touched the wetness between her legs. She was healing a little faster now, not as quickly as Michael and the other Darkyn, but enough to know that the puncture wounds from his teeth had already stopped bleeding and would close in a few minutes.

Her lover turned to lie beside her, gazing into her face with the visible pride and pleasure of a Darkyn male who had satisfied and had been satisfied on several levels.

"Go ahead." Marvel of marvels, they'd done all that to each other and yet she wasn't even winded. "Be full of yourself."

"I am full of you." He bent over to give her a slow, lingering kiss, and she tasted herself on his lips.

Alex was still human enough to be slightly revolted by what they'd done. Blood and sex was still a bizarre mix to her, and what she'd done invoked visions of Lorena Bobbitt. "I didn't hurt you, did I?"

"You can hurt me that way anytime you wish." Michael saw her expression and smiled. "*Non,* I am well. Just when I think I know all about you, *ma belle.*" He cupped her breast and played with her nipple. "You surprise me."

"I have no idea where that came from," she assured him. "All I had in mind was a quick, relaxing blow job for you, to show my appreciation for not leaving me behind in New Orleans with a babysitter. Then there were fangs and orgasms and blood all over the place."

"We have not had much time together of late." He nuzzled

her ear. "I should have warned you that it causes certain needs to arise."

The man was usually a walking erection, but he was right: It had been a while for them. "I never noticed."

"Not only the human desires." He chuckled and pulled her against him. "A Darkyn lord and his *sygkenis* cannot deny each other blood or sex for too long. They share too close a bond. When they do, the passion between them can become uncontrollable."

Alex could have turned that into another interrogation about the Darkyn, but her fangs had begun aching again, as had several other parts of her body.

She let her hand wander down the front of him. "How uncontrollable?" He became rock-hard again the moment she touched him. "I see. I'd say this is a problem that calls for immediate attention by your personal physician, seigneur. How important were those phone calls?"

Michael rolled on top of her. "What phone calls?"

Chapter 8

J. R. "Bud" Montgomery had three jobs to go to before he could call it a night. Then there was his mother, who had called demanding he come over to her house to clean up the trash some dogs had knocked out of her cans and scattered all over her side yard. The last thing he needed to do was waste his time giving an estimate to some hotshot interested in renovating a private grotto. Yet here he was, following a rich man he'd met outside a bar into someone's backyard.

Bud couldn't figure out exactly how the guy had convinced him to check out the job, but he'd certainly been persuasive.

"It was created by an itinerant artist," the potential client told him as he led Bud through a gate and onto the expansive lawn behind the large white house. Beyond the grass ran the charcoal-dark waters of the Intracoastal Waterway. "His granddaughter inherited it but she only comes to Florida in the winter. Over the years I fear she has sadly neglected it."

Bud wasn't even sure he knew what a grotto was. "My men renovate the insides of homes and businesses, Mr. . . ." He stopped when he realized the other man had never mentioned his name.

"I'm Hughes."

"Mr. Hughes." He scanned the yard, which was crowded with odd-looking plaster statues surrounding a pond. "Is this grotto some sort of shed, or what?"

"It is one man's homage to the Word and the Light," Hughes said. "Come, I will show you what this gifted pilgrim did in the name of God." He moved toward the pool.

Another wacky religious fanatic. Probably a Jehovah's Witness, Bud thought as he checked his watch. His mother would start calling his cell phone to bitch at him at any second, and she wouldn't stop until he pulled into her driveway. He hated going to her house; hated the stink and the way her neighbors stared at him. Then there was the daily hour of cleaning up after the cats.

Baker, the neighbor with the dogs, had already threatened to report Nancy Montgomery as an animal hoarder. Bud knew Baker was right—his mother had been compulsively collecting cats ever since his father had died—but as long as she didn't abuse them, he didn't see the problem. So she had thirty-some-odd cats living with her. She kept them inside; they didn't run wild around the neighborhood. He just wished that she weren't so cheap, and that she'd clean up after the damn things herself. He hated scooping out the shit boxes just to save the stinking litter.

He needed to get to his mother's, but he couldn't walk off after he'd promised the rich guy he'd take a look. With a heavy sigh he trudged across the neatly mowed grass to the pool.

The stink of stagnant water reached Bud before he saw that the pool was filled with weeds and black, algae-scummed water. "Hey, they need to clean this out right off," he told Hughes. "Open untreated water like this is a breeding pit for mosquitoes."

"I will suggest it to the family," Hughes said. "What else do you see here, Jason?"

The statues were all of naked men and women. Bud smirked when he saw how small the male statues' cocks were. "Bunch of Roman stuff, right?"

"Actually they are copies of many famous Grecian sculptures. See how cleverly the artist used real objects to adorn the statues? Take this sword." Hughes removed a long, rusty blade from the hand of a naked, blank-eyed warrior. "Go ahead; you can't hurt it. Take it."

Bud didn't want to touch the grody old thing, but found himself holding the handle of the sword, which felt heavy enough to be made of concrete. Uneasy, he held it away from his body. "Cut yourself with this baby, you're gonna need a tetanus booster," he tried to joke.

"True men always carried swords in ancient times," Hughes said. "When they confronted evil, they cut off its head. Unfortunately there were always those who thought they could escape justice. That is the odd thing about justice, Jason. It always catches up to you."

The sword wasn't all that rusty, Bud thought, examining it a little closer. A good scrub with some steel wool, a minute or two on the bench grinder, and the blade would shine like silver. And were those jewels around the handle? Damn if they weren't.

"Yeah, I guess." His cell phone rang, startling him, but the noise faded out almost immediately. "I've got to get going soon." He reached down absently to switch his phone to silent and looked around the quiet little pool. "So what do you need done here, Mr. Hughes? You can have a landscaper clean the pool and scrub up these statues, you know."

"It is so much more than that. You see, I want the ghosts of neglect and cruelty banished forever." A shadow passed over Hughes's handsome face before he smiled again. "You know about ghosts, Jason. Unless you do something about them, they never leave you."

He could sympathize with the rich man on that score. Bud had been living under the grinding weight of his father's ghost for twenty years. "Well, if it's haunted, maybe you should get a priest over here, you know, to bless the place. Then call the landscaper."

Hughes shook his head and sat down on a bird-shit-spattered marble bench. "I think it's better to make a clean break with the past. Demolish it instead of patching and fixing it the way you do."

"Hey, my father started this business," Bud told him, feeling a little defensive now. "I just inherited it and kept it going to make my mother happy." He wondered if he could take the sword with him. His cousin Juana was a jeweler; she could pry out the dark stones and replace them with glass. "I really don't see any work that I can do for you, but let me take this blade to a friend of mine and see what he thinks."

"I can't do that, because you're a thief, Jason," Hughes said. "How many years have you been cheating your customers? Doing substandard work with inferior materials while you charge them for the best grade? How often have you cheated your employees by shorting their paychecks, and firing them if they protested?"

Every word hit him like a fist. How could he have known?

"It was my father that did it." Bud felt tears of anger and frustration stream down his round cheeks. "I've been working night and day since I was sixteen, trying to keep the business from going under, cleaning up his mess."

"You wished to keep your mother in comfort as your father had," Hughes said. "All of those cats of hers cost a great deal. You liked the money as well."

"I'm a fair businessman. There are worse guys out there than me. Why shouldn't my mother have some pets? She's old. She needs the company." Bud wiped the snot from his nose onto the back of his hand. "I'm not a bad guy. I've never had a job flagged for code violation. Not once."

"You are a bad man, a thief. You run a dishonest business to pay for luxuries for a mother who has never loved you the way she loved your father." Hughes rose to his feet. "Your father, who thought you were weak and useless. Your customers know what you have done to them, Jason. They are going to take everything you own and put you in prison."

Panic filled him in a hot, loose flood. "No. That'll kill my mother. They can't."

"God has been waiting for your prayers, Jason. He wishes to forgive you your sins. Why haven't you prayed?"

He was sobbing now. He could hear himself doing it, like a little girl. *Quit your squalling,* his father used to scream at him. *I'm not raising a fucking little girl.* "I don't know. I don't know how." The glowing sword in his hand made him squint. "Help me."

Hughes put his hands on Bud's shoulders. " 'And if thy hand offend thee, cut it off: it is better for thee to enter into life maimed, than having two hands to go into hell, into the fire that never shall be quenched.' "

Bud looked into Hughes's kind eyes. The man was a total stranger, and yet he had revealed so much to him. "That's it? That's all?"

Hughes nodded and led him over to the marble bench. "Here, my friend." He guided Bud to his knees and placed his empty hand on the flat marble surface. "Remove that which has done sin, and rid yourself of the ghosts of your past."

The sword was heavy as Bud lifted it, but he knew that would help make it fast and clean. When Hughes stepped out of the way, he brought it down with a quick chop.

Blood. Agony.

Bud screamed as he watched the sword and his severed hand roll off the marble bench to fall into the grass. "My hand. Oh Jesus oh God no my hand, my hand." He seized his wrist and howled as the skin shifted around the raw, spurting stump.

"You have cut off what has offended thee, Jason." Hughes sounded proud. "Now you can renew yourself and your soul, and ask God to wash away your sins." He gestured toward the filthy pool.

"Shut up, you hear me? Just *shut up.*" Bud panted through the pain as he jerked off his tie and used it to make a tourniquet. "How did you do this to me? I swear to God, I'm gonna take that pigsticker and cut your fucking heart out."

"You will not humble yourself before the Almighty." Hughes stepped out of reach. "You might have purified your soul, but now the evil spills from your very lips."

Bud felt the strange, dragging sadness come over him again. "No."

Hughes picked up the sword and wedged it horizontally between two of the statues. "You know what you must do now."

Blood still dripping from his wrist stump, Bud unwillingly rose to his feet. "No. Cut it out." Something inside him made his legs move backward, putting distance between him and the glittering, beautiful sword. "Why are you doing this to me?" he shrieked just before he began to run toward the blade.

"He did this to you," Hughes said, watching as Bud ran past him.

The blade didn't hurt Bud. He had run into it too fast, and the edge was too sharp. It hurt for only a moment, as it cut into the front of his neck.

Bud didn't think much in that last instant. He only felt relief, and a small amount of satisfaction in knowing that from now on his mother would have to clean up after the damn cats.

*   *   *

The elderly friar who came to wake John Keller just before dawn looked as if he'd been through a minor hurricane. His long, straggly white hair stood on end all around his withered face, while his robe was twisted and the simple cross he wore on a cord around his neck lay flung over his right shoulder. His eyes were so wide that they made his bushy eyebrows appear as if they were trying to escape into his hair.

"Matins, Brother, matins," the old friar said in a hearty voice as he kept shaking John's shoulder. "Get up. Time for prayer. Not to sleep."

"Good morning." John had not thought Mercer would expect him to adhere to the liturgy of the hours, but he was the guest here. Evidently he'd be going to the monastic prayer services given seven times each day. "Give me a moment to dress."

"Wear this." The friar dropped a Franciscan robe onto the end of the pallet and shook a finger at him. "Four minutes. Singing. Praying."

John wondered why the man spoke the way a machine gun fired. "Yes, Brother." He waited until the old man left and picked up the robe. "This is pushing it, Mercer, even for you." He wasn't a priest any longer, and he wouldn't put on the facade of being one to make the friars feel comfortable. If his presence was that unwelcome, he'd call Maurice's brother and get a job fixing roofs.

John hung up the robe in the guest room's small closet. His accommodations were surprisingly modern for an abbey, with a standard twin bed instead of the usual pallet provided for the cloistered. Two white-framed watercolor studies of exotic bird-of-paradise flowers had been hung on the walls, which were painted the color of sea glass. A bookcase with a collection of scholarly religious studies and the omnipresent Bible stood beside a simple writing desk, on which a portable radio and CD player sat. No television, of course, but the radio would keep him in touch with world events. There was even a thermostat for him to adjust the room temperature, which the central air-conditioning unit of the abbey kept at a cool seventy-six degrees.

The guest room had a more personal feel than that of a priest's stark cell or the anonymous one-room-fits-all of hotel accommodations. If he stayed on at Barbastro, John knew he'd be comfortable.

What we could really use is a procurator, Mercer had said. *You'd make a great go-between.*

John didn't want to think about working for the church again even in a civilian capacity. He dressed in the cleanest pair of slacks and plain white T-shirt from his suitcase before walking out of the guest room and following to the sanctuary the sound of bells for matins.

The brothers of Barbastro Abbey were already assembled inside their sanctuary, standing in two rows on either side of the long aisle leading up to the altar, where Mercer was presiding over the morning service. Unlike a parish church there were no pews, only short, narrow knee benches stacked neatly against one wall that would be used for the brothers to kneel on to take the sacrament of communion. Years of burning incense and candles permanently scented the cool air inside the chapel.

Awe and shame battled inside John as he walked in to stand at the end of one of the lines. He still couldn't enter a church without feeling the power of faith, or his own lack of it.

John decided he made a lousy atheist. *I don't believe in this empty ritualistic nonsense anymore, and yet here I am, just one of the boys.*

As the ringing of the last bell of matins faded, the brothers began to sing the opening hymn of the service.

Dies irae, dies illa
Solvet saeclum in favilla,
Teste David cum Sibylla.

It had been so long since John had sung a hymn in Latin for any reason other than to perfect his knowledge of the language of the church that he automatically translated it in his head. *Day of wrath, day that will dissolve the world into burning coals, as David bore witness with the Sibyll.*

Quantus tremor est futurus,
Quando iudex est venturus,
Cuncta stricte discussurus!

*How great a tremor is to be, when the judge is to come briskly
shattering every grave.*

> *Tuba mirum spargens sonum*
> *Per sepulcra regionum,*
> *Coget omnes ante thronum.*

*A trumpet sounding an astonishing sound through the tombs of
the region drives all men before the throne.*

> *Mors stupebit et natura,*
> *Cum resurget creatura*
> *Iudicanti responsura.*

*Death will be stunned and so will Nature, when arises man the
creature responding to the One judging.*

It was a peculiar choice, to say the least, for a matins hymn.
The Dies Irae had been composed in the midthirteenth century
as a meditation on Revelations, when the Catholics expected
Christ to be reborn to the world of man in time for Judgment
Day. John had never heard it sung during any service other than
at a funeral mass or as a mournful requiem for the dead.

Maybe they're celebrating the death of my calling. Disgusted with his endless self-pity, John looked up at the altar. *If
You are in here, God, do something. Strike me with lightning.
Stop my heart. Make my head explode. Give me some reason to
think it all wasn't a waste.*

As usual, God did nothing.

Mercer, dressed in the same humble robes as his brother
friars, knelt before the altar as the men sang, and bowed his
head. That he was praying was obvious, but psalms and passages of scripture were offered after the singing of the hymn,
not during it.

Maybe someone really died around here recently, John
thought, startled to find he was singing the last verses of the
hymn. Gratefully he let his voice fall silent with the others.

Mercer continued to pray for several minutes, then crossed
himself and stood, turning to face John and the friars. " 'Grace

be to you, and peace, from God our Father, and from the Lord Jesus Christ.' "

The friars responded as one with "Heavenly Father, have mercy on us."

" 'Blessed be the God and Father of our Lord Jesus Christ, who hath blessed us with all spiritual blessings in heavenly places in Christ,' " Mercer said, stretching out his arms, " 'according as he hath chosen us in him before the foundation of the world, that we should be holy and without blame before him in love.' "

"Heavenly Father, have mercy on us," the brothers intoned.

John listened to the rest of the abbot's recitation from the first chapter of Ephesians, but he did not join in the refrain, and he let the words roll away from him rather than trying to hold on to them and see some new meaning in them. For him the Holy Scriptures had become like tumbleweeds in the wind: spreading their seed everywhere but the sterile ground within him.

If God truly wanted John to renew his faith and come back to the church, He'd have to do better than hit him with the joyless, misogynistic admonitions of Saint Paul.

The matins service finished with a psalm and more traditional prayer, and the brothers filed out of the sanctuary still in their two lines. John remained standing in his place, so they all passed him. Not one of the brothers glanced at his face. Many made a point to avert their gazes.

"Don't take it personally," Mercer said as he walked down from the platform around the altar. He looked tired, as if he hadn't slept much. "They're not used to visitors, so they tend to be a little shy."

"I remember how it is to be the new brother in the cloister," John told him. He could smell toothpaste on his old friend's breath, but no hint of alcohol—and then he felt ashamed for checking. "Don't worry about it."

"I know what you're thinking," his friend said as they left the sanctuary and crossed the short cement walkway to the refectory. "Who died and made us sing that hymn?"

John looked up at the wide sky over the abbey. It seemed twice the size it had been in Chicago, but there were few tall buildings in this part of the country, and much less air pollution.

A ripple of clouds, like strips of corrugated white paper, began to reflect the intense gold and pink of the rising sun. Florida was a beautiful, unreal place, and to a former Chicago street kid, as alien as Mars.

Mercer nudged him. "You loathed it that much?"

John forced himself to focus on his conversation with the abbot. "It *is* a requiem piece, Mercer. Not exactly how we used to start off our day in the Rockies."

"We're working through some of our own problems here," the abbot said as he opened the door to the dining hall room where the brothers shared their meals. "Some of the older brothers take comfort in the old ghastly stuff. Me, I'd like some John Denver songs, but I don't know how to play the guitar, and you've heard me sing."

"I've heard you screech off-key," John said, shaking his head. "Better stick to the requiems."

Mercer nodded, satisfied. "Exactly. Now, I'm going to ask you to say the blessing over the meal, so stop looking as if you've been sucking jalapeños."

John took the empty seat to the right of Mercer's place at the head of the long trestle table. The abbot remained standing and beamed like a proud parent at the men lining the long benches on either side of him. "Good morning, brothers."

"Good morning, Father," the friars answered in unison.

John felt foolish not replying, but some of Mercer's attitude toward the other friars bothered him a little. It seemed far more patronizing than it should have been, in his opinion, but perhaps that was how Mercer maintained his authority at the abbey.

"Our guest, Brother John Patrick, is joining us for a time here at Barbastro," Mercer was saying. "I would like to thank Brother Ignatius for helping to make Brother John comfortable"——he nodded toward the sour-faced friar who had taken John to his room the previous night—"and I would impose on the rest of you and ask that you do the same. Whatever our position in life, we are all the sons of God, and we serve as one family."

Except me, John thought. *No God, no family, no desire to serve anyone, not even myself. What am I doing here?*

The abbot turned to address him. "Brother Patrick, would you offer thanks for the bounty of the table?"

John nearly got up and walked out, but he found being rude was more revolting than feeling hopeless. So he bowed his head and in a monotone repeated one of the thousand variations of grace that he knew. It seemed the ultimate in hypocrisy to sit with these men of faith and offer thanks after so many months of eating alone without a single word of gratitude to anyone but the occasional waitress who refilled his coffee cup or brought him a bottle of ketchup. It also gave him a sense of moving back in time instead of forward, and that any moment a black cassock would cover his street clothes and someone would want him to offer Mass or hear confession.

"May God forgive us for the weakness of our spirits," John heard himself add on to the end of the prayer. "The gratitude of the wayward soul is the sincerity of the starved dog." He looked up and saw some of the brothers staring at him. "Amen."

The brothers reluctantly echoed his last word and, after an awkward silence, began to pass around the food.

"That was rather interesting," Mercer said as he filled his coffee mug and passed the thermal carafe to John. "What do you say for dinner? 'Blessed be the serial killers, or else the devil would have no one to torment'?"

"If you don't like my act," John replied, "don't put me on a stage."

Breakfast was a Spartan selection of hot oatmeal, cold cereal, and waffles, as the Franciscans believed in ample but plain food. Still, there was plenty of fruit on the table, as well as black tea and orange juice to relieve the blandness of the main dishes.

John expected the brothers to eat in silence, as was traditional at the abbey where he had gone after returning in disgrace from South America. Mercer again surprised him by asking questions and encouraging conversation about the tasks that needed to be accomplished for the day. He listened as the brothers spoke about their individual responsibilities, and offered advice or decisions as needed.

"There was a terrible news report on the radio this morning," one of the younger friars said. "The body of a man was found in the yard of a summer home belonging to an importer and his wife. They said the dead man had been mutilated."

Now Mercer looked as if someone had shoved hot peppers in his mouth. "That is not something we wish to discuss at the table, Brother Robert."

"I only thought . . . it might be a sign of things to come, Father," Robert said, his gaze shifting around the table. "We were told to watch, weren't we?"

"Being watchful," Ignatius told him, "does not mean babbling on about the sins of the world."

"We do work in the outside world, so it is a good thing to keep in touch with what is happening there," Mercer said. "Robert, I would prefer you not listen to the radio in the mornings. The news programs put out a great deal of inappropriate material for their listeners, who are almost always caught in rush-hour traffic. Their stories are entertaining, even shocking, but rarely do they inform us of the facts."

John stared at the abbot and opened his mouth to tell him he was full of it. An image of him hammering nails into shingles made him return his attention to the cold waffle on his plate.

"Someone will have to attend to the services," Brother Ignatius said, at the same time giving Robert a final, hard glare. "Seeing as you were up all night again, Father."

"My insomnia is a plague on us all," Mercer said. "John, if you're feeling rested, Brother Nicholas could use your help in the gardens."

"Brother Nicholas?" He looked down both sides of the table. When the elderly, windblown friar who had woken him for matins lifted his spoon and waved it, John leaned over and said to the abbot in a lower voice, "He's your gardener?"

"It was that or the kitchens," Mercer murmured back. "Try to keep him from using the electrical equipment. He fancies himself a handyman, but yesterday he almost electrocuted himself after rewiring the hedge trimmer."

"Should Brother Patrick make a trip into town for us today?" one of the younger friars, a nervous, fair-haired man in his twenties, asked. "There are several things Brother Paul will need for the infirmary."

"I'd rather stay on the grounds and familiarize myself with

the abbey," John said. He noted the glances the brothers were exchanging with one another, and how some seemed to be fearful. "I'll keep out of the way, of course. I don't want to cause any disruption of your routines."

"You already have, Brother," Ignatius said.

"We will all agree that change is often a good thing," Mercer countered before John could reply. "It gives us the opportunity to examine ourselves and see if we are fulfilling the vows we have made."

"The vow," Brother Nicholas said, pounding the handle on his spoon on the table in emphasis. "Before all others. That is everything. That is . . ." He drifted off, staring at his spoon for a moment before digging into his oatmeal without another word.

"That reminds me," Mercer said. "We have a number of lightbulbs in the cloister that need changing. Brother Joshua, please attend to these. Is there any other business to discuss?" He looked around the silent table. "Very well, then. I would prefer not to be disturbed until vespers. A good day to you, brothers."

"And to you, Father," the men replied in chorus.

"If you're finished pretending to eat those waffles, John," the abbot said as he rose from the table, "I'll show you where we keep the gardening equipment."

Chapter 9

"Why am I here instead of at home trying to sleep through Gloria's game shows?" Harry demanded as he dropped his tray on the cafeteria lunch table.

Sam was tired, too. She'd had the strangest night, dreaming nonstop about making love with Lucan the nightclub owner, of all people. "Garcia decided at the last minute to put us all on switch shifts until the new guys are trained." Which meant she'd be working days and nights for another month or two, assuming she lived that long.

"I still can't believe they're letting that chickenshit bastard come back here." Her partner dropped into his chair hard enough to make the leg ends squeal against the scarred terrazzo floor. "Screw Garcia; take your vacation time."

"I'll run out of that eventually," Sam reminded him as she removed the plastic lid from her coffee cup, "and he'll be here waiting when I get back." She added one sugar and saw her partner grimace and massage his chest. "Take your pills before you eat. Gloria will beat me if you mess up the trip to Cancún."

"Don't know why I've got to take her to *Mexico,* for Christ's sake. We've got the prettiest beaches in the world right here." Harry shook out a pair of tablets from a brown bottle and popped them in his mouth. "She's planning another frigging surprise party, too, isn't she?"

"Next Friday, right after we get off here. She said you'd better look surprised, too, or else." Sam awkwardly used her right hand to push a plastic fork through her fruit-and-nut salad. She'd taken the gauze bandage off her left hand, but it was still sore. "You hear anything about this guy Suarez?"

Harry rolled his eyes. "Ortenza knows him from EC. Says he's not real happy about a female partner, or working graveyard."

"Ortenza is so full of shit that he can play good cop/bad cop by himself," she reminded him.

"Yeah, my feeling." Her partner picked up his chicken sandwich and tried a bite. "The guy is supposed to be tight with Garcia. He recommended Suarez for the slot."

"Good for him." Sam wasn't going to resent Suarez sight unseen. She knew how it felt.

They ate in silence for a few minutes, until a shadow fell between them on the table. Sam looked up into black sunglasses. The man wearing them was about her height, Hispanic, and built like the front end of a truck. He wore a dress uniform with lieutenant bars gleaming on his collar. Blue lights reflected in his coal-black hair, which he wore in a long but neatly combed style.

Ex-undercover, she guessed. *And very, very cool.*

"You Detective Brown?" When she nodded, he held out a broad, square brown hand with discreetly manicured nails. "Adam Suarez. Good to meet you."

"You, too, Lieutenant." She liked the fact that he didn't talk to her tits, as most male officers did when they met her, and shook his hand. From the grip she surmised his strength, which was sinewy and tight, and the fact that he was careful not to use it on her. "My partner, Harry Quinn." She waited until the two men shook hands, and nodded to an empty chair. "Join us?"

"Thanks, but I can't. I've got a briefing to catch." He took out a business card and put it on the table. "If you have a minute, give me a call. I'm on swings in EC until I move to Homicide. Have a good shift." With a nod for Harry, Suarez walked off.

"Woo-hoo, he talks pretty. You see the gleam on that brass?" Harry waggled his brows. "Elvis hair, too. Looks better without the chunky sideburns. Think he plays the girl, or Garcia does?"

Sam snorted. "Why do guys automatically assume that a well-groomed, nicely dressed, polite man is gay?"

"How would I know?" Her partner held up his hands. "I'm the straightest guy on the force, remember?"

She studied his rumpled jacket and the blob of mayonnaise

that had landed on his tie. "If you're the prime example of heterosexuality around here, then the human race is doomed."

"The sun's going to blow up anyway in three billion years," Harry consoled her. "Better to die off than burn up."

Sam picked at her salad. Although she generally enjoyed the unusual combination of flavors, she didn't feel like eating much. The fact that her usual lunch hour was midnight didn't help. Harry gobbled up his meal with no problems, all the while complaining about the retirement cruise he would be taking with his wife.

Last night's dream wouldn't get off her back or, more precisely, out from between her legs. She had had her share of erotic dreams in the past, but this one had seemed so real. There was something else, too—while she'd been rolling around in a tangle of sheets with Lucan, she'd felt different. As if she knew he needed her for something other than the extremely intimate things he had been doing to her body. As if they were supposed to be together.

But why was she having wet dreams about a murder suspect?

Forcing aside her inappropriate fantasy, Sam went back to listening to Harry's ramblings. She envied her partner. After his party next Friday, he had nothing more to do than kick back and relax and putter around the house for the rest of his life. She had to face working with Suarez, who might accept her problem—or use it to make sure that she was bounced off the force.

And then there was Dwyer.

A heavy hand touched her forearm. "You've gotta stop thinking about him," Harry said quietly. "I can always tell when you do. Your whole face turns to glass. You let him see how much he spooks you, and he will get you this time. Be tough, kid."

"I'm really going to miss you, old man." Sam smiled. "There is one thing I need to ask you to do for me."

"I can kidnap you and take you with us to Cancún," Harry offered. "Gloria wouldn't mind. She'd enjoy having someone to talk to while I sleep on the deck chairs." He offered her a weak leer. "Bet you'd look great in a bikini."

Sam had been told she looked stunning in a bikini, not that she'd ever parade around in one away from the pool at her apartment complex.

"If something happens to me, whatever it is, I want you to stay out of it. Let Garcia handle it. No," she said before he could interrupt her. "Garcia knows about Dwyer, and I think he believes my side of things. Either way, he's an honest cop. He'll make sure Dwyer goes down for me." And as Florida was a death-penalty state that loved to execute cop killers, Wesley Dwyer wouldn't have a chance.

"How can you talk about being murdered as if it's like getting a bad write-up?" her partner demanded.

"I haven't had much of a life, Harry, but what I've lived has been okay," Sam told him. "I didn't end up a bored housewife or a corporate monkey. I did something good with what I was given."

She could have done better, if she'd met a guy like Lucan outside the job. Not him personally—guys that rich and good-looking wanted the Lena Caprell type—but someone like him waiting at home every night might have balanced out the stress involved in her job. As things stood, she *was* the job.

A shame Lucan was out of her league, a loner, and an alley cat with women. She had a feeling he was something special in and out of bed. She'd certainly never met a more confident, focused guy.

"Sam, you're not listening to me."

She looked at her partner. "Sorry."

"You're going to be careful, is what you're going to do, and stay away from that sick sack of shit," Harry told her sternly. "Or I will personally walk Gloria's Yorkies over to your grave site and let them piss on it every day. You hear me?"

"Aw." Some of the ice around her heart melted. "You *do* love me, Quinn."

"Yeah." He sighed. "God knows why."

They went back to the squad room to pick up their messages, and Sam saw Adam Suarez and two other men sitting in Captain Garcia's office. As soon as Garcia saw that Sam and Harry were in the squad room, he walked over and closed the blinds.

"Someone doesn't want us eyeballing his briefing," Harry muttered.

Sam felt sick to her stomach. She was almost sure one of the other men in with the captain was Wes Dwyer. "I've got to hit the can before we go," she told her partner. "Be right back."

Homicide shared a restroom with Violent Crimes. At night it was usually deserted, but during the day both genders used it, so the procedure was to knock first before entering. Sam knocked on the door, listened for a moment, then walked in. She didn't think she was going to vomit, but with the way her stomach was rolling, she thought she might wait and see.

Going to the sink and running cold water over her wrists helped. Naturally the prospect of coming face-to-face with Dwyer again was what was making her want to puke. She had never encountered anyone like him in her career. Even worst of the cold-blooded killers she had arrested had some motive for what they did.

Dwyer had none.

That made her side of the story so unbelievable—that an otherwise outstanding officer had fixated on her for no apparent reason. Sam often wondered if she had inadvertently done something to make Dwyer think that she was attracted to him, until she had a chat with a rape counselor from Violent Crimes.

"From the way you describe Dwyer's behavior," the counselor said, "I'd say he's been stalking you."

Sam couldn't believe that. "Isn't that usually a guy who can't accept that his girlfriend has split up with him? Dwyer and I were partners."

"It's more rare than the love-obsessional stalkers, but it happens. It's unusual that Wes was able to pass the academy psych screening—most stalkers are unemployed or underemployed, but they're also more clever than the average felon. Dwyer wasn't married, was he?" When Sam shook her head, the counselor added, "They rarely have successful intimate relationships. It's the reason they so often sexualize their victims, and eventually convince themselves that the object of their obsession deserves what they do to them."

The counselor explained the stages of delusion Dwyer would have built up in his mind as he began forming an obsession with Sam.

"Nondomestic stalkers target someone they have idealized from a distance. They keep their feelings secret at first and will steal personal belongings and other intimate trophies. Sometimes they will build shrines in their homes to the object of their obsession, but eventually the trophies aren't enough. By that time they have worked up to a delusional state in which they believe the target will respond to friendly or even romantic overtures. Rejection only puzzles or angers them, because in their minds, you're already having a relationship."

"But I never encouraged him to think of me as anything but a partner," Sam said. "What would make him believe I could ever want to be with him?"

"It probably was something quite ordinary, a glance, a word, and he was hooked. It didn't matter that you would have treated anyone else the same way; in Dwyer's mind it took on delusional significance and triggered the obsession. Every ordinary gesture or conversation that you had with him would take on even more significance." The counselor's mouth twisted. "I had one stalker describe it as how he and his victim fell in love."

"Dwyer didn't want love from me," Sam assured her. "He only wanted to have sex."

"Stalkers often equate sex with love," the counselor explained. "Frustration over his inability to have a normal intimate relationship, or sexual abuse as a child, or even an unfortunate sexual initiation could have caused him to fixate on sex."

"What could I have done to avoid this?" Sam asked.

"Very little, I'm afraid," the counselor said. "Your ex-partner would have fixated on someone; you were simply in the wrong place at the wrong time. You're an attractive woman who was depending on him to work together as a team; he's a lonely, unattractive man with no sexual outlet. He probably thought he deserved you as a reward for his dedicated police work."

Sam shuddered. "Will he stop now that he's been transferred to Miami?"

"If Dwyer does not have contact with you, it's possible that his fixation will fade in time. However, men who have been unsuccessful at obtaining the object of their obsession and are forcibly removed from it have been known to take extreme measures to be reunited with their victims. In some cases, the only thing that stops them is their death—or the death of their victim."

"So it's possible that the only way Dwyer will stop is if he never sees me again or he kills me." Sam covered her face with one hand. "What can I do?"

"You can move, but with Dwyer's access to police and public records, it would only be a matter of time before he found you. Samantha." The counselor waited until Sam looked up at her. "Half of all stalkers threaten to harm their victims, and over a quarter of those carry out their threats. You are in a very precarious situation. Whatever you decide to do, don't underestimate Dwyer."

Sam washed her hands and her face and went to the paper-towel dispenser. *I am not going to think about Dwyer. I am not going to stand here and throw up a perfectly good lunch. I'll think about Lucan.* Erotic dreams were better than living nightmares.

"Hello, Samantha."

Sam didn't turn around; she knew the voice of the man standing behind her. "This is a coed restroom. It's customary to knock before entering to make sure no one is in here."

"I couldn't wait to see you again," Wesley Dwyer said. "I've been anticipating our reunion for a long time."

Sam put her hand on her weapon. No doubt Dwyer could knife her or shoot her before she could draw it, but maybe she wouldn't die right away. "Officer Dwyer. Please step back."

"You're not afraid to face me, are you, Sam?" Dwyer asked.

She turned slowly. Dwyer stood like an apologetic usher at a movie theater, his hands in his pockets. One of them was moving slightly, as if he were fingering something.

Dwyer was not a handsome man. If asked to describe him, any person on the street would compare him to a weasel, minus the handsome parts. The pinched face, thin nose, and pursed mouth might have given him an ugly/interesting look if he'd been given any sort of reasonable personality; unfortunately Dwyer was as charismatic and charming as the Hunchback of Notre Dame.

Two years at Metro Traffic had changed some things about Dwyer. He had lost more of his thinning brown hair and was now sporting a skimpy mustache. His skin, which had once been a sickly purple-orange from three weekly sessions in a tanning booth, now displayed many small pits and craters from what must have been skin cancer treatments. The horn-rimmed black geek glasses that he used to wear were gone. Sam was sorry about the latter, because now nothing hid the shiny, avaricious gleam of his close-set muddy brown eyes.

Sam watched as Dwyer licked his lips, a nervous habit she remembered him having from the days when they were partners. Seeing his tongue sweep around his thin lips made a surge of bile rise in her throat—he'd tried to put that darting tongue in her mouth too many times—but once his lips were damp, he smiled, showing straight white teeth.

"You do remember that I was fully exonerated in the investigation into your tragic shooting, don't you?" He rolled his shoulders back. "I *did* tell you not to go into that warehouse. You should have listened to me."

She might just shoot him to make the world a better place. "I remember what you did."

Dwyer stared at her chest. "Are you wearing a wire today, Sam? Did Captain Garcia ask you to?"

"No and no."

"Like my new suit?" He tugged at the lapel. "Brooks Brothers. I got it cheap from the last DEA auction."

Only a man like Dwyer would buy clothing confiscated from drug dealers. "Good for you," Sam said, mouth-breathing to avoid the smell of musk cologne. "I'm on duty. Excuse me." She didn't make the mistake of trying to go around him, knowing Dwyer would use the opportunity to put his hands on her, and then she would fire her revolver into his face.

"No. I haven't excused you, Brown," Dwyer said in a very low voice. "I will never excuse you."

The door to the restroom slammed open, and Harry stepped between them. "Sam, Dispatch has another body for us." He took hold of her arm and deliberately knocked into Dwyer with his shoulder as he guided her past him.

"You're a brave old fart, Quinn," Dwyer called after them.

"You're not, you pervert." Harry lifted his fist over his head and extended his middle finger.

Sam concentrated on breathing, and walking, and not puking all over the hallway floor.

When the door closed on Dwyer, Harry took out his inhaler

and gave himself a double shot. "If you gotta pee, Sam, from now on we'll stop at McDonald's. All right?"

Sam nodded, still seeing Dwyer's wet lips and perfect small teeth, knowing it was not all right, and that nothing would ever be that way again until one of them was dead. For a moment she wished she were Lucan's lover. He'd tear someone like Dwyer to pieces.

Which is why he's a suspect, idiot, her conscience snapped. *And you're a cop.*

But then, so was Dwyer.

From the window in Homicide, Adam Suarez observed Harry Quinn leading Samantha Brown away from the lavatory. A few moments passed, and then Wesley Dwyer emerged. He looked as if he meant to follow them, and then abruptly changed direction and walked down to the corridor that led to Central Dispatch.

Ernesto Garcia joined Suarez. They had known each other for many more years than anyone in the department suspected, but they had never had reason to work together until now. Adam wished the circumstances could be different, for he relied on Ernesto as an adviser as well as a compatriot, but there was no choice.

With all that had changed, from now on there never would be.

"What do you think?" Garcia asked in their native language.

"He is a hyena. He will do nothing serious until he can separate her from the old man. We have a few more days to carry out our orders." He looked down at the envelope Garcia was holding out to him. "What is this?"

"Surveillance photographs."

Adam opened the envelope and took out the prints, which showed passengers disembarking in an airport terminal, a man walking toward a building, and two men walking together. They were taken from a distance, but the quality of the camera was such that the subjects in them could readily be identified.

For a moment he couldn't speak, such was his incredulity. Of all the things to happen now . . . "How long ago were these taken?"

"The day before yesterday."

Adam placed them back in the envelope and handed it back to Garcia. "Hold these for now. I will tell you when to deliver them to him."

The captain nodded. "Will we have to kill them, too?"

"That depends," Adam said. "He may wish to do it himself."

Chapter 10

Sam showed her badge to the uniform guarding the gate leading into the yard behind the big white house. "Who found the body?"

"FP and L meter reader," the patrolman told her. "After we got his statement, we had a unit transport him over to North Broward General for assessment and observation." He tapped his chest. "Shock like that does nothing good to a bad heart."

Harry went up on tiptoe to admire a huge boat docked at the short pier at the edge of the property. "Is that a yacht I see, and did someone leave the keys in the ignition?"

"The owners live in New York. The yacht belongs to a neighbor; they let him use their slip when they're not in town." The uniform stiffened. "Excuse me, Detective. Hey. You two. Park it right there." He strode forward to intercept a couple of interested-looking teens who were trying to get a look over the fence.

Sam walked with Harry back to a neglected garden filled with old statues and a reflecting pool in bad condition. She smelled the filthy water from thirty yards away.

"Snowbirds," Harry said with the heartfelt disgust of a native. "You'd think they'd know enough to keep it drained and covered off-season."

The victim had been left on one of the marble benches surrounding the pool. Sam sucked in a breath as she saw the thick legs, pudgy arms, and rounded chest, all of which were soaked with blood. The only other unusual thing about the body was that it was missing some parts.

"Harry?" Sam said, unable to look away. "You ever see one like this before?"

"Kid, I've seen three-week floaters, chain-saw dismemberments, and what happens when you piss off Colombian drug dealers," he assured her in a voice that shook. "But this one tops my gruesome list."

She tore her gaze away and tried to scan the surrounding area. "Where's the rest of him?"

"Some over there," Harry said, pointing to the other side of the reflecting pool.

Sam looked and saw the body's missing head staring back at her from a bench opposite the one the body had been posed on. She circled around the pool and saw that the head was also wet, but with what appeared to be water from the pool, not blood. A puddle of murky fluid surrounded the ragged-edged base of the head. "No hand."

"Killer might have taken it with him." Her partner took another drag off his inhaler before eyeing her. "You need him, ah, all put back together to do your thing?"

The state in which the body had been left had no effect on her "thing," as her partner called it. "It's okay. There's plenty of blood this time."

She went over to the bench to crouch in front of the victim's torso. She had seen only one other headless body before today: that of a biker who had been caught in the middle of a nightmarish three-car smashup while she had been a patrol officer.

A victim of decapitation looked more horrific and unnatural than a corpse in any other condition, but Sam knew few modern murderers chose to cut off their victim's head. It was a near-impossible wound to inflict, for one thing, and one of the messiest ways to kill someone. Unless the murderer had a specific motive involving that kind of mutilation, it was simply less time-consuming to strangle, shoot, or stab the victim.

Harry stepped to the side, blocking the view of Sam from the gate. "You're clear," he said in a low voice.

She took a deep breath, and laid her scarred hand on top of the victim's arm.

I'm sorry, Sam silently apologized to the dead man as she kept the scar that crossed her palm from coming into contact with the blood for a moment. *If there were any other way I could do this, I would.*

She pressed her hand into the victim's blood.

Her "thing" had no official name that she knew of, but since the time that Sam had figured out what was happening to her she had thought of it as blood-reading. It wasn't some sort of mystical ability; she didn't have to close her eyes or mutter incantations. If the victim had been dead too long or she didn't concentrate, it wouldn't even work.

She cleared her mind and focused on the heat spreading over her palm. If she thought anything, it was, *Show me what happened.*

The effect was a little like watching a movie that had been chopped up and spliced back together wrong—a movie that no one could see but Sam. There was no screen inside her head, only flashes of light and color that made brief, disjointed pictures with no sound; glimpses of life through the victim's eyes. Sometimes if there were strong odors, she would pick those up as well.

The gleam of a long, broad blade, like the swords actors used in pirate movies. Two statues that seemed to bounce. Another statue. A short, smug-looking man standing in the shadows. The taint of stagnant water. The sword again, held, slashing down. The blade cutting into a thick wrist.

"Hurry up, kid," she heard Harry say as if from a distance.

The sword kept returning to her mind. She had never encountered such a strong image; it was as if the old blade had meant everything to the victim in his last minutes of life.

Sam ignored the wasplike burn of the blood on her skin and the growing stench of stagnant water as she read further.

Traffic. A crowded parking lot. Unlocking the door to an SUV. The scent of drying seaweed, salt, and suntan lotion. The beachfront. A sidewalk filled with people waiting for admittance to a building. Women's perfume, men's cologne. Neon-lit signs flickering on.

Although touching the blood of the dead gave her only images and scents without sound or much coherence, Sam found herself thinking, *Tell me. Tell me who did this to you.*

She didn't have much time; not only because they wouldn't be left alone long with the body, but because she could read the blood of a victim for only two or three hours after death. If she waited any longer than that, nothing would happen.

Darkness. Tight buttocks under a short black skirt. Little red eyes in the darkness. The sharp odor of hard liquor. A men's room. A measuring tape. Body odor mixed with the smells of pine cleaner over urine and feces. A clipboard with a form on it. An elevator door closing. A tall, broad-shouldered man with silvered fair hair stepping into the elevator. Night-blooming jasmine—

The images vanished as something pulled her hand away from the victim's arm.

"Sam." Harry hauled her to her feet and held her until she was steady. "Sorry, but the photographer's here."

She couldn't speak of what she had seen in front of the other officers and technicians processing the scene, so she gestured toward the water. "Down there." She glanced down at her sore, scarred hand. It was always a little uncomfortable after she read a victim. This time, however, touching the blood had burned so much she expected to see smoke rolling off her scar.

Harry looked worried as they walked toward the yacht. "You okay, kid?" He offered her a paper napkin from the folded stash he kept in his jacket. "You're soaked."

Whatever the weather conditions, reading blood also made Sam perspire badly. Her clothes were sticking to her, and she felt a small but steady stream of sweat pouring down the center of her back. Sam used the napkin to blot her hot, wet face and soaked it; Harry had to give her another before she could dry her face.

She looked back at the grotto of statues. "He was running. That's why they were bouncing."

"What was bouncing?"

"The statues—I mean, the victim. I think he was running away from something just before he died. The killer used a sword." Jasmine suddenly filled her head, and her legs suddenly shook so badly that her knees almost buckled.

"Easy now." Harry was right beside her, and slipped an arm around her waist. "Breathe. You're turning five shades of purple."

She breathed in. Even the reek of the Intracoastal's polluted waters was better than drowning in the delicate, flowery scent. "Why didn't I go into the military?"

Harry gave her shoulder an endearingly awkward pat. "You'd have just ended up getting your head chopped off by terrorists in Iraq."

"Would I." She turned around and stared hard at the statues, recalling the image of the sword wedged between them, and then the sword amputating the victim's hand. "Montgomery ran into the sword that decapitated him—could someone have chased him into it?"

Her partner laughed out loud. "No one's going to cut off their own head to get away from someone."

"Maybe he didn't see it until the last second." Sam knew how ridiculous it sounded, but it was the only thing that made sense of the images. "All I know is what I got from him. There was something else. I think the victim chopped off his own hand first. With the same sword."

"Now you're talking plain crazy," her partner told her. "No sane person amputates his own paw."

"I only know what I saw happen through his eyes." Sam tried to remember what the face of the man standing by the pool had looked like, but all she got was the outline of his body— shorter than her, a bit heavier than Harry. "He was on the beachfront today before he came here, too. I saw the inside of that nightclub where we went to question the owner about the Caprell case."

"Confusion, Fusion, whatever it was?" Harry appeared skeptical. "You sure you're not mixing up two different murders here?"

She nodded. "Whoever this man was, he definitely saw Lucan No-last-name through his own eyes before he came here." That Lena Caprell had been sexually involved with the same man might simply be a coincidence, but her killer had also posed her body sitting up on a bench.

"That Lucan guy was a bit weird, but he didn't strike me as the type to chop up anyone," Harry said. "Look at the way he was dressed. He'd have hired someone to do it."

"We need a motive." She met the doubt in her partner's eyes. "I need you to believe what I saw."

Her partner nodded slowly. "We've used this thing of yours to close too many cases for me to doubt you." He glanced back at the technician who was photographing the remains. "Let's see if we can ID the vic and do the notification. We'll have the uniforms look around for this sword you saw while we go check out the vic's background."

Sam looked toward the water. "Then we have another talk with Lucan."

Sam and Harry left the crime scene after the victim had been tentatively identified as J. R. Montgomery, the owner of Montgomery Construction in Fort Lauderdale. Their first stop was to notify Montgomery's next of kin, which his secretary identified as his mother, Nancy.

Harry called in their next destination to Dispatch as Sam drove. "I hate it when it's the mothers. The old ones always look like it's going to kill them."

"Better she hears it from us than the vultures," Sam said, glancing up at a circling news helicopter.

J. R. Montgomery's mother's home was in an older section of Fort Lauderdale, a neighborhood populated mainly by retirees who preferred to avoid the condo commandos on the beach and live out their golden years in single-family homes.

Nancy Montgomery turned out to be a small gnome of a woman with a blazing halo of dyed red hair. She answered the inside door three seconds after Sam rang the doorbell. She kept the outer screen door locked and peered at them through it with classic old-lady suspicion. "Who are you two? What do you want?"

"I'm Detective Quinn, ma'am, and this is my partner, Detective Brown." Harry held out his open ID so she could see it, and Sam did the same. "We need to speak to you about your son, J.R."

"He's not here, and as soon as he gets here he'll be too busy to talk to anyone." She jabbed a finger toward Harry. "You want to do something for the community? Arrest Mr. Baker next door and take away his no-good dogs."

Harry frowned. "Why would we want to do that, ma'am?"

"He never chains them up when he goes out, and they dig their way out of his yard every time he does. Just look what they did to my trash yesterday." Nancy gestured to the side of the yard, where two garbage cans lay on their sides. Their contents appeared strewn from one end of the yard to the other. "Littering and vandalism and trespassing are against the law, aren't they? And what about keeping pets on leashes? Well?"

"Ma'am." Sam smelled a strong odor of cats and used litter boxes, but was careful to keep her expression neutral. "We need to speak to you about your son in private. May we come in?"

"I suppose." She fumbled to release two inner locks. "Watch out for my babies. I don't want any of them getting out. Mr. Baker's dogs will eat them."

It was good advice, and not just for the cats. The inside of Nancy Montgomery's house was so dark that Sam nearly tripped over what she thought was a furry footstool on the way into the living room.

The footstool got up, shook itself, and waddled off.

The old lady shooed three more fat Persian cats from a small sofa, then picked up one of them and went to sit with it in an overstuffed armchair. Another four cats sauntered into the room to sniff at Sam and Harry.

Sam reached down to scratch behind the ears of a thin but friendly tabby. Loose cat hair in every color imaginable had been shed on the furniture, upholstery, and rugs. It had been so long since Nancy had vacuumed that tufts of the hair had gathered around the baseboards like dust bunnies, and clumped around the bottom legs of the furnishings. There was also a faint but definite odor of decay, as if something had died somewhere but not been found.

"He's gotten himself arrested, hasn't he?" Nancy was demanding of her partner. "What was it? Speeding? Drinking?"

Harry leaned forward with his hands folded. "No, ma'am. Your son J.R. was killed last night in Fort Lauderdale. We're very sorry for your loss."

"Killed?" The old woman looked puzzled. "No, you're mistaken. My son is Jason Ralph Montgomery. You must have him mixed up with someone else."

"We found this on the body, ma'am." Sam took the evidence bag with J.R.'s license in it and handed it to her. "You will need to make a formal identification down at the morgue, but we know it was your son."

"I don't know about this." Nancy stared at the license. "It could be fake. You could be lying to me." Her hands started trembling. "How did he die?"

Harry exchanged a glance with Sam before he said, "We believe he was murdered, ma'am."

"Murdered?" Nancy's voice rose sharply. "By whom? How?"

"We're still trying to determine the circumstances involved, Mrs. Montgomery." Sam took out her PDA. "Do you know of anyone who might want to harm your son? Someone at work, perhaps?"

"No." Nancy looked indignant. "Everyone liked Jason. He was a hard worker, like his father. He was a good son to me." She turned to Harry. "Was he robbed? Did they shoot him? Have you caught them?"

"No, ma'am. It was very quick." Harry kept his voice gentle and sympathetic. "Did J.R. say he was going to meet someone at a club last night? Maybe get together with a friend for a drink?"

Something changed in the old lady's face, and she sat up a little straighter. "My son didn't have time for drinking or going to clubs. Jason was coming here to clean up the garbage Mr. Baker's dogs dragged all over my lawn. I thought about calling the police when he didn't show up, but how was I to know he'd been murdered? What are you trying to say? That this was somehow my fault?"

Like most bereaved parents, Sam thought, she was reacting out of the initial shock. She'd already turned her son into a complete angel; now she would view every question as an attack on her. Which was understandable, but wouldn't help them.

"Not at all, ma'am." Sam pocketed her PDA and looked around. "Did J.R. live with you?"

"He had an apartment, but he spent most of his weekends here in his old room." Nancy waved toward the back of the house. "But what am I going to do about the garbage? Who's going to clean it up now that he's dead? Mr. Baker won't. He'll just laugh at me." Her face crumpled and she began to cry.

Harry rose and gave Sam a nod before going to the old lady's side to offer what comforting words he could. Sam took the opportunity to check out J.R.'s room, which she found at the end of the hallway.

The room might have belonged to Montgomery when he was a boy, but it had not been made into a shrine to his childhood. His mother must have bought the decor straight from a television shopping channel, Sam thought, eyeing the big, painfully bright floral patterns of the drapes, coverlet, and throw rugs. The only thing that didn't match was the wallpaper border around the ceiling, which was of cartoon cats chasing yarn balls and one another. On the nightstand was a copy of *Reader's Digest*, and inside the closet Sam found two pairs of worn sneakers, a couple pairs of old jeans, and some paint-spattered T-shirts.

The real cats in the room—seven of them—were sleeping atop the coverlet on the twin bed.

Harry poked his head in. "She's gone to take a pill and lie down. Find anything besides more cats?"

"Not much. We'll probably do better at his apartment." Still Sam checked each drawer, under the mattress, and in the shoes before gazing around. "No photos, no personal effects. A couple of desiccated hairballs."

"I'll look in the bathroom." Harry disappeared and returned a few moments later. "A toilet, a sink, a roll of Charmin, and three cat boxes overflowing with shit."

Sam felt an unwilling, wretched pang of sympathy for the old woman as she watched five new felines slink into the room to have a look at them. "He probably cleaned them out for her."

Harry rubbed his jaw. "How many animals you think she has?"

"More than Animal Control would want to hear about." Sam smelled the scent of rotten meat again. "I think there might be some dead ones."

"I'll radio Health and Welfare and see who covers this sort of thing." Harry stepped over a pregnant cat having a hissing match with a large silver tom. "You want to hit his apartment?"

"I'd rather have Forensics go in before us. They can dust for prints first." Sam checked her watch. "You need to go home and get some sleep?"

"After seeing that body? I won't sleep for a couple of days," her partner assured her.

Neither would Sam. She had an overwhelming need to see Lucan again, and watch his eyes while she told him about the second murder. "Then let's go grab some dinner, stop by Montgomery's business, and then we'll go to the nightclub."

Chapter 11

Lucan dreamed of the last day he had spent in Rome with his *tresora.*

The floor of the small corner bedchamber Lucan occupied in his night sojourn had become an enormous sundial of sorts; from the gaps in the window shutters thin golden shafts inched steadily across the room. Sitting in the darkest corner allowed him the only comfort to be had while watching them; even so protected, his eyes yet itched. Having memorized the positions of shadow and light on the boards during the weeks he had spent in this room, he could tell that the time was close to four in the afternoon.

Tea, anyone?

Lucan's *tresora,* Leigh, was the sole occupant of the bed on the other side of the room. He had woken at dawn to begin another day of coughing. The spasms had been gradually growing worse, and now he brought up blood with each one: clotted dark expulsions punctuated by sporadic briefer flows of arterial dilution. Morning was always the worst time, yet today there had been no sign of them subsiding, as they always had before.

One aspect of Lucan's loathsome existence was that the death he inflicted was quick and clean. Disease, by comparison, took its time and enjoyed itself. Leigh had been mostly dead for more than a month now.

How long can this posthumous existence of his last?

Lucan wished he could feel some pity or guilt. For days now Leigh could no longer hold pen in hand, or take comfort reading from any of the books Frances had brought for him. He could never be left alone, for he could not rise from the bed unassisted. The ulcerated condition of his throat was such that his weak voice would never carry beyond the walls.

Yet when Leigh was not occupied with the business of dying, he stared at Lucan with open hatred.

Lucan tried to hear the splashing sounds of Bernini's Barcaccia fountain bubbling in the piazza below. Often it had played nursemaid and lulled Leigh to sleep during the bleak winter months when he had still been healthy enough to rail about the unfairness of it all. Now it had become a symbol of all Leigh would never know. No more would he sit on the marble shelf to admire the cascades that poured from the forever submerging boat, or compose sonnets to the crystalline purity of their falling. No more would he dip a cupped hand in its sparkling basin and lift the water to his lips, and drink as much as he chose.

No more would he taunt Lucan because he could not do the same.

"You will never have her," the sodden, thready voice from the bed told him. "Not even when I am gone to heaven."

"Are you so sure about that?" Lucan said, rising and walking over to the bed. "That you go from here to heaven?"

Leigh smiled, showing bloodstained teeth. "I have created beauty. Magnificent poetry that will live forever. What have you given to the world, my lord Darkness, but pain and death?"

Lucan knew Leigh felt bitter about the extreme dichotomy of their situations, but he could not let that pass. "I allowed you freedom. I helped you pursue this poetic life when I could have demanded your seclusion and service. I have never harmed you or yours."

"Why would you? You envied me. You coveted my talent, my family, and my beloved." He paused and lifted a stained handkerchief in a feeble hand to his wet mouth and coughed deeply. "I think you may even envy me this pitiful end I will have."

That struck hard, and was worse than anything Leigh had flung at him. "I could hasten it."

"Oh, yes, do." The damp red crumple of cloth fell away from bloody lips. "That is all you can do, is it not? Take what is not yours and smash it."

Lucan could not strangle his *tresora*; Frances would arrive at any moment. He could not respond, for what Leigh had said was true. He stood, impotent, unable to do more than watch the dying man drift back into semiconsciousness.

A fetid envelope of old blood, sputum, and sweat rose from the wilted linens around Leigh's limp body. Not even the smell bothered Lucan anymore, not after he had breathed it for the endless months they had spent in Hampstead nursing Leigh's brother, who had sickened and died of the same disease. The stink could not sicken Lucan, or affect him in any sense, but it was still poison on the air—poison to Frances, who was still human, and could catch the sickness.

Sometimes Lucan thought she had come to Rome to do just that. She could join Leigh in the grave, as she would never join Lucan in eternal life.

Unable to spend another moment looking down at the dying man, Lucan went to open the shutters. Let the sunlight irritate his eyes. With luck he would go blind, and never again have to look upon Leigh or Frances.

The light was fading. They would need more candles, for only a single half column of tallow remained on the writing table near Leigh's bed. It was the last; part of an ingenious contraption of several candles Frances had linked together by lengths of cotton; as one burned the cotton thread would draw the flame to light the next. She had assembled it after Leigh had pleaded with her never to leave him alone in the darkness.

The door opened, and a tall, graceful Englishwoman walked in. Her dress had been carefully adorned with lace and ribbons to cover the threadbare spots; her light brown hair had been coiled in a simple yet elegant chignon. In her arms she carried a small parcel wrapped in brown paper that doubtless contained more remedies that would not save Leigh, and soft food that he could not swallow.

Frances barely glanced at Lucan. "What do you here, my lord? I would have thought you bound for England by now."

Lucan vaguely remembered threatening to board the next ship for London the night before after unsuccessfully pleading with her again to allow him to move Leigh to a hospital and take her with him to England.

"I fear the servants have deserted for parts unknown," he told her. "They refuse to be near him." He tried to take the parcel from her arms, but she stepped away. "I have done nothing to him but watch," he assured her. "We have not had a single argument." It was the truth; he had not argued with Leigh.

"You will not help him, so what reason is there for you to stay?" She set the parcel down on the writing table. "Go back to England, my lord. Your pity is of no use to us."

He tried to be gallant. "I cannot abandon you, my dear. It would not be the gentlemanly thing to do."

"You are no gentleman," Frances said, her gentle eyes sparkling with new disgust. "If you were you could use your powers to revive him—to heal him. Why will you not do that?"

"It is beyond me. No man—"

"You are not a man." She pressed a hand to her breast and swallowed, gathering her courage to say the rest. "It is said that you can make others like you by giving them your blood."

Lucan looked into her face and saw the mild contempt she had always shown him now swelling into hatred. He saw himself moving to the bed, removing his gloves, and laying hands on his *tresora*—not to heal him, but to put an end to the agony for all of them.

"I cannot heal his sickness. Centuries ago, perhaps, but over time our blood has become poison to humans." He had nothing else to lose; he would tell her all. "Frances, come away with me now. You cannot go on exposing yourself to his disease."

"You are lying." She crossed her arms. "You could not have such powers and be so helpless. Why will you not save him?"

He stared at her midsection and saw why she had been wearing her loose gowns. Jealousy savaged him; here was the only woman he had ever loved, and she was pregnant by another man.

"Did he give you that child in your belly?" he asked. "Is that why you wish me to play God? For the bastard you carry?"

"That is quite enough, sir." Frances went to the door and opened it. "If you refuse to help Leigh then I beg you leave us, my lord, and never come back here again."

"I could give you everything he cannot," Lucan told her stiffly. "Wealth and comfort. Devoted love for the rest of your life. Protection for you, a name for your child. You would be my *kyrya,* my human wife."

"You are too late. Leigh and I were secretly married by a Roman Catholic priest two weeks ago. My child shall bear his father's name." Frances rested a hand on a slight curve of her stomach. "Do you think I would trade my love for the material things you promise? Do you imagine I could bear your touch, knowing you let him die?"

"He will be dead by sunrise, and there is nothing I can do to stop it," Lucan told her flatly. "What will you do when he's gone? You have no money. Your family in England will never take you back. Do you propose to sell yourself on the streets of Rome?"

"Leigh will never leave me." She smiled. "That is what you cannot understand, isn't it? The material world matters not. He and I will be together forever. Death is but a temporary separation. Our love and this child are our immortality."

Lucan thought of killing her. He thought of weeping over her and begging her to reconsider. In the end, he held on to the shreds of his dignity. "I will go then."

"Yes," she said, but her clothing had changed, and her hair had darkened. She wore sunglasses, and carried a weapon. "Go."

He reached out to her. "Samantha?"

"Master."

Lucan opened his eyes, expecting to see Samantha, or Rafael, or welcoming darkness. Instead Burke stood with sunlight streaming around him to pierce Lucan's eyes. He covered his face with one hand. "Is someone dead?"

"No, master."

Someone would be soon. Lucan lifted the edge of his hand to peer at the hovering figure of his *tresora.* "Why then do you wake me before sunset?"

"I beg you forgive me for disturbing you so early, master, but there are so many things happening at once," Burke said, rushing out the words. "I would have consulted Master Rafael, but he has not yet returned, and then the seigneur's seneschal telephoned requesting an audience with you tonight—"

"Cyprien." Despite the ache in his head from the sunlight and the disturbing dream, Lucan smiled. "You said yes, of course."

"I did, master, exactly as you had instructed to, but then the band manager called to confirm the Bastille Day concert—"

"Which you confirmed."

"I would have, but I accidentally disconnected the man when Detective Brown from the police department called to inquire if you were on the premises. I did not know what to say when she advised me that she, too, wished an audience with you, but she didn't seem to require an appointment—"

The damned daylight was going to fry the eyeballs out of his skull. "Burke."

"—and then there was the call from Éliane in Ireland, and I heard the news about the murder, and with Master Rafael gone, I wasn't sure what to do about the concert band or the new delivery—"

"Burke."

"—when she . . . Yes, master?"

"Close the blinds and bring me the phone."

"Oh. Yes." Burke rushed over and began twisting the rod to shut the thin slats. "Master Rafael has summoned guardsmen. They have taken up positions around the building. They report that patrons are already beginning to line up outside."

"We will be opening the club an hour later than usual. Two, if I choose to slaughter the seigneur." Lucan was annoyed by the fact that his seneschal thought he needed guards, but a show of *jardin* force was not an unwelcome thing. Cyprien still thought of him as Richard's creature. It was time his old enemy understood that this was his kingdom, and here he was king.

Lucan recalled the small, passionate face of Dr. Alexandra Keller. He had watched her in New Orleans when she had been arguing with Cyprien. It would be amusing to test how enduring the bond was between the *sygkenis* and her Darkyn lord. Certainly it would drive his old enemy to distraction to watch his lover respond to Lucan.

He dialed the number to Dundellan Castle in Ireland. "Éliane, it is Lucan." He listened for a moment as the frightened voice on the other end of the line described a horror he had long feared. "When will you arrive?" After she told him, he said, "I will see to it." He disconnected the line.

Burke was waiting for instructions, and Luçan forced himself to address him. There were other forms of distraction as well. "Contact Alisa. I will want her and five of her associates to attend me during the meeting with Cyprien."

"Humans? To attend your audience with the seigneur?" Burke fumbled for a tissue and pressed it to his nose. "Master, do you think that is advisable?"

"Do you think it advisable to keep breathing through your mouth?" Lucan asked him. One of the lightbulbs overhead popped and darkened. "I know your nose does not function as it should, but I can create another airway very easily."

"No, thank you." His *tresora* clutched the end of his nose with the tissue. "I will call Ms. Kruk immediately." He turned to leave.

"Where is this delivery?"

"I left it in your sitting room, master," Burke said, gesturing to the door. "Should I bring it in here?"

Lucan got up and pulled on a robe. "No, I will see to it."

The box was from the same florist as before, and Lucan had no doubt it would contain more dead flowers. His admirer was certainly a persistent one. He pulled on his gloves, intending to toss it out into the hallway for Burke to remove. Then he smelled blood.

"Did you send me something more personal this time?" He set the box down and opened it. A dozen blackened, rotting roses lay inside, and buried in the midst of them was something wrapped in bloodstained rags. "A token of your affection?" He prodded the rag and felt flesh inside. "Or someone else's."

He took out the ragged bundle and carefully unwrapped it to reveal a severed hand. As a scare tactic it was entirely useless; he had seen dismembered body parts on the battlefield that would put this humble bit of farce to blush. The rust flakes embedded in the flesh at the severed wrist intrigued him, however. Had his admirer used something more inventive to separate this from its previous owner? Or was the hand treated with copper solution, as the lilies had been?

He put the hand aside and inspected the dead blooms. The thorns had been carefully removed, and thorn-shaped copper spikes inserted in their place. Here was the perfect illustration of his dilemma: beauty that could never be his to hold. Sanctuary that was to be destroyed before it could be fully known.

Vaguely he heard a great deal of glass somewhere nearby shatter.

"Did you think me that careless?" He picked up the box and threw it across the room, shouting after it, "Do you think I am an idiot?"

What was the point of these ridiculously sabotaged dead offerings? To remind Lucan of what he was? Of what he had done? Had he begged God Almighty to curse him with this? No. He had made the best of his lot. Had he not embraced what he was, and learned to control it, it would have put a speedy end to more than him.

The time had come. He had given his word.

As for the taunting, childish offerings, they did not matter. If Rafael did not discover who was sending them, Lucan would. A fool so determined would not keep his distance much longer—and then he would discover just how appropriate his tribute had been.

"Master, the seigneur will be here within the hour," Burke said, stepping gingerly over the dead roses and glass littering the floor. "I will see to having the windows repaired. I left a message on the band manager's voice mail confirming the concert appearance for July fourteenth." He stopped and stared. "Is that a real hand?"

"Are either of yours missing?" Lucan saw that in his anger he had shattered every windowpane in the room. He strode over, picked up the severed appendage and the rags, and stuffed them in the box. "Burn it—all of it."

"Yes, master."

"You will also please stop looking as if you think that I mean to tear your head off every time I address you." He saw Burke wince. "Truly, this cringing of yours will drive me insane. What is it now? Was my tone too loud? My countenance too fierce? I broke too much glass?"

"No, master, it is just . . . the man who was murdered. He was decapitated and mutilated." His *tresora* looked down into the box. "The police have not yet found his hand."

Now he understood why Detective Brown had returned. "Who was the man killed?"

"J. R. Montgomery, master," Burke said.

Lucan frowned. "I do not know the name."

"He owned the company that Master Rafael hired to complete the downstairs renovations," Burke said. "He was here only yesterday."

Sam bought Harry dinner at one of the local salad-and-sandwich shops, ignoring his demand for a chili-cheese dog and bullying him into having a chicken wrap and a diet soda.

"All this dieting and watching my sodium," he grumbled. "I bet I don't live a second longer than I would have on hot dogs and beer."

"But we'll be able to carry your coffin to your grave," she advised him, "instead of having to rent a forklift to move it."

Harry lifted his wrap with a grimace of distaste. "Gloria'll want to bury me by the rosebushes. Just dig a deep hole and roll me in."

Montgomery's office was situated in a strip mall, but the receptionist there had little to offer them but tears and sobs. Through them, she suggested they talk to Montgomery's employees, currently finishing up a job installing drywall in a new medical building downtown.

Sam and Harry found the site, and spent the next six hours in Montgomery's cramped trailer interviewing his work crew. None of the men came out and said that J.R. was a lousy boss, but no one seemed devastated over his murder.

"Bud was okay," Hector Ladega told Sam as he slouched in the folding chair she had set up in front of J.R.'s desk. "Not as bad as some of those *pendejos* down in Miami." His gaze crawled over her, a jittery, hungry spider. "You know who killed him?"

"No," Sam said. "Do you?"

"Wish I did. Get me reward money, ay? Crimestoppers." Four gold front teeth flashed. "You know, you not bad-lookin' for a cop, *chica.*"

Harry had made a run to the Portosan, or Sam would have turned Ladega over to him right then and there. "Did Mr.

Montgomery have trouble with any of the other men on the crew? Have you ever heard him arguing with anyone?"

"Nah. Bud never talk much to anybody except to say, 'Get to work, lazy bum, you.'" He reached down with one plaster-whitened hand to casually adjust his crotch. "So, you married? No ring on your finger. You like to dance?"

What is it about me that draws assholes like a magnet? Sam put down her PDA. "Do you know if Mr. Montgomery frequented a club on the beach called Infusion?"

He shook his head. "Too rich and white for me, lady. I hang at Latino clubs, you know, dance to real *música*." He raised his hands, snapped his fingers, and shimmied in his chair.

Sam saved her retinas by looking at a framed photo on the desk that depicted the company's owner standing in front of his pickup truck. Bud Montgomery had been a little on the beefy side, an average-looking, couch-potato type of guy. He had kept what hair was left on his head short, which Sam thought was more sensible than the ridiculous long-haired comb-overs some balding men insisted on doing to themselves. The skimpy goatee he had worn, however, hadn't done much for his plump face or even faintly disguised the fact that he sported a hefty double chin.

He had his head back and looked down his nose at the camera without smiling, but the effect was more smug than sneering or stern. *I'm the boss,* the photo said. *Don't you forget it.*

"You should go with me some night, *chica*," Hector was saying. "We could have us a party, you know?" His shifty dark eyes finally decided to settle on her breasts. "A *real* good time."

Dwyer had said that to her once, when they were patrolling. *Someday, Samantha, I'm going to show you how to have a real good time.*

She had to stop thinking about the weasel in the department and concentrate on the weasel she was interviewing. "Did Mr. Montgomery ever mention the club? That he liked it, or was going to meet someone there?"

"His *mamacita* find out? She'da kicked his ass." Hector laughed. "She key him up all the time on the radio." His voice rose to a falsetto. "'Jason, I need you get me prunes from the store. Jason, you late for dinner. Jason, come home and suck my saggy old titties.'"

Sam decided she had exhausted Hector's minuscule store of information about his employer and her own scant supply of patience. "All right, I think that's all I need. Thank you, Mr. Ladega, you can go back to work."

Instead of leaving the trailer, Hector stood and leaned across the desk. His breath smelled of some garlicky meal, and under that, halitosis so thick it could probably melt the chrome off a Harley at twenty feet.

"So what do you say, *chica?* You change your mind?" He thrust his chin out and dropped his eyelids as if trying to get a peek down the front of her blouse. "Let's go out tonight."

"I'm not interested, thank you." She rose and walked around the desk, mostly to get away from the stink of his breath.

"Come on, come out dancing with me," Hector said, reaching out.

Sam didn't know why until she felt something squeeze her right buttock. She didn't think; she reacted, and pivoted around to seize his wrist. With a reverse move she'd learned in hand-to-hand in the academy, she slammed his arm down on the desk and held it there.

Part of her saw his openmouthed shock; the other saw the grinning, taunting face of Wesley Dwyer. "You sick little shit."

"What?" Hector was stunned. "I didn't do nothing—"

"You want a dance?" She grabbed his collar and twisted it until he choked. "I can dance on your face, and then book you for assaulting a police officer. Want me to do that?" He shook his head, and stumbled back when she released him. "Let me know if you change your mind."

She didn't have to tell him to get out. Hector shot out of the trailer like a bullet, nearly knocking over Harry, who was on his way in.

"What's his deal?" her partner asked.

"He needs a hand chopped off." Her mobile phone rang, and she slammed the lid down on her temper. Dwyer's transferring to Homicide had her too riled. She switched on the phone and answered, "Samantha Brown."

"Detective Brown, this is Dr. Bill Weylen from the University of Miami. I run the archaeology department down here, and your forensics division asked me to give you a call when I had some results on a cross they sent over for ID and dating."

"What can you tell me about it, Dr. Weylen?"

"It's an excellent forgery, for one thing," he said. "I haven't seen this quality of counterfeiting since the James ossuary. However, the real Noir cross is on permanent display at the Louvre in France."

"Excuse me, you called it the Noir cross?"

"Yes. It was named after its original owner, a Templar knight known as Noir de L'Anfar, and it was made of gold and precious jewels. This fake is pure copper, and the cabochons are paste."

Sam wrote everything down on her PDA, thinking how the forensic tech would be disappointed about his guess on the cross's age. "How does someone make something like that? Can it be traced?"

"Not this time. The cross isn't as old as the original, but no one made it yesterday, either. To be on the safe side, I carbon-dated it. Given the amount of soil and metal oxidation, I'd say someone buried this in the ground about two hundred years ago."

Chapter 12

When they drove down to the strip, Sam saw the line of patrons waiting to enter the nightclub stretching around the block. Most of them looked hot, bored, and unhappy, as if they had been standing there for at least an hour or two. Among them, Sam saw a vivid head of cerulean blue hair, and swore under her breath.

"Problem?" Harry asked.

"I think my new neighbor, the underage brat, is here." Sam felt more like swearing. Hadn't the kid heard anything she'd told her?

"We could bust her for fake ID," her partner suggested.

Sam saw a couple of girls talking with Chris, and relaxed a little. If she stayed in a group of friends, then she'd probably be okay. It was the loners who drew the predators. "I do that, she'll never sign for my UPS packages."

Given the amount of road and foot traffic, and the scanty spaces left by packed-in cars, Sam decided to park in the back of the nightclub and walk around to the front. This time, the bouncer seemed to be expecting them.

"You the cops?" When Sam nodded, he unlocked the entry door. "Enjoy."

"Aren't we friendly tonight," Harry muttered. "Last time we almost had to swear out a warrant to gain access to Mr. Lucan."

"Could be he wants to see us." Sam stopped to let her eyes adjust to the dark interior of the club. "Montgomery would have made the six-o'clock news."

Unlike on their last visit, the bar was almost empty. There were no employees on the floor or behind the counters, and only a few scantily dressed girls sitting at a cluster of small tables that had been pushed together. They were talking, smoking cigarettes, and drinking something with tomato juice out of tall glasses sporting rims of black crystals. One of them, a hard-looking woman with purplish-red hair, glared at Sam and muttered something to the girl sitting next her. They both eyed Sam and laughed together.

"I know that one," Harry said, nodding toward the purple redhead before he started coughing and waving a hand in front of his nose. "Her name's Alice, goes by the name Alisa. We busted her giving blow jobs over at that fetish club on the north side two years ago. Got her tongue stud caught in some guy's cock ring. We had to call the paramedics to get them apart."

"Lovely. We'll catch her on the way out." Sam scanned the room looking for Lucan, and walked with Harry to check the office, which was locked again.

"I beg your pardon, Detective Brown?"

Sam turned to see a worried-looking man hovering behind her. "I'm Detective Brown," she said over Harry's coughing attack, which hadn't abated yet. "Who are you, and where is Lucan?"

"I'm Burke, the nightclub manager. My mas . . . Mr. Lucan is in the penthouse suite, and asks that you join him there." He gestured toward an elevator, but eyed Harry, who was struggling for air. "Sir, would you like to sit down?"

Harry took out his inhaler and used it before he could speak. "Sammy, I've gotta get my pills from the car," he told her. "Meet you upstairs, okay?"

Sam looked at the elevator, torn between helping her partner and getting to Lucan. She needed to see Lucan badly, to know he was all right, and she had absolutely no idea why. "I'll go with you."

"No need, I'm fine." He made a shooing gesture. "Go on; get started on him."

Burke escorted Sam to the elevator but did not step inside. "It will take you directly to the penthouse," he said as he inserted a key that made the doors begin to slide closed.

"Wait, my partner needs to know—" Sam released a frustrated breath as the panels sealed and the elevator began to rise.

* * *

Something was wrong at Barbastro Abbey.

John had a vague sense of it from the day he had arrived. At first he had blamed it on the difference in Mercer Lane. His friend had changed dramatically from the man he had met in Chicago; now he was just like any other pompous, denigrating church official. Sometimes when the abbot was speaking to him, John felt as if he were back in Chicago again, being patronized and misled by Bishop Hightower.

"David might have been a shepherd, but God didn't want him squandering his life on herding sheep," Mercer said during one evening meal when the Bible figure's life was being discussed. "That's why he gave him the slingshot. So he'd practice and prepared himself."

"David composed most of the Psalms when he was a shepherd," John said, surprised at the abbot's militant opinion of the biblical warrior. "Bethlehem, where he herded sheep for his father, is known as the city of David."

"David's humble beginnings were not what made him king," Mercer replied. "They are only to teach us that we must all be ever vigilant, and keep ourselves ready for the Philistines and Goliaths of the world."

Soon after that other, smaller notes of discord became apparent to John.

A seemingly constant, invisible tension kept the brothers at the abbey on edge. They tried to hide it by putting on a false front for John's benefit, but their behavior vacillated between overly friendly and inappropriately lofty. The youngest of the brothers barely spoke to him at all, and they went out of their way not to be alone with him.

They all seemed afraid of something, but what?

It wasn't John. Most of the time the friars were so preoccupied with whatever had them troubled that they noticed John only as an afterthought. No, whatever bothered them was something they were trying to conceal from him. Too many low conversations came to an abrupt halt whenever John came within earshot; too many doors were closed too quickly when he passed by them.

He understood the politics of the abbey, and knew that the cloistered life could instill some odd habits and behaviors, but this was far too obvious to be anything but a cooperative effort to keep him in the dark.

Mercer wasn't any help. For one thing, he slept most of the day, and spent his nights shut up in the abbot's house. The few times John did get close to him, he smelled wine on the abbot's breath. John had counseled enough alcoholics to know that Mercer had fallen off the wagon, hard.

He tried to pry a little information out of Brother Nicholas while they worked together in the gardens, but the old man could hardly string three coherent words together, let alone explain the oddness at the abbey. Thanks to Mercer, John found himself buried in the heaviest yard work and babysitting the elderly friar, who meant well but was also a little deaf as well as feebleminded, which John soon discovered the hard way.

"Need a sign," Nicholas told him one afternoon. His robe was covered in wet sage-green splatters. "Wet paint."

Two hours earlier John had given him a bucket and a scrub brush and instructed him to clean the bronze life-size statue of Saint Frances of Rome in front of the chapel.

"What paint?" He looked down at the scrub brush in Nicholas's hand, which was also covered with green paint, and rushed out to see the brothers gathering around what was now a sage green statue of Saint Frances.

Nicholas came to stand beside him and gestured. "Green, like you said. Green statue of Saint Frances. For Ireland." He nodded, satisfied. "Good color."

John didn't mind the physical labor, or the extra headaches Nicholas sometimes created for him. It gave him a sense of working for his keep, and he had done much worse working in the labor pool in Kentucky. He even attended the liturgy of the hours services in the abbey's chapel, although he came to observe, not to participate. As for Mercer, he never came to meals, and said nothing about John disdaining the robe for comfortable work clothes.

Mercer was also using the brothers to keep John out of his hair, as he had when John had asked to speak to the abbot after vespers about buying some necessary gardening equipment to replace that which Brother Nicholas had destroyed or rendered inoperable.

"I will pass your request along to the abbot as soon as he awakes," Brother Ignatius said. "In the meantime, would you mind washing some dishes in the kitchen? Brother Rupert isn't feeling well."

John went to the kitchen, which was stacked with dirty pots, pans, and dishes from breakfast and lunch—as if they had been saved especially for him. The abbey didn't have an electric dishwasher, so John spent the next three hours up to his elbows in suds. By the time he finished the brothers had left the chapel and were back working at their individual tasks, and Ignatius informed him that Mercer had left the abbey on church business.

The secrecy made John seriously consider leaving the abbey. He certainly didn't owe the church anything; after New Orleans and Chicago John felt that all the accounts had been settled as well as they ever would be. Mercer would probably lend him enough money to make a fresh start. It was the anxiety in the eyes of the youngest brothers that kept him from packing up his suitcase. He'd seen the same desperation in his own eyes after leaving Rome.

Better to find out what was going on first, and then decide how much he wanted to get involved.

John waited until Mercer asked him to drive into town to pick up supplies. Ordinarily Brother Ignatius or one of the senior friars performed the chore, but the abbot told him they were needed for a prayer study.

"Here's the list of what we need," Mercer said, handing him a lengthy tally of groceries and several hundred dollars in cash. "I can trust you with our funds, can't I?"

"If I were a thief, Mercer," John advised him, "I'd blackmail your parents. They've got more money than God, don't they?"

The abbot laughed as he handed him the keys to the abbey's old but reliable station wagon. "Make sure you get the yellow peaches. Brother Nicholas is convinced the white ones aren't ripe and refuses to eat them."

John worried one of the friars might be sent with him, but no one met him at the car. He drove out through the electric gates, using the remote clipped to the visor to open and close them. A few blocks from the abbey was a busy apartment complex with guest slots for visitors, where he parked the station wagon.

I could be wrong, he argued with himself as he walked back to the abbey. *It could just be some crisis of faith, or the brothers wanting to oust Mercer because he's drinking.* The more he thought about it, the more something like that made sense.

John stopped at the chain-link fence at the back of the abbey's property and hesitated. If he did this, he would be in essence betraying his friendship with Mercer. He would be spying on a man who had offered him sanctuary when no one else would.

Mercer has been lying to me, he thought. *I can't pretend it isn't happening, and I wouldn't be much of a friend if I ran away instead of trying to help.*

He climbed the fence easily, and kept to the trees as he walked to where he had left the extension ladder propped against the outside of the brick enclosure wall. He climbed up far enough to see if the way was clear, and then hoisted himself over the top and dropped down.

The grounds were empty, but he could hear the voices of the brothers coming from the chapel. Quietly he walked to the side of the building and edged up to one of the windows to look inside.

The brothers had abandoned their double standing rows and had gathered in a circle on the floor of the chapel. They were kneeling, their hands clasped, and praying in Latin together. After a moment of listening he realized that they were uttering the same prayer, over and over.

"Pater noster qui es in cœlis, sanctificetur nomen tuum. Adveniat regnum tuum. Fiat voluntas tua, sicut in cœlo, et in terra . . ."

John knew the paternoster in English, Latin, and Italian; he had been forced to recite it dozens of times each day while the Brethren had been "initiating" him in Rome. Hearing it from the mouths of the gentle brothers of the abbey made him want to scream his outrage—but it was a prayer used by priests, monks, and friars all over the world. The Brethren had nothing to do with this place. If they had, John would be dead.

It doesn't mean anything.

John felt foolish. All this clandestine nonsense, and the brothers were simply praying together informally, perhaps as

they always did when not called upon to perform for strangers
like him. He moved away from the chapel and retraced his
steps, intending to walk back to the car and run the errands for
Mercer and never, ever question his friend or his motives again.

*Maybe while I'm in town I can see if there's a psychiatrist who
does charity cases.* He certainly needed his head examined.

On his way to the gate, which was his only exit, John saw
the abbot walking with Ignatius toward his house, and realized
Mercer would spot him if he stayed out in the open. Since he
was closer, he trotted behind the little house and waited there
until his friend was inside.

"If you would give the brothers more time, Father, I know
they will be better prepared for what must be done."

John looked at the window that had been left open; Ignatius's voice was coming through it, low but clear enough for
him to overhear. He told himself to stop eavesdropping and go,
but then he smelled the fruity odor of wine.

"You were all trained, were you not?"

That was Mercer, John thought, yet his voice was no longer
mild or kind, but flat and cold as stone.

"We were, but you have to make allowances for the fact that
we have not been activated in twenty years." Ignatius sounded
as if he were pleading.

"They have not had one of their demon lords to lead them
here since they befouled this country with their presence," Mercer replied. "This one that has come, he was the devil who
destroyed our faithful soldiers in Dublin."

"That can't be right. We were told that one was their execu-
tioner—he protects their king—"

John heard the sound of a hard slap, breaking glass, and
Ignatius's sob. He closed his eyes.

"You do not question the word of the Lightkeeper, Brother.
You follow orders, or you violate the oath and die. Now, make
me a drink." Something liquid was poured into a glass. "They
have established another of their infernal nests somewhere
within this area. I have set up the search grids. You will send
groups of three into each one every night. They are to be fully
armed, and use only the copper weapons I have provided,
nothing else."

"If one of my brothers is caught killing these things, they will be arrested."

"Any brethren taken by the police will not live to see trial," Mercer promised. "You will remind them of this. Where is Keller?"

John held his breath.

Ignatius was sniffling. "You sent him into town to pick up groceries."

"It was foolish of me to bring him here. Find another place for him tomorrow and secure the grounds. No more outsiders until we have finished our mission."

"Father, please understand, I am not questioning your orders. I only ask for more time. Most of the brothers here are old men—"

"You were all born to the Light. You will die in it. That is what matters. Give me more of that wine." A bottle gurgled, and liquid poured. "The Lightkeeper has thought up an ingenious way to capture as many alive as possible—by setting traps with their own kind. If you can prove your worth, I may send for one of the prisoners being reserved for your use."

"What if the prisoner uses his powers to escape?" Ignatius's voice was fearful. "Is it not better to keep them in one of our facilities and only make the *maledicti* believe we have one of their kind?"

"The demons always know when we have tried to fool them," the abbot told him. "Live bait is the only thing that works."

John didn't dare look into the window to see if Mercer was getting drunk or Ignatius was having a nervous breakdown. He couldn't believe Mercer was a member of the Brethren. In all the years they had known each other, he had never said a word to John. Of course, if he had, he would have been killed for it.

The first rule of the order is no one talks about the order.

"What of the breeders? Have you secured any?" Mercer's voice lashed out.

"We have only just begun the breeding program." Ignatius sniffed and cleared his throat. "We embraced the monastic life—as we were told to, I might add."

"The Lightkeeper is going to be very disappointed. We need

new men to replace those who are killed by the *maledicti,* and docile women to breed more. You have enough desperate and poor in this community to build a young army in fifteen years. You do know how to set up a proper breeding facility, I hope?"

"I was trained to, yes, but we—none of us—" Ignatius coughed. "Pardon me, Father. The younger men, yes, of course, they will do as they have vowed. But the older men have been dedicated to Christ. They have lived in celibacy since their training. I think it beyond them now."

"I am sure they will remember how to plow a breeder," Mercer snapped. "But if you must, give them demonstrations yourself."

"Is there no alternative for us?" Ignatius's voice bordered on hopeless. "We have done some good things here. Could not others readier to respond be brought in to face this threat?"

"We leave the church work to the members of the church whom we protect. None of you are priests, Ignatius; have you forgotten this? I see you have. None of you belong here. You are not entitled to this life; it is only a farce. If you wish to redeem yourself, then do so in the prescribed manner. Carry on the Light of the World. Burn out the darkness of the evil ones who would extinguish it. Bring forth the next generation of God's warriors, that we may not be plunged into darkness." Mercer sniffed. "Did you cut yourself on that glass, man?"

John felt a distant, nagging pang, and looked down. He had been gripping the car keys so tightly that they had cut into his hand, and he was dripping blood all over the ground.

Chapter 13

Burke rang the penthouse suite to inform Lucan that the seigneur was running late, but Detective Brown and her partner had arrived early. Cigarette smoke had sent the old man back to their car in search of his medication, but Samantha was coming up by herself in the elevator.

"When Detective Quinn returns, keep him downstairs. Inform me when the seigneur arrives." Lucan hung up the phone and turned to his seneschal. "Why can't you trace the flower deliveries?"

"They are not being ordered from, made, or delivered by any floral service, my lord. It may be that whoever is sending them has stolen the boxes and is preparing the contents himself. Burke said in both cases he found the boxes left outside the front door after someone had rung the delivery bell." Rafael pulled on his jacket. "I will greet the seigneur and entertain him until you are ready to receive him. How long will you take with the woman?"

"As long as I wish." Lucan heard the elevator bell.

"I'll take the stairwell." His seneschal hesitated. "She will be armed."

"So will I," he assured him.

Lucan sat down on the wide, butter-soft leather sofa and poured a glass of diluted wine. He sipped from his own, allowing the blood that had been infused in it to warm his cold veins. He had not yet fed, but the bloodwine would keep him from succumbing to the temptation of taking more of Samantha's blood.

When the suite bell rang, he called, "Please come in, Detective."

Samantha let herself in, and came to him. She wore a brown jacket, white knit shirt, and black trousers that Lucan imagined were as crisp and nondescript as everything in her wardrobe. Her straight brown hair—far darker than Frances's had been—had been pulled back tightly from her face again. Even with twenty feet between them, he could smell lemon on her breath and soap on her skin.

Temptation be damned. She was his *kyrya,* or would be before the month was out. He would sample more of her charms before she left.

"Thank you for seeing me," she said, taking out the little electronic device she used to make her notes. "I have some questions—"

"You look as if you have not slept since last we met." He lifted a glass and held it out to her. "Please take it. If you break this one, I have more."

The reminder of what had happened during their last encounter made her frown. "No, sir, thank you. I can't drink when I'm on duty."

"I can make you something else," he said, and moved closer to her. Her eyes were not dilated, and she didn't appear to be in any danger of falling under his voice control. Then he felt a gust of air against his back and remembered the windows were gone. The combination of her resistance and the unsealed room would make it twice as hard to lure her to him with *l'attrait.*

Good. Lucan preferred a challenge.

Samantha looked past his shoulder. "Where are your windows?"

"I grew tired of opening and closing them." He gestured to the sofa. "Please sit down, Detective."

She approached his furniture with an endearing amount of admiration and mistrust, as if she wanted nothing more than to stroke the fine leather but expected to have her hand slapped if she did so.

Lucan also knew what she was feeling at that moment. He had planted the suggestion in her mind, and now she would be fighting the compulsion to tell him everything about the murders, as well as the less obvious desire simply to be with him. The fact that he was implicated in both murders clashed with her needs, making her intellect war with her instincts.

He decided to test her resolve. "Have you made any progress in discovering who killed the woman?"

"Her name was Lena Caprell," Samantha said. "We have some new leads to follow. We . . . I can't discuss the details."

Yes, fight me. Lucan admired her all the more for her strength of character. That she could deny him meant that whatever she gave him would come from her own desire, not a reflection of his. He wanted an equal, not a servant.

She deliberately looked into his eyes. "What can you tell me about a man named J. R. Montgomery?"

"Only that he is dead. My assistant told me of his unfortunate demise." Lucan enjoyed returning her scrutiny. She did not blush, as any other bespelled human female would, and the set of her mouth indicated she was neither enchanted nor absorbed by his physical presence. "A terrible thing."

"Is it true that you hired Mr. Montgomery and his company to renovate part of your nightclub?"

"I'm certain that one of my people did. I don't involve myself in the business at that level." She wore no jewelry again, but she had the skin for pearls. Lucan imagined wrapping her in long, long strands of them: white and gold and pink and black. . . .

Samantha ticked off something on the device in her hand. "Do you know anything about a cross that belonged to a Temple knight named Noir de L'Anfar?"

"I believe the term is Templar," he said softly. He liked hearing his priestly name on her lips. "And no, I avoid crosses and men with complicated names."

She eyed him. "But you did see Mr. Montgomery shortly before he was murdered."

"Did I? I can't recall." While contemplating which pearls would look best against her breasts, he realized he had never gotten a proper look at them. "Why don't you take off your jacket? You'll be more comfortable."

She gave him an exasperated look. "Lucan, if you want me to help you with whatever trouble you're in, you've got to stop making moves on me."

"Is that what I'm doing?"

Shaking her head, she pocketed her device and stood. "I'd better go downstairs and check on my partner."

"I did not ask you to strip to the skin, Samantha." He hid his smile behind his wineglass. "Of course, if you are inclined to, we can move our discussion into my bedchamber. My lack of windows affords pleasant ventilation but little privacy."

"I'll be back in a minute." She pivoted to go.

"If you leave," he warned, "I will not answer any more of your questions without my attorney present. I believe he is in Barbados for the next two weeks."

Samantha swung back around, and he saw that he had made her angry. Incredible. She had more resolve than any human female he'd ever known.

"You'd better start taking this seriously, Lucan. A lot of people who were involved with you are being murdered." Temper improved her color and made her eyes come alive.

He wondered if fucking her would make her glow from within like this. A week in bed with him and he'd make her blaze like a fire in midwinter. "Is two a great deal?"

"One is too many."

A week wasn't going to be enough. He'd need a month, perhaps two. "Alas, the world is a vicious place, and we but the wretches who must navigate through its horrors." He got up and walked toward her. "I do like Fort Lauderdale, so I am counting on you to make it a safer place for me."

"First your lover is murdered, and now a man who was working for you. It's as if someone wants to shut down your business and your life." She skirted around the sofa, putting it between them. "Are they trying to get to you; is that it? Have you been threatened?"

"Why would someone threaten me but kill two other people?" he asked as he came after her. "It would make more sense to kill me."

She avoided him neatly by mirroring his movements. "Has anything like this happened to you before you came to Florida?"

Too many times. "No." As the word left his lips, the wineglass on the coffee table cracked.

Samantha's expression turned uneasy as her eyes shifted from him to the wineglass and back again. "Let's take a break. I'll be back in a minute with my partner." She headed for the elevator.

Lucan beat her to the door, putting out a hand and closing it with a small slam the moment she tried to open it.

"You are not leaving." He braced his other arm against the wall, cutting off her last escape route. "Turn around and look at me, Samantha. Only look."

Slowly she turned, a leaf on a mild breeze, her chin tucked in, her frame vibrating with some brittle emotion. "I'm flattered, Lucan, really, I am, but I'm not interested in you."

His gladiatrix, so determined never to surrender. "Is that why you dreamt of me?"

Her hazel eyes turned as green as dark emeralds when she was angry. "How did you know that? Are you some kind of hypnotist?"

"I dreamt of you. I feel the same things you feel. I know what you hide from the world." He tapped his chest. "We live in here, alone. No one gets close. That's why I know we were meant to be together."

"Together." She chuckled. "You and me."

He leaned closer. "Don't you want me?"

She stared at his mouth. "No."

"But you're not trembling with anger. Your heart isn't pounding with fear." Lucan reached out and traced the subtle curve of her narrow brow. "I have an indecently good sense of smell, you know, and I can smell you, Samantha. When you change your clothes tonight, you'll see the evidence, all wet and glistening and wasted." He dipped his head down far enough to make her flinch. "That is the most erotic perfume in the world, you know. The scent of an aroused female going wet between her legs."

"I'm a lesbian," she said flatly.

Lucan threw back his head and laughed. "No, you're not, dearest heart. However, I will tell you a secret. Whoever you've bedded in the past doesn't matter to me. Frankly I don't care if you've been keeping a herd of goats for your personal pleasure." He ran a finger along the open vee at the front of her collar. God, her skin was so soft and thin that it seemed to flow like water under his touch. "Soon they won't matter to you. No one else will. When you and I come together, you'll think only of me."

She abruptly shifted tactics by dropping her head and staring at his chest. "Why pick me? I'm not like Lena. There are fifty women standing outside who make me look like a dog. Seduce one of them; you'll have a better time."

Frances had been supremely confident in her power over men. Samantha, with her hidden arsenal of magnificent curves and the open challenge in her gemstone eyes, didn't even recognize her own.

"I prefer a battle." Lucan almost laughed when he felt the nudge of a barrel against his side. "Not that sort."

"You want to scare me? Not a chance." She raised her chin and glared at him. "I'm about to make your birth certificate a worthless document. Back off. *Now.*"

An alien tenderness flooded him. "Oh, Samantha, don't be afraid of it. It's the price of this degree of wanting." He reached down and wrapped his hand around her weapon, not attempting to take it from her but keeping his big hand over hers. "If you fire this, you will ruin my jacket. I am expecting guests, you see, so I would rather you not."

"God, you're a cold-blooded bastard."

"More than you will ever know. Now there is something that *I* wish to discover. Are you incorruptible, Samantha?" He bent forward and let his hair brush her cheek as he murmured against her ear, "If you do not know, would you like to find out if you are?"

"I ought to haul your ass downtown." Without looking away from his eyes, she lowered the weapon and slid it back into her shoulder holster. His hand chased hers, catching her fingers and bringing them back up to his mouth. "Why me?" she asked again, utterly perplexed.

"Why not you?" Lucan felt annoyed at her continued resistance. This close, she should have responded at least a little to *l'attrait*. It was apparent now that he would have to ensnare her in the traditional manner. "Aside from your appearance, which seems to trouble you so."

"I'm a cop investigating two murders; you're my prime suspect," she reminded him. "Stacked against that, sex is not only inappropriate, it's meaningless."

"It isn't only the sex, which I daresay will bring new meaning to both our lives." He brushed his mouth over hers, a whisper of a kiss, and tugged the band on the end of her braid. "It's about getting under your skin." He wasn't particularly gentle about unwinding her hair, and saw how her eyes darkened. "Taking you somewhere that you've only imagined." He felt his fangs extend fully, and closed his arm around her waist. "Somewhere you never dared go with anyone else. You'll be safe with me, Samantha. I swear you will."

"You don't even know me," she muttered, staring at his mouth. "Quit playing vampire."

"I'm not playing."

Until she saw the fake fangs, Sam thought she was in serious trouble. There was just too much Lucan in too small a room and no way out.

Now the situation had gone from dire to ridiculous.

"I didn't come here for this," she said slowly, in case he was too drunk to understand her. He had been knocking back a lot of that wine. "Like I said, thanks for the compliment, but no."

"Then you should not have come here." Up close, his face was prettier, all smooth skin and beautiful shadows framed by that gorgeous silvery mane. She raised a hand to push him back. He caught it so fast she didn't see him move then, or when he kept her follow-through punch from breaking his nose. "Don't fight me."

Their hands met at the exact same moment—another shock, for her left hand opened and threaded her fingers in his. His hand felt wrong against her scar, cool and heavy and too hard, and when she tried to jerk free, he used their entwined fingers to hold her there.

There is something seriously wrong with this man, something babbled inside Sam's head as Lucan's pale eyes came level with hers. He hadn't bent over; he'd lifted her off her feet, pinning her against the door with his hips and their entwined hands.

She had met men to whom she'd felt an instant, irresistible attraction. This wasn't that. It felt too strong, too eerie. Being shot three times hadn't scared her this much, only there was no room to pull away, and if she stayed like this she might do something extremely stupid, like—

"Listen to me, Samantha," he said. "You want to, don't you?"

She had never thought of herself as the obedient type, but just like that, she wanted to. The idea of him snapping his fingers and her jumping should have disgusted her, but instead it thrilled her. Everything about him did, especially the heat of his big body and the way he smelled. Men who wore cologne usually repelled her, but they didn't smell like. . . .

"Jasmine." She breathed in. "It's you. It's coming from you."

He muttered something that sounded like a curse in another language. Then he bent down, his mouth open, as if he meant to kiss her. But he wasn't aiming for her mouth. He forced her hand up, turning it until his breath touched the scar on her palm.

Lucan bit her.

For several moments the room went away. So did the world, and time, and all that was became Sam and Lucan, together in the darkness that was the universe.

Samantha opened her eyes. She was surrounded by beautiful women in long gowns in every color of the rainbow, and handsome men in old-fashioned suits with short jackets and frothy white lace spilling from their cuffs and collars. They spoke in low, cultured voices; now and then a woman would titter. No one seemed to mind that she was wearing her dress uniform.

"You should have gone into the military."

Lucan came to stand beside her, but he wasn't dressed like the other men. He looked as if he'd just come from a costume party. His costume was supposed to be that of a knight, Sam guessed, but he hadn't taken very good care of it. The metal gauntlets encasing his forearms were blackened and dented; he'd used too much fake blood on the rest of it. The center of the dingy white tunic he wore had been ripped, leaving a hole in the shape of a cross through which dull, dark chain mail showed through. From his shoulders hung a long, black cape dripping with blood and gore.

Sam smelled smoke and sweat and fury. "You should have taken a bath and gone to the dry cleaner's."

"What would be the point? I'll never be clean again." He tossed a huge sword, dripping with blood, onto the punch table, and drew a shorter dagger from a sheath strapped to his upper arm. "Give me your hand."

Sam tried to draw her gun. Out of her holster came a bunch of jasmine.

Lucan regarded the flowers the same way he might a weapon. "Why do you keep fighting me off? Are you going to be like Frances?"

Who's Frances? "I'm just trying to arrest you."

"You're nothing like her, you know. You're everything she might have been, if she had let me save her." With that, he drove the dagger through the center of his left hand.

"God damn it." Sam dropped the flowers and seized his wrist. "That was a silly-ass thing to do."

"So is this." Lucan jerked the dagger out and grabbed her wrist with his wounded hand, slicing the scarred palm open with the tip of the dagger before turning his hand and shoving his bloody fingers through hers.

Their wounded palms came together, bound by his grip and their blood.

Sam saw so many things at first that she nearly fainted. Oceans. Castles. Endless forests. Countries exotic and dismal. Palaces of gold. Ships of rotting timber. Horses. Islands. Black sands. Dark men and fair women. Kings. Beggars.

A golden cross covered in red and black jewels.

Night skies, a hundred, a thousand. Beyond them, something darker. Something worse than the infinite darkness of despair and death.

You've never been made to leave your homeland because of your curse, Samantha. I see why you've hidden it from the others for so long.

She turned around, smothered by the airless blackness, trying to find her way out and back to her reality and him. *As soon as I stop hallucinating, you're going to jail.*

Wouldn't you rather stay with me?

She felt his hand touching her face, his mouth skimming

down the side of her throat, and dragged in a quick breath. *With the way you get your jollies? No, thanks.*

Laughter vibrated against her skin. *Such astonishing endurance. You simply won't give in. I find myself utterly dazzled by you.* A mouth kissed her forehead. *How long do you think it will be before you can't hold me off any longer?*

Sam thought of Dwyer. *How's never? Does never work for you?*

The laughter died away. *No, Samantha. I am not like that worm who harassed you. Allow me to prove it.*

Another explosion of images filled Sam's head, this time of her and Lucan. She was wearing one of the beautiful long gowns this time, and he held her in his arms and waltzed her around a room.

The movements of her feet bewildered her. *I can't dance.*

You can do anything that you've dreamed of with me, he promised.

The ballroom blurred into something darker, a bedroom filled with huge, ornate furniture. Sam fell back against an enormous bed. Lucan was on top of her, kissing her, pulling down the bodice of her gown to get at her breast.

It was the feel of velvet on her skin that broke the spell. She looked down at the burgundy velvet gloves he wore, and then everything dissolved into a frantic rush forward, hurtling her through days and nights and months and years, until she was back in the penthouse suite, pinned against the door, with him all over her.

She didn't know how he'd gotten her T-shirt pulled up or her bra unclipped, but all the evidence was there, along with his mouth. Lucan lifted his head reluctantly, and Sam heard a phone somewhere ringing. "Put me down."

He lowered her to the carpet, where she shoved her foot back into her shoe. "Tell me about your talent."

"Tell me how you made me hallucinate like that," she countered.

"It's not important." He seized her hand, running his thumb along the scar on her palm. "This is. You use blood. You use it to see murders. Tell me, Samantha."

She didn't want to, until she heard the words coming out

of her mouth. "After I was shot, I died for a few minutes on the operating table. It wasn't like it is in the movies. I don't remember anything, no tunnel, no bright light, no dead people welcoming me. It was just dark. A few months later, when I was back on the job, I accidentally put my hand in a puddle of blood from a victim. From the blood touching my scar, I saw some of the very last things that happened to him before he died."

"I see." He looked appalled, and released her hand.

"I've shared; now it's your turn," she told him. "How did you make me see those things in my head? Are you psychic?"

"No." Lucan opened the door and gestured toward the elevator. "You had better go and find your partner."

She wasn't moving a centimeter. "Lucan, if you want me to let you in, it has to go both ways."

"Master." Burke emerged from the elevator. "You're needed downstairs." He was so agitated that he completely ignored Samantha.

She arched a brow. "Master?"

Lucan didn't look at his assistant. "Tell him to wait."

"My lord Rafael said—" Burke halted as he finally noticed Sam. "Detective Brown. My goodness, I thought you had already left."

"Is my partner downstairs?" she asked.

"I'm sorry, but I'm afraid Detective Quinn never returned to the club."

She faced Lucan. "When Harry and I come back, I'd appreciate it if we could go over this one more time. Without hypnosis."

He started to say something, and then went back to the table where he had left his wine and retrieved it. "I believe that you'll find something more material linking me to the place where you found Montgomery. Something old, like the cross left on Lena. But I tell you now, whatever evidence you find to the contrary, I didn't kill them, Samantha."

How did he know about the cross? "You believe you're being framed for the murders? By who?"

"I don't know." Lucan glanced at her. "But I'm the only one who can help you find out."

"I don't need another partner." Samantha turned on her heel and stalked out.

As tempted as Lucan was to follow her, he had to attend to the seigneur. Then, after Michael was reduced to a suitable state of ineffective rage, he would hunt down Samantha and finish converting the stubborn detective into his lover and willing *kyrya*.

"How many guards did Cyprien bring?" he asked Burke.

"Twenty, along with his *sygkenis*. She is as beautiful as they say." His *tresora* slipped a throat lozenge into his mouth. "The seigneur's seneschal is Phillipe of Navarre, isn't he? I've read about him in our history books. Did he really—"

"Yes. He really did." The odor of wild cherry from Burke's breath was too much like the Darkyn high lord's scent, and immediately put Lucan on edge. "Burke, I trust you know what I expect of you when other Kyn come to have audience with me?"

"I believe I do, master, but you have only to say," Burke said.

"Then shut up and don't speak again until I tell you to do so." He watched Burke open his mouth to reply, close it, and nod. "We make progress. Excellent. Continue in just such a vein, Herbert, and you should live long enough to retire to the old *tresori*'s home."

Chapter 14

Michael Cyprien watched a human female walk out of Lucan's private elevator. She did not appear to be one of the courtesans Lucan had provided for their entertainment, but she bore a striking resemblance to another woman whom until that moment he had quite forgotten.

"How much you want to bet Lucan made her that angry?" Alexandra murmured as she watched the woman stride past. She smiled, but all the other woman gave her was a terse nod in return before leaving the club. "And what's your arch-nemesis doing talking to a cop? Is he having trouble with the law now?"

"I wouldn't know." Her question intrigued Michael on several levels. "How do you know that she's a member of the police?"

"She was wearing a shoulder holster and a gun under that jacket, for one thing," Alex said. "For another, her picture was on the front page of the *Sun-Sentinel*. She's the detective investigating that woman who was murdered a few days ago."

Michael let his hand follow the curve of her spine. "You are a veritable font of interesting facts and observations, *ma belle*."

"Do not grab my ass in public, Lord of Eternity, or I'll assume that means I can do the same thing to your dick." As his hand stopped to rest against the small of her back, she gave him a guileless smile. "Also, if you're not going to watch television, at least pick up a newspaper once in a while. It'll open up a whole new world for you."

"Why must I, when I have you to do this for me?" He avoided her elbow before she could drive it into his side. "Yes,

I know, like any other Frenchman, I am the lazy sexist chauvinist swine. I bow before your shining example, *ma belle.*"

"I'm just going to start arbitrarily slapping your mouth once a day," Alex decided. "It'll save time and probably our future relationship."

"Why, when there are so many other, far more enjoyable things you can do with my mouth?" He enjoyed seeing that he could still fluster her on occasion. "This policewoman, do you recall her name?"

"Something Brown." His *sygkenis* thought for a moment, and then snapped her fingers. "Samantha, that's it. Samantha Brown."

Michael beckoned to his seneschal. When Phillipe joined them, he said in French, "That human female who just walked out of here is a police detective named Samantha Brown. Alex tells me her photo was in the newspaper today. I want to know what you can learn about her, especially in regard to her family background and her involvement with the suzerain."

"Of course, master." Phillipe nodded toward a dark man who had taken up point position among Lucan's personal guard. "With your permission, may I have a word with my counterpart? He will know why she was here."

Michael knew Rafael from the long and brutal years they had spent as Templars in the Holy Land; they had fought together once during the last of the battles to hold back the Saracens. Had circumstances been different, he would have greeted him directly, but that was not Kyn practice. "Yes. Give him my regards."

Phillipe nodded and went over to speak to the other seneschal.

"Do you want to play with me?" a sexy female voice asked.

Michael looked down to see one of Lucan's prostitutes posing before him. Her augmented breasts nearly spilled out of the low front of her bodice, and she exuded a strong odor of too-sweet perfume and other, less appealing chemicals. The taint of drugs on her breath and skin was echoed in the constricted pupils of her eyes. "No, thank you."

"We can go into Lucan's office." She put a hand on Michael's sleeve and made a caressing motion. "You can do whatever you want to me. Have me any way you like me." She reached up toward Michael's face.

"Uh-uh. Mine." A small, strong hand caught the prostitute's wrist. "That's right. You can look at him, dream about him, even proposition him, but that's all."

The woman's small, glassy eyes shifted to Alexandra. "I'll lick your pussy." She sounded desperate. "He can fuck me from behind while I do."

"What a trooper. You know, you just don't meet that many full-service hookers these days." Alex stepped between the woman and Michael. "Unfortunately, we're kind of old-fashioned when it comes to things like threesomes, so go find someone else to play with, honey."

The prostitute glanced at Michael before flouncing off.

"We're old-fashioned?" Michael murmured as he wrapped his arms around his *sygkenis* from behind.

"We are now." Alex scanned the room. "I'm getting a very creepy low-watt buzz, lover." Her brows drew together. "Nothing specific, but it's getting stronger. Someone here wants to kill something."

Michael eyed the elevator, which had returned to the penthouse suite and was now descending again. "Lucan."

Lucan's *tresora* had been herding the prostitutes out of the club, and after the last was gone, he secured the outer doors. Rafael went to unlock the elevator.

It had been hundreds of years since the last time Michael Cyprien had seen Richard's chief assassin, but time melted away as Lucan stepped off the elevator. The red and black— Richard's colors, which they had all taken as their own as members of his, the first *jardin*—favored his old enemy. Against them he seemed taller, broader, and more powerful than any man in the room.

Richard had amused himself by making Michael wear the red and Lucan the black at his tourneys. *Red Prince of Blood, Black Prince of Death.*

Michael reached for the inner peace he had found since Alexandra had repaired more than his face, and watched his men assume their places around him.

The Black Prince came forward with his men in the appropriate positions around him, and executed a bow that would have pleased the starchiest of monarchs. "Seigneur, you grace our humble *jardin* with your presence. Welcome to my domain."

"Suzerain." Michael returned the bow without the unnecessary flourishes, and brought Alexandra to stand beside him. "This is my *sygkenis*, Dr. Alexandra Keller. Alexandra, this is Lucan."

"I have been eager to meet this miraculous new addition to our ranks." Lucan bowed again. "Your beauty leaves me speechless, my lady."

She eyed him. "You seem to be talking fine, and you could have met me in New Orleans. You remember. When you spied on us and assaulted my nurse?"

Lucan straightened and grinned, unashamed. "Nurse Heather was so sweet and compliant that I almost took her with me. How is she?"

"Alive, no thanks to you." Alex would have said more, but Michael caught her gaze, and she huffed out some air. "Fine. I'll be quiet now."

"Rafael." When the seneschal came forward, Lucan formally presented him, after which Michael did the same with Phillipe, and then they began the same with their men.

Michael knew Alexandra was bored two minutes after they had begun the formal ritual of presentation, but while he could often forgo it with suzerain he considered friends, it was vital to ensure that Lucan knew all of his men, and for Michael to know all of Lucan's. *Jardin* wars had begun over a single Kyn intruding on the territory of a lord paramount to whom he had not been presented.

At last all of the Kyn present had been named and acknowledged, and Lucan and Michael sat down with their seneschals at a long table swathed in ivory linens, upon which bejeweled silver chalices sat.

As Alex sat down next to Michael, Rafael offered them bloodwine. "Thank you, no," Michael told him.

"Rafael will taste it first, if you like," Lucan drawled.

Michael returned the cool gaze. "Alas, we have already fed."

"While I have not." Lucan sipped from the glass Burke filled for him. "My seneschal tells me that you seek a member of your *jardin*. Have you so many that you cannot keep track of them, seigneur?"

The men behind Michael tensed.

"My new duties can be somewhat distracting," Michael said, acknowledging the problem without reacting to the insult of Lucan pointing it out. "That is why I must soon select a new suzerain for New Orleans."

"I had thought you would give Thierry Durand his own clutch," Lucan said, "now that he has found sanity."

"Thierry does not wish to serve as suzerain, and Phillipe refuses to abandon me." He smiled briefly at his seneschal. "I was hoping to rely on you for a recommendation. But then, you have your own distractions. Under those nondescript clothes, I would think Samantha Brown is quite attractive. She certainly reminds me of a woman who was once part of your entourage a long time ago."

"Indeed." Lucan's eyes turned to ice. "A pity that I have already claimed her for myself, seigneur. You remember the old traditions, I trust?"

Michael was appalled and fascinated. "Detective Brown is your *kyrya?*"

"She will be."

"Hello." Alex waved a hand between the two of them, breaking their eye contact. "Some of us here still don't speak much fang lang."

"A *kyrya* is a Kyn's human lover. We began taking them when we found we could no longer change humans to Darkyn. *Kyryas* are usually immune to *l'attrait*. I cannot remember the last time a Kyn lord took one outside the ranks of the *tresori*. In these times, we trust only those sworn to serve us." Michael filed the information away and smiled at Alex. "There, *chérie*. You have just had a short history lesson on the Darkyn."

"Perhaps you could get to the reason for coming into my territory," Lucan said.

Michael told him about the situation with the Pavieres, and of Faryl's escape from New Orleans. "The family believes he comes to you for a merciful dispatching."

Lucan nodded. "Likely it is so. I have had no contact from Faryl, however. His brother is not with you tonight."

"Gard is out in the night, hunting him," Michael said. "Your seneschal was informed, and granted him safe passage."

"I am delighted my decisions are being made for me." Lucan gave Rafael a brief look before addressing Alexandra. "Why do you come here, Doctor? To keep your lord entertained, or do you wish to see a changeling put out of its misery?"

Alex looked bewildered. "A changeling?"

"I refer to Paviere's brother Faryl. His condition is irreversible." Lucan's mouth curved on one side. "I see. Our new seigneur hasn't told you all of it."

Michael stood. "We will take our leave now."

"Don't run away just yet." The big man also rose. "I'm so disappointed in you, Michael. You create the perfect mate for yourself, after centuries of the rest of us failing to do the same, and yet you are actively deceiving her. I wonder if we should consider a form of divorce for our kind. I think you may be in need of one soon, Alexandra."

She looked at him and then at Lucan and back to him. "Michael told me about Faryl feeding on animals, if that's what you're hinting. I get the whole fleshrot thing."

Lucan laughed. "Faryl, my dear doctor, is not rotting. He's molting."

"That's enough, Lucan." Michael helped Alexandra out of her chair. "We're leaving."

"You're leaving." She dragged her arm out of his grip. "I'm going to hear the rest of this. Lucan, what do you mean by molting?"

"Exactly that," he told her. "His body is changing from human into something else. It is a process that involves many such moltings until he attains his final form. Our high lord endures the same trials, as Michael will tell you."

He should have hunted him down and killed him in New Orleans. "Richard's condition is not the same as Faryl's, nor is it something we discuss."

"What is Faryl molting into?" Alex demanded.

"What he will become. You have heard the saying, 'You are what you eat'?" Lucan gestured to her. "You drink human blood, so you remain in human form. But if you drink animal blood, and you feed only on that long enough, you shed your humanity like the skin of a snake. You become whatever you feed upon."

Alex's eyes were huge. "You're telling me that Faryl is mutating into another animal species? Like an alligator or a rat or something?"

"A two-legged version of whatever he has been feeding on, yes. You might make yourself into a magnificent leopard woman. You would only have to go to Africa and feed on them for a century or two." The suzerain reached out to touch one of the curls on her shoulder. "Then the process begins with—"

Michael threw his fist into Lucan's face, and with deep satisfaction felt it connect with the bigger man's jaw.

"Don't touch her," he snarled as the suzerain staggered back. "Don't ever touch her again."

All around them daggers and swords appeared as the men began taking defensive positions.

"Do you fear she will prefer mine to yours?" Lucan asked, his voice silky.

Michael took pleasure in striking back, this time with the truth. "At least my touch will not kill her."

Rafael and Phillipe took up their positions as second to their respective lords.

"Master, I think it would be wise to conclude this meeting now," Lucan's seneschal said. "Before any blood is spilled."

Phillipe put Alexandra behind him. "I agree, master."

"It appears that despite our best efforts, our people will not permit us our squabble," Lucan said. "If you require anything while you are in my territory, seigneur, you have but to contact Rafael."

Michael was so angry he could not manage even the thinnest of polite farewells, and turned to go.

"If *you* are in need, Alexandra," the suzerain called after them, "do come to me."

Sam was happy to get away from Lucan.

As she had left the club, she saw the prostitutes were finally earning their keep by mingling with a lot of tall, handsome men in beautiful suits and one short brunette woman wearing a gorgeous ivory silk dress. The odd thing was that while the hookers were drinking and chatting and laughing, the men were simply standing around in a loose circle around the woman and one tall man with white-streaked black hair in a ponytail.

Shrewd brown eyes met Sam's, and the woman smiled. Sam nodded before she stalked outside.

The unit wasn't in the alley behind the nightclub, and for a moment Sam felt like screaming. But Harry had been having a bad attack; maybe he'd gone over to Emergency. As Sam walked out of the alley and onto the street, she dialed her partner's cell phone and waited for him to answer.

"Hello?" a muffled male voice answered.

Sam knew it wasn't Harry. "I'm calling for Detective Quinn. Who is this?"

"He can't come to the phone right now. He's waiting for you in the park by the fire station."

"Who is this?" Sam demanded again.

The line clicked.

She tried dialing Harry's phone a second time, but got only his voice mail. The fire station was six blocks away. She began walking, and then fear set in, and she ran.

The unit was parked under a cypress tree by the small pond in the center of the park. Sam felt relief flooding her as she saw Harry's silhouette through the driver's-side window. He had his window open, and a hand propped against his head.

He was taking a nap.

Christ, is he going to be mad when he finds out someone reached in and stole his mobile.

Sam still slammed the door out of principle as she climbed in behind the wheel. "Can't you wait for the deck chairs on the boat, old man?" Harry didn't answer her, so she reached over and shook his shoulder to wake him up. "Come on, wake up, wake—" She pulled back a wet, red hand. "Oh, my God." She grabbed Harry's head and pushed it up. "Harry. *Harry.*"

Blood from his slashed throat transferred from his jacket to her hands, and without thinking she picked up his hand to check for a pulse. Their palms brushed.

Cigarettes. Tiny red lights. Streetlights. Briny, humid air. Angry faces. Bored faces. The darkness of the alley. Harry's inhaler. The smell of its medicated spray.

Sam was seeing his last moments—as they had happened. Harry hadn't been dead long, or they would have come to her backward. Maybe she still had time—

A stray cat, carrying something in its mouth, darting out of the alley. Harry's watch. The door of the unit. The windshield. The glove box. A prescription bottle. Two tablets on Harry's broad palm.

"No," she heard herself saying.

A flash of silver from the rearview mirror. The blade slashing the air. The fist around the hilt. The bare arm.

Sam closed her eyes and screamed, but the images didn't stop.

The huge spray of blood. On the dashboard, on the windshield, everywhere. One bloody, trembling hand held up in the light. Reaching for the tiny crystal dolphin, Sam's good-luck charm, hanging from the rearview. The hand falling. Darkness.

Darkness.

Darkness.

"I'm sorry," Sam whispered. "I'm sorry."

A soft white glow. The smell of pine trees. Stars falling all around her. Rain made of light.

The roof of the unit. The alley below. The cooling towers, the rooftops. The block, the street, the city, all falling away. The lights of the living dwindling to tiny jewels on black velvet.

Above.

Sparkles of light, white and pure and untouchable. Stars swelling into suns. Stars melding with other stars. Stars exploding. More light, growing, blazing, consuming everything that was and would be—

Darkness.

The last thing Samantha remembered clearly doing that night was calling Dispatch on the radio to report her location and the fact that her partner had been murdered. After that, most of her brain seemed to simply shut down.

She was aware of things, distant, unimportant things. Like the fact that the first people to arrive on the scene were fire rescue; they simply walked over from the station next to the park. She knew that one of them checked Harry for a pulse, while another talked to her through the window. There were questions asked that she didn't answer. She could hear them debating with each other on whether to move her or let her stay.

She stayed with Harry.

There were pretty colors on the dappled surface of the lake in front of her. Flashing blue, white, and red lights. More of them lit up the park as squad cars and an ambulance pulled in on either side of Sam's unit. More voices tried to talk to her, but she still saw no reason to speak. Her partner was dead, murdered, right there beside her. If they couldn't figure it out, then they shouldn't be carrying badges.

"Sammy, come on." Ortenza's voice, strained and pleading, penetrated the haze of pain and disbelief. "Snap out of it."

Peterson answered for her. "Leave her alone."

Wise, sensible Peterson. Sam wanted to thank him, but nothing would come out of her mouth. Then Garcia was there, not asking, not begging, not saying a word to her. It was his hands she allowed on her, his strength that guided her out of the car and put her into another one.

"No," he said to someone asking angry questions. "Tomorrow. Tomorrow."

The captain didn't question her, which was fine with Sam. He seemed to be reading her mind, though, for he pulled off the road twice so she could get out and vomit into the grass. Both times he knelt beside her, an arm around her shoulders, a hand holding her hair back.

Everything after that came in briefer flashes, blinks of reality.

Stairs. Blue hair, black leather, worried young eyes. Chris. Low voices, an exchange of keys. Doors opening, doors closing. Taking off her jacket, pushing her onto her narrow bed.

She'll be all right. Sam's tougher than you think.

She wasn't this tough, Sam wanted to argue. This surely was going to kill her.

Chris's voice returned, soft and sweet as she read from one of Sam's books.

" 'Perhaps everything terrible is in its deepest being something helpless that wants help from us.' "

Harry had wanted help from her, but Sam had been too busy playing with Lucan to be there for him. Now he was dead.

" 'Life has not forgotten you . . . it holds you in its hand; it will not let you fall.' "

Chris kept reading. The words hung over Sam, mobiles of moving beauty, memories of another life's pain. No one should have to suffer such things as this.

Harry never would again. Harry, who had left her behind, was safe.

Sam started weeping. Not sobbing; her throat refused to let out a single sound. Tears streamed down her face until the low, sweet voice stopped and Chris was beside her, holding her in her arms and rubbing her back.

"Keep breathing. That's all you have to do now, Sam. Keep breathing."

Lucan had to discover whether Richard had left Ireland and where in Florida he would be residing, as well as prepare for the coming battle with Cyprien. All of that went out of his head the moment Rafael told him that Harry Quinn had been robbed and murdered not a half dozen blocks from the club.

"Samantha?"

"She was found on the scene with him. She was in shock, so her superior took her home. A neighbor is with her now. My lord, about this situation with the seigneur—"

"Not now." Lucan scooped up the keys to his Ferrari and strode out of the club.

Once he was standing outside the door to Samantha's apartment, however, his determination deserted him. Lucan had seen Samantha and Quinn together. All of the reports indicated theirs had been a close and affectionate relationship. She would not stop until she brought the old man's killer to justice.

She would be in shock, horrified, suffering for the loss of a man she held in great affection. What could he do for her now? Seduce her? Even he was not so callous as to take advantage of her grief.

She will wish to be alone. I would.

The door to the apartment abruptly opened, and a young woman with the most astonishing head of blue hair stared out at him. "I thought I heard someone out here." Her eyes widened. "I know you; you're—"

"Samantha's friend," Lucan said, taking a step closer so that the space between them filled with the scent of jasmine. "I've come to see her."

The girl's eyelids drooped, and she smiled. "Of course you have." She opened the door wider. "Come in."

Lucan stepped inside and smiled down at the girl. "I will care for her now. You should go home and sleep."

"Sleep." The girl yawned. "Yes. Good night." Without protest she walked out and went into the apartment across the hall.

He saw some candles burning here and there, but most of the electric lights had been switched off. Samantha lay curled up on her bed, still dressed in her day clothes, her eyes staring at the ceiling. At the threshold he again hesitated.

"I heard you talking to Chris," she said, not looking at him. "Come in."

"Rafael told me about Detective Quinn." Cautiously he approached the bed and stood at the foot of it. "I am very sorry for your loss, Samantha."

"That's what we always say to the victim's family. Right before we ask them who might have wanted the victim dead." She sat up, looking a little bewildered. "How did you know where I lived?" Before he could reply, she rubbed her eyes. "You've had me investigated. Why?"

"I wanted to learn more about you." That seemed the blandest way of putting it. "I know you're a very private person. I apologize for intruding."

"Don't. I'm flattered." She swung her legs off the bed and tried to stand, but had to grasp the headboard for support. "I'm not doing too well right now, though. Maybe you could hit on me another time."

"Samantha." He went to her, catching her as she tumbled forward, holding her against him. "It wasn't your fault."

"I should have been with him. I'm his partner. Was his partner." She rubbed her hand. "I saw how he died. Brutal, but quick. He didn't suffer long. I suppose that's better than dying slowly in a hospital bed."

He had forgotten about her talent. "I wish I could have spared you that." He would find whoever killed Harry Quinn, and he would gut them slowly. That much he could do for her.

She uttered something like a laugh and lifted her hand, exposing the puckered scar across the palm. "You know, you're the only person I can trust now. You know about what I do."

He wanted to protect her, but he was the very thing she despised. All his plans to make her his *kyrya* seemed slightly obscene now. "You shouldn't trust so easily."

She looked from her hand to him. "Twenty people at the club confirmed your alibi; they saw you there the entire night when Lena was murdered. You weren't the man in the garden with Montgomery. And you were with me when Harry was murdered."

She was going to rip the heart out of his chest. He put her down on the bed and drew his hands away from her. "I will go and bring the blue-haired girl back here."

"I want you." Her hand curled around his velvet-covered fingers, and she moved over, making room for him. "Stay with me."

Lucan fought a silent battle with himself and lost. He pulled off his jacket, slipped his feet from his shoes, and lay down with her. Her bed was a third the size of his, and barely accommodated his length and bulk. He had never been more uncomfortable in his life, including the years he spent on his knees praying under the stern eye of the Templar master.

Then Samantha was curling up against him, and he forgot everything but putting his arms around her and holding her there.

He would not mouth empty platitudes; surely she had heard enough of those. "What will you do now?"

She thought about it. "Take a few days off. Bury my partner. Try to find a reason to stay on the job. They won't let me investigate Harry's murder because I was his partner, so I'm running low on reasons."

He would not permit her to go on risking her life to serve the police force. The man who had killed her partner could have easily done the same to her. Samantha didn't realize how much she needed his protection. She would also resent any insinuation that she did.

"Perhaps," he said carefully, "there is something else you could do besides police work."

"If I wasn't a cop, I'd be nothing. It's all I have." Her hair tickled his chin as she looked up at him. "You said you could help me find the man who killed Lena. Was that part of the come-on, or did you mean it?"

"Yes." Lucan hadn't considered how much of her self-esteem was involved in her work. He needed to show her what her life would be like with him, to give her a clear choice. But that would have to wait until after she had had proper time to grieve. "We will talk about it in a few days."

"I can't believe I'm in bed with you." Her voice slurred on the last words, and her eyes closed. "It's like a dream."

Lucan pulled the covers up around them. "Then go to sleep, Samantha."

Chapter 15

"Father, do you know where Brother Patrick is?"

Mercer looked up from the chapter in Kings that he was pretending to read. "Not here, I hope."

"He's disappeared," Ignatius said. "He never came back from town with our supplies yesterday. He never came back at all."

"That's odd." Ignatius's voice was piercing the fog of wine Mercer had so carefully built over the last hour, but the old friar wouldn't go away until he showed some interest. "Did Brother Jacob receive a phone call from him?"

"I already checked, and no, he did not." Ignatius began pacing the floor in front of Mercer's desk. "You gave him cash to buy the supplies, didn't you? That was foolish. He has probably run off with it."

"Of course I gave him cash. John couldn't very well take the checkbook." Mercer wondered if Ignatius devoted all of his waking hours to looking for trouble. "Have you acquired new accommodations for him?"

"Not yet." Ignatius inserted his hands in the ends of his sleeves and assumed what he considered his most dignified posture. "There is something wrong with Brother Patrick. He shouldn't be here. He asks too many questions about us. I think we should report him to the Lightkeeper."

"I think you should remember who is in charge here," Mercer suggested. "I decide what Rome needs to know."

"Of course, Father." Ignatius's paranoia turned fearful. "Please do not think that I was questioning your judgment. I was only concerned. You have been under so much stress lately." He looked pointedly at the wine bottle on the desk.

Mercer magnanimously ignored that. "Ignatius, I am depending on you to hold things together here when I take the men out tonight to look for the *maledicti*. Please don't make me think I've made a poor choice."

"You haven't, Father." Now the guestmaster was babbling. "I have devoted myself to our cause, as you well know. Part of our promise to the Lightkeeper is to obey without question. I wouldn't dream of—"

"You needn't be so afraid of me." Mercer smiled. "Even Jesus questioned the Lord once. Go now."

After Ignatius left, Mercer contemplated his night's work. He had been sending the brothers in pairs to search the downtown clubs and report any suspicious activity, but he couldn't keep doing that, not after Rome's latest fax. The order was looking for a former priest named John Patrick Keller, and he was to be taken and detained for interrogators if possible, or terminated if not.

That pushed Mercer over the edge. He took out the bottle from his desk, began drinking, and hadn't stopped since.

That he had deviated from his mission now did not bother him in the slightest, for the order had asked too much of him this time. He was so close to finishing his work, after which he had planned to retire here at Barbastro and live out the rest of his life in peace. If he was careful, it was possible that he could. Over the years he had occasionally lived the life of a real priest; he longed to do so again. But the order was not willing to release him from their clutches, and no one ever left the order.

Death and destruction, that was all that mattered to them.

Mercer could not wantonly destroy life; it went against everything he believed in. That was what had driven him to look outside the order, to consult with the priests of other faiths. His lengthy search had revealed one cult that wielded true mystical powers.

The *santeros* of Lukumi.

Mercer had not believed it the first time he had witnessed the old man practicing his witchcraft, or the second. The third time he tried to dismiss it as hysteria. Then one of the younger brothers had been caught in a minor scandal involving a young Cuban girl, and Mercer had gone to the *santero* to ask for his intervention. The old man had done better than that. He had made the problem vanish into thin air.

Even Mercer couldn't do that.

He picked up the phone and dialed a number in Little Havana, where the *santero* kept his church. The old man spoke only Spanish, but Mercer knew enough to make himself understood. They agreed upon a meeting time, the price to be negotiated. Then he called a local cab company and ordered a taxi to pick him up at the front gate within thirty minutes. When asked his destination, he told the dispatcher that he would give the address to the driver upon arrival.

"Whaddya mean, you want to go to Little Havana?" the cabdriver asked when Mercer climbed into the back thirty minutes later and gave him the address. "Do you know how far that is?"

Mercer handed him three twenties. "If the meter runs over that I have more."

"Whatever you say, pal."

The drive to Little Havana took over an hour, but it gave Mercer time to consider his options and to sober up a little more. The cabdriver stopped in front of the little church at the address Mercer had given him.

"You sure you want to get out in this neighborhood, Father?" The cabdriver looked at a posse of Cuban teenagers strolling casually by. All had knives and handguns tucked in the front pockets of their baggy jeans, and examined the cab with negligent interest. "You're gonna end up getting mugged or something."

"I'll be perfectly safe," Mercer assured him as he handed him another twenty. "Would you return for me in an hour, please?"

"Yeah, if you're still alive." The driver was still shaking his head as he drove away.

Mercer walked up the narrow sidewalk to the front of the little church. The hand-painted sign above the door read, CAPILLA DEL SAGRADO CORAZÓN DE OGÚN in small, poorly sized lettering. Dents and rust blooms defaced the cheap tin siding, while an unadorned wooden cross, nailed to the roof peak, cast a skewed shadow with its sagging crossbeam.

Mercer had cast off most of his fears over time, but there was nothing on earth he feared more than walking through this door. The last time he had, Mercer had sworn he would never do so again. And yet, here he was. Come to beg for help from the helpless.

The stink of cigar smoke and rum greeted him as he stepped inside. To honor Babalu Aye, the Afro-Cuban version of Saint Lazarus, the worshipers here smoked cigars during church services, and drank from open bottles. There were no Bibles, no prayer guides, no canon or formal texts in this religion. The story-telling traditions of their native land combined with the need for secrecy kept them from permanently recording anything about their religion. Everything was passed along by word of mouth alone.

"*Hola, Padre* Lane," a young, sly voice greeted him. "*Mi abuelo* is expecting you."

Mercer told himself it was the heat that made him sweat as he moved farther into the church. Everywhere cheap votive and tealight candles flickered; no matter what hour of the day or night they were always left burning. The young grinning Cuban boy sitting by the altar waiting for him had a long, thick Havana cigar in his right hand. He tucked it in the corner of his mouth as he jumped up.

"*Abuelo* say for me to translate for you this time," the boy told him, and seized his hand with one small, dirty paw. "He say your Spanish suck."

Mercer wanted to laugh at the little church, the cigar-smoking boy, and his wicked, wicked grandfather. He wanted to run outside where the air was clean, where desperate men didn't consort with the unholy. But this man had helped him before, and each time everything he had promised had happened.

Lukumi was not that much different from Catholicism. Certainly it had embraced the practices and rituals of the church. Some said that it had also corrupted them with evil pagan practices born in Africa and brought to Cuba by slaves. Whatever it was, sometimes Mercer thought it might be the only true magic left in the world. It had been born in the cradle of civilization and had been blended with the greatest of the world's faiths. Perhaps that was what made it so powerful.

The old man was sitting in his usual rocking chair, dressed in a faded Panama Jack T-shirt and frayed boxers. He had a quarter of a bottle of rum in his hand, from which he took a drink before he rose on unsteady legs.

"*Padre.*"

"*Santero.*" Mercer did not touch him, but bowed with respect. "Tell your grandfather that I need to remove a threat to our abbey. Tell him I must do this in secret, as before."

The boy nodded and rattled off a great deal in Spanish. "*Mi abuelo* call on his orisha," the boy said. "He will ride him and tell you what you to do."

Mercer knew little of the unholy spirits the *santero* called upon to possess him in his trances. He knew the old man's followers believed that every person was born under the guardianship of a particular orisha, and that several hundred of them ruled over everything in the universe, and beseeched them through prayer and ritual offerings to help them live better and cleanse their spirits. There were colors and numbers and days of the week involved with each one that the followers honored with beaded necklaces and household shrines.

The old man sat back down in his rocking chair and carefully put aside the bottle of rum. He gripped the arms of the chair and began chanting a prayer in monotone Spanish, bracing himself as he did.

The boy brought the rum bottle to his grandfather's mouth, but instead of swallowing the liquor he spit it in four directions on the floor around his chair. His face turned dark red, and he shook all over, as if going into a seizure.

"Orisha comes," the boy whispered.

The old man slumped over, and then slowly straightened. His entire posture and bearing changed, becoming as straight as that of a much younger man. He glared at Mercer and barked out something in a deeper, frightening voice.

"Ask what you want," the boy said.

"There is a man whom I believe will destroy me," Mercer said. "I have to do something to stop him, but I don't know how. It cannot be anything that could be traced back to me, or it will be for nothing."

The santero snickered and asked something.

"Orisha ask if you have heart to do what must be done," the boy translated.

Mercer nodded. "Anything."

The old man took a pouch from the pocket of his shirt and handed it to the boy, along with a string of orders.

"Orisha say you use this. Do not mix with anything. Pour into mouth." The boy handed him the pouch.

Mercer felt his knees quake. "What is it?"

The old man grinned and said in perfect English, "Heart killer."

"I can't *do* my job if you *keep* things from me," Phillipe heard Alexandra shout.

"There are matters involved here that you cannot understand," his master said, sounding as calm as his *sygkenis* was furious. "I have explained this to you."

"Did you just call me *stupid*?"

The seneschal reined in a sigh and finished giving orders to Cyprien's personal guards. "Patrol the grounds until dawn. Be alert for any signs of the suzerain's men." Something crashed into a wall and shattered. "Stay away from the master's *sygkenis*."

"He should beat her," Maren muttered as he checked copper rounds in his pistol and pocketed it. He had been one of the last survivors of a *jardin* in Burgundy that had fallen to the Brethren during the Revolution.

Kamisor, who had served Cyprien since the holy wars, sighed. "I would lock her in an attic with no one to feed on for two weeks. That would sweeten her wasp's tongue."

"The mistress is a modern woman," Phillipe reminded them. "They expect many things our women did not, such as being regarded as an equal partner and being consulted over matters of importance to their lord."

Maren snorted. "Oh, so she wishes to be a man."

"Bizarre." Kamisor shook his shaggy head.

"She will come around. She always does." Phillipe nodded to them as they left, and then went back to his daily chore of screening the seigneur's e-mails. It was not long before he heard the front door of the beach house slam, hard enough to make the entire edifice shake. A few moments later, Alexandra burst into the kitchen.

"Where are the guns?" she demanded.

Knowing this might take a while, Phillipe shut off the laptop's screen. "Why?"

"I need to shoot a jackass vampire. I won't need a scope, either, because he's very easy to spot." She began talking to herself as she rummaged through the cabinets. "Tells me I can sit around here and wait while he and the boys take care of things." Her voice climbed an octave and assumed a deadly imitation of Cyprien's light French accent. " 'Be patient, Alexandra.' 'This is none of your concern, Alexandra.' 'You can't understand, Alexandra.' " She stopped, turned, and glared at him. "How have you put up with this shit for seven hundred years?"

He rested his chin on his hand. "I listen and try to help instead of shouting and looking for guns?"

"Jesus Christ, you're just as bad as he is." She turned back to the open cabinet and slammed it shut. Her back went rigid. "Does he own me? I mean, really, I don't get this relationship. One minute we're all lovey-dovey; the next he's wrapping me in a chastity belt and locking me in a damn closet."

Close, daily proximity to Alexandra had improved Phillipe's English by great leaps and bounds, but there were still moments when she confused him. "You are wrapped in clothing, and this is the kitchen, which is not locked."

"It's an analogy, Phil." She came over to fling herself in the chair beside him. "If I ask you some questions, will you answer them? Just answer them?"

"I will try." She didn't realize how much she was asking, as Phillipe and the other men had specific orders from Cyprien on what they could and could not discuss with her. Still, he might be able to work around that. For her he would make the effort.

"Are there a lot of changelings among the Kyn?"

Of course, the very thing Cyprien did not wish her to know. "To be honest, I cannot say." He was not lying; he had never counted them.

"All right. How many have you met?"

"One does not meet a changeling," Phillipe told her. "What happens to them removes the humanity from them. One is attacked by a changeling, or one hunts one down and puts it out of its misery."

"But Richard the black-hearted is one of them." When he

nodded, she pinched the bridge of her nose. "Right. So if he's all that animalistic or whatever, why is *he* in charge?"

"The high lord has never . . . succumbed to his condition." Phillipe knew Cyprien would be furious with him, but he also understood his mistress's burning curiosity, and how much she needed the answers in order to stave off despair. "Richard never chose to be less than Kyn, like the others. He was *made* a changeling by the Brethren."

"They can do that?"

He inclined his head. "It is how the first changelings came about. They tortured Kyn by feeding them only animal blood."

"Michael ordered you not to talk to me about this, didn't he?" She watched his face. "It's okay; you don't have to lie. I figured he had." She shoved her chair back.

He caught her hand before she stood. "The master knows what must be done to protect us. He tries to do the same with you, but you were born in another time. He does not yet fully accept that you are not like the women we have known and changed. None of us quite understands you, Alexandra."

"I want in. I want to be a part of this. All the way." She threw up her hands. "Is that so hard to get?"

"Please, will you not listen to me now?" He saw the anger fade from her expression as she sank back into the chair. "What the master tells you about Lucan is true. He is very dangerous, and will not hesitate to use you to hurt the master."

"I can handle this guy," she insisted. "You let me go over there with a couple of guards, and—"

"—and the guards will be killed, and you will be made his prisoner. That is what men of our time did, and still do." Phillipe shifted tactics. "The master has managed to hold on to his soul all these years. If he had not, he could not love you as he does. Do you agree with this?"

"Some days I don't think the handsome snot has a single brain cell to his name, much less a soul," she said. Then, after a glance at him, she shrugged. "Okay, I agree. With certain reservations to be invoked the next time we have a screaming match."

"Lucan lost his love two centuries ago. He buried his heart with her in England." Phillipe touched the scar on his face. "He did this to me, trying to get at Cyprien."

Her chin dropped. "*Lucan* did that to you?"

He nodded slowly. "You yourself have seen what those who have no feeling left in them can do to another. You have repaired the damage to their faces and bodies and spirits. This is what the master fears. Why he will not let you go to question the suzerain. Every time he looks at me, he sees the same thing happening to you."

"But if I can't talk to Lucan, and no one is allowed to talk about Richard, then how can I help the Kyn?" When he would have answered, she shook her head. "This change that happens from drinking animal blood, it has to be directly related to the change that turned me into Kyn. Don't you see? It could be the most important element to my research into finding a cure."

"We will find Faryl," he promised her. "Dead or alive, his blood will give you the answers that you seek. Until then, please, Alexandra, do as the master says. If Lucan were to kill you . . ." He did not want to think about the bloodbath that would ensue.

She gave him a rueful look. "I think it would make him pretty happy right about now."

"*Non.* It would put an end to the master's sanity. I know it. You have seen how powerful he is," Phillipe said. "Imagine Cyprien with no temperance, no restraint. No heart left to care for anyone."

"That's why we have to cure this thing," she said. "No human being—mutated or otherwise—should have the power that we do. We can't handle it. Power corrupts, Phil. It makes us into monsters."

"You have the power to destroy a body as much as you may rebuild it," Phillipe reminded her. "Yet you devote yourself to healing instead of harming. Who is to say you will not someday become corrupted? Should you be permitted to have such a thing?"

"Aside from butt implants and breast lifts, there is no dark side to reconstructive surgery." She sighed. "All right, you've got a point. A small one. I'd hate you if you weren't so damn cute."

He sat back. "I am not cute."

"You are." Her lips curved. "And that scar makes you look very sexy, in a dangerous, De Niro, don't-fuck-with-me kinda way."

It was probably a compliment. "Thank you. So you will not break any more things on the wall? Our damage deposit was considerable, but so is your aim."

"No more breaking things." Something shifted in her eyes. "I promise, from here on out, to do my best for the master and the Kyn." She leaned over and kissed his scarred cheek. "You're a peach, Phil."

When she left, Phillipe wondered if he should relate everything he had said to her to Cyprien. If he had not convinced Alexandra to abide by his master's wishes, then the only one who could stop her was Cyprien.

No, she truly loves him, and she trusts me, he thought, switching on the laptop's screen. *She will keep her word.*

Chapter 16

Three days after her partner was murdered, Samantha Brown helped carry the casket containing the body of Harry Quinn from the hearse that brought him from the church to his final resting place. As she and five other Homicide detectives bore their burden to the grave, hundreds of other uniformed police officers from Dade, Broward, and Palm Beach counties who lined both sides of the narrow cemetery road snapped to attention.

Harry's widow, Gloria Quinn, stepped forward to place a large sheaf of orange blossoms and lilies beside her husband's casket. She looked at Sam for a moment, as lost and bewildered as any woman who had to face living the rest of her life without the man she loved.

Sam listened to the graveside service, conducted by the department's chaplain.

" 'Finally, all of you be of one mind, having compassion for one another; love as brothers, be tenderhearted, be courteous; not returning evil for evil or reviling for reviling, but on the contrary blessing, knowing that you were called to this, that you may inherit a blessing. For

> *"He who would love life*
> *And see good days,*
> *Let him refrain his tongue from evil,*
> *And his lips from speaking deceit.*
> *Let him turn away from evil and do good;*
> *Let him seek peace and pursue it.*
> *For the eyes of the LORD are on the righteous,*
> *And His ears are open to their prayers. . . . "' "*

After the chaplain had finished his final offering, one by one commissioners and captains and other officials who had known Harry stepped up to the grave to offer prayers, words of praise, and short remembrances. Family members had done the same after the funeral Mass at Harry's church.

Captain Garcia and two other department chiefs removed the American flag from Harry's casket and performed the ceremonial folding. The chaplain took Gloria's flowers and laid them in place of the flag. The folded triangle was formally presented to Gloria Quinn by Garcia along with the traditional expression of gratitude for her husband's supreme sacrifice in the line of duty.

Every word struck Sam like a stone thrown from the inside, where no one could see. By the time the service was over, she was battered, but she had one last thing to do before leaving Harry in peace.

She waited until everyone began to leave, and walked forward to place her rookie shield under the huge bouquet of Gloria's flowers. Harry hadn't known her when she'd been a rookie, but he had taught her more than any other cop on the force. She rested her white-gloved hand on the surface of the casket, wishing she had more to leave with him besides an old badge and what was left of her heart.

"I guess I'm supposed to say that you were like the father I never had," she murmured. "But you weren't a dad to me, Harry. You were my partner and my friend. You kept me straight. You showed me how to work a case the right way. You made me see the good in cops, instead of all the bad. You saved me, Harry, because without you, I wouldn't be a cop anymore. I'd have given up and quit."

The funeral director, who had come to stand on the other side of the grave, made a polite coughing sound.

Sam ignored him. "I know what you saw. I'll find him, whoever he was, and he'll pay. I promise you."

"Detective."

She looked up and saw Garcia. "Yeah." She took her hand from the casket and stepped back. The funeral director gave her a small, grateful smile as he flipped the switch that lowered Harry's casket into his grave.

Sam turned and walked down the path through the cemetery toward the parking lot.

Garcia caught up with her. "I'll take you home."

Sam looked over at the people gathered around Gloria at her car. She was white-faced and clutching the flag to her chest. "Gloria—"

"—needs her family now. You haven't slept since the night it happened, have you?"

She wasn't going to think of Lucan. Not here, not now. "I don't need to sleep." She saw the approaching trio of Peterson, Ortenza, and Dwyer and started to move on.

"It wasn't your fault," Garcia said, pacing her.

Oh, yes, it was. In spite of the heat of the day and her heavy dress uniform, she couldn't feel anything but cold. "I'm going back to Infusion tonight. I'll canvass for witnesses again. Someone had to see something." Lucan would help her, too. He had promised.

Garcia shook his head. "Ortenza, Peterson, and the task force from VC have already questioned everyone within a six-block radius."

"Someone might remember something they forgot."

Adam Suarez came to stand beside Garcia. He had his shades on like everyone else, but the rigid set of his face seemed a little kinder than before. "Detective Brown. I'm sorry about your partner."

Everyone said the same thing, but sympathy wouldn't find Harry's killer. Sam would. She didn't need a new partner getting in her way, however. "Are you officially on the squad yet?"

"Suarez will be partnering with Ortenza for a few weeks," the captain told her. "As of today, you're starting three weeks of vacation."

"No, I'm not."

Garcia shrugged. "You'll take the three weeks, or I'll suspend you from duty for the same length of time. Your choice."

Sam curled her hands into fists and pressed them against the flat seams of her trousers. "You can't suspend me. I haven't done anything wrong."

The captain regarded her steadily. "After your behavior at the crime scene, I can suspend you until you undergo a psychiatric and are cleared for duty. That would take about three weeks."

"Take the time, Detective," Suarez said gently. "I'm not going anywhere."

Before Sam could reply, Dwyer paused by them long enough to say, "She's a good partner, Suarez. Just don't lay a finger on her, or she'll scream rape."

Sam didn't scream, didn't make a sound, but she went for Dwyer. Garcia grabbed her just in time to ruin her roundhouse punch, and Suarez's strong arm blocked her second try.

"Get him out of here," Garcia snarled at Peterson, who with Ortenza's help hustled the grinning Dwyer away from Sam. "That's enough, Brown. Pull yourself together, or I *will* put you in for testing."

Gloria Quinn appeared, sans flag. "You two can let go of her. Samantha. Come on." She held out her hand, and Sam took it. "You're coming home with me."

"Mrs. Quinn," Garcia said, his expression turning blank and polite. "I'm sure Detective Brown wouldn't wish to intrude on your family time—"

"Samantha was my husband's partner, and a good friend to both of us," she coolly informed him. "That makes her part of my family."

Sam's rage faded into humiliation and embarrassment, and as she walked with Gloria to her car, she tried to apologize for her behavior.

"Oh, be quiet," Harry's widow said. "I saw what that grinning, rat-faced Dwyer was up to the minute he made a beeline for you. Harry often told me he regretted being a cop only because he couldn't shoot that nasty piece of work in the head. All I can say is, thank the good Lord I'm not carrying a gun today, or he'd be minus his male parts."

Sam stared at the woman who had always been so gentle, kind, and devout that she never raised her voice or said a bad word about anyone. *"Gloria."*

The widow produced a grim smile. "Just so you know. Now the only cop I trust to find the scum that killed my Harry is you. You can't do that if you're on suspension for disobeying Garcia's orders or punching out Rat Face."

Sam's shoulders slumped. "If I don't take my vacation, he'll suspend me anyway."

Gloria guided her around a couple of uniformed patrolmen, nodding to them as they passed. "Do you know what they're saying about the motive for Harry's murder, Samantha?"

"Only that he was probably killed for his phone and his wallet." That was the popular theory Peterson and Ortenza were supporting, anyway.

"Tell me, if it was a mugging, why didn't the thief dump Harry on the ground and take the unit? Pefect getaway vehicle; no one would have been looking for it for a few hours. He also left Harry's wedding ring on his finger. I just had the band re-sized for our anniversary so he could get it on and off without using soap. It's solid gold with three diamonds." Gloria's voice quavered. "One for every time he asked me to marry him before I said yes."

"He still had his service revolver, too." Sam sometimes forgot how smart cops' wives could be. "Has anyone been calling the house?" she asked carefully. "Did you have the feeling that Harry was keeping something from you?"

"The hot dogs he was always sneaking while he was on duty, yes. I knew you'd catch him most of the time. But a threat, or some felon threatening him? Never. Danger to him was danger to me, Samantha. He always told me when he was worried about something." The widow's spine straightened. "So. Now we go back to the house, and you're going to eat, and talk, and share wonderful funny stories about my husband with our family. You can stay over, shower, sleep, and get a fresh start in the morning. How are you going to spend your vacation?"

"Looking for Harry's murderer," Sam promised.

"That's my girl." She patted her cheek. "Come on; let's get out of here."

Lucan ordered Burke to replace some of the electric lights in his suite with pillar candles. Of all the things he disliked about modern living, electricity topped the list. Certainly it was versatile, and instantly available, but it lacked the warmth and ambience of his natal era. To read by candlelight or sit before a good fire to contemplate the flames had been some of the few pleasures of his human life. One could not do the same with a soft white lightbulb. And where was the romance in a fluorescent tube?

Everything had to be perfect for Samantha.

He would have to change several things about his primary residence to make her comfortable. She would want bookcases for her books. A new wardrobe, too. He planned to cast every article of clothing she presently possessed into the building's Dumpster. After he put them through his office shredder.

Making Samantha his *kyrya* would have to wait, though. First he had to kidnap Cyprien's lover and hold her hostage.

Rafael watched him light the columns of beeswax in a three-tiered standing iron rack Burke had placed on the foot table. "Cyprien's refuge is well patrolled. When the seigneur is not present, his seneschal never lets Dr. Keller out of his sight. We cannot use a conventional attack."

"I want Alexandra brought here," Lucan repeated. "I don't care how difficult it is to take her. Find a way, get her, and bring her to me."

"There are two possibilities. It is said that Dr. Keller has not made a proper transition, and that she is still as vulnerable to Kyn talent as any human. If that is so . . ." Rafael reached out and snuffed one of the candles with his fingertips.

"No wonder Cyprien guards her like an attack dog." He thought of the many talents among his *jardin*. "What is the other possibility?"

"The high lord's *tresora* sent these by special courier." Rafael opened a case and took out several transparent darts filled with blue fluid and an odd-looking pistol. "According to Éliane's letter, the fluid acts as a sedative on us. I tested it on Alvaro last night, and one dart rendered him helpless for two hours. Evidently Dr. Keller invented it."

"Then why do you complain?" Lucan asked. "With these darts and your talent, you can take her whenever you wish."

"The consequences of this are what concern me, my lord. By doing this, you risk starting a *jardin* war," his seneschal warned. "The seigneur has but to issue a summons and every Kyn in the country will swarm to his side, most particularly Locksley, Jaus, and Durand. We could never prevail against them and their men."

Lucan thought of Cyprien and the way he had looked at his brazen *sygkenis,* and blew out the taper in his hand. "He will not risk her."

"Doing this will solve nothing between you. It will only make things worse."

Wineglasses lining the shelf above the wet bar began to crack as he turned to regard his seneschal.

"As Burke has gone to so much trouble to have the windows replaced," Lucan said in his mildest voice, "it would be prudent to stop questioning me and follow my orders."

"Yes, my lord." Rafael picked up the reports Lucan had ignored. "Quinn was buried today. According to our information, Detective Brown has been forced to take a paid leave of absence, but she still intends to investigate Quinn's murder on her own. She is staying at his widow's home tonight." His dark eyes glinted with tiny reflections of the candlelight. "Should I have her kidnapped as well? You might start your own harem."

"Get out."

Rafael bowed and departed.

Lucan heard the music creeping up through the ductwork from the nightclub below. He had been in a constant state of temper since the ill-advised meeting with Cyprien and spending the night comforting Samantha after her partner's murder. Now that he had agreed to be her partner—ironic as it was—he could not stop thinking about the murders, particularly Harry Quinn's. There were no icons found on the old man's body, and no more dead flowers had arrived. From the manner of the killing it would seem a random street crime. An article in the newspaper the day after suggested that because of the unmarked vehicle and Harry's plain clothes that the thief had not realized he had murdered a cop.

Too convenient, that.

No prints had been found on the vehicle but Quinn's and Samantha's. Why would Quinn drive six blocks away to sit in a park while his partner was questioning a suspect? Why had he not been found behind the driver's wheel? If the motive was thievery, why had the killer taken his wallet and phone but not his weapon or jewelry? How could anyone reach into the car to cut the throat of a veteran cop like Quinn without any signs of a struggle?

Lucan had killed enough men to know when something was being staged.

The murder had also derailed his plans for Samantha to abandon her life as a member of the police to be his *kyrya*. At first he thought it only a temporary setback, but the Kyn's contact within the department sent a detailed report on Detective Brown's reaction to Quinn's death. She had been devastated and exhausted the night she had spent in Lucan's arms, but since then she had been hounding everyone involved in the case.

She is staying at his widow's home tonight. Should I have her kidnapped as well?

He need not rely on Rafael to do everything for him. Lucan picked up the house phone and dialed his *tresora.* "Burke, I want Quinn's home address."

"Quinn, master?"

"Detective Brown's partner. The one who was murdered. She is staying with his widow. I am going there tonight."

"But master—"

Two wineglasses shattered. "Give me the address."

Burke recited the address, and then asked, "May I say one thing?"

"No."

As he went to replace the receiver, Lucan heard his *tresora* say, "But Detective Brown is here, master."

He didn't bother with the phone or the elevator; the stairs sufficed. His goth patrons had by now begun treating him like a prince, and willingly drew back as he moved through the club. That allowed Lucan to see Samantha sitting at a corner table by herself. She was watching the dancers and drinking what appeared to be water.

"You should try the Douglas Clegg Daiquiri," Lucan said as he came up behind her. "It makes hot buttered rum taste insipid."

She put down the glass and traced her finger around one side of the cross-shaped red cocktail napkin under it. "I didn't come here to drink."

"I would hope that you came to see me." He couldn't read her expression, but he could feel her anger. She almost vibrated with it.

"I've been thinking a lot about these murders, and I keep getting the feeling that you know something about them that I don't." Now she looked at him. "Three people who came to this club are dead. You are the only connection between them."

Someone called to him. Lucan ignored it. "Come upstairs with me, where you can hear me."

"I don't want to cuddle and cry this time," she told him. "I need answers. Straight answers."

The self-contempt saturating the first part of what she said made Lucan wrap his hand around her right wrist, so she couldn't reach for her weapon. He trailed his fingertips down the knotted cable of her hair. It was silky-fine, the color of bitter chocolate, and smelled of the rich, dark-roasted coffee she liked to drink. He wanted to take it apart to see it on her shoulders again. He wanted to bury his face in it.

"I know what you need, and I will give it to you. I promise." He gave her braid a tug. "Come with me. Be with me, Samantha."

He could see her pulse speeding up, the way her breasts lifted and fell as she tried to control her breath. Her muscles were so tense they were almost coiled.

"Harry's dead." She got to her feet, but instead of jerking out of his grip, she came to stand between his thighs. Lucan looked down as she rested her hands on either side of his waist. She dug her fingernails in, not to hurt, but to hold. "I want his killer."

"I want you."

Their faces were at opposing angles, the light from the bar masking hers in shadow. He wanted to put her on the bar and have her right there. Her scent flooded his senses, blanking out everything but the heat radiating from her, and the other, darker hunger gnawing inside of him.

She leaned forward. "So how are we going to do this?" Her cheek grazed his, and her voice became a murmur. "You being my partner and all?"

Someone called his name again. Louder this time.

"What would you have me do?" He stared at her mouth.

"I want you to tell me what the deal is here." Her lips grazed his cheekbone. "You'll tell me everything, won't you?"

She was trying to *seduce* him into helping her. Lucan didn't know whether to be offended or laugh—or throw her over his shoulder and carry her upstairs.

The front entry door to the bar swung open, and two of Lucan's guards rushed in. *"¡Ayuda!"*

Annoyed as he was by the interruption, even Lucan knew that Kyn guards didn't scream for help unless there was something they couldn't handle. There was very little on earth that qualified.

"I have to attend to this." Lucan picked her up off her feet and sat her back on her stool. "Stay here."

He met three more of his guards at the door and followed them out to where humans were staggering about rubbing at their eyes. Traffic had come to a complete halt, and panicked drivers were stumbling out of their vehicles.

In the center of the street, Rafael stood, surrounded by a nimbus of golden light. Several yards away from him stood what appeared to be a six-foot-tall snake with arms and legs. The latter was sinking eight-inch fangs into the neck of an unconscious Kyn.

"Faryl." Lucan stripped off his jacket and gloves. "How kind of you to call."

The changeling lifted his head and hissed, grabbing up his prey in his jaws and dragging him down the street and around the corner. Lucan nodded to Rafael, who took two guards and went the opposite way, while Lucan and the remaining men followed Faryl.

They found the broken body of Faryl's victim in the doorway of a tourist shop. The glass of the door had been shattered. Lucan looked through the space between the shop and the next building to see Rafael and his men covering the rear exit.

"What are you doing?" he heard Samantha say. "Is that man dead?"

Somehow Samantha had blundered past Rafael, or perhaps his seneschal had been overwhelmed by the number of humans on the street. Whatever the case, Samantha could obviously see everything that was happening.

"Get back to the club." Lucan scanned the front of the shop before turning to find her just behind him. "Do as I say, woman!"

"You don't have the authority to go in there." She drew her weapon. "I do."

He reached over and kept her from going into the shop by grabbing the back of her jacket. "This is not something your law covers. Mine does. Get out of here before you get hurt."

"I'm not that easy to hurt, and you're being a lousy partner. Is he armed? Is he alone?" The sound of the metal being torn apart drew her attention back to the shop. "What was that?"

Lucan seized her and pulled her against his chest, covering her head with his arms as the front window of the shop exploded out on them.

Sam wasn't sure what had happened. She had hurried out of the club straight into a light so intense that it had virtually blinded her. She froze, but after a few seconds her eyes grew accustomed to it, and by squinting she was able to walk out of it. She saw Lucan running with his men and went after him.

Now he was giving her orders and treating her like some helpless female. Didn't he understand that *she* was the cop, and *he* was the private citizen? Just as she was about to slap the cuffs on him, he pulled her into a bear hug. She realized why as the enormous plate-glass window in front of them shattered outward, pelting them both with cutting shards. Along with the shower of glass came an aluminum-and-Formica table that flew out, bounced onto the sidewalk, and came apart.

As Lucan dragged her backward, three men came running down toward them from the nightclub.

As men went, they were rather ordinary, if one overlooked the brown bathrobes. They were shouting in some foreign language that sounded vaguely like Spanish, and were armed with some kind of spears. And, it appeared, they were serious.

"The hell." She stared. The spears had big ax heads and dagger-shaped spikes on one end. "Are those . . . are those battle-axes?"

"Halberds." Lucan moved, putting himself between her and the men. "Run, Samantha. Obey me. *Run.*"

She almost did. Almost. But whatever weird hypnotism he was using on her faded away in the next moment, and she regained control.

"I am a police officer," she called out in a loud, clear voice to the men. "Stop where you are and put down those weapons." They kept running, and in another block, the men would be on top of them. She repeated her order in Spanish, and when the men didn't slow down, she bent and picked up a broken table leg made of aluminum pipe.

"T'ta a facc', arruso!" one shouted as he charged forward at Lucan.

It might have been choreographed, the way Sam went right and Lucan went left. Simultaneously they both ducked the slash of the halberd. As she slammed the assailant in the back of the kneecap with her pipe, Lucan caught the shaft of the halberd and wrenched it out of the man's hands. She didn't see what happened after that, but their attacker let out a horrendous scream before he toppled over, clutching his chest.

Lucan turned his head in her direction. "Behind you!"

Sam pivoted around and without thinking swiped up the pipe in her hand in time to parry the ax coming at her face. Metal screeched and sparks flew. Her arms absorbed the jolt, but only just. It got her close enough to see the man's face and the fury in his eyes.

He hauled the ax backward and swung again. *"Donnicciola!"* Sam ducked and dodged, but he reversed the swing and caught the side of her head with the blunt end of the halberd's staff. Stars burst in front of her eyes, but before the blade descended, incredibly it shattered in midair. She came around and blindly used the pipe like a baseball bat, driving it into his spine from behind.

The ax man roared and arched, but Sam tottered back two steps and kicked him squarely between his legs. The ax fell to the road and he went down, short-squealing and clutching his crotch.

"Next time," she panted, "put down the damn weapon when I tell you to."

Lucan appeared, clamping his hand on the back of the man's neck. The man convulsed, went stiff, and hit the asphalt like a sack of rotten tomatoes. Lucan stepped over him to get to Sam. "Are you injured?"

She rubbed her head and checked her hand for blood. "I'm

all right. Where's the third . . ." She saw another body in the gutter. "Is he dead?"

Instead of answering her, Lucan turned as louder crashing sounds came from inside the shop. "Samantha, don't shoot what comes out of there."

"Why not?"

He pushed her behind him. "It won't stop him. It will only make him angrier."

What came out of the shop wasn't human, exactly. It had the vague shape of a man, and arms and legs, but that was where everything human stopped and something else took over. Its neck was as long as Sam's forearm, and had huge, bulging tendons on either side that ran up and formed a ridge around an oblong-shaped, hairless head. It had yellow, lidless eyes the size of lemons, and its mouth was a lipless, blunted snout.

Sam could see it, but she couldn't believe it.

The thing's barrel-shaped torso tapered down into ridges that disappeared under a ragged pair of trousers. Between its legs, a long, thick tail dragged on the ground behind it. Instead of skin, mottled green, brown, and yellow rectangular scales covered its entire body. The slitted eyes shifted from side to side. A thin, forked pink tongue flickered out to taste the air.

"It's a . . ." For a minute Sam thought her eyes would pop out of her head. "Snake-man?"

It heard Sam's voice, drew its head back, and hissed, displaying enormous, curved white fangs.

"Faryl, stop," Lucan said. "No one else needs to suffer this night."

Sam turned to stare at him. "You *know* this thing?"

"He was my friend once." Lucan moved forward, holding his empty hands out in front of him. "You came here to me, Faryl; do you not remember? I will help you, brother, I promise. But for me to do that, you must control yourself."

For a moment the snake-man seemed mesmerized by Lucan's voice, and swayed a little.

"My lord!" someone shouted, and a short arrow flew past Lucan's head and buried itself in the snake-man's right arm.

Faryl screamed in a horribly distorted human voice and lunged for Lucan. They went down on the ground, grappling.

Sam couldn't fire her weapon, not with them wrestling each other, and if her gun was useless, as Lucan had said, then shooting it wouldn't help. She snatched up one of the halberds and waited, and then brought the ax down on the snake-man's tail, cleanly cutting off the end.

Faryl screamed again and rolled away from Lucan before pushing himself to his feet and running off into the night. Four of Lucan's guards went after him.

Sam went to Lucan, who had deep puncture wounds from Faryl's fangs in his shoulder and a diagonal slash wound across his face. "Don't move." She straddled him, tearing off her jacket and covering his chest with it to keep him warm. "I'll get an ambulance." She fumbled for her mobile.

His pale silver eyes opened and he wiped the blood from his face with his sleeve casually, as if there weren't a two-inch-deep gash bisecting it. "That will not be necessary, Detective."

Sam started to argue, and then her eyes widened as she saw the gash filling in and the edges drawing together. "Your face."

"No, watch it, Samantha." He yanked on his gloves and caught her hips as she tried to rise, holding her in place. "This should be more convincing than my *dents acérées.*"

"Your what?" she whispered, completely enthralled by the sight of his wound closing and shrinking.

"My fangs."

When it was over—and it took only twenty seconds or less—the wound was gone, and there was no scar on Lucan's face. He appeared as if he'd never been slashed. She looked down at the bloody, ragged holes in his shirt, but where there had been fist-sized puncture wounds, now only smooth skin showed through. Sam took hold of his shirt and ripped it, looking for the injuries—and found nothing.

She took in a deep, slow breath and released it. "So your friend is a snake-man, and you're . . . ?"

"Darkyn." He put an arm around her waist and sat up so that she straddled his lap. "Something like a vampire."

"*Something* like a vampire." She nodded as if it all made sense. Not that it ever would.

Men surrounded them, and Lucan stood, holding Samantha

with one arm until she found the ground with her feet. "What of Faryl?"

"He beheaded Reyes and escaped by water, my lord," one of them replied. "However, your woman wounded him, and we have his scent now."

"He will go into the swamp to feed and heal. Track him, but do not try to corner or capture him," Lucan said. "Locate his lair and report back to me."

"Yes, my lord."

Sam heard distant sirens wailing and drawing closer. For a moment she considered staying on the scene and reporting to the responding units what had happened. Then she saw that the three men who had attacked them had vanished—along with the section of tail she had chopped off Faryl.

"How do I write up an incident report involving a snake-man and a vampire?" she muttered. Her mouth felt dry, and her head was starting to spin.

"You don't." Lucan looked down at her, and his mouth twisted. "If only I had Cyprien's talent."

Sam didn't know what that was, but she had a good idea why she couldn't feel her legs, and the reason her vision was dwindling down to something small and insignificant at the end of a long, black tunnel. As the ground tilted, she asked, "Can you catch?"

Evidently he could, for as she went down she never felt her head hit the ground.

Chapter 17

The brothel didn't resemble the ones Sam had occasionally raided during one of the DA's semiannual Clean Up Our City Streets campaigns. There were no televisions tuned to the triple-X-rated Dish Network channel. No thin, hollow-eyed girls in skimpy, tattered lingerie turning their arms in to hide the track marks.

Why she was here, and how she knew it was a brothel, she had no idea.

The furnishings were crude wood minus upholstery: benches, chairs, a small table with a pewter candleholder that looked like Beowulf had used it to find his way around. The walls had some pretty lengths of cloth hanging from hooks, but they were loosely woven and dyed a not very appealing brown. There was a huge oak cask in one corner, and another table with wooden mugs beside it.

Sam smelled alcohol fumes—strong wine—and started to move away from them. When she saw the two men, though, she stopped and stared.

The pair sat on the bench next to the big cask. They were large, sweaty, and dirty twins, with shaggy heads of dark hair and scraggly beards. One of them had been hit in the face with something that had left a half-inch-deep old scar. The scar ran from his forehead through a white blind eye and down to tug at the corner of his mouth. It distorted his mouth into a snarl. The other one threw back his head and laughed, flashing lots of gaps, sore gums, and a couple of chipped, brown teeth.

She hoped whoever was running the place planned to charge extra for kissing privileges.

Men of my time rarely kissed.

Sam gave the pair one more cautious look before she turned
toward the voice. In front of her was a plain wood-planked door
that opened with a latch string. Going through that led her down
another unfurnished corridor into a second chamber, this one
filled with women lounging around on pillow-strewn chaises.

This bunch were slightly cleaner than the two waiting out
front, but their hair and gowns definitely needed washing. Sam
saw something small with wings fly off the top of one girl's
head. *And maybe delousing.*

She cleared her throat. "Did someone call me?"

At the sight of her, the women rose, some of them yawning
and stretching. All of them worked up smiles of varying degrees for her.

"She be the marster's?" one of them, the youngest and prettiest, asked in a kind of strangled whisper.

An older one sighed. "Aye."

One woman with a wandering left eye and a grease-stained
tunic stepped up to Sam. "I say she fancies sommat with tits."
Her breath could have been bottled and labeled EAU DE LAND-
FILL. "Ye fancy wenches, do ye?"

"Not today." Or ever, thank God.

"Makes no never mind ta me." The youngest girl present si-
dled up, slinking her arm through Sam's. "Marster gives us
many toys." She trailed grimy nails over Sam's forearm. "I
could bring you."

The lives she could change here with a hose, a scrub brush,
and two hundred bars of strong deodorant soap. "I bring my
own, thanks."

A woman in an ivory gown emerged from the shadows.
Compared to the other whores, she was so clean she might have
come from a different planet.

"Indeed you could, Maribel," she said, "but the lady has de-
clined your services. Cease making a nuisance of yourself, please."

Sam eyed her. The body and dress resembled Cinderella's
on a good night, but the face and voice were identical to her
own. "Who are you?"

"The woman he loved." She swept a beautifully executed
curtsy. "You are very welcome here."

Sam looked around. "Where is Lucan?"

"He will not come within these walls unless you permit it," she said. "May I bring you wine?"

The women began sneaking out of the room. "I don't drink."

"You did, once." Her twin adjusted the lacy cuff of one sleeve and then folded her hands in front of her. The ladylike movements made Sam uneasy, probably because she was watching her body do it, and hearing her voice coming out of that primly held mouth. "I would be happy to acquire some fetching males from the slave quarters for your pleasure, if you so wish it."

"You have slave quarters? You have *slaves*?" Before she could answer, Sam shook her head. "Never mind. How do I get to Lucan?"

"He doesn't want you," she said, her voice bland. "He wants me."

"But you are— Never mind." Sam sat down on the edge of a chaise. "What kind of wine have you got?"

"I will fetch it." Her twin slipped out of the room.

Sudden, cold weight yanked at Sam's feet and legs. She looked down. Large black metal plates ran up her calves to encase her thighs.

"Christ." She jumped up and slapped at her leg. Metal clanked as the jointed gauntlet on her hand hit the hinged knee plates. She pried at the gauntlet, but she couldn't budge them. More metal began crawling up her body. "Someone—help me," she shouted.

Her voice echoed in the empty room. No one answered it.

The living armor ignored Sam's efforts to get it off her body and grew up toward her face. Things began overlapping it: a wide belt, a chest strap, another gauntlet that left her palm and fingers bare. The suit of armor didn't eat her; it just grew on her like a metal skin. She felt her hair being sucked back, and the feel of a leather strap snaking across her forehead. Bladed and blunt weapons attached themselves to her thighs, hips, and forearms.

At last it seemed the special effects were over. A complete set of armor enveloped her, along with enough weapons to outfit an entire commando squad.

"I'm . . . RoboCop?" Gingerly she took one of the shorter blades out of a sheath strapped to her left thigh and examined it. It looked pretty real, and when Sam pressed a fingertip to the edge, it cut into her skin with razor-sharp efficiency. "Ouch." She licked the blood away, and it tasted like blood. "Medieval hookers, snake-men, self-dressing armor, and vampires. I've finally gone off the deep end."

You're dreaming the brothel, the whores, and the armor. Everything else was real.

She turned around. "Where are you?"

In the dungeon.

Sam saw a rat peer out at her from under one of the chaises. "Have an Orkin man down there?"

Her well-dressed twin came back with two goblets, and handed her one. Sam checked the contents and saw bits of wood and pulp swirling around the top. "Got a strainer?"

"I beg your pardon?"

"Never mind." It was dream wine, so why was she worried? Sam tasted it and nearly choked on the thick, sickly-sweet liquid. "Nice and, ah, chunky."

Her twin took a dainty swig of her own. "It does revive the spirits."

"If it doesn't etch the enamel off your teeth first." Sam set the goblet down on the little table. "What happens now?"

"You take the castle or the dungeon."

Sam frowned. "Take them where?"

"You take what you wish," her twin said with exaggerated patience. "The castle in the air"—she pointed to one narrow window—"or the dungeon below."

Sam felt suspicious. "Does this involve another snake-man?"

The other Sam's mouth stretched wide over pearly white teeth. "You cannot have one without the other."

The stones of the floor under their feet began to crack like melting ice. Sam tried to step back, but the stone under her heel fell away, leaving a black hole.

"It appears," her twin said as she floated up to the windowsill and perched on it, "that he wishes to decide for you."

All of the stones came apart and tumbled into the black hole beneath them, taking Sam with them.

Sam fell. She scrambled for a handhold, anything she might grab, but there were no walls. Beneath her she saw no light, no bottom, only darkness. She fell for what seemed like hours. She fell until she didn't care how hard she landed, or if it would kill her, if she could just stop falling.

The long fall didn't end until someone reached out and snatched her out of the darkness from behind. Hands settled on her shoulders, holding her steady.

"Grapes are out of season here, Samantha," Lucan said against her ear. "Should I order some pomegranates?"

She was still in complete darkness, but too relieved to have stopped falling to care that he had just scared the living shit out of her. "I'm not hungry."

"But you are."

Sam tucked her chin in and turned her head a notch, and saw that the left hand sitting on her shoulder wasn't covered by a velvet glove. It wasn't even a human hand, not with those six-inch curved black claws sprouting from the ends instead of fingernails. Then she looked over at the other hand, which was tanned and had a beautiful manicure. On the ring finger of that one was an old-fashioned signet ring with a gothic letter L.

"Why am I here?" She watched the human fingers sink in a little. "Is this the dungeon?"

"You can't have the pleasures of the world without the horrors, Samantha." The human/monster hands began to turn her around. "You're a cop. You should know that."

Why should I know that? She had had damned few pleasures in her life. Then again, if Lucan represented the bulk of them—which if she thought about it, he probably did—then what did that say about her?

Her left side was against his chest now, and she was going to see his face in another few seconds. Somehow she knew that if she faced him—if she so much as *looked* at his face—she would be his. Those ghost eyes of his would suck the brains out of her skull, the way they had every other woman who had loved him.

He doesn't love me. He loves her.

"No." The claws ripped into her shoulder as Lucan jerked her to face him. "You'll not run from this now. Not when I've brought you this far. Wake up, Samantha." He shook her. *"Wake up."*

Lucan had been trying to wake Samantha from the catatonic trance she had fallen into after Faryl's escape, with no luck. He had tried cold compresses, a capsule of ammonia from Burke's first-aid kit, and brandy. Nothing roused her.

Burke had suggested calling the authorities, but Lucan refused. He would not allow them to lock her up in some asylum. He had put her into this trance; he would wake her from it.

He had talked to her, and rubbed her hands, and immersed her in a warm bath. He had held her, and rocked her, and lain down with her on his bed, trying to warm her. He even considered singing to her. Nothing worked, until at last he lost his temper and propped himself over her, shaking her shoulders.

"Bloody hell, woman, you won't do this to me. You can't find Harry's killer if you're a bloody damn vegetable. Obey me, Samantha. Do you hear me?" He shook her again. *"Wake up."*

The blank stare in her eyes receded, and her eyelids closed and opened until she focused on his face.

"Thank Christ," he said.

"Hello," she said, like a polite child. She glanced around her. "We don't have to chase that snake-man again, do we?"

He was so relieved that he couldn't answer her. He could only snatch her up against his chest and hold her tight.

"Lucan." Her voice was muffled against his ragged shirt. "I can't breathe."

"Forgive me." He laughed, so great was his relief. "I had thought I might never bring you back."

Samantha relaxed against him. "That bad." She sat up again and stared at his face. "You were all cut up, and then you healed in a few seconds. I wasn't hallucinating."

"No." He cursed himself for allowing her to see him heal. "You were not."

Her expression grew solemn. "How do I even begin to believe in something like you?"

"Not easily. I know what even the fact of our existence can do to the sanity of a human," he told her, brushing the hair back from her face. "But you are stronger than that, Samantha. What you saw tonight was a Kyn version of the humans you hunt."

She shook her head. "He was easy to spot. Human snakes wear their skins on the inside."

"I would have spared you this." Ironic, that she had been made to face what human monsters could do, and now had to endure knowledge of those among his kind. "Then again, perhaps all of your life's miseries were to prepare you for what I would do to you."

Now she seemed bewildered. "What have you done to me?"

"Witnessing the rage of my old friend Faryl wasn't enough?"

"Did you make him that way?" When he shook his head, she smiled a little. "I didn't think so. Was he what you said you were? Something like a vampire?"

He hid his fear, but he could not keep back the words. "I'd rather not tell you something that will made you turn back into a beautiful carrot—"

"Don't tell me," she said. "Show me."

"You've been through enough." If he touched her now, he wouldn't be able to control himself.

Samantha reached up and took a handful of his hair in her fist, and dragged his face to hers. He was so starved for her that the kiss he gave her must have bruised her lips, but she only nestled closer to him. As he kissed her, he felt her fingers touch the juncture of their mouths. Their lips parted, and she inserted a fingertip, rimming the edge of his bottom teeth, turning her hand to do the same to the top.

Desire made his *dents acérées* slide from the recesses in his palate. She felt them as they extended, and the taste of her blood sweetened his mouth as the sharp, elongated point of one fang pierced her skin.

Her eyes were only inches from his. In them, he could see the reflection of his, and how the pupils in his eyes instantly contracted, becoming narrow, vertical black slits.

"Jesus," she breathed, not repulsed but riveted. "You really are a vampire."

Lucan caressed the length of her finger with his tongue as he savored the small wound he had inflicted on her. The scent of

jasmine rose around them, thick and deep. Reluctantly he released her finger, kissing the reddened dimple in the skin.

"I live on human blood." He would tell her the rest. "My
wounds heal instantly, and I do not age. My kind are difficult to
kill. We have been living among you since the Middle Ages,
when the first of my kind rose to walk the night. I was born in
the thirteenth century."

"Are you like the vampires in the movies?"

"No. The cross doesn't burn us, and sunlight only makes us
tired. Wooden stakes are useless; our weakness is copper. We
don't drain all the blood from humans or make them into our
kind." He thought of Alexandra, but explaining her would only
complicate matters. "We are different, but we try to coexist
with you."

"You have sex with humans."

He gave her a wicked smile. "Whenever possible. We are
very hungry, very sensory creatures, and you . . ." He breathed
in her scent. "You are a movable feast." He felt her pulse
change. "What more can I show you?"

"One last thing," she said. "Take off your gloves and show
me your hands."

"I can't touch you."

"I know. I remember." She looked down at them. "You did
something with them to stop those men who attacked us. That's
why you wear gloves all the time."

"Each of the Kyn has their own talent, but some are particularly rare and powerful," he said, hearing the bitterness in his
voice and despising his own self-pity. "Mine affects anything
that breathes, whether it is animal, vegetable, human, or Kyn.
That is why I am feared, Samantha."

"Why? What do you do?"

"I can shatter bones, tear flesh, and rend veins. Nothing living can withstand the touch of my bare hands if I wish it harm."
He looked down at the weapons he could never be rid of. "My
former master called me the Black Prince of Death. Black like
a plague that can never be stopped. Death for my hands."

"Why does glass break around you?" she asked. "That's not
a living thing."

"It happens sometimes when I'm angry, or close to losing

my temper. Rather like a warning signal." His mouth curled. "I never have enough wineglasses."

She nodded slowly. "I still want to see your hands."

Lucan considered the thin layer of velvet that kept her safe. If this was the price for her sanity, then so be it. Slowly he stripped off his gloves and held out his hands.

Her expression changed to surprise. "They're not black."

Of all the things he had expected her to say, that was not one of them. "I'm not a black man."

She looked up quickly. "In my dream, one of them was black."

"Was it the left?" When she nodded, he picked up his gloves. "I was born left-handed. It was considered unlucky in my time." He froze when she touched his hands with hers, and jerked them away. "Samantha, I told you, nothing living—"

"Can withstand your touch, yeah, I got that. I also know you don't want to hurt me. If you did, you wouldn't have been so careful." She took his bare hands in hers again. "I trust you."

The only flesh Lucan had touched without gloves protecting it for the last seven hundred years had suffered or died moments later. Yet here was this foolish, ridiculous human female, cradling his killing hands between hers, bending to them, bringing them to her face—

The feel of her skin under his fingers made Lucan close his eyes.

Like a blind man walking without cane or guide, he let himself live dangerously for a moment. He moved his fingertips over her face, sweeping over the lines and curves, learning her, feeling her. At first he raced, eager to take in as much as he could before it was time to release her, but then he began to linger, testing a texture here, a softness there.

Her lashes were gossamer, her lips warm satin. The bones beneath her flesh were strong, angular things made graceful by the resilient stretch of muscle. The tiny hairs on her skin worked like fine velvet against him, finer than any glove he had ever worn. Her breath warmed his skin, as tender as a lover's caress.

Too much.

He opened his eyes and pulled his trembling hands away,

ashamed of himself for risking her safety all for the rapture of knowing her under his hands. He reached for his gloves.

"Don't put them back on." Her voice sounded as ragged as his grip on his self-control. "Please."

He stared at her in disbelief. "Have you gone carrot-brained again?"

Samantha lay back against the pillows of his bed, and pulled up the hem of her T-shirt, tugging it up and over her head. Under it she wore a plain white bra. "I like feeling your hands on me." She touched the clip at the front, but didn't release it. "Don't you want me?"

She wasn't afraid. She had seen what he could do with his hands, and she wasn't screaming in fear. Lucan couldn't think. "I want you."

"Then take off my bra."

If he put both hands on her, he would rip her bra to shreds, so Lucan used only two fingers to release the clasp, and one to peel back the thin cotton cups. Her breasts were neither too small or too large, pretty round globes that promised to fill his hand. Her nipples were the same color as her lips, a delicate pink only a shade or two darker than her skin, but as he looked at them they turned rosy and tightened.

"Touch me," she whispered.

Lucan had to taste her first, and so he bent his head to her, watching the tiny vibrations of her heartbeat under her skin, and opened his mouth over her, and took her nipple in. He tried not to curve his hand around the luscious weight of her breast as he sucked, but that, too, he could not resist, and the sensation of his fingers sinking into the firm mound brought his other hand to her.

He felt her hands on him, moving over his shoulders, skimming down his back. He was on top of her, pressing her into the bed, his bare hands filled with her, his tongue lashing her. Her thighs parted and he settled between them, inching the heavy weight of his cock back and forth against her.

He lifted his head to look into her eyes. He saw no pain, no hesitation, no doubt. "I want to put my fingers inside you."

Instead of answering, Samantha reached down and unfastened the waistband of her trousers, and opened the zipper beneath it. Lucan lifted up, first to watch her, then to help her. He stripped off the trousers, tossing them aside, but left her white cotton panties, which he found as unbearably erotic as her plain little bra, in place.

"Spread your legs for me," he told her, watching her shift, relishing the play of her muscles as she opened herself to his gaze. He used one finger to pull the cotton crotch out of his way, discovering a light dusting of dark curly hair over more delicate pink flesh, and with two fingers of his other hand he explored the plump outer curves of her labia. She was all damp and flowering, his Samantha, her hips moving in a small, subtle roll as he parted her with a fingertip and found the narrow, tight place that made his fingers ache.

Lucan might have looked at her for the rest of the night, had her hand not found his to urge him against her. He bent to press his mouth to her thigh, and then rested his face against it as he slowly pushed one finger up inside her.

Samantha made a low, keening sound.

"Yes." He penetrated her as deeply as he could, feeling the clench of her against him, sliding through wetness and tender, swollen flesh until the tip of his finger brushed the mouth of her womb. Slowly he drew his hand back, easing out of her, and then entered her again, this time with two fingers.

His hands were big, and she was tight; he knew he was stretching her as he fit her to his palm. When he had his fingers inside her as deeply as they would go, he put his mouth to her, opening her again with his tongue, caressing her and tasting the silkiness his fingers were drawing from her as he pushed them slowly in and out, fucking her with his hand.

"Lucan." Her fingers were in his hair, restless, tugging.

He used his fangs to tear the panties from her, and worked his tongue against her until he felt her thigh muscles tense and strain. Sinking his two fingers into her, he pushed his thumb up and into the tight cleft of her buttocks, opening and working it into her there.

Samantha cried out, a beautiful sound of longing and wanting and a little fear, and then she came on his hand, writhing under his mouth, drenching his fingers as she squeezed them and tugged them deeper with the contractions of finding her pleasure.

Lucan rode her climax, licking and petting and stroking her
to another, and when her head fell back, he slowly withdrew his
fingers from her body. His entire hand was wet from her, and
he painted her breast with the satiny proof of her satisfaction
before he stood and began shedding his own clothes.

Through dazed eyes she watched him undress. "What are
you doing to me?"

"Everything." He stood for a moment by the bed, as naked
as she was, looking down at her. He put his hand around his
cock, stroking it as she watched. "I'm going to fuck you,
Samantha. It's what I've wanted since the moment I first saw
you." He took hold of her hips and flipped her over onto her
belly, pulling her to the edge of the bed. He curled one arm
under her, lifting her hips as he followed the tight curve of her
buttocks with his other hand. She was still wet, still seething
with heat. He guided the head of his cock to where his fingers
had danced inside her, and pushed it inside.

His fingers weren't as thick as his penis, so Lucan had to
penetrate her by slow increments. He pushed into her, and then
withdrew, forcing her to take a little more of him with each
small, slow thrust.

"Oh, God." As he worked his way into her, Samantha's fists
knotted in the dark satin of his sheets.

"You can take me," he murmured, reaching under her to cup
her breasts.

She braced herself against the bed, pushing back against
him, helping him penetrate deeper inside her. He had only another inch or two and their bodies would be fully meshed.

"I'm going to taste you again." He bent, curving himself
over her until he could put his mouth to the nape of her neck.
"Here, while I take you. Do you want that?"

Samantha pulled her hair out of the way, baring the side of
her throat, the line of her shoulder to him. For a moment Lucan
stilled, wanting to preserve the image in his mind forever. Then
the aching hunger inside him swelled, and he put his teeth to her,
sliding his fangs through her skin as he buried himself in her
completely.

Her head fell back and she groaned, shaking uncontrollably
as she reached her peak, and took him to his.

Lucan drank from her throat and poured into her body, and when he could take or give no more without harming her, he wrenched his mouth away and lay down beside her.

"Don't leave me alone," Samantha murmured.

No, he wouldn't be doing that. Not for the rest of her existence.

Lucan held her to him with the hands that had been denied the simple comfort of touch for so long, stroking her with them as she drifted to sleep, and stared past her at windows Burke had replaced. It took a few minutes to realize what was wrong with them.

I trust you.

Every glass pane in the brand-new windows was covered with a spiderweb of brand-new cracks.

Chapter 18

Alexandra woke up expecting to be alone, although she didn't know why. She felt warm and contented, as if she'd been basking in the Florida sun all day. Her eyes weren't swollen shut, though, so she assumed she hadn't.

"Faryl attacked Lucan and his men," she heard Phillipe say in French outside the door. Thanks to her lousy French, she could make out only a little of the rest of what he said, but the gist of it seemed to be that Faryl had escaped into the swamp, and hunters had been sent after him. There was also something about the Brethren, but she couldn't make out that part.

"Send three of our men to aid them," Michael said. "Gard and I are going to check the churches. He thinks Faryl may try to enter one to pray."

Alex opened her eyes as Michael came into the bedroom. She rolled over to see him set a case on the table beside the bed and open it, revealing an extensive collection of daggers, through which he began to sort. "I hope you're not planning to use one of those on me."

Michael sheathed the long, wicked-looking hunting knife with a copper-coated blade and set it aside before coming to her. "Why would I wish to do that?"

She smiled up at him, lifting her face for his kiss. "I don't know. I'm usually in the doghouse for something." She stretched, and tried to draw him down on the bed beside her. "Bored with me already?"

"Never." He gave her a rueful smile. "I must leave you again, *ma belle*. Faryl was seen on Bahia Mar last night. He attacked Lucan and his men, and killed two Kyn before escaping. Gard and I are going to the swamps to aid the trackers."

That wasn't what he'd told Phillipe, but maybe he meant after he checked the churches. "Faryl got away from big, bad Lucan? So much for his rep. Did the Brethren mess it up?"

"Three attacked while Lucan was trying to subdue Faryl," Michael said.

"Bastards have the worst timing, don't they?" She yawned and sat up. "Can I come out and play, too?"

"With Faryl on the loose, and the Brethren involved, I would rather you stay here with Phillipe and the guards." He kissed the top of her head. "You do not wish me to be distracted by worrying about you, yes?"

"I do not wish, yes." She pulled on her robe. "Have fun. Don't be very late, either, or you'll have to wait until tomorrow night before I molest your body."

"I will return in fifteen minutes," he assured her. "Perhaps ten."

Alex went into the immense master bathroom and indulged herself over the next hour with a bubble bath and a pedicure. While her toenail polish dried, she experimented with new ways of doing her hair. She'd never be like Marcella Evareaux, who could tie back her raven tresses with a piece of frayed jute cord and make men swoon, but since living with Michael she'd found some magazines and tried to look a little more feminine.

It was more for Michael than anything, but she had to admit, since moving in with him, the whole hair/makeup/clothes girl thing was starting to grow on her.

Another thing that had changed: her hair. Thanks to the strange spurts caused by her mutated metabolism it was four inches longer than it had been yesterday. The occasional Rip van Winkle effect also made her fingernails grow overnight. One evening she'd woken up, tried to rub her eyes, and nearly gouged out an eyeball with the six-inch nail that had sprouted from her index finger.

She couldn't do anything with her hair this long, so she took a pair of shears from the bathroom cabinet and went to hunt Phillipe.

The seneschal was in the kitchen, his favorite room in any house, arranging flowers.

"Pretty." Alex came over to admire the large basket of colorful tropical blooms. "If we need some extra money for the *jardin,* I'm opening you a florist shop."

Phillipe added a twig of vivid red-green-and-yellow crocus leaves to one side and viewed his handiwork critically. "Tropical plants are interesting, but I prefer working with roses. They are more orderly than these wild things."

"Oh, you're always sucking up to the boss." She set the shears on the table. "Have you got time to give me a trim?"

"Of course." Phillipe retrieved a towel to drape around her shoulders, then brushed out her hair. "Four and a half inches in one day. A new record."

"Mmmmm." Alex closed her eyes and enjoyed the soothing motions of the brush through her curly hair. "Why does it always feel better when someone else brushes your hair?"

"It is one of the first things our mothers do for us," he said. "Mine always devoted a few minutes each morning and night to combing my hair."

She was charmed. "What a great mom you had."

He picked up the shears and began snipping. "In my time, it was more to remove nits and lice than for grooming."

"She must have really loved you. I'd have just dipped you in RID." Alex looked down at her fingernails. They were still the same length, but she hadn't bothered with a manicure for a while. She had been in such a rush to get down here for . . . something. She frowned. "Phillipe?"

He had the comb in his mouth. "Hmmmm?"

"Why am I here?"

His hand went still for a second before he continued cutting. "Because you wished me to trim your hair."

"Here in Florida."

"You are here to be with the master while he and Paviere hunt Faryl." He was trying too hard to sound casual. "You did not wish to be left behind, as always."

"There was another reason." She caught his hand and stopped him, turning around to face him. "And I can't remember it. Isn't that funny?"

Phillipe said nothing.

"You can't tell me because he ordered you not to." She got

to her feet. "That son of a bitch. That scheming, conniving, cold-blooded, manipulative jackass. This time, I will kill him."

"Alexandra, please."

She whipped up a hand. "No. Don't you dare tell me this time that it was because he loves me. I'm his *sygkenis*, his life partner or whatever the fuck it means. I gave him back his face, Phil. I've reassembled his friends. I stopped being human because of him. I took a goddamn copper bolt in the chest for him."

"It is because of your hard work, love, sacrifice, and devotion," Phillipe said, "that he wishes to protect you."

"Protect me how? By picking my brain apart? By deciding for me what I can or cannot handle? Nothing could be that bad." When the seneschal remained silent, she whirled. "Fine. I'm out of here."

Phillipe set down the scissors. "You cannot leave."

"Who's going to—" She turned around. "You wouldn't."

The seneschal came around the table. "He is my master."

Alex fought him for as long as her physical will remained her own, but then the room filled with the sweet scent of honeysuckle. Her mutation did not protect her from any Kyn talent, and Phillipe's was the ability to take over a human being's body and operate it by remote control.

"How long can you keep this up?" she asked as her body calmly walked back to the chair and sat down. "A few hours? Two days? A week? You have to rest sometime, you jerk."

Phillipe picked up the scissors and finished trimming her hair in silence.

Alex fought with everything she had the compulsion to remain still and acquiescent. Nothing could dent the seneschal's hold over her, though, and she was held as spellbound as the first time Phillipe had used it on her, when he had compelled her to operate on Cyprien's shattered face without any proper anesthesia.

He turned her to face him. "When the master returns, I will release you. I am sorry, Alexandra."

She was sorry, too, because she would never again trust the oversize bastard. Tears of frustration pricked her eyes, but through them she saw the door to the kitchen slowly open, and a man step inside. In his right hand was a tranquilizer gun.

"There's a man with a gun standing right behind you," she told Phillipe.

The seneschal removed the towel from her shoulders and brushed some cut hairs from her shoulders. "Distracting me will not—" He stiffened and tried to turn around. "Rafael."

"Forgive me," the other seneschal said.

Alex was released from Phillipe's compulsion as soon as he fell unconscious to the kitchen floor. She jumped out of the chair, but a blast of golden light radiated out, enveloping everything around her, until she could see nothing but the light. She still tried to run, but collided with a pair of hard hands.

"You will be blind until I release you," the man said, "but I mean you no harm, Doctor."

She struggled, but even her Kyn-augmented strength was no match for his. She couldn't pick up any murderous thoughts from him, either. "Then why are you doing this? Who are you?"

"I have my orders."

Alex felt him pick her up in his arms and carry her out of the kitchen. She screamed for the guards, and then felt something sharp and burning stab into the side of her arm. The familiar feel of her own Kyn tranquilizer flooded through her, ending her struggles, silencing her last cry.

John didn't return to Barbastro Abbey for several days. He left the abbey's station wagon parked in town where it could be easily found, but he used the cash Mercer had given him to rent a room and feed himself while he thought of what he could do. He knew he was committing the sin of stealing, but Mercer had lied to him. In his readjusted view, that made things even.

His first impulse was to move on, leave Florida and find another place for himself. That the Brethren had corrupted another good man was no business of his. The only thing that kept him from leaving was remembering how ruthlessly he had abandoned the homeless kids he had supervised at the Haven runaway shelter in Chicago, just as he had his sister and the priesthood. If he didn't stop running away every time he faced tragedy and adversity, in time he'd never find a place for himself.

He began by doing something ordinary: He called Maurice's brother, Lamar Robinson, and asked him for a job interview.

"I don't have no office, brother," the roofer told him. "But you want to meet for a meal, okay."

John took the bus to the restaurant in North Fort Lauderdale. Heaven's Kitchen had once been a gas station; the concrete pad converted to a parking lot, the food mart section serving as a diner, with kitchen in what had been a drive-through car wash. A pair of black youths stood outside the front door, but both gave him only the briefest glance as he walked in.

The months of working outdoors had darkened John's skin, just as Dougall Hurley, the bigoted shelter manager who had been killed in Chicago, had predicted it would. Apparently now he passed as a black man.

Lamar Robinson rose from the booth where he was sitting as soon as John came in and walked over to shake his hand. A tall, heavily built black man with hair gone mostly gray, he looked more like Maurice's father.

"Robinson," he said, shaking John's hand. "You hungry? Good."

They sat down and a pretty teenage waitress with braces brought John a glass of iced water and took their orders.

"You don't try the barbecue sandwich lunch platter," Robinson warned him, "you're gonna regret it the rest of your life."

John dutifully ordered the meal and a glass of iced tea to go with it.

When the waitress left them, Robinson gave him the once-over. "You got any outstanding warrants on you?"

The question almost made John choke on his water. He started to say no, and then thought of the car he had left in town, and the money he had stolen from the abbey. "Not that I'm aware of."

"Good answer." Robinson called to the waitress to bring him a cup of coffee. "Cops come looking for anybody on my crew, I hand them over. Keep my ass out the county lockup. I work a four-day week, from Jupiter to Biscayne and anywhere in between, so you'll need a car. You can't get one, let me know, I'll fix you up."

"I've been passing as Caucasian since I was a kid," John suddenly said. "I've made people think I am. I've never . . . I've not lived as what I am."

Robinson peered at him for a moment, and then he chuckled. "Boy, if I could bleach this old black hide of mine, I'd make 'em think I was a white man, too." He put his hand on the table next to John's. "Lawd, look at that. Like night and day. I know some brothers don't trust no mix-color folk like you, but I say a man's more than his skin. Most white folks not like that, though, are they?"

John shook his head.

"So tell me where you been working the last year."

Feeling curiously relieved, John recited the names and places where he had been employed; there weren't that many. When he mentioned the labor-pool job in Kentucky, Robinson nodded as if that had some weight. "I've been staying with a friend of mine, but that didn't work out."

Robinson sat back as the waitress brought their orders and placed them on the table. "You need a place? My cousin runs a pay-a-week place out on U.S. One. He'll take you on until you get your first paycheck."

John looked at the delicious food in front of him, and then at the man on the other side of the table. "You'd hire me. Just like that. No résumé, no job application, no background check?"

Robinson shrugged. "Maurice sent you to me. That makes you all right."

"But you don't know anything about me," John persisted. "I could be lying to you."

"You could." Robinson picked up his sandwich and took a bite. "I'll tell you about my little brother, Maurice. He the baby; came along when I was twelve. My daddy died, and I was married and out the house by the time he got old enough to give our mama trouble. Got into enough of that, too, and like to kill her with worry. Time I bail him out for burglary, he only sixteen. I told him, 'You get busted again, I take you out to the 'glades, leave you for the gators.'"

"That convinced him to straighten out?"

Robinson shook his head. "He did time up until he was seventeen. Then one of them gangsters he ran with got himself shot up, and my little brother saw what his future would be. It was just that one thing, but that was it. Maurice came to me after his friend's funeral and asked me for a job. I threw him out of my house. He came back the next day, and the next, till I stopped slamming the door in his face. So I put him on the crew, and I worked his skinny ass harder than anyone else. Took him a bit, but he turned out to be my best man."

John couldn't resist the tangy odor of the barbecue any longer, and took a bite. The pulled pork was as tender as butter, and the savory, smoky sweetness of the sauce made him take a second bite, and then a third.

"I told you." Robinson watched his expression with smug satisfaction. "Rest of your life."

"How did Maurice end up with the bus company?"

"He always liked to drive, Maurice did. While he was on my crew he took a course on bus driving. Quit roofing when he got a place with the county school system. Went from there to public transit, and then to the big companies. Now he drive all over the country." He took a drink from his glass. "The whole time Maurice been driving, ten years now, he give my business card to just three men. One of them married to my daughter and own a shoe shop in the mall. The other's the chief of my crew. And here you are. But you ain't looking for a job, brother."

John put down what was left of his sandwich. "I'm not."

Robinson shook his head. "You ain't no roofer, not with the way you talk, man. There's something about you, too. I'm thinking you already got yourself something lined up. You just ain't made up your mind how you gonna do it, or where."

John thought of telling this simple, decent man about the church and the Brethren. About his struggle to hold on to his faith, which had been as solid as sand, and had slipped through his fingers just as quickly. Then there was Mercer, and the monster hiding under his smiling mask. But Lamar Robinson had earned his peaceful existence, keeping the roofs over people's heads, looking out for men in trouble, and doing his small part to make the world go on.

"Everyone I've trusted has left me, lied to me, or used me," he said slowly. "I don't know who I am anymore. I don't know where I belong."

Robinson nodded. "You got to make a change, then. Way Maurice did."

John suddenly knew with a deep, unwavering conviction
that he would never possess the kind of contentment that Lamar
Robinson radiated, unless he chose, once and for all, between
the two great forces on either side of him.

They ate the rest of their lunch in a companionable silence.
When the waitress brought the check, John took out his wallet,
but Robinson shook his head.

"I'm working; you're not. 'Sides, how often a man get to
buy himself and his friend a little bit of heaven?" he asked,
winking at the waitress, who giggled.

"Mr. Robinson, the food was delicious, and I appreciate
your seeing me about the job." John stood and held out his
hand. "I'm sorry I wasted your time."

"It don't work out for you, this thing you got going, you call
me." He grinned. "I can always use another strong back to haul
shingles and slap down tar for me."

John checked the bus schedule, and determined what con-
nections he had to make to go from Heaven to hell. It was time
to make a stand against the order. As the first step toward his
personal salvation, he could do worse than saving an old friend
from them.

It took changing buses three times to get within walking distance of the abbey. He took his time, reaching the front gates just
as the sun was beginning to set. He rang the bell, and as soon as
Brother Jacob heard his voice he opened the electronic locks.

Mercer met him halfway between the gate and the cloister.
"John, I was so worried about you. Where have you been? The
police called us about the station wagon being left in town.
Were you robbed? What happened?"

John smelled the wine the abbot had been drinking coating
every word, hanging in the air between them, another silent
slap at their so-called friendship.

"We need to talk." He looked over the abbot's shoulder at
the other brothers walking toward them. "Alone."

"Of course, after vespers—"

"I know about the Brethren and the Darkyn, Mercer," John
said in a low voice. "They're the reason I left the priesthood.
We talk alone, or we talk here."

Mercer turned to address the brothers. "Brother Patrick has returned safely to us. I must speak with him about his misfortune in town. Go on to services without me."

The friars exchanged uncertain looks before obeying the abbot's orders.

Mercer had gone shock-white when he faced him. "Why didn't you tell me that you knew? Are you part of the order? How in God's name—"

"The Brethren pretended to recruit me, but they were only interested in using me to get to my sister." He gestured toward the abbot's house. "Shall we?"

Acting as if they were being pursued by demons, Mercer hurried him inside, locking the door behind them.

"I'm so relieved you know about them," the abbot said. "I hated keeping it from you all this time. But you can't talk about the order openly. They've killed everyone who has tried to expose them."

John sat down and let him babble on. He could see how Mercer's alcoholism would have given the Brethren a hold over him. The order knew how to ferret out any weakness—and exploit it—to get what they wanted.

"I came here to get away from them, John," his friend was saying. "I swear to you, I thought they'd forget about me, the way they did Bromwell. And they have, until now. We've been able to live and work as the Lord intended us to here."

"You're not a priest, Mercer."

"No, not officially," the abbot conceded. "But you can't argue with the good we've done here. We've helped this community so much. I can't tell you how many families we've brought back to God. We've all found true serenity and peace in devoting ourselves to good works."

John rubbed his eyes. "What about the breeding program? How you threatened Ignatius? Was that all part of your good works, Mercer?"

Mercer's hesitant smile disappeared. "I don't agree with everything I'm told to do, but Brethren's mission is to protect humanity. These things that they fight, they are evil incarnate. I have no choice but to follow their methods."

"Their methods. Not yours."

"I can't kill them." The abbot went to his desk and took out the wine bottle inside. "I found out that I'm a coward, John. I couldn't take it. I couldn't even stand on the sidelines and watch it. I knew what they were doing was right, and necessary to protect the real church, but it got to me. It would have destroyed me."

John watched him pour the dark liquid into a glass. "My sister is one of them now."

Wine spilled onto the desk. "What did you say?"

"The *maledicti*. The Darkyn. They infected my sister, and she changed into one of them." John stood up and crossed the room to take the bottle out of the abbot's hand. "Alexandra has become a vampire."

"Oh, John. No. Not Alex." Mercer's face screwed up, until he glanced down. "What are you doing?"

"Ruining your next binge." He picked up the glass and the bottle and carried them out to the kitchen, where he emptied them into the sink. The abbot followed but didn't attempt to stop him.

"I don't need it," Mercer said. He began making a pot of coffee. "It's the Brethren, you know. They made me like this."

"What will be your excuse next time, Mercer?"

The abbot poured measured grounds into the drip filter. "There won't be a next time." He added water to the machine and switched it on. "I promise."

"You have to get help." John slid the phone book Mercer kept on the counter toward him. "Alcoholics Anonymous could be the first step. The local chapters are listed under A."

"I can't seek outside help. The Brethren would never permit it. Even if I did, I can't change." Mercer took two cups from the cabinet. "Did they make you torment the demons? How do you live with what you've done?"

"I didn't know—I still don't know what the Darkyn are. I know what the Brethren are. I know my sister." John thought of how angry he had been with Alexandra, and how little she deserved it. "She's no demon. She may not believe in God, but she's never harmed anyone. I used to pity her because she had no faith. Now I see how she must have pitied me for mine." He looked at Mercer. "The killing has to stop. On both sides."

"Yes." Mercer filled the coffee cups and gave one to him. "I'll make my last toast, John. To life."

The coffee was hot and bitter, but John drank some to be polite.

Mercer didn't touch his, but turned his back on John and set it on the counter. He stayed that way, moving his hand to his face for a moment. "I was going to poison you just now. The order wants you dead." He turned to look at John's expression and grimaced. "I changed my mind at the last minute."

The abbot clutched his chest and fell to his knees. John grabbed him to hold him upright. "Jesus, Mercer, what have you done?"

"Lukumi poison. Looks like a heart attack or a stroke." The abbot went limp.

John eased him down on his back, and saw an empty vial fall out of his friend's hand and roll across the kitchen floor.

The abbot clutched at his arm. "Go to a nightclub on the beach. Infusion." He dragged in a labored breath. "Go down there and warn them. Bastille Day."

"I don't understand."

The fierceness emptied out of his face. "Have to bury me on consecrated ground. Fool God, the devil to pay." Mercer uttered a weak chuckle. "But my masters . . . will be so . . . disappointed." He gave the ceiling a look of mild surprise, and then his hand fell away.

John put his hand on the abbot's face, and gently closed his friend's eyes. A persistent ringing brought him to his feet, and he picked up the phone.

"Father Lane," Brother Jacob said, not waiting for John to speak, "why didn't you answer the phone? The Lightkeeper called for you from Rome."

"Brother Jacob, this is John." He tried to think of what to say, and decided to show his friend a final mercy. "The abbot has had a heart attack. Call an ambulance."

"But . . . what about Brother Rupert and the others?"

John almost swore. "What about them?"

"They never returned last night," Brother Jacob said.

Chapter 19

"Hey." Someone was shaking her. "Time to make the dough-nuts."

Sam groped for a pillow, found one, and put it over her face to block out the noise and the light. "Go away."

"I'd be happy to, Officer, but you're in my apartment."

The pillow lifted, forcing Sam's eyelids to do the same thing. An exasperated Chris was sitting on the edge of her bed. No, on Keri's bed. As the first time she'd woken up in the exact same spot, Sam couldn't remember how she'd gotten there. Now she was so thirsty she could barely speak.

She eyed the kid, who looked disgustingly cheerful. "Did I sleep with you?"

"Nope. I bunked out on the couch."

Lucan.

"I was at the nightclub." Sam sat up carefully. "How did I get here?"

"A nice man with a bad head cold carried you up the stairs. He said that you'd gotten hit on the head. You also had a lot of bumps and bruises, and you were really out of it, so I told him to bring you in here. I woke you up a couple of times to make sure you weren't lapsing into a coma or anything." Chris handed her a cup of coffee. "I borrowed the stuff to make this from your place. I can't afford coffee yet."

"I'll buy you twenty pounds." Sam attacked the cup, drink-ing it down in a couple of swallows and scalding her tongue in the process. "Is there more?" When Chris nodded, she handed her the empty cup and tried not to whimper. "Please?"

Chris disappeared to get more coffee, and Sam crawled out

of bed and went into Keri's bathroom. She ignored the hollow-eyed, banged-up woman in the mirror and sat down to pee for what felt like an hour. An image of her own sweat-slick hands gripping satin flickered through her head, and the tenderness between her legs and throbbing in her breasts backed it up.

I had sex with Lucan.

At some point last night she'd gotten completely soaked; her bra and panties were still damp. There were tiny cuts on her hands, probably from the flying glass, and dried blood. One hell of a knot under her hair, where one of the nutcases in the brown bathrobes had smacked her with the halberd's shaft. It was looking at the little nick on her right index finger that filled in the rest of the blanks.

Lucan has fangs. He's a vampire. She searched under her hair until she felt the two small puncture wounds on the side of her neck. *I let him bite me.*

"What did you do on your vacation, Sam?" she asked her toes, and then answered for them. "Oh, chased a snake-man, slugged it out with ax killers, and had mind-blowing sex with a thirsty vampire. Nothing special."

Lightning didn't shoot through the window to reduce her to ashes. The world didn't stop spinning. She didn't feel shame, or remorse, or even mild annoyance with herself. She wanted to go back. She wanted more.

Right after she chewed off Lucan's ear for letting her wake up alone in the strange bed.

Thirst and what felt like an oncoming fever made her strip and climb into the shower, where she turned on the cold spray and drank directly from it. She was so dry she thought she might start to swell up like a water balloon. It was the blood loss. If they were going somewhere with this . . . *relationship?* . . . his diet was probably going to be an issue.

We are very hungry, very sensory creatures, and you . . . you are a movable feast.

There was a strange logic to it, too. Lucan was a vampire who could kill with his hands; Sam could read the blood of murder victims with her hand. It couldn't be a coincidence.

It had been just as stupid for her to have sex with a material witness and potential suspect in two murder cases as it had been

for him to jump in the sack with her, the cop investigating his
ex-lover's murder. But the fight with the snake-man and the
three bozos with the axes had torn down a lot of barriers between them. Making him take off his gloves to touch her . . .
The warm water poured over her as she closed her eyes to
remember.

Lucan's hands looked perfectly normal. It was when he
started caressing her face with them that she realized the difference. Something happened every time his fingers and palms
touched her; they created a strange, low hum beneath her skin.
It had felt almost like being stroked by the velvet gloves, except
the velvet had been charged with heat and some kind of weird
energy. Then the hum had deepened, sinking into her, so that
every touch on the outside echoed inside, flowing through her
like silent music.

Sam didn't feel a scrap of shame about how she had offered
herself to him. She couldn't help herself; she'd so badly wanted
to feel that mysterious sensation on her breasts, and when she
saw his reaction to touching her face she'd pulled off her T-
shirt. As long as she stayed in control, she thought she could
handle whatever he did to her.

Then he took over, and control ran shrieking out the door.

The things he'd done to her . . . taking her with those long,
lethal fingers of his, putting them so deep inside her she'd
thought she'd shake apart. When he added the refined torment
of his mouth the hum had become a soft, insistent roar. She'd
come all over him. As she tried to catch her breath, he'd
dragged her half off the bed and demonstrated that his hands
weren't his only instrument of torment.

Sam reached down and touched the lingering soreness between her legs. They'd been like a couple of teenagers; he'd
barely gotten into her all the way before they'd both gone over.
Lucky for her, because much more of that would have reduced
her to a mindless, babbling love groupie.

You can take me.

Could she?

Sam turned off the shower, took a towel from the rack outside the curtain, and dried off. She wrapped the damp towel
around her and stepped out, but had to whirl and drop down in

front of the toilet as her stomach heaved and she brought up all the coffee and water she'd chugged.

"You guys must have partied hard." Chris was there, pulling her wet hair back and supporting her with an arm. It was so like what Garcia had done the day of Harry's funeral that Sam puked up the rest of what was left in her belly. "I got you. Bombs away."

When she finally sat back on her haunches, Chris handed her a washcloth to wipe her face.

The damp cloth felt good and cold against her burning face. "I need some clothes."

"On the bed," her neighbor replied. "I've never seen anyone with so many plain T-shirts and ugly suits, and that's all you have. You should splurge one time; get a striped skirt or a pair of tie-dyed shorts."

Sam trudged back into the bedroom and dressed. Chris stayed in the bathroom, evidently to preserve her modesty.

"I'm decent," she called out, wincing at the sound of her own voice as she pulled on her jacket.

Chris emerged. "Mrs. Quinn called while I was over raiding your closet. I told her you had the flu. Sounded better than a hangover."

"I don't have a hangover." What she had was a vampire for a lover, and a snake-man wreaking havoc through the streets of Fort Lauderdale. "I'm sorry Burke dumped me on you." She looked at the cup of coffee Chris held out to her. "No, I'd better not; my stomach's still a mess. Thanks for helping out."

"Next time I get wasted," Chris advised her, "I expect you be there to help *me* worship the porcelain goddess."

"I'm there." Sam had to get to a phone, find some aspirin, and decide how she felt about her new lover drinking her blood, but Chris was giving her an odd look. "What's wrong?"

"You and that tall, gorgeous guy, Lucan? You got together last night, right?" Chris grimaced. "I know, none of my business, but . . . did he get you drunk?"

"Sort of. What about it?"

"He didn't, like, force you or date-rape you, did he?" Before Sam could answer, she added, "Guys at bars can drop shit like roofies into your drink that make you go a little wild. But he can't do that and get away with it. You can't let him."

Considering the actual events of the night, Sam almost laughed, but Chris's concern and anger were genuine, and it touched her more than anything else the kid had done. "I was willing."

"But Keri said . . ." The younger girl looked ready to squirm now. "I know you're a dyke, Sam. I mean, it's cool with me that you are. You don't have to pretend. I don't think any less of you. I might freak out if you make a pass at me, but it's okay."

Other women at the department had made variations on Chris's speech, and Sam had ignored them. Most people took interest in someone's personal problems only so they could feel better about their own. But the kid had looked out for her, and she'd earned the right to hear the truth.

"I'm going to tell you this once and then we're going to drop it, okay?" When Chris nodded, Sam said, "I got drunk one night and ended up in bed with Keri. But as gorgeous and sexy as she is, I found out that being with her didn't do a damn thing for me." She pushed the damp hair back from her face. "It wasn't fair to pretend I did, either, so I broke it off with her right away."

Chris frowned. "The way she tells it, she makes it sound like you chickened out and went into denial. That as a cop you couldn't face coming out."

Was that how Keri thought about it? No wonder she'd been so pissy.

"I was never *in*, Chris. Maybe Keri thought I was, or she wanted me to be, but I'm not a lesbian." She rubbed her face. "I made a big mistake, and I've tried to apologize to her a million times. But she didn't do me any favors, either."

"She told me she went down to the police department and had it out with you in front of the other cops."

Sam tried hard not to remember the ugly scene. "She had a tantrum; I just tried to calm her down. Things got pretty loud. The fallout was that it affected a sexual-harassment complaint I had filed against another officer. He got away with what he did to me because that scene with Keri had everyone on the force thinking I was a gay woman with an ax to grind. A couple of weeks later, that same asshole nearly had me killed."

"God. That sucks."

Sam nodded. "I know. I screwed up that night with Keri, but I think I've paid for it." She looked around until she spotted her keys, and picked them up. "I hate to puke and run, but I've got a million things to do. What kind of coffee do you drink?"

"Colombian Supreme," Chris said instantly. "Some glazed doughnuts would also be excellent. You know, to dunk."

Sam grinned. "You got it, kid."

Her first call when she got back to her own apartment was to Gloria Quinn, to apologize for running out on her. Harry's widow felt well enough to politely rip her head off about it, and then surprised Sam with the news that she had decided to go on the cruise she had planned for Harry's retirement.

"It's that or sit here with two patrolmen babysitting me until Harry's killer is caught," Gloria explained. "One of my friends from church lost her husband last year, so I invited her to go with me. What I want to know is that you're okay before I go."

"I'm okay."

"I mean it, Samantha." Gloria's tone was firm. "If you want me to stay, you could move in here for a few weeks. I'd love to have you, and the department might even consider that adequate protection for me."

"I know I was out of it, but I'm a lot better now." Not counting the head injury, the low-grade fever, or the fact that she'd fucked a vampire. "I think it's terrific that you're going on the cruise, and I know Harry would, too. Don't worry about me; I've got plenty to do here."

"You be careful. I know you're a cop, but you're on your own now."

She thought of Lucan, and some of her bones melted. She wasn't alone; that was the difference. She had him, and he would protect her. "I will."

Her next call was to Infusion, and was answered by Lucan's assistant, Burke.

"Mr. Burke, I understand you brought me home last night," Sam said.

"Yes, Detective Brown. Excuse me." The sound of a muffled sneeze came over the line. "The master thought it was best that you be returned to your home."

"Your master has never woken up alone in a strange bed."

And she'd give him some grief about it. Nerves made her wander over to the window and open the blinds. "Does he sleep all day, or can I speak with him?"

"Master Lucan is not available."

So he slept all day. Sam looked down at the parking lot to see if Burke had left her car in front of her building, which he had. Next to it someone had parked an unfamiliar blue sedan backward so that the windshield faced her building. She could see a man sitting behind the wheel and pointing a telephoto lens at the window of her apartment. "Can I leave him a message?"

"No, madam," Burke said. "The master does not wish to speak to you, and I have been instructed to inform you that you are no longer welcome here."

Sam thought she heard him wrong. "Could you repeat that, please?"

"The master regrets that you were caught up in Kyn business," Burke said, as if reading it from notes. "He is grateful for the assistance you provided, but no longer wishes your involvement. He wishes you good health and happiness."

I hope one day someone gives you what you really need, Samantha, and takes it away from you the minute you start enjoying it.

Keri wasn't getting her wish. "Put Master Lucan on the damn phone."

Burke smothered a cough. "I cannot, Detective. He does not wish to speak to you."

"What if I come down there and drag his ass out of his coffin?" Sam suggested. "Will he speak to me then?"

"The master does not sleep in a coffin," Burke told her. "If you come here, you will not be admitted to the premises."

Sam couldn't believe it. He was ditching her like a one-night stand? After everything they'd been through together? "Your master is still a suspect in two murders that I'm investigating."

"You are not on active duty, Detective, and those cases have been reassigned." Burke's voice went low and cautious. "The situation has become too dangerous for human involvement. It would be best for you if you forgot what happened last night."

"What situation?" Sam demanded. "Burke, what is going on?"

"I have no further information for you, madam. Good day."
Burke hung up.

Sam stared at the phone, and then back at the man taking
pictures of her. He had put down the camera and was pulling
out of the parking space, and as he turned to leave the complex,
she got a clear look at the side of his face. It seemed that Wesley Dwyer was stalking her again.

Cake, she thought dully. *Iced.*

Lucan walked into his office and overheard the last of what
Burke said before he hung up the phone. "For whom do you
have no further information?"

His *tresora* looked up at him. "That was Detective Brown,
master."

He had showered twice to remove every trace of Samantha's
scent from his skin, and yet hearing her name filled his head
with her dark perfume again. After she had fallen asleep in his
arms, he had summoned Burke to take her home. She had been
so exhausted that she had not woken when he had put her in his
tresora's arms.

"She is well?" he tried to ask casually, thinking of the windows.

"She seems fully recovered. I related your instructions and
wishes to her." For the first time since coming to serve him,
Burke didn't sound particularly afraid of him. "She was upset."

Samantha had given herself to him, and he had rejected her
as harshly as he could. She had the right to be upset. "There is
a change to the program for tomorrow night's concert. The performance artist will not be torturing herself for our patrons. Call
Alisa and tell her I require her services for the show."

"Will she be replacing the artist, master?"

"No. Alexandra Keller will."

Lucan went out to the empty bar and sat down in front of the
small stage upon which the club's Friday- and Saturday-night
bands played. It was hardly large enough for his purposes—
Carnegie Hall would be more fitting—but he would make do.
He had only to create an illusion for his guests, one that would
provoke the necessary response.

As he had with Samantha. As he had with Frances.

Lucan had left Frances in Rome with her dying lover, and

gone back to his duties to Richard, and pretended to forget about her for the next forty years. For his own amusement—or so he told himself—he had her kept under close watch. She had never remarried or taken a lover, but devoted herself to raising her child. Toward the end of her life, when her son had left England to seek his fortune in America, she sold most of her belongings and retired alone to a tiny country cottage, where she grew flowers and walked the moors alone.

Business for Richard brought him to that part of the world once, and Lucan had made the mistake of going to see her.

She had recognized him as soon as she unlatched the door. "My lord darkness." She did not seem at all surprised to see him. Instead of inviting him in, she stepped outside. "Let us take a turn through my gardens."

Frances had always been able to coax the most amazing things from the dark earth, but as he strolled with her down the narrow aisles of grass between her flower beds, he looked down at her. She had aged, her hair silver and wrinkles marring the fine skin around her eyes, but she was still as slender and straight as the fierce young woman he had left with her dying lover in Rome.

"Why have you never come for me?" she asked. "I expected you to. I would not have resisted long, I think."

Lucan had a thousand scalding retorts prepared. He heard himself tell her the truth instead. "The boy. He deserved a mother to care for him."

She paused and looked up at him. "As yours never cared for you."

"Yes."

Frances nodded. "I will thank you for my son, then, sir."

He forced himself to apologize for the one wrong that still haunted him. "I regret that I left you in Rome. You should not have had to watch him die alone. I should have arranged a companion for you."

"It happened a few days after you left, while I was out at market buying more candles. By the time I returned, they had already removed his body." She walked a little farther, then slowed and sighed. "You do well to avoid old age. My rheumatism keeps me on a short leash."

Lucan had escorted her back to her cottage, but refused her invitation to tea. "I must go. Is there anything you need? Funds, a housemaid, better lodgings? You have only to say." He looked around the tiny house with disdain. "I would be delighted to arrange it for you."

Frances smiled and shook her head. "Your last gift to me was all that I could ever wish."

"My last gift?"

"You let me go, my lord." She folded her hands in front of her like a young girl. "My life may not seem grand to you, but it has been a good one. I have been happy. I have been loved. I have watched my son grow to be a fine man. And soon I will be with his father again."

"I could have given you so much more, if only you had come with me," he heard himself say. He reached out to touch her cheek with his gloved hand. "You are the only woman I have ever loved, Frances."

"I know. That is why your gift was so precious to me. Good-bye, my lord." Gently she closed the door in his face.

Lucan had stood there, one hand against the wooden barrier that separated him from Frances, for what seemed like forever. She never came to the window to look out. She never opened the door again.

The next day, after he had executed an inquisitor responsible for the deaths of five Kyn in Canterbury, he received word that Frances had hanged herself in her pretty little cottage the same night he had gone to see her. He waited until she had been buried before he sought out her grave. He placed a single white lily atop it, along with what was left of his heart, and walked away from her for the last time.

The sound of Rafael's voice interrupted his reverie, and he looked over to see that his seneschal and a small group of humans had gathered at the front of the club.

Rafael was issuing orders to the guards to station themselves at various points around the building and the entire block. When the men dispersed, Lucan called him over.

Rafael came to him. "My lord."

"I assume you were successful."

"We were, my lord. I took the liberty of installing Dr. Keller in the safe room." He set down the case he was carrying and checked his watch. "The last dose of sedative I gave her should be wearing off now. Should I use more to keep her unconscious?"

"I will wake our Sleeping Beauty." Lucan turned on his heel. "Arrange a Kyn nurse for our guest. She will need to be fed by IV."

"She will be more compliant if you starve her."

Lucan glanced back and saw the contempt on his seneschal's face. "If you wish to be released from my service, Rafael, you have but to say, and I will set you free. You have made your place among humans. I would not deprive you of the joys of serving them."

"My place is at your side. My duty is to advise you." He removed one of the copper daggers he carried and placed it on a table. "She is blameless in this thing between you and Cyprien. If you mean to kill her, do not cause her to suffer first. Give her the dignity of a clean and merciful death. You can say whatever you wish to him; he will never know how she died."

"She carves the very heart from your chest with those eyes, doesn't she?" Lucan smiled as his seneschal flinched. "Don't be offended. I nearly stole her from him in New Orleans, just so I could keep her for myself and wallow in her light. Get the nurse."

He went up to the floor below his suites, where the offices had been renovated to serve various functions. Rafael had placed Alexandra Keller in the safe room, a suite that had been reinforced to contain the most unwilling of guests.

Lucan checked the room's security monitor and saw Cyprien's *sygkenis* on the wide, comfortable bed before he released Kyn-proof bolts on the outer door. Inside, her lavender scent perfumed the cool air, drawing him into the master bedroom to look down at her unconscious form. She wore a short negligee and a diaphanous robe in a shade of peach that complemented the sun-kissed golden bloom of her flawless skin. Rafael had taken the additional precaution of chaining her to the bed with copper, he noted, but had protected her wrists and ankles by lining the manacles with flannel padding.

"Sleeping Beauty, indeed," he murmured, using his finger to dislodge a curl of hair that had tangled with her long dark eyelashes. Fangs flashed, and Lucan barely had time to pull his hand away before Alexandra sank her sharp teeth into them. "Good morning, Doctor. I trust you slept well?"

"Bite my ass."

"I should be happy to." Ah, she was beautiful when she snarled. "Roll over."

Chains rattled as she strained against her bonds. "Let me out of these fucking things."

"I would like nothing better," he assured her, "but I must insist you stay as you are for the time being."

She stopped jerking on the chains and glared up at him. "This has got to be the stupidest thing you've ever done."

He thought of Samantha, naked and willing under his bare hands, and his smile faded. "Not quite."

"Cyprien will be back by now. Your walking lightbulb didn't kill everyone. Phillipe saw him, and will tell Michael what happened, and he'll come for me. He'll bring the whole freaking vampire army with him, too. But that's what you want." She peered at him. "Can't you guys just kiss and make up?"

"Your master has taken everything from me that I ever wanted." He sat down on the side of the bed, keeping just out of her reach. "Now he will experience firsthand what that feels like."

"Another vampire pissing contest. Marvelous." She looked at the copper bars on the window. "So he comes here and you two battle it out until someone dies. Is that the plan?"

He ran his glove along her bare leg. She had very shapely legs, and arched, dainty feet. "You could choose to stay with me of your own volition."

"Oh, yeah, I'm going to do that." She laughed.

"Sacrificing yourself for the one you love is such a noble thing." He traced the spaces between her toes, admiring her pink-polished toenails. "I wouldn't kill him if you became my woman."

She jerked her leg away as far as the chains would allow. "Now? You're dreaming."

"I'm not the monster you think I am, Alexandra." Here was a solution to both of his problems. He could rid himself of his inconvenient longing for Samantha and strike a crippling blow to Cyprien at the same time. "Think of all the lives you would save."

"I'd rather screw a snake, thanks." She bit her lip as he climbed over her and settled himself on top of her. "Lucan, wait. *Wait.*"

"I have, my dear. Two hundred years and better."

Alexandra was smaller than Samantha, more delicately made. Her scent was softer, rather sweeter than he had expected, but it suited her. He could see why Cyprien had taken so many risks to take and keep her. She was the kind of woman a man would gladly gamble his life to have and to hold. In fact, he was counting on it.

"Don't do this," she said, turning her face away from his when he came closer. "You can't ever take it back."

"I should hope not." He pinned her manacled wrists on either side of her head, and bent to put his mouth to her throat.

Chapter 20

Richard Tremayne, high lord of the Darkyn, walked through the empty private airport terminal and out to the waiting car. He was well aware that this was likely to be his last journey away from Ireland, so he took his time, enjoying the warmth of the tropical night air, and the sight of palm trees silhouetted against the moonlight sky.

Paradise.

This trip had cost him dearly—buying out every chartered flight scheduled to land at the small commercial airport within two hours of the arrival of his private jet had been only one of many expenditures involved—but he allowed himself so few amusements that he did not count the expense. He had been working diligently to orchestrate certain matters so that his two prodigal sons would be properly positioned and motivated to engage in their final battle. That they had anticipated him was simply the universe agreeing with his logic. Whoever prevailed would be worthy to lead the Kyn, and Richard would at long last be shed of the last of his responsibilities.

Only the strong survive.

The driver took him to the private oceanfront estate owned by an international rock star presently on tour in Europe. To Richard's eyes, which had admired centuries of some of the world's greatest architecture, the sprawling contemporary villa had as much aesthetic appeal as a refugee camp. His choice of lodgings was unhappily limited to that which provided adequate security, and the only other privately owned domicile that met those standards and was available for short-term lease was located one hundred miles to the north.

His *tresora*, Éliane Selvais, waited patiently at the top of the winding drive. She dismissed the driver and escorted Richard into the house. "Your trip was uneventful, my lord?"

"As ever." He viewed with distaste the cacophony of modern furnishings that crowded each room. "Is there somewhere we can sit that does not celebrate the triumph of idiots over art?"

Éliane opened the doors to a small library. Although most of the books were devoted to modern music, something Richard often compared to recorded bouts of public flatulence, the furnishings were more traditional leather and wood, and did not attempt to illustrate the entire spectrum of the rainbow.

His *tresora* first brought him a glass of bloodwine, then sat with her legs crossed at the ankle with a notepad waiting in hand. Éliane's cold, pale blond beauty infuriated Richard's wife, Elizabeth, whose carefully cultivated facade of gold seemed brassy in comparison. It had nothing to do with Richard's relationship with his *tresora*, naturally. Elizabeth's real hatred came from being made to remain in Ireland while Éliane was permitted to travel with Richard all over the world. Still, aside from a few petty indignities she occasionally inflicted on his patient *tresora*, Elizabeth did not protest her usurper. She had not tolerated Richard all these years only to relinquish her portion of his kingdom to avenge herself on a pretty human servant.

Richard did not remove his mask. To drink the wine and look upon Éliane without impediment was tempting, but his beast had been caged inside an airplane for twelve hours. "Tell me what has happened since I left Dundellan Castle."

His *tresora* consulted her notes. "Faryl Paviere attacked Lucan last night near his nightclub. Both were wounded slightly, and two Kyn guards were killed, but Faryl managed to escape by water. The seigneur is searching the swamps with Gard Paviere and has yet to return. He does not yet know that Lucan's seneschal abducted Dr. Keller."

Richard nodded. "Where is Dr. Keller?"

"She is being held captive inside Lucan's household. The last report indicates she is still alive." Éliane looked up at his empty glass. "Do you wish to feed, my lord?"

"Not now." He would have to temper his hunger before he

indulged it; feeding had become, like almost everything else, a dangerous business for him of late. "Lucan will not kill the doctor unless it serves his purpose. Michael presents the immediate problem."

His *tresora*'s nose wrinkled. "She is his *sygkenis*. He will never forgive the suzerain for taking her."

"Which is precisely why Lucan took her." Richard felt the itch of desire, always stirred by bloodwine, and beckoned to Éliane. She set aside her notepad and came to stand before him. "We must prevent my children from slaughtering everyone around them as they settle this thing." He watched her strip down to her skin, appreciating the perfection of her body and her self-discipline. "On your back, if you please."

Éliane stretched out on the settee opposite Richard, making herself comfortable. "You would risk making another public appearance?"

"At the very least I will be present to monitor the engagement. I will see that the battle is fought fairly." He rose and walked over to her, opening the front of his trousers before he knelt between her legs. The changes his condition had wrought had left nothing untouched, not even the cock in his fist. His *tresora* kept her eyes averted as he pressed it into her. Only when he had worked himself deeply inside her did he say, "Now, Éliane."

His words broke her composure as swiftly and completely as one of Lucan's rages shattered crystal. Éliane kept her eyes closed as she moaned and shuddered, twisting under him as he held her slender body in place and took her with slow, deliberate strokes.

He allowed himself to swell inside her, but kept his other hungers locked inside the iron cage of his will. To do otherwise would deprive him of a very valuable servant and personal outlet, and Éliane of her life.

His *tresora* knew exactly how much she was permitted to respond to his fucking. She did not climax until after he had jetted inside her and withdrew, and even then she did so in silence. Later, he knew, she would retire and manipulate herself to another, more satisfactory orgasm. He sometimes watched her through the cameras he had installed in her rooms at Dundellan.

He never begrudged her those solitary pleasures, for when she reached her peak, it was still his name that she cried out.

"Thank you, my lord." She went to retrieve her clothing, and hesitated. "What should I do about replacing the servants at the castle?"

"The servants?"

She did not look at him. "The ones you dispatched before we left Ireland."

Such domestic matters bored him. "Hire replacements, of course."

"Yes, my lord." She began to dress as quietly as she had come for him.

Richard fastened his trousers and drank the rest of his wine as he watched her neat, economical movements. He could not play voyeur with her until they returned to Ireland, nor could he hunt in unfamiliar territory, so he would work. "Contact Jaus in Chicago. I would have news of what is happening there with the good brothers."

"Yes, my lord." His *tresora* went to the phone and dialed a number.

Richard looked at the wineglass in his hand. Another man would see it as a thing of fragile beauty, to be admired for its form even when empty. The high lord of the Darkyn saw a vessel, pleasing to the eye but essentially useless until it was filled. Rather like a woman.

Éliane brought him the telephone. As he spoke to Valentin Jaus, Richard did not see his *tresora* slip from the room. He never knew how she closed the door to lean back against it, or saw the thin, trembling hand that she pressed over her eyes, or the tears that rolled down her cheeks as she wept in silence.

Sam had no doubt in her mind that Lucan could successfully keep her out of the nightclub—and his life—for the rest of hers. That wasn't going to stop her from investigating Harry's murder, or having her say. If what had happened between them was so meaningless, he could tell her that. Personally.

She wouldn't throw a fit the way Keri had. She could be civilized and reasonable. All Lucan had to do was say, "No, thanks," to her face, and they could go back to being cop and suspect.

Lucan owed her that much.

"Getting to you won't be easy," Sam muttered to herself as she switched on her laptop, "but I will. I might be only human, with no superpowers, and I need a gun to kill someone, but I'm still a cop—and you're not."

Sam logged into the department's database system from home using her remote-access password, and pulled up the blueprints for Lucan's property. Under the new terrorist laws, the department had scanned all of the blueprints for every building in the city, and kept them updated. Sam had done rotations through SWAT and burglary, so she knew how to locate entry points that weren't readily apparent to civilians.

According to the diagram, Lucan's building had two fire escapes, but they weren't accessible from ground level until they were lowered from an upper floor. However, there was a chiller room with an outer door at the back of the club that connected to the emergency stairwell through two walk-through passages.

That was her way in.

She dressed in her darkest clothes, using her gun belt instead of her shoulder holster to give her more unrestricted movement. After she slipped a jimmy and her set of lock picks into her back pocket, she grabbed her keys and headed downstairs.

As she drove to the beach, Sam went over in her head every moment she had spent with Lucan. She knew she was doing the typical woman thing—trying to figure out what she'd done wrong—but it also helped her get a handle on her own feelings.

Granted, they hadn't had that much time together, but what they'd shared had been explosive. Lucan had come on to her in his office that first night, and again when she'd returned for a second visit. She felt sure the attraction between them had been real on both sides. Lucan might be the type to jump into bed with any woman, but when she'd given him the green light, he'd been more concerned with protecting her. A man who wanted only to screw a woman didn't worry about her personal safety.

Now this stunning, absolute rejection.

It just didn't make sense. Something else had been added to the mix. Something she wasn't involved in.

What had Burke said? *The situation has become too dangerous for human involvement.*

That had to be it—but what situation, and what had made it so dangerous?

Sam parked down the street from Infusion. There was the usual crowd waiting to get in, and a couple of Lucan's guards posted at five-yard intervals all around the front of the building, but the alley road behind the block appeared to be empty. She walked down one block and approached the building on foot from the alley side.

The locks on the outer door to the equipment room yielded to the jimmy—for all Lucan's security, no one had bothered installing dead bolts—and Sam slipped inside. One of the big chillers that cooled the building cycled on as she passed it, the motor whining a little as it came up to speed, but no one appeared to order her out of the building. She followed the walk-throughs to the stairwell access door, which had been left unlocked. There Sam paused, listening, but all she could hear was the air-conditioning equipment running.

It didn't reassure her. *This is too easy.*

She took out her weapon as she climbed the dimly lit stairs. It took a few minutes to walk all the way up to the pent-house level, but once there she opened the access door an inch and put her ear to the gap. She heard only silence, and saw an empty hall through the small square window in the door, so she stepped inside.

The lingering scent of jasmine followed her around the suite, but a quick search revealed that it, too, was empty. She could hear the sound of music from the nightclub six floors below, and when she checked the elevator she saw it was also down on the first level. She'd have to wait here for him to come to her.

A thumping sound under her feet made her jump. She crouched down, listening, and heard it again. It wasn't mechanical; it sounded like someone kicking something. She went over to the air-conditioning duct and put her ear to the vent, and heard it again, this time accompanied by the sound of an angry, muffled voice.

Someone was one floor down. Someone who didn't want to be.

Sam went back to the stairwell and descended one floor. Here the access door had been locked, and took a little more finesse to open. She then walked down the hall, listening at each closed door for the thumps. The only odd thing was the locks on the doors, which looked as if they'd been made of spiky copper. A series of muffled yelps coming from behind the last door made Sam pull out her picks and go to work on the lock.

After ten minutes of messing with the tumblers, Sam got the lock open and walked inside. The room behind the door was a formal guest room, done in walnut wood, cream and hunter green. There was no one watching the big-screen plasma TV on the wall, so she wandered into the adjoining bedroom.

On top of a messed-up bed, someone had left a half-naked woman gagged and chained to the wall. For a second Sam thought she was dead, until her brown eyes opened and she gave a muffled shriek.

"Don't scream." She hurried over and untied the silk scarf covering her mouth. "I'm a cop. I'll get you out of here." Sam picked up one of her wrists to have a look at the manacle around it. "What's your name?"

"Alex Keller." The brunette turned her head to look at the window. "Were there a bunch of big guys with swords down-stairs yelling at each other in French or Latin?"

"Can't say," Sam admitted. "I came in through the back." The locks on the manacles weren't like anything she'd ever seen. "How the hell do I get you out of these?"

"You don't," Alex told her. "They don't open without the electronic key. There's no time for that anyway. I need you to stop a war."

"I'm a cop, lady, not the U.N." Sam smelled lavender, felt a pleasant tug inside her chest, and stared down at Alex. "You're like Lucan is. You're a vampire."

"Don't hold it against me; it wasn't my idea. How much do you know about Lucan and the Kyn?"

Not enough, apparently. "Everything," Sam lied.

"Good." Alex pushed herself up as far as she could. "Lucan is trying to bait my lover, Michael Cyprien, into storming the castle here. You've got to get to Michael before he does and tell him I'm all right, or a lot of men are going to die."

"Maybe I should find Lucan and you two can talk this out," Sam suggested.

"I tried that, but the dumb blond asshole won't listen to me," Alex told her. "I guess it's easier to kill people. Assassin mentality."

"He's not an assassin." Sam took a step back from the bed. "He's a nightclub owner."

The other woman peered at her as if she'd lost her mind. "I thought you knew . . . Oh, shit." She strained against the copper manacles. "Why does it always have to be me? Am I a surgeon, or a fucking shrink?" She fixed her gaze on Sam. "Listen, these guys have a king named Richard. Lucan was Richard's hit man. Then he got tired of it or whatever and came here to America to start his own *jardin*. But he's really only interested in settling a score with Michael. Are you following me?"

Lucan was a hit man. Richard's hit man. Whoever Richard was. Something inside Sam was tearing itself apart. "How many people has Lucan killed?"

"That's not important now, sweetie. The point is to keep him from—"

"How many?" she shouted.

Alex's expression changed from urgent to sympathetic. "I don't know. No one talks about him, and they never let me get near him long enough to get his story. I can tell you what they've told me. When there was a problem with the Kyn or the Brethren, Richard sent Lucan to take care of it, and he did. Everyone he touches with those hands dies. He's the best."

The best. The best killer. The best assassin.

Sam felt muddled, as if someone had drugged her. "The Brethren?"

"They would be the fanatic humans who pose as priests and are trying to wipe us out," Alex said slowly, watching her. "More shit he didn't tell you, right? It's all tied up with religion and history and the Crusades and God knows what else." Alex sighed. "Jesus, even hearing myself say it, it sounds like bullshit."

Sam came back to the bed. "Lucan said you don't kill human beings. Was he lying to me?"

"The Kyn have gotten the whole blood-dependency thing down to an art, and he's right: We don't kill people," Alex assured her. "Unless they're insane, changing into an animal, or in cahoots with the Brethren."

Like that made it better. "Is he going to change into a snake?" Sam asked, thinking of the thing that they'd battled on the street.

"He doesn't need to; he's . . ." She grimaced. "You've got feelings for him, obviously, and I'm sorry. I know what it's like to love one of these guys and face what they are. But I can't let Lucan kill Michael. I need you to stop him."

"She doesn't have any copper weapons, Alexandra," Lucan said from behind Sam. "No tranquilizer darts, no holy water to throw in my face." He caught Sam before she got to him and held her by the wrists. His expression as he looked down at her was merciless. "She's only a human. She can't stop anything."

"You son of a bitch," Sam whispered.

He smiled. "Exactly."

Sam didn't let him drag her out of the room without a fight. Dimly she could hear Alex in the background, yelling at Lucan to let her go, but she had to focus on trying to hurt him. He ignored her kicking feet until they were out in the hallway, where he snatched her up and flung her over his shoulder.

Sam kept fighting all the way down the stairs and through the walk-through. She almost managed to wriggle free in the maintenance room, but he clamped an arm over her legs and used his shoulder to open the access door. Someone had moved her car; it stood just outside.

He put her down on her feet and opened the driver's-side door. "Get in."

"Go fuck yourself," she replied.

He picked her up and tossed her into the car like a rag doll, sliding in behind her.

"Sit down." He turned the key in the ignition.

"What are you doing?"

"I'm taking you home," he said as he jerked her seat belt over her and started the engine.

"No, you're not." She grabbed the door handle, and then found herself pinned under his arm. She punched him in the face, cutting her knuckles on his teeth.

"If you try that again," he told her pleasantly as blood dripped from his mouth, "I will hit you back."

He would, too; she could see it in his eyes. "Do you like

kidnapping women? When are you going to drown Alex? Am I next on the list?"

"I'm not going to kill Alex, and I didn't kill Lena. You, I am seriously considering. Shut up and hold on." He gunned the engine, making the tires squeal as they shot out of the alley.

He drove too fast, dodging slower cars and running red lights without hesitation. Any other night they'd have attracted the attention of a dozen cops, Sam thought, but as luck would have it, they didn't pass a single squad car on the way to her apartment.

Not that a cop would have stopped him. Humans meant no more to him than a cup of coffee did to her. The scent of jasmine grew thick, and Sam opened her window a crack to let in some fresh air. How could she have thought they might have a chance at some kind of relationship? He was an excellent actor; that was how. He'd made her think they would burn each other alive, when in reality that sex with her had probably been as exciting for him as boinking a cheeseburger.

As soon as Lucan pulled into the parking lot Sam went for her seat belt release, but his hand shot out and seized her wrist. "A gentleman always sees a lady to her door." He opened his door, released her clip, and pulled her across the seat after him.

"You're an assassin, not a gentleman," she snarled.

"Then it's a good thing that you're no lady." He took her arm, and when she tried to jerk it away, added, "We can walk up to your apartment calmly and quietly, and not draw the attention of any other humans, or you can create a scene and I will have a snack before I go home." He flashed his fangs before he picked up her scarred hand and pressed his bloodied mouth to it. "Your choice, dearest."

"How about I shoot you in the face?" she asked, drawing her weapon with her free hand. "That work for you?"

"If it makes you feel better, by all means, do." He seized the gun and shoved the muzzle under his chin. "If you can manage to sever my spine, you'll kill me. Miss it and you'll just make an ugly hole, but you're a fair shot, aren't you?"

Sam tried to pull the gun back but he wouldn't let her. Her scar burned under the blood on her hand, and jasmine and images began flooding her head. At first she thought it was something he was doing to her, because her thing only worked with dead people.

Until now.

Sam saw what was like a fast-motion silent movie running backward in her head. Lucan coming to Florida. Hunting in New Orleans. Crossing the Atlantic. Facing Richard for the last time. Carrying the wounded from their cells. Killing the sadistic inquisitors who had tortured them. Hunting for the Durands.

"Stop it," she whispered.

The movie rolled faster. Never staying in one city, one country. Reviled by his own kind. Capturing things like the snake-man and killing them. The human women he used, trying to forget Frances. The grave where she was buried. Years of defending the Kyn. Seeing Frances in Rome. Falling in love with Frances.

Frances, who could have been Sam's twin sister.

He smiled. "Don't hesitate now." He let go of the gun, but his metallic eyes never left hers. "You're an officer of the law, Samantha. Do your job."

She really should pull the trigger. What he did, what he was, all of his life was inside her now, and it was completely beyond her comprehension. Feelings, so new and foreign and terrifying, were welling up in her even now, demanding she put down the gun and beg him to explain everything she'd seen so that it would make some sense. She'd probably believe anything Lucan told her, too.

Sam slowly put her gun away and shuffled back. "No."

"I won't stop you. You'll save Alex and her lover. The Kyn will thank you for it." He spread his arms wide. *"Shoot me."*

"I can't." She turned away, and whispered the rest. "I think I'm in love with you."

Chapter 21

Sam walked blindly to the stairwell and climbed the three flights to her apartment. When she got to it she stared at the door she couldn't open. Lucan had her keys. He had everything.

Then he was there, reaching past her, crushing the knob as he forced the lock, his other velvet-gloved hand shoving her inside.

"Say that again." He backed her into the living room, his velvet grip on her throat as unyielding as the look on his face. Somewhere a glass shattered. "Say it to my face. Say it so I can hear you properly this time." He shook her, and Sam heard an ominous cracking. "Say it."

Why was he so angry? "I'm in love with you." Now he'd laugh, and stroll out of her life, and kill some more monsters, and she'd never understand what he was.

"In love." He released her and circled around her, looking at her from all angles as if deciding where best to bite first. "That's simply not possible, Samantha. You hunt human killers. You send them to prison. You take vengeance for their victims. You can't love death."

His scent changed, growing hot and almost smoky, as if someone had wrenched jasmine out of the ground and thrown it on a bonfire.

"You don't kill humans." She closed her eyes and willed him to go away, but when she opened them, he was still standing there. "Don't worry; I'm sure I'll get over it." In thirty or forty years, if she were lucky and found a good, patient therapist.

"Remember what I did to you last night. How I made you feel." Velvet fingertips trailed down her arm as his breath warmed her ear. "It was glorious, wasn't it?" When she nodded, he gripped her waist. "That's what you love. Not me."

The cracking sound grew louder.

"You can't tell me how I feel." She dragged in a quick breath as his gloves slid up to cup her breasts. "I can't do anything to you. I don't matter to you. What do you care?"

"I don't." Lucan spun her around, shoving her against the nearest wall. "Neither do you."

Sam shook her head, scraping her forehead against the drywall. She regretted her feelings for him, but she wasn't ashamed of them. "I'm in love with you, whatever you are."

"Poor Samantha." Lucan curled his hand over the back of her collar and tore off her jacket with a single motion. "You're right; you really have no idea what I am. What I can do to you."

He reached around her, jerking open her blouse so fast that buttons popped and fell like tiny coins around their feet.

She stared down at them. "I can guess."

"I think not. Shall we test the limits of this love of yours? My crimes haven't killed it yet. Neither has my indifference to your feelings. Perhaps something more personal will persuade it to give up its hold on your heart." He slid one hand over her breast, catching the nipple between two fingers and pinching it as he massaged her.

Sam squeezed her eyes shut. "Don't do this. Leave me alone, Lucan, for God's sake."

"I stopped serving the Almighty a very long time ago." He caught the lobe of her ear between his teeth, grazing it with the tips of his fangs. "Now I rule in hell. This is who you love, Detective Brown. Death."

Sam heard a popping sound like a bullet through a silencer, followed by muted tinkling, coming from her kitchen.

Lucan slid his hands up over her shoulders, where he ripped her blouse down the middle of her back. He peeled the sleeves away, gripping her wrists and stretching her bare arms out on either side of her, pressing her hips and breasts against the wall.

Sam discovered she was between two of her bookcases, and grabbed the side of each one, trying to brace herself. She felt his breath on the back of her neck, and then his tongue on the spot

where he had used his fangs on her last night. She tensed, expecting another bite, and flinched as she felt his mouth grazing
her back. His mouth branded her an inch at a time down the
length of her spine as he pulled her trousers and panties down
until they were a tangle around her ankles.

"No more pleas for mercy?" Velvet stroked the curve of her
bottom. "I like hearing you beg, Samantha. It makes my cock
hard. Ask me again to leave you alone and I'll fuck you until
you scream."

Sam pulled one foot, then the other out of the puddle of
clothes. With her legs free she could run. "I'm not afraid of you."

"Oh, yes, I quite forgot. You *trust* me." Velvet ripped, and
then his bare hand spread over her belly, sending small shock
waves through her skin. The other hand glided down, spreading
the humming warmth along the cleft of her buttocks before it
pushed between her legs. "Do you trust me now?" His fingers
went still, and Sam felt her own wetness as they pressed against
it. "Your body does your pleading for you, Samantha. It begs
for mine. Mine will be happy to oblige."

"The only reason you want me is because I look like your
old girlfriend," she said tiredly. "Her name was Frances, right?"

One or more of the windows in her bedroom shattered.

He flipped her around, slamming her back against the wall.
"How did you know?" He bent until their breath mixed and she
could see nothing but the ghosts in his eyes. Lightbulbs in her
lamps began to explode, sending sprays of sparks into the air.
"Who told you?"

Sam felt an overwhelming sadness that had nothing to do
with what they were and everything to do with what they might
have been. They'd found each other too late; they'd gone in different directions. It made no difference. Whatever Lucan was,
she knew that he was the man she had been born to love.

"It doesn't matter." She touched his cheek with her scarred
hand, felt him flinch. "I still love you anyway."

His eyes narrowed. "Do you."

The plate glass in the sliding door came apart, the pieces
sliding down to fall out of the frame and crash onto the concrete
pad of her balcony.

Lucan dragged her down to the carpet, laying her out on her

back as he tore at the front of his trousers. Sam latched onto his shoulders, curling her legs around his as he came between them, his hand around his cock, the head punching into her like a fist before the shaft followed, slamming into her with so much force that she slid back on the carpet.

Sam's shoulders ground into the rug fibers as Lucan draped her legs over his arms and lifted her hips, fucking her hard and deep, ramming through the sudden, terrifying orgasm that racked her without stopping. Holding on for the ride was all she could do, and then he picked her up and got to his feet, still working her over him as he walked across the room. He bent, using his arm to sweep everything off her little dining room table, and then pulled out of her, dropping her on her feet.

"What are you—"

He whirled her around, pushing her down against the tabletop, using his knee to separate her legs from behind. When Sam got her hands under her and tried to lift up, he gripped the back of her neck and held her down, pushing her cheek against the smooth wood surface.

"Don't move." His voice sounded guttural, thick with anger and desire. "I'm not done with you yet."

Sam felt his fingers push into her, and saw one of her kitchen cabinets fly open and release a burst of broken glass. Then she realized why he had brought her here. Directly above her was a hanging light made of dozens of pieces of dark gray glass that had been shaped to look like flowers.

If it broke, it would fall on her.

He felt her muscles clench against him. "Are you worried about something, Samantha?" he murmured against her tangled hair. "I thought you loved me."

Lucan was deliberately trying to goad her, as if nothing were more important to him than tearing down her feelings for him by flaunting his power. On some level Sam knew that if she fought him now, he wouldn't force her, but he'd win the battle of wills.

She was exhausted, and ready to let him win.

What he didn't realize was how he'd given himself away by not hurting her. He may have broken every glass, window, and light in the apartment, but not a single piece of glass had touched her. His bare hands were all over her, but she wasn't being torn apart.

He doesn't want to hurt me, even when he's trying to. That knowledge made her blink back hot tears.

"I do love you." Sam made herself go boneless under his hands, only lifting her hips a little to give him better access to her.

"What are you doing?"

"Giving you what you want."

Again she felt Lucan go still against her, and then the smooth head of his cock replaced his fingers. With a slow, steady pressure, he pushed, wedging himself inside her body.

The hanging glass above her crackled.

Lucan's hand curved around her hip, his fingers inching down to the top of her sex, where his thumb pushed into the soft notch. He stroked the pad of his thumb over her clit as he pressed deeper, and Sam trembled between pleasure and panic. She could feel his big frame shaking now, and heard a deep, rumbling sound that might have been a groan. The tight bulge of his scrotum brushed her vaginal lips as he sank in to the hilt.

"Brave girl." With a curse, he started to ease out of her. "I'll make you a happy one. I'll leave you alone."

Sam reached down to catch his hand and brought it back to her clit. "No." She pushed back against him before he could withdraw completely, using the muscles that had tried to keep him out to clamp down on him and hold him inside her. "Do it again."

"I'm frightening you."

"Not really." She glanced up at the hanging light. "If that thing falls, it'll hit you first." She pushed her fingers between his and used both to rub her clit. "Finish it, Lucan. Come inside me. Make me come."

Sam didn't think he could, not when he pressed slowly back into her. The only thing that kept her from looking at the glass above her head was their stroking fingers—and the suspicion that something was waiting for her just out of reach, something more important than being afraid.

"Samantha," he breathed as he withdrew and pushed back in smoothly, one hand on her hip to steady her, the other working her aching clit without mercy.

Samantha felt the fear inside her change to heat, and then all that mattered was the melding of their flesh. She didn't know where he was taking her, but there was no holding back now, not against something as primal as this.

His hips slapped against her buttocks, swift kisses of damp skin as he slid in and out of her with thorough, relentless repetition. The tops of his thighs brushed hers as he pulled her back, making her meet him as he buried himself inside her.

"Give it to me, Samantha," he muttered, tensing every muscle pressed against her as he went impossibly deep. "Now."

He did something with his fingers and hers, dragging them over her labia and then her clit as he twisted his hips against her, and Sam shattered into a horrendous, endless climax that sent her rocketing up and over and back again until she thought her heart might explode. A moment later Lucan stiffened and flooded her, holding her so tightly as he did she thought bones might snap.

The gentleness with which he drew out of her made her catch a sob, and then he had her in his arms, lifting and cradling her against his chest. "If you start to weep, so will I."

That was all that was left now, Sam thought as he carried her through the bedroom and into the bathroom. The crying part. What had he said to her, the first time they'd made love? *Perhaps all of your life's miseries were to prepare you for what I would do to you.*

She let Lucan put her in the shower, standing silent and docile as he washed her from head to toe. All the glass in the bathroom had shattered, so he wouldn't let her put a single foot on the floor or touch anything. He did everything for her, drying her with a soft towel, carrying her naked to her bed, and lying down with her in his arms.

"Look at me."

Sam did, and saw that the icy metal of his irises had softened and darkened—with pain, with regret, she couldn't tell. But the rage was gone, and he was handling her as if she were made of silk. "I'm okay. You didn't hurt me."

"Liar." His hand moved down to stroke the curves of her bottom. "Come here."

Sam didn't think she could, and then she was on top of him, and he was sliding into her, not pounding or taking but gliding easily, caressing her from the inside. The sensations became sweet and thick, as if she'd been covered in cream and slowly licked clean, and when he brought her mouth to his she moaned.

"Remember this, Samantha." He tasted her mouth again, catching her lower lip with his teeth for a moment before releasing it and rolling with her until she was under him and he pushed into her with smooth, firm strokes. "Remember us like this."

Sam was so tired she shouldn't have been able to move, but he wouldn't stop, and her body refused to lie there and do nothing. She arched, shifting her legs to cradle his hips, bringing him deeper.

Lucan never stopped kissing her. His tongue went deep, curling around hers, making her return the kiss. He would pull back to trace her lips with small, light brushes of his, and then coax them open to come inside to taste her again. She felt his fangs brush her lips more than once, but he was so careful that he never drew blood, even when he kissed her so deeply that she couldn't tell where his mouth ended and hers began.

It couldn't last forever, even when she thought it might. Her breasts heaved as she felt herself tighten from her toes to the back of her neck, and something gave way inside her, making her clench and gush around him at the same time. As her orgasm shimmered through her, as bright and silent as sunrise on the ocean, Lucan buried himself in the center of it, lifting his head and watching her eyes as he released his semen in slow, heavy pulses.

When it was over, he kissed her again, then shifted to his side, staying inside her as he held her against his heart.

They lay together until Samantha was almost asleep, and then she felt him rise and leave her. He came back dressed, and used a damp washcloth between her legs before he dressed her in panties and an old T-shirt. He disappeared again before bringing a large glass of water and two of her granola bars, which he set on the night table beside her.

"I'm okay." She looked at the empty bucket he'd also put by

the side of the bed. Did he think she was going to be sick? "I'm going to pass out. I don't need anything."

"You will." He took her right hand in his. He'd put on another pair of gloves, she noted absently; of course he would carry spares. The way she wore a backup piece. "You'll never forgive me for this, but I am sorry, Samantha." He bent down and put his mouth on hers, kissing her as though starved for her, as if he'd never touched her once the entire night.

Sam didn't resist until she felt cold metal on her wrist, and heard a familiar snick. But by the time she rolled, he'd already handcuffed her to the headboard.

"When it's over tomorrow night, Burke will come and release you." He stepped back, took one long, last look at her, and left.

Michael Cyprien tracked Faryl Paviere for fourteen hours before the sun and exhaustion forced him and Gard to take cover for the day in an empty, abandoned boathouse. He felt uneasy being away from Alexandra for so long, so he called a halt to the search. A pair of passing fishermen willingly provided nourishment and transportation back to where they had left their vehicle.

"I do not understand why he does not fashion a permanent lair for himself," Gard said as they drove back into the city. "It is as if he moves nightly. But why? Why has he not given himself to Lucan?"

"I cannot say, but we will find him." Michael felt as weary and defeated as Gard, but he could not air his own suspicions. If Faryl had lost the last of his humanity, then he would be living as an animal, attacking humans without discretion or restraint. He could not tell Gard that his brother would have to be executed the moment they found him.

Michael wished he could extend some mercy to Faryl, and permit Alexandra a chance to try to help him, but there was more at stake than the life of a Kyn gone mad. In the past, the American Darkyn had been able to manipulate detection of such changelings to make them seem like things of myth or hoaxes, which had resulted in such human legends as Sasquatch, the manitou, and the New Jersey Devil.

Times had changed, and humans had become more technologically advanced. In this age nearly everyone sported some form of digital recording device. Photos of Faryl in his changeling state could be taken with something as innocuous as a mobile phone.

Then there were the human authorities, who had become far more sophisticated in their quest to control crime. Compared to the devices available to private citizens, their surveillance equipment was the stuff of science fiction. Faryl would have to be caught and killed by whatever means were necessary, or the Darkyn risked exposure.

Michael's brooding thoughts shifted as he saw his seneschal running down the drive toward the car. There was only one thing that could have made Phillipe carry as many weapons as he did, or look so fearful.

"Alexandra. No." Michael slammed on the brakes and jumped out of the car. "He has taken her?"

Phillipe stopped and nodded. "Last night. They shot the guards with tranquilizer darts. There was no warning."

Michael knew he should not have left her. Not after the way he had seen Lucan look at her. "Recall the men. Have you sent word to Orlando, Atlanta, New Orleans?"

His seneschal nodded. "Byrne is here and his men are prepared to fight. Locksley, his men, and ours are en route. Other *jardins* are standing by awaiting your summons. As we are, we will be fully assembled in three hours."

"We cannot march down the streets of Fort Lauderdale." Had they been in New Orleans, they might have used the underground tunnel system they had successfully built and concealed from the world for three centuries.

"Byrne came by sea, and has staged his men here." Phillipe gestured toward the marina across the street, every sloop of which was occupied by large, powerful boats. "He suggests the inland waterway, at midnight."

"There is to be a concert for the humans tonight." He remembered the posters advertising it plastered on the outside walls of the nightclub. "That should provide additional cover. Bring Byrne to me." He started to walk toward the house.

"Master, there is something else you must know." Phillipe

caught up to him. "Éliane contacted me this morning. The high lord is here in South Florida. He is to attend this concert tonight."

"Good." Michael didn't slow his stride. "Then he can watch me kill his bastard son."

Chapter 22

Lucan stepped into the security room, where Rafael was monitoring the hidden cameras that showed the interior of every room in the club as well as the exterior of the building. It was how he had watched Samantha break into the building.

Dawn was only minutes away, so it was unlikely that Michael would attack now. Still, there were any number of humans at the seigneur's command. "Any sign?"

"Nothing yet, my lord." His seneschal turned to face him. "Were you able to persuade Detective Brown to cooperate with us?"

Lucan didn't want to think of what he'd done to Samantha. "I left her handcuffed to her bed. If I die tomorrow night, do send Burke to release her. Who told Detective Brown about Frances?"

Rafael looked mystified. "Who is Frances?"

"It's not important." Another mystery to go unsolved. Lucan's life was rife with them.

"Cyprien will come with every Kyn he can recall," his seneschal warned him. "There is still time to end this."

No, there wasn't. "Be ready, Rafael."

Lucan took the stairwell up to the secured room where Alexandra was being held. A nurse sat dozing in the front room, so he closed the bedroom door behind him. Alex was not sleeping, and someone had thoughtfully replaced her gag.

He removed it. "Have you changed your mind?"

"What did you do to the cop?" she demanded.

"Before or after I raped her?" Even as he despised himself for uttering the ugly words, a perverse part of him enjoyed seeing her cringe away from him. "You should learn to curb your reaction to unpleasant realities, Alex. There are many among our kind."

"Did you tell the nurse to take a unit of blood from me?" When he nodded, she touched the place on her neck where he had bitten her. "Why not go au naturel again? You seemed to enjoy it enough last time."

"I drank a little of your blood to see if I could acquire some of your scent. Unfortunately yours doesn't seem to transfer through feeding, as ours does. I'll have to put a little from the bag on my skin before I face your lover tonight."

"He'll smell me on you. He'll think you . . ." She swore.

"Why do you think I went to all the trouble of taking you? You are my one advantage against him. Of course he'll smell you on me, and assume that I took you, blood, body, and soul." He pulled the covers she had kicked off up and over her. "You needn't worry, Alex. It's a well-known fact that I've never beaten Michael in a fight. Even wearing your blood on me, I rather doubt my luck will turn."

"Then why do this? He'll kill you. He'll make you suffer first."

"That is a certainty." He smiled down at her. "But a man should be able to choose the day he loses his head, don't you think?"

"You're more messed up than any vampire I've ever met, including Thierry Durand when he was insane, but you're not suicidal," she said immediately. "Call Michael; explain whatever this game is. Ask for another truce. He'll give you one."

"This is how these things have been done for centuries, Alex. You can't change the Kyn." He looked down to where she had wrapped her hand around his wrist. "You'd do well to remember that in the years to come."

Her pupils contracted to slits. "You didn't rape me, and I don't think you raped that cop. I saw how you looked at her. You don't even want to kill Michael. It's as if you're trying to . . ." Her eyes became huge. "Oh, my God."

He removed her hand from his arm. "When it's over, will you go to her and give her a message?"

"Her?" Dazed, Alex stared up at him. "You mean the cop?"

He nodded. "Her name is Samantha. Tell her that I loved

Frances, not her. That everything I did to her was because of my love for Frances. She doesn't respond to *l'attrait*, so you'll have to make her believe it by words alone."

"That's stupid," Alex muttered. "Who is Frances, and why am I telling the cop this bullshit story?"

"Do you know, if you had come to me instead of Michael, I think I would have been just as lost in you. You are such a brilliant, beautiful thing." He rested his gloved hand against her cheek for a moment. "Will you tell her what I said?"

"Still need a why."

"Why." Lucan could say it, this once. "Because I love her, Alex."

Sam spent several hours trying to free herself without success. Despite her best efforts, she discovered what thousands of criminals already knew: that standard police-issue handcuffs were impossible to wedge, pry, or hammer open. Toward dawn she dozed, jerking awake when she heard any sounds from the floor below, but when she called out no one answered her.

She had to get to the nightclub and stop this thing Lucan had planned. How, she didn't know, but Alex Keller might help her. If she believed her, and if Sam could get her out of Lucan's chains, and if she could stop Michael Cyprien from killing Lucan . . . Sam jerked at the handcuffs again.

Nothing worked. After she'd inflicted a new set of bruises, Sam fell asleep, and didn't wake until late that afternoon, when she heard the door across the hall slam.

"Chris?" She sat up and drank some water to soothe her hoarse, dry throat, and then started shouting the girl's name.

"Sam?" Chris called back from outside her apartment door. "You okay?"

"No," she yelled. "Kick in the door."

"With all these dead bolts? Not hardly."

Sam looked frantically around the room, and then caught sight of her balcony, which was only two feet away from Keri's. Lucan had shattered the door last night. "Can you climb over from your balcony to mine? Be careful; there's a lot of broken glass out there."

"Okay. Hang on."

A few minutes later glass crunched, and then a disheveled Chris appeared at the sliding door. "Glad I'm not afraid of heights. Who broke your sliding glass"—she looked at Sam's handcuffed arm—"door?"

Sam sagged with relief. "The spare key's in my top dresser drawer. Get it for me, please."

Chris found the key and released her from the cuffs. "Your poor arm, it's all bruised up." She saw the water, food, and bucket Lucan had left for Sam. "Nice burglar. Do you know he broke, like, everything in your apartment?"

"It was a lousy date." Sam rubbed her wrist as she got out of bed, stretching her cramped limbs. She was sore and mad and needed a shower, but otherwise all right.

"Want some coffee? Aspirin?"

The thought of drinking or eating anything made Sam's stomach turn. "I'm okay. Make it for yourself if you want some." She stared at Chris's all-black outfit, and an idea began to jell. "What time is it?"

"About five thirty, I think."

"Got any plans for tonight?"

"Besides sleeping? Nope."

Sam gestured toward her clothes. "Can you make me look like that? Like a goth?"

Chris frowned. "The bondage and bad date weren't exciting enough?"

"I have to go undercover at that nightclub, Infusion, and I need you to help me dress the part. Look in my closet and see what might work," Sam said as she headed for the bathroom. "I'm going to take a shower."

When she came out ten minutes later, Chris had thrown most of her suits onto her bed.

"Boring." The younger girl added a brown suit to the pile, and then examined the other black suit she was holding. "Ugly *and* boring." She glanced at Sam. "Does your great-grandmother, like, buy *all* your clothes?"

"I'm an orphan."

"You dress like one." She tossed the black suit on top of the brown one. "Let's go over to my place. I've got some stuff that might fit you."

There was a knock at the door, and Sam jumped a little. *Burke isn't coming until it's over,* she reminded herself. She looked at Chris and pointed to the pile of suits. "Hang those back up."

"You're sure I can't burn them?" Chris grumbled.

Sam had her weapon in hand when she checked the peephole, but tucked it into the pocket of her robe before she unlocked the dead bolts.

Adam Suarez seemed almost as surprised to see her. "Detective Brown. You're . . . home."

She was on vacation. Where else would she be? "What can I do for you, Lieutenant?"

"I came by to check on you." He looked over her shoulder, and then back at her face. "Are you staying in tonight?"

A wave of images came over her, but she resisted the memories. Now was not the time to freak out in front of Suarez, and she wasn't even sure of what she'd seen in her head. What had he asked her? Something about staying in. "No."

"You should, Samantha."

"We're not partners yet, Adam. Wait until we are before you start trying to run my life." She started to close the door, but his hand stopped her. "Was there something else you wanted?"

"If you're going down to the nightclub, you'll need some backup. I'm off duty." He checked his watch. "I'll come back in an hour and pick you up."

"I'll drive myself, thanks." She couldn't see his eyes through the sunglasses he wore, and his expression gave away nothing. She couldn't confirm what she suspected until she saw him without the glasses, either. "What do you know about Infusion?"

"Only what I've read from your case files. There's supposed to be a big concert there tonight. I'll meet you outside at seven." He turned and left.

Sam slowly closed the door. "Okay."

"Was that the bad date?" Chris asked as she came out of the bedroom.

"No, that was my new partner, checking on me."

"Nice someone cares besides me." Chris linked her arm with

Sam's. "Come on, Officer. Time to walk on the dark side of the moon."

John returned to the abbey from the hospital and gathered the brothers in the chapel. Ignatius protested for a moment, telling him that he had no authority over them, until John looked at him. The friar abruptly quieted and marched into the sanctuary after the other friars.

He stood for a moment outside the chapel and looked out at the abbey grounds. Bromwell and Mercer had tried so hard to keep the outside world at bay, but it would not be denied. The needs of the people of the world could not be held back by fences and brick walls. And, whether John liked it or not, the Darkyn were a part of this world.

John walked inside. He didn't take the abbot's place at the altar, but stood at the back of the little church. "Father Lane committed suicide," he told them without preamble. "Before he died, he said something about a nightclub and Bastille Day. What did he have planned for it?"

"The abbot was delusional, Brother Patrick," Ignatius said at once. "I'm very sorry, but you must know that he had started drinking again. You know how irrational alcoholics can be—"

"I know about the Darkyn, Ignatius," John told him. "They took my sister. She's one of them now." He ignored the pale faces and the muttered prayers. "I also know what the Brethren do to the vampires they capture. They brought me to Rome on the pretense of having me join the order and drugged and tortured me."

No one spoke for a long time, and then Brother Jacob asked, "What are you going to do, Brother Patrick?"

He wasn't running away anymore. "Mercer told me that you all have been living as real priests here. Doing good works, devoting yourself to the faith, and repenting for the wrongs you did in the name of the Brethren. Is that the life you want?" He watched the men nod. "Then it's time you left the order."

"You know nothing," Ignatius said, stepping out of his line, his face contorted with anger. "No one leaves the order. We are born to it, we live it, and we die for it."

How much control did the Brethren still have over these men? After twenty years, John suspected, not much.

"You will have to leave the abbey and change your identities, but there is enough money in the accounts to help you start over," he told them.

The old friar thrust his hands in his sleeves. "Steal from the church? Never."

"That money doesn't belong to church, and it didn't come from the church. The Brethren have always funded you," John reminded him. "It's your choice." He turned and walked away.

Ignatius caught up with him outside. "Bravo, Brother Patrick. You've achieved with one speech what my brothers and I could never bring ourselves to do in twenty years. My brothers are even now deciding how to leave Florida and where we should settle."

John thought of the many states through which he had traveled. "The Carolinas are nice, and there are a lot of needy people in the hills."

"North Carolina." Ignatius's tone softened. "I drove through it once, when I was a younger man. It's very green there." He sighed. "I don't suppose you'd like to adopt Brother Nicholas."

"Not even if you paid me. Don't worry; he'll have lots of leaves to blow around in North Carolina. What he and the other men need is a steady hand to lead them to that new life." He gave the guestmaster a sideways look. "Abbot Ignatius has a nice ring to it."

"Abbot William," Ignatius said. "If I am to become a fugitive from the order and change my identity, I am not passing up the chance to be rid of this hideous name of mine." He stopped with John at the front gates. "You are going to the nightclub Father Lane wished us to attack." When John nodded, he frowned. "What do you intend to do?"

"What Mercer should have done," John said. "Find a way to call a truce."

"Mercer?" Ignatius looked. "You mean Father Lane? But his Christian name was Leigh."

Chapter 23

"People think the goth lifestyle is just clothes and hair and silly shit," Chris said as she finished combing the dark rinse through Sam's hair.

Sam's bathroom mirror hadn't survived the night with Lucan, so they were using Keri's. "It's not?"

"The world judges you by your appearance, you know. Right now you look like a cop, so people respect you. Maybe you've earned it; maybe you haven't—but you still get the respect no matter what."

Sam rubbed the scar on her palm. Seeing Lucan's life through his blood had confused her more than anything. "So how do people treat goths?"

"How do *you* treat them?"

"I don't," Sam admitted. "You're the first one I've met."

Chris nodded. "And that's only because I moved across the hall from you, made coffee for you, and rescued your ass from your mean boyfriend, who I still think you should dump immediately. If you saw me on the street, or in a store, or hanging out downstairs, would you have even said hello? Be honest."

"Probably not." She eyed Chris's head. "The blue hair is a little scary."

"Exactly. I don't look like other girls. I'm way different. An outsider." She took a hair dryer from the bathroom cabinet and plugged it into a wall outlet. "So you treat me like one."

Sam sighed. "That doesn't make sense. Why dress like you do if you don't want people to treat you like an outsider?"

"Well, one, because I like it. Two, because I don't like your phony society with all its uptight rules." Chris switched on the hair dryer and went to work on Sam's damp head.

Sam didn't look in Keri's mirrors—she'd stopped looking after the kid had gotten out makeup that looked like different shades of heavy-duty shoe polish—and rewound the silent movie of Lucan's life that had been playing in her mind since he'd left her.

He'd lived longer than she could fathom, and traveled to places that no longer existed. He'd been a priest, of all things, and had fought in wars all over the Middle East. That was when it had happened—he'd come back from the Crusades with some kind of sickness, and died from it. Sam almost threw up as she relived Lucan's memories of clawing his way out of the mass grave outside London where he'd been buried.

She also thought that might be why she could read his blood: He had died, and he had been buried.

With a cop's methodical patience, she sifted through and examined each memory she had been able to retain. Lucan was definitely a killer; he had killed more people than she could count. The problem was, he had never wanted to—he had been sent to kill them.

She could understand that, too. From the memories she'd taken from Lucan's blood, the Kyn he had killed had been insanely dangerous, like the countess who had been deliberately trying to infect the crown heads of Europe with Kyn blood so she could become queen, or changelings like Faryl Paviere who had lost their humanity and went on rampages, killing humans until they were stopped by Lucan. A few others had been traitors, preserving their own lives by passing information or handing over Kyn to the Brethren.

No law, cop, or prison in the world could hold the Darkyn. The only thing to stop them had been Lucan.

The Brethren were the hardest thing for Sam to wrap her head around. According to Lucan's memories, they had begun, as the Kyn had, as Catholic priests. The Brethren had instigated the Crusades, but they had never fought the holy wars themselves. They had sent Lucan and the Templars instead. They knew about the sickness that caused the Kyn to rise from their graves, but instead of helping them, they demonized them and began hunting them.

Throughout his human and inhuman lives, Lucan had never let anyone get close to him. Frances had been the only one to get past his walls, and she had been in love with another man. It made Sam angry to see how callously Frances had used Lucan to pay for her lover's debts and care for him as he died. All he had wanted in return was a little kindness from her, and she'd thrown him out like garbage.

As for the killing, Lucan had never used it for his own profit. He served as the only final authority among the Kyn. He was, in essence, their only cop.

The hair dryer clicked off. "You better not cry," Chris told her. "You'll ruin your mascara."

Sam blinked and glanced at the window. The sky outside was a rich dark purple; the regal color of twilight. She stood up. "Are we done yet?"

"Clothes." Chris shoved her toward the bedroom.

The outfit the kid had picked for her had more straps and rigging than a circus act, but Sam dutifully pulled and buckled and strapped everything until Chris stepped back and nodded.

"You're done." She gestured toward the full-length mirror behind Sam. "Behold, Officer Goth."

Sam turned and yelped. In the mirror stood a raven-haired witch in gleaming black leather and red spandex. "That's me?" She peered at her face, which might have been a beautiful mask. "Why did you glue sequins on my face?"

"They're crystal bindi, from India, and they're very hot right now. Don't mess with them. Lean down." When she did, Chris lowered a tangle of silver and black necklaces over her head. "Don't smile, and try to look a little more haunted."

"Haunted."

"Goth is about the dark side of life. Death, sorrow, pain, unrequited love, passions of the heart and blood. Watch this." Chris put the back of her hand against her forehead and dropped into the nearest chair, sighing, her eyes half-closed. "Goths are all about accepting and celebrating the dark things that scare people like you. We drink absinthe, write beautiful poetry about loss and pain and angst, and make ourselves living, breathing art."

"I don't scare that easy." Sam studied her. "And I'm not drinking absinthe."

Chris flipped her hand over to cover her eyes. "Don't talk, okay? It destroys the facade. Just look mildly pissed off—yeah, like that. Perfect." She got up and grabbed her purse, a square of beaded ebony satin hanging from a braided leather strap spiked with pointed studs, and handed Sam a college student's ID that stated her name was Shane Meredith and she was twenty-one years old. "I made you up to look like her. Remember to answer to Shane." She picked up a black dress and headed for the bathroom. "Give me a second and I'll be ready to go."

"You're not going. It's too dangerous."

Chris turned. "Excuse me? I believe I have saved your ass twice now, Officer. Plus if you leave me behind I'll just follow you. You know. Like Lassie to the rescue." She barked a few times.

Sam didn't have time to argue. "When this thing goes down, I want you out of there. I'm counting on you to be safe."

"As long as you stay away from handcuffs, blondes, and anything made of glass," Chris replied. "You don't have too much luck with them."

When they walked out into the night, Sam looked around the nearly full parking lot before going to her car. No one stopped them, and as she got in behind the wheel, she focused on what she was going to say when she saw Lucan at the club.

The blue sedan didn't pull out immediately after Sam's car. The driver was in no hurry. He already knew where she was going.

Byrne came out of the shadows, the hem of his greatcoat swirling in the faint mist. He pulled back the scarf covering his head, revealing bloodred hair that fell over his shoulders in waves, some of which had been woven into thin, tight braids. Byrne's garnet mane contrasted sharply with the enigmatic swirls and lines of the dark blue tattoos on his face. He moved with the quick, easy power of a man accustomed to climbing mountains on foot.

"Seigneur." He sketched a quick bow and gestured to the slim girl beside him. "My seneschal, Jayr."

As Jayr duplicated her master's bow, Michael took a moment to study her. He had never met the only female seneschal among the Darkyn, but he had known of her lethal reputation for centuries. Like Thierry Durand's son Jamys, she had been young when she had risen to walk the night, and retained her youthful appearance. She kept her hair cut very short and dressed as a modern adolescent boy, and carried more daggers than he could count.

Michael inclined his head. "I thank you for answering my call."

"My men are in position, and Locksley waits with his lot to the south." The soft brogue of his homeland still colored Byrne's voice, but he spoke in the same archaic French Michael and Phillipe had been using. "You have but to give word."

Michael sheathed his battle sword and covered it, as Byrne had, with a coat. He went to the map spread out on the table in the kitchen. "Phillipe and I will go in with our men through the crowd at the front. We have to separate Lucan from the humans if possible, so we will attempt to force him outside, here." He pointed to the alley behind the building. "When I signal you, block off all sides and keep the alley clear."

Byrne gave the map a skeptical look. "Close quarters for such a battle, my lord. Jayr?"

The girl took a look. "Too many windows." Her voice was clear as a bell, with no accent whatsoever. "Suzerain Lucan's talent can cause them to shatter and fall down."

"I don't intend to let him live that long," Michael told her. He offered his hand to Byrne. "Your loyalty is appreciated."

Byrne's mouth twisted. "May it not be piss in the wind."

Phillipe drove Michael to within a block of the nightclub, but from there they walked. With every step, Michael felt the coiling fury inside him tighten. Was she alive? Had Lucan tortured her, the way he had the servants after Michael left France? When this was over, he would never again permit Alex to leave Louisiana. He would capture and bring her as many changelings as she wished.

As they came closer, Michael noted Lucan's guards in position. "He is expecting us."

"Of course he is."

Michael turned to see a figure in a black cloak approaching them. "My lord." He was too astonished to bow. "How do you come to be here?"

"My princes are about to test their swords against each other without my permission," Richard said, his beautiful voice as compelling as the waves rolling up to the sands. "How was I to stay away?"

Michael stiffened. "There was not time to contact you. Lucan attacked my men. He took Alexandra."

"I know, my dear boy." Richard rested a gloved hand on his shoulder, tilting his head back to better look at Michael through the slits in his mask. "Come. I draw too much attention out here, and I wish to find a good seat for the festivities."

"The guards," Phillipe said, glancing at them.

"They will not molest you," Richard said. "Not when they see that I am your escort."

Michael was not above using the high lord to get to Alexandra. "Let us go inside."

Only one of the guards stepped forward to challenge them, but Richard uttered a few low, melodic-sounding words and sent him shuffling back to his place.

"Special charge for the concert." The bouncer didn't even glance at Richard's mask. "Forty bucks each."

Phillipe paid him in cash, and the human stamped the back of his glove with the number 714. He did the same to Cyprien, but the dimensions of Richard's inhuman hand in its custom-fitted glove gave him pause. He handed Phillipe ten dollars back.

"What is this for?" Michael's seneschal asked.

"Discount for the handicapped dude. Move along." He waved them toward the door to the club.

"I am a 'handicapped dude,'" Richard murmured as they went into the crowded club. "Imagine that."

The decor had been altered slightly from what it had been during Michael's meeting with Lucan. Gold had been added to the red-and-black theme, in the form of medieval crosses, chalices, and banners bearing Richard's standard, the lion rampant.

Michael stared at the banners. "He knew that you would be here." He turned to Richard, but the high lord had vanished. "Phillipe."

His seneschal scanned the crowd. "It appears Lucan's entire *jardin* is here as well. They are not armed."

So it was to be single combat under the banners of the high lord. All they needed were horses and lances. "Signal Locksley and Byrne. Tell them to cut off all access to this place, but to keep their men outside." His eyes narrowed as he saw a face he thought he recognized and worked his way through the crowd toward him.

John Keller had lost weight and grown a beard in the months since Michael had last seen him in Chicago. His skin was also much darker. If not for the regular photos of him sent weekly to Michael, he might not have recognized him at all.

Although Alex was unaware of it, Michael had kept her brother under surveillance since he had left Chicago. He knew exactly how John Keller had made his way across the country, and that he had had no contact with the Brethren. He had not expected to see him in Florida, but doubtless a report was waiting for Michael back in New Orleans detailing how John had come to be here.

Alex's brother recognized him from three feet away and closed the distance between them. "Cyprien. What are you doing in Florida? Is Alexandra . . ." He looked around. "Is my sister with you?"

"She was abducted by the Kyn who arranged all this." Michael doubted Lucan had recruited Keller; John avoided the Darkyn as much as he dodged the Brethren. "Why are you here?"

"The Brethren," he said simply. "They know about this place. Something is going to happen tonight. Something bad. I'm here to play mediator, I guess."

Michael clamped down on his irritation. He didn't have time for the Brethren to interfere in this; it was Kyn business. "This could easily become a full-scale melee," he told John, who had been witness to one such battle in New Orleans. "You cannot negotiate peace between us. If you are intelligent, you'll seek safety."

"My sister is involved, and a friend of mine killed himself because of this." John thrust his hands in his pockets. "I'm not going anywhere."

*   *   *

Burke escorted Alisa up to the penthouse suite. She had dressed exactly as Lucan had instructed her, in her black patent-leather dominatrix costume, and carried a coiled black whip and various instruments of torture.

"I've missed you," she said, hurrying up to him. "Do we have time for a quickie before the show? Who am I going to flog?"

"Sit down and be quiet," Lucan told her.

Surprised, Alisa did just that.

"I can dress you in your armor in a minute or less," Burke said. "Please, if you do not wear it . . . at least take this much advantage, master."

His *tresora* thought he was going to lose. They all did. Lucan didn't know whether to be annoyed or depressed.

"Thank you for your concern, Herbert, but armor will only weigh me down." He finished buttoning his full-sleeved white shirt and pulled his boots up over the calves of his dark, fitted trousers. "You have served me well, and I have written a letter to your family commending your service. You should be placed with another Kyn lord within the year." He smiled at the other man's dumbfounded expression. "I would suggest somewhere away from the various allergens that torment you here in Florida."

Burke's stammered response was lost, drowned out by the sounds of heavy footsteps, a woman shouting, and chains rattling.

"Put me down," Lucan heard Alex yell as Rafael carried her into the suite. "I mean it. The minute I can see you again, bright boy, I'm going to sink fangs in you."

Alisa perked up. "Who's that?" The moment Rafael came into view, she squealed and covered her eyes. "I can't see."

"Join the club," Alex snarled. "Lucan? I know you're here; I can smell you. Your insidious plot is safe; I'm not going to run away wrapped up in chains. So tell the lightbulb to turn off the high beams, will you?"

"Rafael," Lucan said.

"Forgive me, my lord"—he set Alex down with a grunt—"but she is very strong, and very determined." He wiped drying blood from his nose. "She did not wish to wear the gown you provided for her."

"You got that right." Alex's dazzled eyes cleared and she looked down in disgust at the cloud of white silk floating around her. "I've been able to dress myself since I was two." She looked at Lucan. "Aren't you pretty tonight." Her gaze shifted to Alisa. "Ick."

Alisa returned the sneer with interest. "Let me whip her, Lucan. I won't charge extra."

"I liked the cop better." Alex looked around the suite. "Is Michael here? You haven't started this circus act yet, have you?"

"The seigneur was just seen entering the club." Lucan had watched him by remote monitor, gauging Cyprien's emotional state. With a final bit of prodding, his old enemy would descend into a blood rage.

"I'll talk to him for you," Alex said quickly. "I know he'll listen to me, and we can settle this thing without chopping off heads and arms and stuff."

Lucan gazed down at her. She was so young, so determined. "It's too late for that, Alexandra. Events have been set into motion now that must be resolved." He took her arm. "Rafael, alert the men downstairs. Come, Alisa. It's time to start the show."

Lucan had Burke take Alisa down the stairwell, while he and Alex rode alone in the elevator. The band playing onstage was so loud that the mirrored tiles above the musicians' heads vibrated in time with the music.

"I've been thinking about the changelings," Alex said unexpectedly on the way down to the club level. "You've been near Faryl when he was human and after he changed. Has his scent changed?"

Lucan shrugged. "What has Faryl's scent to do with anything?"

"It could prove my theory about the changelings," Alex told him. "If they go through this physical change because of their blood choices, it must mean the pathogen is adapting them to its new diet."

"Perhaps." Lucan didn't care about the changelings. After tonight, someone else would have to hunt them down and kill them. "Faryl's scent didn't change. It disappeared. He doesn't smell like anything."

"Anything that would appeal to a *human* nose," she corrected him. "You said it yourself: You are what you eat. Or you adapt to hunt what you eat. Think about it." She shifted, making the chains around her rattle. "The Kyn are uniformly strong, fast, and very good-looking. You don't age and your wounds heal incredibly fast. You have *l'attrait* to lure humans to you. That all has to come from the pathogen, because you didn't have those things as humans. The pathogen also needs human blood as nourishment, so it makes sense that it would cause the specific mutations that it does."

"So Kyn change into monsters when they feed on animal blood for what reason?" he asked. "To scare their prey to death?"

"Camouflage, Lucan. The pathogen can't shrink you, but it can make you attractive to what you live on. If it's human beings, it gives you a pretty face, a pretty smell, and other perks. If it's snakes, it makes you a snake that is beautiful to other snakes."

Lucan led her out of the elevator. "I fail to see your point."

"Once a changeling begins feeding on animals, they never go back to using humans again, do they?"

He shook his head. "The blood makes them sick."

She smiled. "I knew it." She frowned as Lucan picked her up and carried her into the backstage area, where Burke and Alisa were waiting. "What are you doing?"

"I'm carrying out my insidious plot." He set her down in front of the cross and began removing the chains around her. "I don't want to do this to you, Alexandra, but it has to look real. It shouldn't take long."

Alex looked from him to the eight-foot-high cross to Alisa, who had uncoiled her whip and was making some practice lashes. "You can't be serious."

Chapter 24

Sam saw Lucan's guards out in force around the entire block surrounding Infusion, but Chris's disguise was so convincing that she might have been invisible.

Dozens of goths waited patiently to get into Infusion. Chris claimed those who followed the lifestyle disdained conformity, but Sam noticed a number of the girls dressed in dark variations on an early Madonna-like theme: sexy tattered clothes, dozens of bracelets and necklaces, pouty makeup, and black-dyed hair spiked in similar styles.

"They're posers," Chris told her, following the direction of her gaze. "They want people to look at them and think they're goth."

Sam looked at her young neighbor. "While you . . . ?"

Chris grinned. "Don't care what people think. I'm art."

The band had already begun playing by the time they reached the entry, where the bouncer was interested only in collecting the steep cover charge. Sam was about to pay it when Adam Suarez came out of nowhere and told the bouncer to let them through.

"You know that guy?" Chris asked Adam in a loud voice as they walked into the crowded club.

"He's a friend." Adam glanced at Sam and bent over to say to her, "You look different."

Without his sunglasses, so did he. His eyes weren't the usual dark brown most Hispanics possessed, but pitch-black with flecks of yellow so bright he looked as if someone had sprinkled them with glitter. The citrus cologne he wore was a little overpowering, too.

"Thanks." The music was too loud for conversation, so Sam left it at that and started looking for Lucan. She didn't see him or Alex, but there were plenty of other Kyn present. She recognized some of them from Lucan's memories.

"There's nowhere to sit," Chris complained. She brightened when she saw three girls waving frantically at her. "There are some of my friends—do you need me to hang with you guys?"

Sam shook her head. "Just remember what I told you. If it gets bad—"

"I know; get out." Chris winked and started elbowing her way over to her friends.

"Why do you go by Adam?" Sam asked Suarez as they circled the edge of the crowd.

"It's my name."

"No, it's not, Rafael." Over the jumping, gyrating bodies in the crowd, she saw Lucan's men gathering toward the front of the stage.

He stopped and stared at her, genuinely shocked. "How do you know who I am?"

"I didn't until you took off the shades." She had to shout the rest to be heard over the band's screaming finish. "You never wear them around him, seneschal."

"You cannot stop this," he told her. "I have been trying for weeks. Lucan means to kill Cyprien."

"Cyprien is only bait." She didn't want to think of all the duels Lucan had lost to Alex's lover, or the distinct possibility that he would die before he could carry out his final job as the Darkyn's cop. "If we can get Alex away from Lucan, we might be able to delay things long enough for me to tell Cyprien the real story. I think he may be the only one who can stop Lucan without killing him."

"Alexandra is already backstage, being prepared for the finale." Rafael turned, looking. "Cyprien is at the front of the crowd, there." He pointed.

"I'll go to him. You get Alex." Someone bumped into her from behind as the stage curtains closed. "Hurry up, Rafael."

It took precious minutes to press through the crowd and make her way to where Cyprien and another grim-looking Kyn stood before the stage. Sam was out of breath and the band was carrying their instruments offstage by the time she reached him.

"Michael." The scent of roses wafted over her as he turned to look down at her. "My name is Samantha Brown. I'm a homicide detective. I need to talk to you."

Gardenia blended with roses as a dark-haired man came to stand beside Cyprien. His golden eyes flicked over Sam before he looked up at the stage. "Do we wait for him?" he asked Michael, who nodded.

The other Kyn with the scarred face came to stand beside her. "Come away now, mademoiselle." He reached to take her arm.

"I saw Alex yesterday," she said quickly, shrugging off the big man's hand. "She was okay. She asked me to find you and warn you about what Lucan has planned."

Cyprien didn't look at her. "Phillipe, take her out of here."

"It's not what you think. Lucan doesn't want to kill you. This was all a show to lure him here." That got his attention. "He's going after the high lord. He plans to kill Richard."

Cyprien's dark brows drew together. "Richard?"

That was all he had time to say. Music blasted through the speakers overhead as all the lights inside the club went dim, and the curtains onstage silently parted.

Sam's heart nearly stopped as she saw Lucan step out into a spotlight. He was dressed as he had been the first time she'd come here, in a plain white shirt and black trousers. He moved to the heavy rock music, dancing like a rock star, spreading his hand over the bulge at his crotch. Voices shrieked their approval as he slipped his hand down the front of his trousers and pulled out what looked like his penis.

It might be as long and hard, but Sam had intimate knowledge of Lucan's cock, and she knew it wasn't black. So she was the only female watching who didn't scream as he kept pulling, taking the handle of the whip and then the long braided lash out of his pants.

She saw Rafael standing in the shadows behind Lucan, but he disappeared a moment later. The spotlight widened, gradually shining on the purple-haired prostitute Harry had recognized. The crowd fell silent as the eight-foot-tall cross that stood directly behind Lucan was also revealed.

A woman in a white gown had been tied backward to the cross, her bare back facing the crowd.

"Alexandra," Sam heard Cyprien say in a terrible voice before the crowd in the club began cheering and screaming again.

Lucan tossed the whip to the prostitute, who shook it out and strode forward, making a practiced arc with her arm before lashing out. Alex stiffened, and Sam saw a diagonal slash of reddened skin appear across her back.

The prostitute turned and pouted at the wild shrieks of the crowd. "One," she shouted before turning back toward Alex. Yet as she raised her arm, the scar-faced Kyn beside Michael stepped forward, his face intent, and she froze.

Alex shouted something.

Sam saw that the weal on Alex's back was bleeding, but then the blood stopped trickling and the lash wound slowly began to shrink.

A hundred voices demanded more by chanting, "Two! Two! Two!"

The prostitute dropped the whip and, like a windup toy, marched off the stage. Lucan watched her and went to pick up the whip. He flicked it out to its full length as he walked toward the cross.

"Mercy," Alex was shouting. "Michael, mercy."

Sam shut her eyes as a blinding golden light filled the club, and everyone around her began shrieking and groping. The light vanished as suddenly as it had appeared, and she saw Lucan's seneschal fighting with someone who picked him up and literally threw him across the room.

"Let them see," someone bellowed.

The crowd began to run for the exits, still screaming.

Lucan had turned to keep an eye on Cyprien, but he didn't see what happened to Rafael. As the club emptied, the music abruptly shut off. "Welcome to the show, seigneur. You've chased off my assistant. Perhaps you would like to join us?" He moved up to Alex, putting his mouth to her back and licking some of the blood from her skin.

"Knock it off," Alex snarled. "Michael, can you hear me? Find mercy. He's going to—" The rest of what she was trying to say was muffled by Lucan's hand.

Cyprien made a low, brutal sound in his throat, but the golden-eyed man beside him put out his hand as if to keep him from jumping up on the stage.

"Wait," he murmured as he drew a sword from under his long coat. "Something is not right with this."

Sam saw that Cyprien and the scar-faced man were already holding swords, as was every other man left in the club.

Someone began clapping, and the Kyn parted as a cloaked figure walked toward the stage. "Beautifully done, Lucan. I never appreciated your sense of the dramatic until this night." He stopped in front of the stage, a few feet away from Michael. "Don't stop now. I find myself absolutely riveted."

Sam saw the instant of relief in Lucan's eyes as he looked down at Richard, and drew the whip back as if to use it on Alex again. At the last moment he pivoted, changing the direction of the lash, which wrapped itself around Richard's neck. He jerked the whip, yanking the masked Kyn to the edge of the stage as he drew off his glove with his teeth. "It is time, my lord. As you commanded."

"How is it time?" Richard choked out.

"You butchered twenty of your own servants in Ireland," Lucan told him. "There was no reason for it."

A quartet of girls dressed in goth clothes rushed onto the stage, surrounding the cross.

"Cyprien, what are you waiting for?" someone shouted, pushing men aside as he came forward. He had Alisa under his arm, and threw her down at the foot of the stage. Her hands were curled around a blade, which she stabbed one more time into her own belly, and then went limp. "He touched your woman. He defiled her with those filthy hands. *Kill them.*"

Sam saw Chris on the stage, trying to get Alex down, and looked over at the man shouting at Michael. He was dressed like an ordinary businessman and had a thin, pale face. The smell of stagnant water filled her head.

Lucan also stared at the man shouting at Michael. "Leigh?" The whip fell out of his hand, and Richard staggered back from the stage, pulling the lash from around his neck. "It can't be. You're dead."

"They came for me in Rome, where you left me to rot," the

man he had called Leigh snarled. "They didn't leave me alone, Lucan. They took my soul. They made me a demon like you."

"No." Lucan jumped down from the stage. "How could this happen to you? You were human. Frances told me they had buried you."

The scar-faced man pressed a dagger into Sam's hand, and looked at Alex and the girls trying to get her off the cross. She nodded and slowly edged toward the end of stage, ducking into the shadows to climb up and make her way to the cross.

"Oh, yes, they buried me. Buried me in the bowels of their hell, working their witchcraft on me, until I finally died." Leigh drew a rusted sword. "But I didn't stay dead. God rejected me, Lucan, because you polluted my life with your touch. He sent me back to cleanse the others so they would not share my damnation."

"Sam," Chris hissed as soon as she saw her step up behind Alex. "We can't get the ropes untied."

"Hang on." Sam began to saw her way through the ropes binding Alex to the wooden beams. The thick cords were bound with paper-thin strips of copper, but she was able to cut through them. "Are you okay?" she whispered to Alex.

"Better now." As soon as she was free, Alex jumped down and grabbed Sam's arm. "You need to get these girls out of the way."

She glanced over her shoulder at Lucan. "I can't leave him."

Chris eyed the sword-wielding Kyn. "Oh, we're so not staying. Sam, should I call the cops?"

She shook her head. "The police can't stop this. Only the guys here can." She gave Chris a kiss on the cheek. "Get your friends out of here, and thanks."

The lightning smile flashed. "Anytime, Officer."

"What are you talking about, Leigh?" Lucan was asking. "What cleansing? What others?"

"I've never let you settle anywhere. You're like a cancer, infecting everyone around you." Leigh glanced at Cyprien. "He came to your estate after you left for America. I made your servants tell me the truth. Your king planned to give it to him. I let them find absolution, and then I cleansed them all with fire."

Cyprien lowered his sword. "*You* burned my estates in France? *You* killed my servants?"

"They killed themselves. I only gave them absolution," Leigh insisted. "They are in heaven now, with my beloved." He smiled at Lucan as two Kyn came on either side of him and took hold of his arms. "You thought you were being clever, waiting until Frances was an old woman before you poisoned her with your touch. I got to her in time, that very night. She thought I was an angel. She was the only one who didn't resist my cleansing. She was happy to hang herself after I told her what had been done to me."

"The Brethren tortured you," Richard rasped.

"Mercer." A bearded man stepped out of the crowd. "I don't know what they did to you, but I can help. I'm your friend. Let me."

That was what Alex had been shouting, Sam thought. *Mercer,* not mercy.

"My name is Leigh, not Mercer." Lucan's former *tresora* sneered at the dark, bearded man. "You don't know. You're still human. You even believed my faked suicide."

The bearded man looked at Cyprien. "This isn't his fault. The Brethren have destroyed his mind. He's not responsible for what he's done."

"I can show you the Light, John," Leigh said. "I can make you feel the weight of your sins. That was the dark gift they gave me, you see. I don't have to kill anyone. Once I make you face the wrongs you've done, you will find absolution for yourself. Death is only a doorway to heaven."

Richard stepped up to Leigh. "The Brethren made you Kyn? How?"

The *tresora*'s face took on a sly look. "You would only make more demons to serve you." A terrible scream rang out in the club. "I caught one of your beasts. I brought him with me to be part of the cleansing." While the guards were distracted, he broke free and ran toward Lucan.

The golden-eyed man moved so fast Sam barely saw him before he swung his sword at Leigh, decapitating him. She turned her head away from the gruesome sight, and spotted the outline of an oblong head moving in the shadows behind Lucan.

"Oh, God, Faryl, no," Alex called out.

"Wait," Sam shouted, running out in front of the snake-man before he could get to Lucan. "Don't hurt anyone."

"Stop, Faryl," Alex said, joining Sam. "I can help you. You came here for help, remember? There might be a way to reverse what's happened to you."

Behind each bar, glasses began to shatter and bottles to crack.

"Samantha, Alexandra," Lucan said as he stood and faced Faryl. "He has no mind left. Step away from him."

Lightbulbs all around them began bursting like popcorn.

"I know what I'm doing." Alex actually moved closer, holding out her hands. "Please, Faryl. Let me help you."

A gun went off twice, and Faryl shrieked, leaping across the stage, grabbing Alex, and diving from the stage. Cyprien and the other Kyn gave chase.

Sam didn't understand what had happened until she looked down and saw the wet spot spreading over her right side.

"What?" She touched it, and her hand came away red with her own blood. She'd been shot . . . but no one had a gun but her.

A pale, perspiring Wesley Dwyer stepped out from behind the cross, still holding his weapon pointed at Sam. "That thing won't die," he said in an unsteady voice, "but you will. Just like Harry did when I cut his throat. This time you will."

Sam's legs gave out and she dropped to the stage, but Rafael was there, and his arms kept her from falling over. Then Lucan stepped between them and Dwyer, and took off his other glove.

"It takes a brave man to shoot a defenseless woman," Lucan said.

All around the club, full bottles of liquor began exploding like bombs, spraying anyone near them with their contents.

Dwyer's hand shook as he pointed the gun at Lucan. "You stay back. I'll shoot you."

Lucan bared his fangs. "Be my guest."

Every lightbulb that remained intact in the club exploded simultaneously. Dwyer shrieked and pulled the trigger as Lucan reached out to him, and fired again when Lucan's bare hand touched his chest. Then the gun fell from his fingers and he began to shake all over, convulsing, choking, blood pouring from his nose and ears and mouth, bones cracking, limbs flopping helplessly as he crumpled to the stage.

Wesley Dwyer was almost dead when his body exploded.

"Rafael." Sam closed her eyes, the cold pain in her side spreading over her. "Make sure Chris is all right." She coughed, and felt something liquid in her lungs.

The seneschal looked up. "My lord, come quickly."

Sam saw Lucan's face over her, and watched his lips move, but the pain was dragging her away from this world, and she knew she couldn't stay with him any longer. Then she felt his hand on her face, and arms lifting her, and let him carry her off into the night.

Michael chased Faryl out of the club and into the alley, where they had prepared for a more civilized fight. Alex managed to wrestle free of his grip, but the changeling threw her against a wall, knocking the breath out of her.

"Faryl." Michael held his sword ready, circling around as he matched the changeling's sinuous movements. "Your brother is here. Your family is suffering. Do you wish to return to your life as Kyn?"

The changeling went still, his enormous eyes blinking as he tried to focus on Michael. Out of his throat came a single, distorted word. "No."

Michael nodded. "Then allow me to end your suffering as Lucan would. Quickly and cleanly."

Faryl released a long, low sound, and then dropped to his knees in front of Michael.

Alex staggered to her feet. "Michael, don't kill him. I think I know how to cure him."

"There is no cure for what we are." He brought down the sword, severing Faryl's head cleanly from his body with a single stroke. He looked at his *sygkenis*'s horrified face. "That is what he hated. Being Kyn."

Gard came forward and dropped down by his brother's distorted body. He looked up at Michael helplessly. "Thank you, seigneur."

Alex shook her head slowly. "We can't keep doing this. Killing them isn't the answer." She trudged back into the club.

Michael sheathed his sword and saw Byrne and Jayr approaching. "It is over."

"Congratulations on winning, my lord," Byrne said.

Michael's eyes went to the pathetic figure of Gard Paviere. "No one prevailed here tonight," he assured the suzerain before he went in after Alex.

The Kyn were already removing the physical traces of what had happened in the club. The bits and pieces of the body of the human male who had shot Detective Brown were gone. Because of the manner in which he died, Michael knew Lucan's men would destroy the remains rather than allow them to be recovered.

Thierry was standing guard over Richard, who told Cyprien, "Your *sygkenis* went upstairs after Lucan and the human female who was shot."

"What will you do to Lucan for his betrayal?" Michael had to ask.

"He did not betray me." Richard drew his cloak on. "I commanded him to assassinate me when it became apparent that I was losing the battle with my affliction." He paused. "He seems to believe that I have."

Michael knew the high lord was struggling with his change. The knowledge that he had wantonly killed his own servants was also disturbing. "Have you?"

"Not yet. Not for some time yet, I think. Shall we go and see how Lucan's little human fares?" Richard gestured to the elevator.

The high lord's blandness about the assassination attempt should have been a warning, but Michael was too concerned about Alexandra to give it much thought.

Michael heard Alex shouting at Lucan as soon as the elevator stopped on the penthouse floor. He followed the voices through the front room and into Lucan's bedroom, but the curious tableau there made him stop in the doorway.

Lucan sat with Detective Brown unconscious in his arms, while his seneschal was holding Alexandra back from the bed. Someone had started an IV of whole blood for the human female.

"She can have the surgery she needs at the hospital," Alex was yelling at the suzerain, who was pressing a cloth against the gunshot wound in her side. "There's still a chance to save her."

"I have seen enough wounds among humans to know this

one is fatal," Lucan said, looking up to see Cyprien and Richard watching them. "This is the only way."

"Giving her blood won't help. She'll just bleed it out." Alex whipped her head around and saw Michael. "Do something."

Michael smelled lavender coming from two directions, as if there were two Alexandras in the room, and finally understood why his old enemy had started the IV. "Lucan isn't giving her human blood."

Alex went still. "You wouldn't." The next moment she went berserk, jerking free of Rafael's hold and launching herself at the bed. Michael caught her before she could rip the line out of Samantha Brown's arm. "You want her dead? My blood is poisonous, you moron."

"Perhaps." Lucan lifted the cloth he had pressed to the wound and studied it. He looked up at the high lord. "Perhaps not."

"I have been studying the medical data you have sent me, Michael," Richard said. "The results seem to indicate that there is a difference between us and these new Kyn women in America. They have some of our gifts, and yet they remain more human than we."

Michael swore under his breath.

"The medical data." Alex whipped her head to stare at Richard. "What medical data?"

"The seigneur has been kind enough to send me copies of all your research, my dear." The high lord made a casual gesture. "It has kept me abreast of your progress."

"Is this true?" Alex demanded of Michael.

"It was necessary, Alexandra." He had to stop this before Richard turned her against him. "If I hadn't your brother would be dead, and Richard would have taken you from me."

"I might have borrowed her," Richard said reasonably, "but I would have given her back. Eventually."

Alex covered her eyes for a minute. "You lied to me. You stole my research. You took my memories. Do you love me or *hate* me?"

Michael took her hands in his. "Everything I did was to protect you and your brother. Please believe me."

"Yeah," Alex said, gripping his hands hard, "I guess I do. But next time, Michael, ask."

"What would you need, Dr. Keller," the high lord said, "to research how to reverse the changeling process?"

She gave him an uneasy look. "Some time, a lab, a couple of assistants, and some changeling blood and tissue samples. Maybe some test animals."

"Indeed. Is there anything else?" Richard asked politely.

"I don't know, some bone marrow and spinal fluid. The change affects every part of the body." She shrugged. "With the Pavieres' permission, I can harvest what I need from Faryl's remains."

"But it would be better to work on a living changeling subject, would it not?" When she nodded, Richard turned to Michael. "Sending me copies of the data simply isn't enough anymore, seigneur. I hope you understand." Before Michael could react, the high lord's voice swelled to a level he rarely used, the one with which he could control other Kyn. "You will not speak. You will not interfere." He turned to Lucan, who was rising from the bed. "Neither will you."

Michael could not resist the voice, and stood helpless as the dark lord took Alexandra by the arm and guided her out of the suite. The effect of Richard's voice disappeared a few moments later, but when Michael ran downstairs, Phillipe and Thierry stood paralyzed, and Richard was gone.

He waited with his seneschal until Phillipe emerged from his bespelled state. "The high lord took her with him, master. I could not stop him."

John Keller joined them. "Neither could I. What is he going to do to my sister, Cyprien?"

Michael stared at one of the golden banners hanging from the ceiling of the club. "He'll try to use her to find a cure for himself."

"Your blond friend said he killed half of his own servants." John turned to him, his fists clenched. "Will he do the same to Alexandra if she doesn't find this cure?"

"I don't know," Michael admitted. "I don't know what he's capable of anymore."

John considered that for a long moment. "All right. Where will he take her from here?"

Thierry answered for Michael. "To Ireland. To his kingdom in hell."

"You can't let him have her," John said. "What are we going to do about it?"

"We will go into hell." Michael looked into the dark, fierce eyes of Alex's brother, and saw a determination that matched his own. "And we will take her back."

Lucan lay next to the woman he loved. It had been six days now, and still she lingered, not dead or alive, but caught in some purgatory between the two. He had not left her for a moment since the night of the concert.

Samantha did not move on her own. She never woke.

Cyprien had come to see him before leaving Florida. They had settled many things, and while they would never be friends, the days of being enemies were over.

"I think Leigh must have been responsible for all of the crimes and deaths the Kyn believed you committed for your own amusement," Cyprien told him.

Lucan had long believed Cyprien guilty of similar crimes against him. "He was a victim of the Brethren."

Michael held out his hand. "So were you."

Each day Lucan washed Samantha and brushed out her hair and rubbed her skin with silky lotions to improve her sluggish circulation. He kept her naked but covered with the softest linens.

He talked to her for hours. He told her about Gwynyth, and his childhood at court, and how it had been to live in such dangerous times. How proud he had been to be selected to join the Templars, and how crushing the grim reality of living as a warrior-priest had been. He told her how he had learned to fight on the sands of ancient deserts, and the horror of the battles waged there. He even told her of the years after he rose as Kyn, when he had sworn his oath of loyalty to Richard, and carried out his orders, and how, gradually, he had come to know that he could not spend his life ending those of others, whatever their crimes had been. Most of all, he told her the truth about what he was, and what he had done.

Samantha never reacted, never showed a sign that she could hear him.

After the last of Alex's blood was gone, Lucan used saline

solution to keep her hydrated. He feared giving her any form of
human nourishment, but as her weight dwindled, he tried clear
juices and broths. She instantly regurgitated everything he fed
her. He was too afraid of poisoning her further to try giving her
his own blood.

On the seventh day, Lucan left the bed to stand at the third
set of windows Burke had installed. Alex's blood had healed
the wound in her side, and kept her alive, but that was all it had
done, and he did not have the knowledge or means to discover
what else was happening to Samantha. For all he knew the
blood could be slowly poisoning her from the inside out.

It was time to let her go, to put her back in the hands of her
own kind.

Lucan had never wept in his life. Any show of tears before
his mother had resulted in an immediate, vicious beating for
him, and during his years in the Holy Land the sun, the hatred,
and the merciless march of death across the sands had desiccated his emotions. Richard and the Kyn had finished the job,
turning him into a killing machine. No, he could no more weep
than he could bring life with his touch, but as he went to sit beside the woman he loved, he wished he could.

Lucan took her scarred hand between his, and bent over to
kiss her lips and breathe in her scent. He would spend a few
more hours with her, and then he would summon Rafael to take
her away from him. He closed his eyes as their lips met.

"Mmmmm."

He jerked back at the sound, sure he had imagined it, and
saw her eyelashes flutter. "Samantha?" He slid his hands under
her shoulders, lifting her up. *"Samantha?"*

"Shhh." She groped until she could press her fingers against
his mouth. She grimaced. "My mouth hurts."

Lucan tipped her face back and opened her mouth. Inside,
two newly formed apertures made dark holes in her palate.
"Those are *dents acérées*," he said, almost laughing the words.
"You've grown fangs, my love."

"Sucks." She closed her mouth and glared at him. "Do I?"

He nodded. "I gave you some of Alexandra's blood. I didn't
know if it would work, but I couldn't let you die. You're making the change from human to Kyn."

She thought about it for a while. "Thanks."

"You're welcome."

"I'm not Frances," she said suddenly. "I only look like her. I'll never be her."

He uttered a shaky laugh. "I don't want Frances."

"I'm a cop. I'm not giving it up." She shifted. "You are done being the Darkyn's cop."

"Yes." He thought of Richard and Cyprien. "I think I am."

"Do you love me?" When he nodded, she sighed and closed her eyes, snuggling closer to him. "Hold that thought, and me."

Lucan rested his cheek against the top of her head. "Forever."

Read on for a preview of
Lynn Viehl's next novel of the Darkyn

Night Lost

Coming from Signet Eclipse in April 2007

"I'm not afraid," Nicola muttered under her breath as she followed the smell of evergreen. "There's nothing to be afraid of."

Nick didn't mind lying to herself. The truth never set anything free.

The woodsy scent seemed to be coming from a large tapestry at the far end of the cellar passageway. As soon as Nick trained her flashlight on it, she set down her bag and stepped back to have a proper look. At first it seemed to be only a threadbare frame for the rat and moth holes eaten through it, and then she picked out what the weaving had once depicted: a pale-haired woman standing beside a tree. The lady had wrapped her arm around the trunk; the tree's branches curled down around her as if the tree were trying to return the embrace.

The Golden Madonna, perhaps?

Even as hope rose, Nick's memory quashed it. She had walked the circular room devoted to the six famous Lady and the Unicorn tapestries at the Cluny in Paris. They had the same bloodred background as this one, and in them the maker had woven the same black banners with three crescent moons. No way could this be one of them; it had to be a reproduction or a knockoff. Who would leave a national treasure hanging unguarded in the basement of a crumbling ruin to feed the rat population?

When Nick reached up to feel along the upper edge, her

touch made the entire tapestry fall. A cloud of dust, dirt and rotted wool fragments enveloped her. Coughing, she covered her nose and mouth as she examined the wall behind the weaving. New red brick filled in the space of an old entryway, to seal off a room. The mortar must have been mixed wrong, as the seams between the bricks were riddled with holes, and some of the bricks were loose enough for her to push in with her fingers.

"Hello." Nick crouched down and pulled the pile of tapestry away from the wall. A thick layer of mortar dust obscured the base of the new bricks, caked as if it had been there a while. "Father Claudio, you'll never land a job as a bricklayer."

Come to me.

Falling back onto her ass didn't improve Nick's mood, nor did scraping her palms on the stone floor. She stood and put an ear to the brick before stepping back again. "Is someone in there?"

Silence.

"If you hadn't noticed, this is private property, and I'm trespassing," she told the wall. "The French police aren't very fond of Americans breaking and entering, either." She waited for a response. "If you really want my help, friend, tell me if you're in there."

Silence.

Nick realized something. "Do you speak any English?" She repeated that in her phrase-book French, along with, "Are you stuck in there?" Brilliant question. "Do you want me to get you out?"

Silence, and evergreen.

"We'll call that a yes." Feeling ridiculous, Nick bent down, unzipped her bag and took out a hammer and chisel. After a glance at the brick, she put them back and removed a small sledgehammer. "If you're near the door, move back. Shit is about to hit the fan."

A hail of mortar dust followed the metal-on-stone slam of the sledgehammer. Bricks shifted, two falling into the space behind them. Grinning, Nick swung the heavy steel head again, and a foot-wide hole appeared.

Seeing that much brick implode made her stop and bend over to peer into the gap. Air rushed around her face as if the pitch-black room on the other side were sucking it in. Invisible branches of evergreen seemed to close around her.

"They didn't even leave you a night-light? Cheapskates." She shoved in a brick, scraping her knuckles, and something dark and wet dripped onto the back of her hand. Blood, and not hers.

Beneath the blood, her scratches disappeared.

"Fuck." She paused long enough to put on her leather gloves before she wrenched around the edges of the hole at the brick, pushing it away and widening the space. A strange urgency hammered inside her head, as if an invisible alarm clock had gone off on the other side of the wall. *I have to get him the hell out of here before they come for both of us.*

The hole was finally large enough for Nick to squeeze through. "Here we go." She poked her head and then her shoulders inside. The evergreen scent on the other side of the wall didn't cover the other, awful smell—as if someone had emptied a couple of trash cans in the hidden room—but she'd smelled worse. She climbed in, groping for a handhold, but her fingers found nothing but floor. More brick collapsed under her weight, and she fell on her face. Something long and hard bruised her thigh.

Flashlight. She pulled it out and switched it on.

The tiny room still held the empty racks where some long-dead aristocrat had kept his best bottles of wine and brandy. From all the tangled, dusty cobwebs hanging from the ceiling, it appeared as if no one had entered the space for years. Nick stood up and slowly swept the flashlight around her. A rickety-looking table and two old, scarred chairs waited empty in front of a dead fireplace overflowing with ancient ash.

No sign of life, however. "Where are you?"

Chains rattled behind her.

She turned around and pointed the flashlight toward the sound, and saw him. The light wavered before she controlled her hand. "Bastards."

They'd crucified this one.

Nick saw she was partially wrong—chains had been wrapped around his neck, arms, waist and legs—but two huge copper bolts had been hammered through his wrists. He'd worked at one, apparently, and could move it enough to rattle the chains around that arm. A black rag had been tied over his eyes, and a wide band of copper covered the lower half of his face. Dark green tattoos mottled his naked body, along with dried blood, open wounds, and filth.

Despite his sad condition, he still looked beautiful, the way they all did. This one resembled a green god, carved from dark jade.

Nailed to a cross.

The holy freaks had done this to him. Nick had never seen one this bad, but the deliberate, mocking crucifixion had the same feel as the others she had found. The question was, why? If they wanted them dead, why not just kill them? Why the torture and humiliation?

The prisoner turned his head slightly and moved his hand, disturbing the chains again.

Nick lowered the flashlight as she walked to him. "Sorry." She didn't know why she was apologizing. None of this was her doing, and if she had an ounce of brains left, she'd run out of here before the old man found her screwing with this thing. Lucky for this one she was an idiot. "How do I get you off this without tearing you to shreds?"

The chains rattled a third time as he gestured toward the wall beside him.

Nick reached out through the hole and groped until she grabbed her bag and pulled it inside. Once she had retrieved her bolt cutters, she looked around the crude wooden cross. The chains had been threaded through rusted iron rings driven into the wall around him. She started there, cutting open the rings and tugging away the loops of chain. The weighty copper links felt icy and sticky, and wherever they had touched him, left dark impressions of their links on his skin.

This close, Nick could smell nothing else but the evergreen

scent he radiated. How long had he been sealed in this room? Weeks? Months? His matted brown hair shifted and his head moved back, as if he was trying to see under the edge of his blindfold.

"Want to have a look at me?" She stopped cutting long enough to remove the black rag from his eyes. His closed eyelids didn't open, and he sagged a little. "I'm Nick," she told him as she went back to work on the chains. "And you're a mess."

She freed his neck and arms, and examined the copper band gagging him. It had been welded there, but it was thin, and her tinsnips cut through it nicely. The raw skin under it began to heal at once, and she flung the copper to the floor in disgust.

"I've got to pry these bolts out." His mouth matched the perfection of his body; she saw that right away. Were any of these things ever ugly, or even a little plain? "It's going to hurt, maybe as much as when they went in."

Nick heard a jerking, tearing sound.

"Ce n'est pas nécessaire." The voice sounded as dry and shredded as the feel of the trembling hand that pushed her back. "I can do the rest. Leave me, girl."

Like an animal in a trap, he'd ripped his wrists free of the bolts. Maybe that's all they were: gorgeous, two-legged animals.

Not very grateful ones, either. "You want me to leave *now*? Before you thank me, and say good-bye, and tell me to have a wonderful life? Tell me, is that what Jesus would do?"

He leaned forward, his eyes still closed. "If you remain, and if I look upon you," he murmured, "I will kill us both."

He sounded like the genie that had been kept too long in the bottle: enraged and wanting some payback. Of course, he needed blood, and she was the only source present. In this state he'd lose control and try to drain her dry.

"I'm not leaving until I cut through enough of these so that you can get out on your own." She went back to work on the chains.

Bugs found their way into the room and began flying at her

head. Absently she swatted at them until she remembered that all the bugs were upstairs in the chapel.

She hadn't left the cellar door open. How had they gotten down—

Father Claudio was right there, his walking stick raised high, and then he clubbed her across the head with it. Nick couldn't avoid the blow, and in the explosion of pain that followed, she felt her scalp split, and the heat of her own blood. She went down like a sack of stones.

The last things she heard and saw before the night took her were chains falling on the floor, and two bare, dirty, beautiful feet walking across the stone.

J.R. Ward

DARK LOVER

THE DEBUT NOVEL IN THE BLACK DAGGER BROTHERHOOD SERIES

In the shadows of the night in Caldwell, New York, there's a deadly turf war going on between vampires and their slayers. There exists a secret band of brothers like no other—six vampire warriors, defenders of their race. Yet none of them relishes killing more than Wrath, the leader of The Black Dagger Brotherhood.

The only purebred vampire left on earth, Wrath has a score to settle with the slayers who murdered his parents centuries ago. But, when one of his most trusted fighters is killed—leaving his half-breed daughter unaware of his existence or her fate—Wrath must usher her into the world of the undead—a world of sensuality beyond her wildest dreams.

0-451-21695-4

"A midnight whirlwind of dangerous characters and mesmerizing erotic romance. The Black Dagger Brotherhood owns me now."
—LYNN VIEHL, AUTHOR OF *THE DARKYN* NOVELS

Available wherever books are sold or at penguin.com